D1164738

Howard, Hanna C.,author.
Our divine mischief

2023
33305255417101
ca   10/12/23

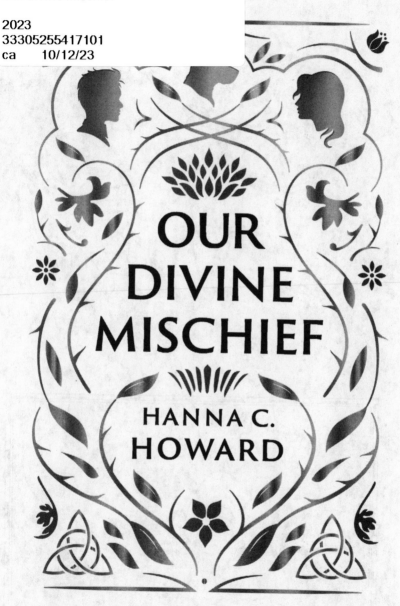

OUR DIVINE MISCHIEF

HANNA C. HOWARD

BLINK

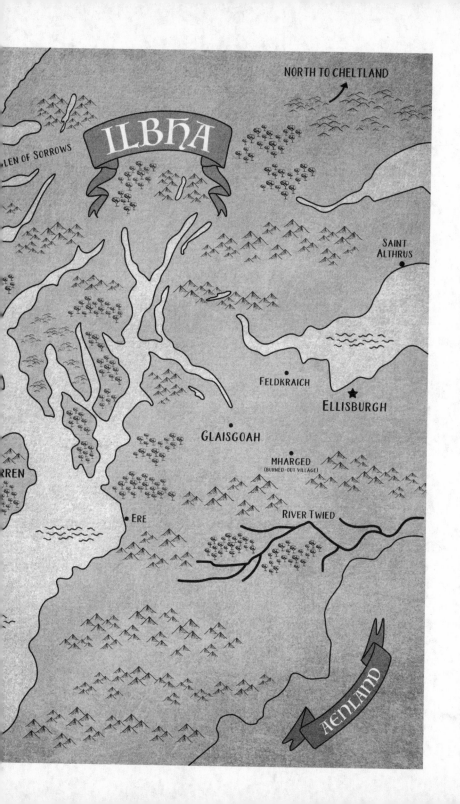

BLINK

Our Divine Mischief
Copyright © 2023 by Hanna C. Howard

Requests for information should be addressed to:
Blink, *3900 Sparks Dr. SE, Grand Rapids, Michigan 49546*

ISBN 978-0-310-15618-5 (audio)

Library of Congress Cataloging-in-Publication Data

Names: Howard, Hanna C., author.
Title: Our divine mischief / Hanna C. Howard.
Description: Grand Rapids, Michigan : Blink, [2023] | Audience: Ages
    12 and up. | Summary: Told from three perspectives, outcast Hew and
    wish-granting canine Orail help seventeen-year-old Ália through a series
    of divine Ordeals, but there is more at stake in the kingdom than just
    Ália's future, and Orail may be the key to saving them all.
Identifiers: LCCN 2023023706 (print) | LCCN 2023023707 (ebook) |
    ISBN 9780310156222 (hardcover) | ISBN 9780310156055 (ebook)
Subjects: CYAC: Fantasy. | Magic—Fiction. | Belonging—Fiction. |
    Dogs—Fiction. | Human-animal relationships—Fiction. | BISAC:
    YOUNG ADULT FICTION / Fantasy / Historical | YOUNG
    ADULT FICTION / Fantasy / Romance | LCGFT: Fantasy fiction. |
    Novels.
Classification: LCC PZ7.1.H68773 Ou 2023 (print) | LCC PZ7.1.H68773
    (ebook) | DDC [Fic]—dc23
LC record available at https://lccn.loc.gov/2023023706
LC ebook record available at https://lccn.loc.gov/2023023707

Publisher's Note: This novel is a work of fiction. Names, characters, places,
and incidents are either products of the author's imagination or used
fictitiously. All characters are fictional, and any similarity to people living or
dead is purely coincidental.

No part of this publication may be reproduced, stored in a retrieval system,
or transmitted in any form or by any means—electronic, mechanical,
photocopy, recording, or any other—except for brief quotations in printed
reviews, without the prior permission of the publisher.

Cover Design: Micah Kandros
Interior Design: Denise Froehlich

Printed in the United States of America

23 24 25 26 27 LBC 5 4 3 2 1

For Daniel, love of my heart. Jamie
Fraser has nothing on you.

And for Ophelia, my Orail, whose heartbeat
is preserved in the pages of this book.

Author's Note

Friends, whatever happens,
remember this: I detest books
like *Where the Red Fern Grows*.

—*HCH*

"What is't? A spirit?
Lord, how it looks about! Believe me, sir,
It carries a brave form. But 'tis a spirit.

◆ ◆ ◆

I might call him
A thing divine; for nothing natural
I ever saw so noble."

—WILLIAM SHAKESPEARE,
THE TEMPEST, ACT I, SCENE II

"Golden Light and Thistle"

O'er the heath, where hurcheouns sleep
All cradled by the solum, O,
The westly winds arise and pen
A tune both bright and solemn, O;
The pipe and drum first creaky hum,
I turn to hear the whistle, O;
Lyk night hae daw, ilk freeze hae thaw
An' golden light and thistle, O.

Golden light and thistle, O!
Golden light and thistle, O!
The pipe and drum begin tae hum
Of golden light and thistle, O.

Auld Gaelan turns, her lantern burns
The last of evening fuel, O,
An' shakes the bed of leafy reds
An' doffs her crown of jewels, O;
Her gowning white is set to side
And hang'ed with the mistletoe.
She dawns a robe of Ilbhan rose
An' golden light and thistle, O.

Golden light and thistle, O!
Golden light and thistle, O!
She dawns a robe of Ilbhan rose
An' golden light and thistle, O.

Nigh the ledge, the water's edge,
Is found a willow bower, O,

All branches twined, and there I'll find
My true love crowned with flowers, O.
Clear and bright, though meek and slight
We watch as day will bristle, O;
And as it stirs, the smell of firs
An' golden light and thistle, O.

Golden light and thistle, O!
Golden light and thistle, O!
As it stirs, the smell of firs
An' golden light and thistle, O.

In the rest o' the zephyr's breath
The swallow takes the tune, O;
Then chorus formed, an aeriform
Organ sings and croons, O.
'Neath the dew the buds accrue
To draft this great epistle, O.
Which spins a tale of warmer gales
An' golden light and thistle, O.

Golden light and thistle, O!
Golden light and thistle, O!
It spins a tale of warmer gales
An' golden light and thistle, O.

Golden light and thistle, O!
Golden light and thistle, O!
The flowers tell of warmer spells
An' golden light and thistle, O.

—Traditional Ilbhan folk song

Part One

SEA

Chapter One

ÁILA

"Tack!" my father shouts. "Tack now!"

Rain lashes the deck of *The Golden Thistle* while a vicious wind whips the sails overhead, and pulleys clap a loud staccato against the main mast. My father's crew rush to obey his orders—and I do my best to stay out of their way.

"LacTalish, are you sure there's nothing I can do?" I yell over the roar of the storm as my father's first mate and two of the crew dip the lugsail and begin the process of wrestling it down onto the deck. He barely glances at me as he squints up at the flapping canvas.

"You know there isn't, lass," he barks, cords of muscle standing out on his forearms like sail lines. "Just stand clear!"

I duck as the yard plummets, narrowly missing the side of my head.

Salt and scales.

"Áila!"

I wheel toward Da's voice. He's at the stern, one hand gripping the tiller, the other braced against his driftwood crutch. Rain streams down his face. "Out of the way!" He taps his forefinger twice against the translucent, green medallion lying against his chest—as if I need reminding why I'm not allowed to help.

Only goddess-approved seafarers should be working right now. Those who've been to Yslet's island and secured her blessing.

Gotten the medallion. Done the apprenticeship. Earned their place on this boat and in our village.

My chest pinches slightly, like I have a hunger cramp there.

Sighing, I slip and slide over the deck, taking care not to get in anyone's way. The boat climbs waves big enough to swamp us while I grip the gritty mizzenmast and focus on keeping my feet below me. Trying not to think about the fact that everyone else my age went to the island years ago, or that in a year I'll be eighteen and too old for the Goddess Trial. Trying not to dwell on the fact that this birthday, *again*, Mother said no.

Da is still bellowing orders to his crew, his voice blending with the howl of the waves, the smell of brine, and the frigid plopping of rain across my skin. After a few minutes, the tension knotting my shoulders slips away, taking my tangled-up anger at my mother along with it. I am once again present with the whipping wind, the icy seawater, and the urgent possibility of capsizing.

All less formidable than my mother during an argument.

"I think we're through it!" shouts Da.

I blink out over the water to find the clouds rolling off east and the way ahead starting to clear. Da's crew slumps in relief as they start to pick up the mess of overturned barrels, snarled rope, and storm-flung fish that litter the deck.

"Lir has seen us safely through!" Da calls, to ripples of shaky laughter across the boat. Propping his crutch against the tiller and putting his weight on his good leg, he smiles ruefully at his crew. "Aye, the sea god isn't always easy on us," he says, "but he's on our side. And he knows what it is to suffer, remember."

I may not have the sea glass medallion that declares me a goddess-blessed fisher, but as far as Da's concerned, I am still qualified to help clean up after a storm. Just as I'm qualified to mend nets, prepare bait, and handle the lines in fair weather—like the good, untrained grunt I am. So I wander the deck alongside the sailors as Da begins a familiar tale.

"Lir was in the ocean the day his daughter Ona died. Some say he was there because the whales needed guiding in their migration, some say he was feuding with Atobion and had to protect the boats from the sky god's winds. And others say it was Arial's doing, that the trickster goddess led him away from our isle of Fuiscea, far out to sea so that he would not be able to help when the wolves attacked Ona."

Everyone here has heard the tale of the sea god's greatest loss more times than they can count. But Da's telling of it still loosens the tension wrapped about us after the storm and eases us back into peace as we head for home.

"Whatever the reason, Lir was not there to hold his wee lass in his arms when her lifeblood slipped away, nor was he there to comfort his wife, Yslet, as she begged the healing goddess Belaine to do something despite it being too late. But Lir is not a god of destruction, and so even after he learned of this great loss, he did not rage or wield his tempests. He did not sink any ships or drown any swimmers. The seas were quiet as a forest pool for a whole month after Ona died, as Lir poured his grief into a new work."

I steal glances at the crew as the storm's mess is tidied away. They are spellbound by Da's voice, calmed by his confidence. As usual, his lame leg is no impediment to the range of skills he wields as a captain.

He continues. "Though water was his usual craft, Lir turned his hands to the island on which his daughter had died, determined to make it a monument for Ona: a place of stark and tragic beauty. He pushed back the wild forests where the wolves reigned, forcing most to flee across the channel to a new land. He raised up sheer cliffs, with bare faces where the waves could beat out his grief forevermore. He brought hills low and made

4

them boggy, ripe with peat to make whisky: the elixir that dulls the blade of loss. And he covered the heath with beautiful purple heather and sharp, spiny thistles as a reminder of beauty forever intermixed with pain."

I can feel Lir's anguish as if my father has spoken it into being within me. It aches in my bones and tightens my throat.

Da pauses, and I look around to find his eyes fixed ahead, on the very cliffs he just described. West of them, the docks of Carrighlas swim into view. My heart pinches with something fierce and desperate as I, too, watch our village drift nearer.

I have lived here nearly eleven of my seventeen years, and I still don't feel quite like I belong—though I want more than anything to believe that I do.

I glance back at Da, and he jerks his chin, inviting me to join him at the helm. As I cross the deck, he concludes his story and guides us into port.

"And thus *our* Fuiscea was born," he says, "and the people in it were knitted to a land forged by the pain and love of the sea god and held together by the guidance of the goddess of beasts and birds. This land holds us in its arms, we the children of two gods whose first daughter was slain upon our shores. Her blood has become our blood, so that whatever we do, wherever we go, this will always be our home."

There is an audible sigh from some of Da's crew, and a few scattered cries of "Aye!" But I roll my eyes. Da's stories end too soppily for me; it's not as if being born in a place is all it takes to make it your home. Da's hand rests briefly at the top of my neck and gives me a little squeeze, as if to say he knows what I'm thinking. Then he says, too quietly for anyone else to hear, "Talk to your mother again. Explain why you want to go."

I grip the railing until my chapped fingers turn bone white. "I've told her, Da. She doesn't care."

"You give in too easily," he counters gently. "She believes

that, like her, you could be content without a medallion. Let her see what I have seen. The way you look at my crew like they're goddess-touched, the way you yearn to help with the harder work. *Aila.*"

I turn to meet his blue eyes, earnest in the clear, salmon-pink light of the setting sun. I think of the way his crew looks at him—so different from the way he was treated in Learchlas after the accident that ruined his leg. He is esteemed among them, counted as their own. Because the work he does helps the village. And everyone can see his skills have been blessed by Yslet.

"I know you," he says. "You'll never be at peace until you've gone to the island yourself."

I bite my lip, imagining for the thousandth time what it might be like to do the Goddess Trial, to meet Yslet, to come home with an apprenticeship and a medallion of my own. Sea glass, perhaps, like my father's, inscribed with the word *fisher.* Or polished hoof, bearing the word *shepherd.* Proof I have a job to do in Carrighlas, that it's truly my home.

"Let her see what I see," Da repeats softly.

I almost never push back against my mother, whose will always seems immovable compared with mine. Nothing ever feels worth the fight. But perhaps *this* is.

"We'll take care of the *Thistle*," he says. "I'll see you at home."

When the anchor plunges into the black waters of the sea loch, I have already crossed the deck to the starboard bow. I leap easily over the railing, and land on the dock with a thump of my boots. Some of the fishers shout their goodbyes, and I wave back at them, breaking into a jog, heading toward the village.

I wish I had time to go run the cliffs—nothing clears my head and quiets my thoughts like a long, breathless gallop beneath the endless sky—but I need to talk to Mother before I lose my nerve. I push myself into a jog, and the turmoil inside me quiets to a low murmur beneath the hum of my moving body.

Chapter Two

HEW

The golden hour is that strange, brief time of day when I can see nothing in the world that needs fixing, because every inch of it seems gilded by the great goldsmith Credne himself. Even the peat slabs I have been digging since this morning glow like bars of warm copper in the setting sun as I finish piling them on the bank of the trench. I strap the harness of my wagon—filled with last month's dried peats—over my sore shoulders, then begin the peaceful trundle back toward the village. It is my custom to watch the sun set while pretending that this golden version of life is reality, and that everything around me is perfect.

Even me.

The fantasy always dies the moment I cross into the streets of Carrighlas, because not even the bewitching shimmer-light of dusk can make the villagers forget what I am.

Unblessed. The first in a generation, and most likely the last.

They aren't cruel, except for the very young, the very careless, and my brother-in-law, but there are times I think I might prefer cruelty to the pity and indifference I get from folk. I used to smile, but the effort grew heavier the longer my smiles went unreturned. Now I just keep my head down and pull my cart.

Which is why, right outside of the kirk in the village square, I run into someone.

"I'm sorry!" I gasp. I jerk to a halt so abruptly that my cart knocks me in the small of the back—and then I realize who I've hit. Heat washes through my body from scalp to soles.

"LacEllan," sighs the priest, his voice dripping with irritation as he steps away from me. "What are you doing?"

I stand there like a stone crag for a moment, gaping for an explanation that might make me look less incompetent. I had hoped to speak with the priest soon, but nearly knocking him off his feet beforehand was not part of my plan. The voice inside that's always lightning-quick to remind me how substandard I am perks up its head and tells me I've ruined my whole life.

Again.

"Fáthair Firnan," I stammer, bowing my head. "I'm sorry, I was just on my way to deliver the peat."

He frowns. "You're taking a circuitous route, aren't you?"

"Aye," I mumble. "Sorry."

He pulls his cloak tighter and starts to walk away, but—

"Wait!" I gasp. "Fáthair—could I have a word?"

The priest turns toward me, looking like he regrets stopping to talk at all. "Quickly then, LacEllan. I'm late for supper."

I hurry on, afraid of losing my chance. "I was just wondering whether you'd, er, have any extra time. To tutor me. In theology. I mean to say, I know Unblessed aren't welcome at prayers, but I do aspire to be a priest one day myself, and without an apprenticeship, I find I don't know how to learn what I need to know . . ." I trail off, noting his expression. It's somewhere between doused-with-cold-water and slapped-by-a-fish.

"Hew," he says, sounding flabbergasted. "You are *Unblessed*. You're not even allowed in our holy spaces. Why in the name of all the gods do you think you could ever become a *priest*?"

I stare at him, wondering if he and the voice inside me get together from time to time to share a dram and compare notes. The breath leaks out of me in a slow stream.

The truth is, I don't have any idea why I think I could. I know what it means to be Unblessed better than anyone, but my yearning to serve the gods—which has been with me for as long as I can remember—didn't shift at all when I went to the island and got my blank, gold medallion from the goddess Yslet. It didn't shift when I moved into the monastery because Auntie Denna refused to house me anymore. And it didn't shift when the chieftain of our village, Greme LaCail, told me I'd be cutting peat until I died.

My desire to learn the ways of the gods and lead people into greater understanding of them has never wavered, and I suppose it never will.

I feel much smaller than my six-foot frame as Fáthair Firnan frowns up at me. It's impossible to imagine him sympathizing with any of those thoughts, so I button in my words.

"You're welcome to the library at the monastery, LacEllan," he sighs at last. "But that's all I can offer. Remember to clean the books when you're done with them. Off with you and your peat." He waves his hand rather wearily, and I nod, feeling a slender shoot of hope pushing up inside my chest.

The library is not as good as personal tutelage, but it's much better than nothing. I adjust my shoulder straps and pull the cart back into rickety motion.

Perhaps with devoted study, I'll learn enough to convince Fáthair Firnan to reconsider, to even petition the gods for an exception. I take a deep breath and raise my fingers to the tiny icon I've painted of Lir, which hangs around my neck by the same length of twine that holds my medallion. Humming a prayer to him, I head up the street toward the distillery with my load.

Chapter Three

ÁILA

I push through the door of our stone cottage and smell bread baking, which is a good sign: Mother only bakes when she's cheerful. I take several deep breaths, then pick my way through the sitting room into the kitchen, where Mother is bent over the cooking fire, using a long-handled iron spatula to rotate the loaf.

"Good day today?" she asks without turning around. "I worried that squall would swamp you."

"Fine," I say. I cross to take the kettle off its shelf and fill it with water from the barrel before leaning around Mother to hang it on its hook. She smiles at me.

"How were things here?" I ask. My hands shake slightly as I rummage for tea leaves and the pot.

"Aye, well enough," she says, and I only half listen as she embarks on a rambling description of her trip to the market, the quality of milk from Trese LaKinnin's cow these days, and the wild rumors about conflict on the mainland.

"And *I* say that dastardly King Porrl should come and drag his son home by the hair," she says with a flourish of her hands. She is sitting back in her chair by the fire while I set the tea to steep, pull the bread out to cool, and start to assemble a tea tray. "Aenland is just lucky our good King Fireld hasn't taken the Usurper Prince more seriously, or we'd have open war on our borders even now. Gods know what would happen to our wee island in a war. If the LaCail decided to fight, he could call every last one of us to march alongside him, whether we wanted to or not.

And of course the Aenladers do things much differently from us. If the Usurper succeeds, I daresay he'll stomp our traditions into dust. It's just there, dear," she says, pointing to a high shelf where the milk pitcher crouches behind a jar of pickled herring.

She ceases her familiar monologue about the Usurper Prince—the crown prince of Aenland who has reputedly been trying to overthrow our king in mainland Ilbha for the better part of six months—and I serve us both, calmed in spite of myself by the steam rising up from the tea. Cradling her clay mug in her hands, Mother leans her head back and shuts her eyes.

I pull a wooden chair up beside hers, focusing on the warm, yeasty scent of the bread. And it all comes out in a rush.

"Mother, I want to take the Trial," I blurt. "Everyone I know already has their medallion, and I'm the only one in our family who doesn't, and it's almost too late. I'll be eighteen this year. I want to help our village. I want to do whatever I was *made* to do. Please. Please, will you arrange it with Fáthair Firnan?"

She doesn't open her eyes, but her body stiffens like she's turning to stone. "Áila," she says, eyes still closed. Her voice is hard now. "There's nothing wrong with taking the other path. Not everyone goes to the island, you know."

By which she means, *she* didn't go to the island.

"You didn't live in Carrighlas as a girl," I press on, though my insides feel like a dinghy in a tempest. "And Learchlas was different. Not everyone could be apprenticed, even if they wanted to be. Fewer people did the Trial there than they do here." I want to point out that had she learned a craft, we might not have been asked to leave Learchlas after Da's accident. But as they say, only a fool pokes a beithir in an old wound, and I'm not a fool.

"You're not ready," Mother says, dark brows contracting as she opens her eyes. "And even if you were, why should you need to go? If you're tired of the boat, you can always stay home and help me."

"I'm *not* tired of the boat. I'm tired of being useless. And I'm useless without a medallion."

"So you think I'm useless, then?"

"No," I say quickly, hearing the dangerous edge in her voice. "No, that's not what I mean." I take a deep breath, and suddenly I have to fight to keep my voice from wavering. "Today, during the squall, the most help I could give was in staying out of the way. I wanted to do more, but I couldn't. I wasn't allowed. I'm dead weight there, Mother. I don't want to be dead weight."

I can't be.

Images flood my brain before I can stop them, the searing memory of the day that doomed my family's life in Learchlas.

The accident happened in the middle of the winter I was six. While Da was out on the boat with his crew, the top of an old mast broke away after a sharp gust of wind pulled hard at the sail. My brother Matan was down at the docks when the boat came back, and when he saw Da lying on the deck with men swarming around him like bees around a thistle, he lit off for home and broke into our croft shouting that Da was dead and the priest would soon be here to consecrate him.

I don't think I breathed until the healer arrived.

She bustled in just behind the fishermen, who were bearing Da on a wide plank, cursing the trickster goddess Arial with language as colorful as any of the sailors'. Da wasn't dead. The only indication he was even in pain was his clammy pallor; every word he uttered emphasized his irritation at the accident and his desire not to be made such a fuss of. I felt weak with relief to hear him complain, even if the sight of him on a plank made the world feel wrong.

After a long time, the healer stood back and looked at my mother, brow furrowed deep enough to plant seeds in.

"He won't walk easy again, if he walks at all," she said, and everyone went silent. Even Matan, always chatty, seemed lost for words. I glanced at Da and watched his blue eyes, bright and piercing, as they bored into the back of the healer's head. "The bone is shattered," she went on. "I'll bind it up, but the pieces will not easily fuse together again. At best, he will limp. Badly."

"What will happen?" asked my sister, Deirdre, in a hushed whisper, once the healer had gone. "How will we eat? Shall I go to Yslet for my medallion?"

"Of course not," said Mother. "You're far too young. We'll bide with my sister." She clapped her hands together briskly, as if it was all settled. "Mara'll make sure we don't go hungry."

But Auntie Mara had five children and problems of her own. She sent us a basket of tatties and leeks, but that was all she could offer. And the winter had not yet given its worst.

The LaKinley, chief of my mother's clan, came to see us from time to time to deliver what food he could wring from the other families. But his face grew grimmer with every visit, and the offerings became more and more sparse.

One day, he came with nothing at all.

"This is a cruel winter," he said. There was no tea to offer and no peat for the fire, so he sat empty-handed and cold like the rest of us. "Crueler than any I've seen before. And folk are getting nervous."

"Nervous?" said Mother with an unmistakable edge to her voice.

"Aye. Nervous the accident was an omen. That the winter is another."

Da's expression darkened from his place on the bed. "An omen of what, exactly, Laird?"

The LaKinley shrugged his shoulders beneath his plaid and furs. "Of the gods' wrath, Angas. Folk are concerned you might've offended them somehow."

A long silence crept over us all, colder than the air outside. Finally Da ground out, "And what do you propose we do?"

"You can't work on that leg," the LaKinley said, holding up his palms. "And the rest of us can barely feed our own families."

I squinted up at him from my seat beside Deirdre. She was squeezing my hand so hard my fingers were going numb, but I couldn't work out why she was scared. Did the LaKinley mean for Mother to work, even though she had no medallion?

"We could go to the island for our Trial," said Matan, leaping to his feet. "Deirdre and I are old enough. We can work."

"It would be years, lad, before your apprenticeship was done," said the LaKinley gently. "Years before you earned enough to feed a family. I'm truly sorry, Angas. Genivieve. I think you have kin in Carrighlas? Best try them." He nodded again at Da, whose jaw stiffened.

In anger, I realized. Not just pain.

And then I understood what the LaKinley was telling us. We couldn't stay in Learchlas. We had to leave the village.

Heat flooded my face, and I suddenly wanted to run out of our house—to run and run and run, until I couldn't run anymore. I wanted to run right out of my skin.

The LaKinley bowed to each of us individually, as if a bow could make up for what he was doing. As if a bow could give us a new place to live, or a means to earn our way in.

When it was my turn, I gave him a gracious smile—and planned to dump fish guts into his ale the next time his back was turned.

But I never had the chance. Da and Mother made us ready to leave that very night, and I never saw the LaKinley again. But I have not forgotten the price of being unable to work a craft—nor the shame I felt during our first year in Carrighlas, living off my uncle's labors while Da healed. I can still feel the ice of the villagers' stares when we went with Uncle to the kirk: the family who only took, never gave. It wasn't until Da was fit enough to captain a ship again that the people of Carrighlas stopped treating us like strangers.

The idea of facing that kind of life once more makes me feel cold all over.

Mother is watching me, and though her lips are still tight, her eyes have gone soft and sad. I wonder if she, too, is remembering that winter day more than ten years ago.

"When we had to leave Learchlas," I say quietly, "and come here . . . The way everyone looked at us. I never want to feel that way again."

Her eyes glitter suddenly like a prism caught in sunlight. She draws in a sharp breath, but tears are already beading on her lower lashes. "My darling—" The words come out thick and hoarse. She nods, swallows, and tries again. "My Áila. If it's really what you want, then yes, you may take your Trial. I hoped I could keep you here . . . with me." She swallows again, then chokes on a sob. "Oh, my sweet, wee lass. What will I do when you've gone? You've all gone now."

I hurry to kneel beside her, pulling her into a hug as she shudders and weeps. Without a craft, I realize, being a mother was all she ever had in this village. *We* were all she had. I squeeze her tighter and rest my temple against her head.

"Thank you, Mother."

She fumbles for my hand and grips it tightly. And even though a part of my heart is breaking for her, the rest of it is singing.

I will finally have my chance to go to Yslet's island. To meet the goddess. To be granted an apprenticeship, a future, a place in my village.

I find that I am crying too.

Chapter Four

ÁILA

It's been a week since I spoke with Mother, and it is my last day on Da's boat. I'll miss the salty wind on my face, the physical challenge of the work, and sharing days with my father. But I don't mourn the change. I feel like I am made of sea spray—light, leaping, free—as I look toward the life I will be given tonight. Tonight, when I finally make the journey to Yslet's island.

It could be fishing.

It could be farming.

It could be *anything*.

But even fishing will feel different if it is given to me as a task—a purpose—from the goddess. If it comes with her approval and her seal.

I can almost feel the medallion around my neck.

When we are nearly back to Carrighlas, one of the fishermen claps me on the back and tells me he'll have his fingers crossed for the sea glass medallion.

"Aye, wee LacInis," calls another across the deck. "Tell the goddess this job is the only one worth its salt!"

I roll my eyes but laugh along with him as Da brings us into port. The docks are busy this afternoon—and with more than just fishers and sailors. Our deck goes quiet with interest as we pull alongside a crew that have hoisted a whisky barrel onto their boat and are passing around drams.

"To Ilbha and King Fireld!" the blacksmith bellows from the pier, tossing back his whisky to roars of approval.

I sweep my eyes over the boardwalk, curiosity driving the Trial momentarily out of my mind. Just a few feet from the *Thistle's* railing is a tall, dark-haired young man I have never seen anywhere near the docks before. His warm brown eyes flicker to mine before I can look away, and he smiles broadly.

"Áila!" he calls. "Have you heard the news?"

My belly swoops like a falcon diving. I smile back and shake my head. He pushes his way toward me and offers a hand down onto the dock—which I take, even though I don't need it.

An itinerant scribe from the northern isles, Morgen LaCree arrived in Carrighlas with his sister two weeks ago and has been staying in the monastery while he writes a book about regional religious customs. His manners are impeccable—not quite what I expected from a Cheltlander—and his smile makes me feel like I'm turning into a jellyfish.

"What's the news?" I ask, throwing another glance at the ship handing out whiskies.

"From the mainland," he says, grinning. "The rising has been squashed out! The Usurper Prince is finished—shipped back home to Aenland. Ilbha's strength and traditions live on!"

I smile back, thinking how pleased Mother will be. Then I remember—*Mother*. She's expecting me.

"Salt and scales, I have to go," I gasp.

Morgen raises thick, black brows, striking in his olive-skinned face. "Your Trial is tonight, aye?"

I nod, but I'm already moving away. "See you later!"

He waves, still beaming, as I squeeze through the crowd and start to jog up the pier.

No news, even news about the Usurper, is likely to distract my mother when there is something as important as a Goddess Trial to prepare for.

It's traditional for a Trial applicant's family to help them prepare, so it is to my sister's stately hilltop home I run today. Mother is pacing up and down the front garden when I trot into view.

"Goddess be praised!" she cries. "What took you so long, child? I told your father to have you back hours ago! Gods, did you run here? You look like one of the wee folk, wild and feral off the moor!"

I don't point out that I would have been even later had I walked. Instead I just nod, and she shunts me through the door, toward the staircase. "Deirdre's got your bath ready. Hurry! Don't run!"

I can't hold back a laugh this time, and I try to oblige her with the fastest walk I can manage. Matan is at the top of the stairs burying a smile of his own. He has his hands full with a gaggle of my nieces and nephews, whose dark heads I muss as I stride by.

"Don't run, ye mad brownie!" Matan hisses after me. I flash him a wicked grin as I break into a jog.

When I poke my head into my sister's bathing parlor, Deirdre is sitting in an emerald velvet wing-backed chair. She's humming to herself while stitching green fabric with violet thread: my Trial dress.

"There you are!" she says. "Your bath is getting cold. Come here."

She helps me out of my wet, reeking wools, and I climb into the brass tub. It isn't hot anymore, but it's warm enough to be a relief from the cold ocean winds that've settled in my bones. I scrub my chapped skin and Deirdre goes to work on my hair, tangled with salt and grime. I take up the song she was humming—"Golden Light and Thistle"—feeling warmth seep past my skin and into my bones at the melody's familiarity.

Deirdre joins me in the chorus. "*Golden light and thistle, O! Golden light and thistle! The pipe and drum begin tae hum of golden light and thistle, O.*"

Our father's boat was named for this line. It's a song about all of Ilbha, so as many people know it in Carrighlas as they did in Learchlas. If a song can feel like home, this one does, and it seems fitting to sing it as I prepare to receive the medallion that will seal my place in Carrighlas for good.

The water is tepid by the time Deirdre finishes my hair, and I am grateful to step into the thick towel she holds. While she stitches the final touches on my dress, I sit with my back to the large hearth—burning bright with logs, instead of peat like we use at home—and rotate my head back and forth to dry my long hair.

"Right," says Deirdre after a quarter of an hour. "Come. Supper will be ready soon."

She directs me to the vanity and applies her artistic eye to my hair. I imagine for a moment what it would be like to be as rich as Deirdre, who married the LaCail's son—but the idea of marriage capsizes my thoughts entirely. Goddess Trials are often followed by weddings in Carrighlas, and I've been so focused on the former I've barely considered the latter. My stomach churns. Binding myself to someone in lifelong love and companionship is far from unappealing—my siblings both seem happy with the arrangement—but I can't think of a single soul I'd *want* to bind myself to.

Except . . .

I am once more on the deck of Da's boat, grasping Morgen LaCree's hand as I climb onto the dock. I see him smile, hear him laugh. The nervous feeling in my stomach doesn't go away, but it veers toward something pleasant and warm.

I don't want to marry him or anything—

But he's not a bad subject for daydreams.

"Are you scared, Áila?" asks Deirdre.

I start at her voice and steer my thoughts back to the Trial. For a moment, I'm seized by a doubt—familiar because it feeds my greatest fear. Yslet, it seems, tends to bless the children of Carrighlas in the areas they already show interest or aptitude: Deirdre loved working with a needle, and Yslet blessed her with embroidery. My father was obsessed with sailing, and Yslet gave him an apprenticeship as a fisherman. My friend Fiona loved children, and she came away from the island a midwife. And Matan . . . I smirk. Well, Matan would have been most pleased to be made Carrighlas's chief whisky taster, but the goddess blessed him with the cork medallion of a distiller instead. They were all given apprenticeships to match the things they already loved.

I would be delighted to stay on Da's boat, but I can't honestly say I love fishing itself. Apart from my family, I am not entirely sure *what* I love. The awareness makes me fidget. What will Yslet do with me?

Something, I pray. *Do something with me, please.*

Deirdre's eyes are sharp as the needles she wields so skillfully. Her hands pause in my hair. "What is it?"

I meet her eyes in the mirror. "I was just thinking . . . What if my medallion is . . ." I swallow. "Gold."

Gold and blank: the rare medallion of the Unblessed. Our ancient laws tell us the precious material is the goddess's kind compensation for the heartbreaking truth betrayed by its blankness. For they are only given to those who have no aptitude in any of the crafts done on the island of Fuiscea—to those who, as a result, most need a means to begin a new life. Gold medallions are often melted down and used to buy passage to the mainland or elsewhere, where few keep our traditions. It is a rare person who chooses to stay and live the hard, thankless life of an Unblessed on Fuiscea.

A darkness comes into Deirdre's hazel eyes. I recognize it as fear. But her stubbornness wins out, and a moment later they're gleaming with ferocity. "It won't be," she says in a low growl, which I know she means as a warning to the goddess. "If Yslet tries to give you an Unblessed medallion, you tell her you won't take it, and I'll slip you mine when you get back to the docks."

I laugh at this plan. Only my sister would think defying the goddess and lying to the village was a viable strategy. My amusement disarms Deirdre's intensity, and she smiles again.

"But you won't be Unblessed, Áila," she says. "There's only been one new Unblessed since we came to Carrighlas. And you're too talented, too smart, and too beautiful to waste like that."

I squeeze her hand in gratitude, thinking of the poor Unblessed boy she mentioned. He stayed in Carrighlas, and though I have always wondered why, I suddenly think how hard it would be to leave everything and everyone you know. Even if the cost of staying was to live as an outsider.

I shiver slightly. Whatever that boy did to make the goddess think he was useless, I hope I have done better.

"There. What do you think?"

Deirdre has finished weaving white stonecrop into my wavy, dark hair, and the flowers gleam like tiny stars in the candlelight. Her excitement sinks into me, warm as her hugs, and banishes thoughts of Unblessing. I stand up to slip into my green-and-purple dress.

Green, the color of life; purple, the color of the gods. Proclaiming acceptance of whatever future they might have in store for me. The thin linen swishes, much lighter than my usual wools, and I savor the feeling. I try not to think of how cold I will be on the journey to the island.

Deirdre surveys me. "Mother's going to be a shipwreck," she says, and we both burst into giggles.

"Come on," I say. "We'd best give her plenty of time to cry before we leave."

Chapter Five

ORAIL

mud

      smell

      I

      smell

      smell

      green

      salt salt salt

      I

            am—

          who

              am

          I?

      mud roll mud roll mud

      smell

      hungry

      but salt

      only salt

    is smell

wet

      dark

      drops drip wet

where

      who

I
am

sniff
air
sniff

what
body
is
Me?

23

Chapter Six

HEW

Despite the laws prohibiting Unblessed like me from engaging in religious practices—formed from the belief the blank medallion is a sign of divine rejection—I have felt the gods to be both loving and gentle in the years since I had my Trial. It's not like me to disobey rules of any kind, but in the case of prayer, I simply cannot stop; it leaks out of me like water from a cracked cup whenever I try and keep it sealed away.

As I prepare for my first visit to the library, I am brimming with prayers. And in my cold, mirrorless room in the monastery's cellar, I do my best to make myself presentable. Instead of mud-stained work clothes, I pull on the gray wool robe the monks gave me—a hand-me-down iteration of their thistle-green ones—and since it's especially chilly this evening, I belt my plaid over my shoulders for warmth. I have only one pair of shoes, the same boots I wear every day on the bog, so I clear the paints, brushes, and half-finished icons from my desk and spend half an hour bent over the muddy leather, scraping and buffing until it gleams.

The stone corridors of the monastery are empty, the only sounds the echo of voices from the monks cleaning up the dining hall. Tonight is someone's Goddess Trial, I seem to remember, and I wonder if I will have the library to myself. I watch my feet as I walk, disappointed to see a smudge of dirt already marring the toe of one of my boots.

The librarian is a short, dark-haired monk named Bráthair Gibrat, and he scowls at me when I enter the cavernous room.

I have apparently interrupted a conversation he's having with Morgen LaCree, a stranger to our island, but one who has proved himself capable of charming almost anyone on it—including, it would seem, the crabbit librarian, who technically shouldn't allow anyone access to the records behind his desk without express permission from the laird. Still, the book is open for LeCree to peruse, and he stands with his mouth slightly open, like he's broken off midsentence. Unlike Gibrat, however, he gives me a friendly smile.

Bráthair Gibrat frowns. "You took a wrong turn, *mallacht*," he says. "The peat bog is outside and to the north."

"Thank you," I say through my teeth, suppressing the flare of anger I feel at his use of the word *mallacht*—"cursed" in the old tongue. Only Gibrat and my sister's husband, Colm, are ever coldhearted enough to use it. "But I'm not looking for the bog. Fáthair Firnan said I could borrow books."

He looks annoyed, but waves an open palm toward the rows of towering shelves, pale face splotching like stained parchment. "Fine, then. Help yourself."

"Theology . . . ?" I venture.

Gibrat's eyebrows go up, and he almost smiles. Mocking me, undoubtedly. "Second row to the right," he says, "and all the way back. But hurry, *mallacht*. LaCree and I need to get to the kirk."

I'm a little dazzled by the gold-embossed spines as I walk along the shelves, but I decide to start at the beginning and make my way through them in order. I fully intend to read them all eventually, and this way I won't miss any. I pile the first five into the crook of my arm and bring them back to Gibrat for approval.

He levels his gaze at me. "What are you taking out?"

"These, obviously."

"I mean," he says slowly, and with obnoxious emphasis, "what are their *titles*?" He smirks at Morgen, who looks just as confused as I feel.

I crack one open, its yellowed pages sending a puff of dust into the air. The title page is easy enough to find, but the words on it are incomprehensible. I frown. Whatever the language is, it's not one I've been taught to read.

"This must have been on the wrong shelf. Looks like foreign language, not theology."

"No, that's theology," says Gibrat, and there's a mean hardness in his voice. "One of the classics. *Life of the Divine* by Altus."

"Then where's your common-speech copy?"

"I don't know what you mean."

"Fine, just—" I flip open the next book in the stack, and stare at the cover page in disbelief. This one, too, is written in that same language—one I definitely can't decipher. Leaving Gibrat and Morgen at the desk with my stack, I turn and stride back to the shelves marked *Theology* and begin to pull down one book after another. Heat floods my limbs as I realize not one has been translated into the common speech.

I walk slowly back to the desk where Gibrat is now smiling with the lazy satisfaction of a kitchen cat who has mortally wounded a mouse. Beside him, Morgen seems conflicted, like he can't decide whether it's his place to intervene. "Guess you won't be borrowing anything after all, *mallacht*," says Gibrat.

Mouth clamped shut on my fury, I leave the books on the desk and stride out of the library without a word. I keep walking, all the way to the double doors of the monastery and out into the night.

For a while I don't even notice where I'm going—I barely register the monks chatting and guffawing as they tromp through the mud, or the rain falling in a cold stream over my hair and down my neck, or the ocean wind ruffling the heather beside the cliffside path that leads down to the village. I don't even think to raise my hood until I am almost to the kirk itself.

He knew. Fáthair Firnan *knew* all the books in the library that might teach me more about the gods were written in the old tongue. He knew offering access to them was as much a refusal to help me as denying my request for tutoring, and he knew I would be humiliated when I went to find them.

He was doing you a favor, says the voice inside me. *You know you could never* study *your way into the priesthood. You're nowhere near clever enough for that, even if it* was *allowed.*

Outside the chapel, I find a bench in a shadowed alcove where no one will notice me. Putting my face in my hands, I breathe a prayer to Lir, god of the sea. The god I feel the most kinship and connection to.

"Why do people like Firnan and Gibrat get to serve you?" I growl into my palms. "I'm not perfect either, but at least I'm *trying* to be."

Despite my plaid, I shiver. The night is damp, and there's a bitter wind blowing in from the north; it will be a hard, cold row across the water for tonight's Trial-taker.

"LacEllan?"

I lift my head to see Bráthair Wellam, one of the few monks who doesn't treat me like sheep dung. I step out from the alcove, feeling suddenly exhausted. For the first time since my own Trial, I consider what probably should have been my decision the moment Yslet handed me that gold medallion: leaving Carrighlas for good.

"Y'alright, man?" Wellam inquires. Like mine, his robe is sodden from the long walk from the cliffs, and the dark skin of his face is glistening with rainwater.

But his words seem to reach me from a long way off. The idea of leaving has sunk into me, sudden as an iron anchor plunging beneath waves, and it drives everything else out of my head. There is plenty more to Ilbha than just our island—and the medallion tradition is unique to Fuiscea, even if the rest of the kingdom worships the same gods we do. So why should I stay in a place that calls me Unblessed—*mallacht*—when there are other places I might be allowed to serve the gods I love? Especially now that the Usurper's war has been stamped out and the mainland is on its way back to peace and order.

But of course, I know why.

I was only thirteen when I had my Trial, and I stayed afterward because the idea of leaving my sister Vira was unimaginable: she was my closest friend, and since our mother's death I had felt it my duty to protect her, even though she was older by two years. I told myself I would leave as soon as she had her own Trial—because I had nothing to offer her if I was Unblessed—but then Auntie Denna did something unthinkable. Instead of sending Vira to Yslet's island, she betrothed my sister to a man who seemed every bit as cruel and lazy as our dead father had been. Young and without a medallion or apprenticeship to give her status, Vira could do nothing except marry the man . . . and eventually bear his child. Imprisoned, like me, in a life she had not chosen.

How could I leave her?

But it has been five years since then, and Colm has proven more apathetic than cruel in that time—except, of course, in his interactions with *me*. Vira tells me he has never harmed either her or their daughter, Gemma, and swears she could protect them even if he tried. Lately, she has been begging me to leave Fuiscea, insisting my life would be better somewhere else.

I have always disregarded her advice . . . until now.

I meet Wellam's eyes. "Aye," I say with a relief that is sudden and almost painful. "I think I *am* alright."

He gives me a bracing grin, and we both head toward the kirk's side door. "See you after," he says when we reach it, and I stay outside while he goes in to sit with the other monks. I may not be allowed inside the chapel, but I can watch the Goddess Trial from the small doorway, left open to admit a cool draft into the overcrowded space.

I hunch down to lean against the frame—as close as I can get to the service without committing blasphemy—and gaze inside, still feeling slightly dizzy from my sudden epiphany. After a few moments, someone calls for quiet, and a series of shushings echo like soft rain through the timber and plaster chapel, clearing my head. Fáthair Firnan enters from the front vestibule, there are a few moments of squirming, excited silence, and then—

"Let the postulant enter!" he cries, and the heavy front doors creak open.

A family I recognize as the LacInises trail inside—including a gaggle of young children processing like dancers around a Maypole before tonight's Trial-taker: Áila LacInis.

A year or two younger than me, Áila is wearing traditional green and purple, and her long, dark hair is woven with tiny white flowers. Her tanned skin is flushed with excitement, and her sea-green eyes are alight as she proceeds down the center aisle toward the priest. Her family is giddy with anticipation, and I can't quite repress a pang of jealousy at the sight: Vira was the only family member at my Trial who cared enough to be excited, and her hopes for my future were thoroughly dashed.

The ceremony is brief, and soon the liturgy of the Trial is spooling out from the priest's lips to cover Áila like a spell. Then Firnan reaches to the table behind him for the quaich, which he fills from a crystal whisky decanter beside it. He turns, holding the shallow cup by its two handles, and offers it to Áila.

I see her brother give her a wink—he is a whisky distiller, I seem to remember—and she grins back before lifting the quaich and taking a sip of the glowing amber liquid inside.

The villagers roar with approval as she hands the cup back to the priest and turns for the door, her face radiant. Áila's green eyes sparkle like the stained glass windows of the kirk at midday, and it couldn't be clearer that the village expects great things. But for all their beauty, it is not her eyes that hold me captive as I watch her conclude the ceremony. It is her smile.

She gives the villagers its glory and its glow as she sets her face toward the door of the kirk and what lies beyond it: a small rowboat bobbing in the choppy, black waters of the sea loch.

I touch my icon and breathe another prayer to Lir—this time for her safety—as I unfold myself from the doorway and join the stream of villagers following Áila down to the docks. My resolution to leave Fuiscea tickles my thoughts, but there will be time to plan out the details of my departure later. For now, I decide, I will pray for the girl with the sea-green eyes and the sunlight smile as she conducts the Trial that will alter the course of her life.

I have prayed for many Trials since my own, but this will be the last—my final act of goodwill toward this village that has scorned me—before I turn my back on Carrighlas forever.

Chapter Seven

ORAIL

all mud

        is

world of mud

and salt

is

       this

         Is

this

saltmud world

      my

         now?

Yet.

the universe

      tilts

         shifts

           breaks

           is born

I

     sniff

     air

     sniff

someone

not me

someone

is.

She
is.

I

am
born.

Chapter Eight

ÁILA

I have never been more grateful for my years on Da's boat than I am at this moment. The dark waves pitch and churn beneath the tiny rowboat that feels like driftwood just now, and I grip the oars, muscling them against the whitecaps. I look over my shoulder and strain to see the glimmer of light—the lantern—that will lead me to Yslet's island, but all is darkness. Water crashes over the side of the boat, soaking me through, and I gasp at the piercing cold. However pretty I felt when I left Deirdre's house, I now heartily wish I had on my usual practical wools. I'll be lucky if I don't freeze to death before I reach the island.

And yet, I grin. Every pore of my body sings with exhilarated energy. I am almost giddy at the thought of what's waiting for me on the island: Yslet, our great, wise goddess, who will tell me where I belong.

Icy rain lashes my face—an extra challenge to the usual nighttime setting of the Trial. I brace my boots against the rowboat's floor and pull harder on the oars, bellowing as I fight the waves. My arms—strong from hauling sail lines—ache, but my fingers are numb, which is far more concerning. If they slip off the handles, I could lose the oars to the sea. I grip harder. Pull harder.

Salt and scales!

Yslet's island is only about halfway across the sea loch, but it feels like hours before I catch a glimmer of firelight through the sheeting rain and thick mist. My limbs go limp when the boat finally grates against the pebbly shore. For a moment, I sit with tingling muscles, and give thanks to Yslet for guiding me safely to her island. Then my heart lurches as I remember the goddess is *here*, possibly mere yards away. Possibly watching me even now.

I climb out of the boat, wet sand sucking at my boots as I haul the vessel up the bank onto a mossy rise. Then I stand back, hands clasped behind my head to catch my breath and my wits. To reassemble my nerves before I meet the goddess I have spent my whole life praying to.

Apart from a single lantern—a rustic joining of iron and sooty glass hung from an old peat cutter some long-dead priest once planted in the bank to be lit by the monks on Trial nights—there is no light on the island. I linger beside it, assuming Yslet will meet me here. Neither of my siblings ever mentioned finding Yslet lurking in the dark, after all. But the goddess does not come, and I have never been one to stand still for long.

I try detaching the lantern from its post, but the rope securing it is too tight and too old. So I yank the peat cutter out of the squidgy ground and carry it before me like a staff as I stride into the trees to find Yslet.

My heart is a bodhrán drum, pounding in my skull. Where should I go? What will I say when I find Yslet? "Hello" seems casual to the point of blasphemy. "O great goddess" feels too much like a priest's prayer. And "Good evening" makes me think of a fine lady ushering guests in to tea.

Why did I never think to ask anyone these things before now?

I keep walking, half my mind now sifting through greetings.

The island is small, barely bigger than the village square, and entirely covered with trees. I pick my way over damp bracken and squashy moss, grateful for the branches that deter the rain. When I was a small child, I believed Yslet must live here all the time, as I lived in Learchlas. I imagined she had a cottage in the trees, right in the center of the island. I even thought that if I stood on the docks on a clear day and squinted toward the island, I might see her sitting on the shore, weaving a net, perhaps, or fishing. It's been years since I dismissed the fantasy as childish—gods do not live in cottages on islands, even if they do claim parts of the mortal world for their own—but in the darkness on this strange, stormy night, the old image is difficult to repress.

Not least because a warm cottage stocked with hot tea sounds wonderful.

At first, I walk cautiously through the wood, looking for Yslet around every tree. My siblings say she is tall, with fire-colored hair and green garments, and that she always has her gray unicorn, Cire, at her side. Easy to recognize even if she *weren't* the only other person on this tiny island. Every now and again, I'm sure I hear the tread of soft feet over bracken. But I do not find her. As the minutes accumulate, my tiptoeing turns to tramping, and my cautious peering becomes a frantic search for any movement that isn't raindrops disturbing leaves. And then, as I notice the oil in the peat-cutter lamp dwindling, a terrible thought occurs to me: What if Yslet isn't here at all?

The idea is so disturbing that I stop dead, frozen by the fear of it. I've never once thought to worry about *not* finding Yslet on the island. Even the Unblessed meet her when they come. Could she have missed the priest's invitation? Is it even possible for a goddess to make such a mistake?

My lungs feel empty.

I plunge toward the center of the wood, body suddenly screaming for action. I tell myself I have assumed the worst with no reason to be afraid. Yslet will be just ahead, waiting with her blessing at the ready. She will tell me how I should apprentice, tell me where I belong.

She'll tell me I *do* belong.

Then—ahead—I hear the rustle of leaves, the snap of a branch. I nearly sob with relief. She is here. She is coming.

Thank the gods. Every last one of them.

I slow to a walk, trying to collect myself. My panic has gotten the better of me, as it almost never does, and I feel silly with embarrassment. But perhaps Yslet will not have noticed. I take one, two, three steadying breaths before I push back a low-hanging branch and step into a clearing.

The rain has stopped.

Yslet is not here.

There is only a small, muddy animal with eerie gold eyes. It takes one look at me, yips, and leaps at my chest.

Chapter Nine

ORAIL

she

    she
    she
    she
    she

      is

        here
      is
      mine
    Is

lick, salt, lick

"Ow! No!" says

but she is
      here
      mine
        Is.

lick

hungry still, hungry
    sniff
    sniff salt still

sad
        hungry

but

she she she she she

is
        mine

Is.

Chapter Ten

ÁILA

My brain bends with incomprehension as the animal leaps again, smearing mud across my dress. It's difficult to tell when there's so little light and the beast is a blur of motion, but I think it is a puppy. I shove it off for a third time, and press my fingers into my temples, wondering what in the name of all the gods to do.

I came to meet Yslet. To receive an apprenticeship, a medallion—a blessing. A way to find my place in Carrighlas. And I need the answer to that question almost as much as I need to breathe. What will I do if I can't get it?

And why, *why*, is there a dog here instead of the goddess?

I look down at it, now rolling on the ground as if the mud were sweet-smelling clover. My last remaining hope—that perhaps the dog is Yslet in disguise—vanishes like morning mist. No goddess worth the title would roll in mud.

I spin around, half-wild. "Yslet!" I cry. "Yslet, are you here? Please come! Please, don't leave me alone!"

Don't leave me with nothing.

I'm looking so hard into the surrounding trees that my eyeballs ache. The lantern sways on its peat cutter, throwing bleary gold light in patches over the ground, but Yslet does not appear.

Panic snaps whatever tether is holding me still, and I take off running. The dog is close on my heels, lolloping on legs that seem too long for it. Once or twice it trips me up, and I snarl at it to keep out of the way. But it only seems delighted to have earned a scrap of attention, and leaps to snap at my sleeve.

I feel like I might scream.

I do scream.

"YSLET!"

But she does not come.

I keep running, determined to comb every inch of this place. To make sure I haven't missed her somehow. But for once, running is not enough to banish my fear. My anger.

I scream again.

I have raced around the entire circumference of the island and crossed its middle so many times I might have traced a giant star pattern with my footprints. I have probably touched every tree.

I've never heard of someone coming for their Trial who didn't find Yslet waiting for them. Never heard of her arriving late. But maybe she isn't here because I don't actually belong at all. Because I'm not worth even the blank gold medallion of the Unblessed.

Still running, I glare furiously up at the cloud-swathed sky and scream all the curse words I know. Halfway through the last—and foulest—one, I trip over something and fall hard onto my face. A warm, muddy body wriggles its way through my ankles, paws clamber onto my legs and along my back, and a wet nose pushes down through the space between my shoulder and my head. It finds my cheek, which it licks.

I weep into the ground.

What will I do without a medallion? How will I tell the village what happened?

I think of all those shining, confident faces in the kirk as the priest announced my Trial. Of Morgen LaCree and his sister Flora, leaning across the pew to cheer me on as I made my way out of the chapel. Of my family, riotous over dinner with hope for my future. The idea of admitting failure makes me want to throw up my supper.

I push myself onto my elbows to sit up, and the puppy slides down my back and lands in the mud with a soft flump. It clambers into my lap, trying to lick my face again, but I restrain it. I settle its small, wet body between my crossed legs, where I begin to pet its muddy coat in slow, methodical strokes. I'm not really thinking anymore, just breathing in and out. Trying to arrive at a point where the chaos in my mind subsides enough for me to stand up again and go home. To whatever awaits.

Salt and bloody, bloody scales.

I hum "Golden Light and Thistle" quietly, almost unconsciously, and the familiar melody does what movement could not. It calms my anxiety and stills my thoughts. It's raining again, and I realize I'm shivering, so I nudge the dog out of my lap and push myself up. Somehow, I must find the strength to row back across the waves.

It isn't until I've dragged the rowboat down the bank again that I realize the dog is inside it: tail wagging as it gazes up at me with eyes that glow like a pair of Unblessed medallions. For a moment I consider tossing the mutt back onto the bank, but even the idea makes me feel exhausted.

Don't leave me with nothing, I prayed earlier. Well. This is not what I meant, but there can be no doubt that this creature is *something.* What's more, it's a something that seems determined to follow me. Perhaps the priest or the LaCail will have some idea what its presence might mean. Perhaps they'll know a way I might earn my medallion even yet.

Bolstered by this thin hope, I push the rowboat into open water and leap into it. On the floor by my feet, the puppy shakes, wriggling from nose to tail, and I can see that its short, dark coat is covered in even darker spots. Markings perhaps, or persistent mud. I'll only find out if we can survive the passage home.

Some don't. Not often, but it's not called a Trial for nothing.

I clench my teeth against their uncontrollable chattering, grip the oars, and once more begin to pull against the tossing sea.

Chapter Eleven

HEW

What makes the Trial so gratifying to most people is precisely what made it a horror for me, which is that the entire village is waiting to receive you when you row back across the sea loch with your news of how the goddess has blessed you. My Trial happened as early as the custom allows, because I had no parents left to make the decision for me, and my aunt was impatient that I start providing for myself. If she'd known what was coming, perhaps she would have waited, for all our sakes.

But then, perhaps not. Auntie Denna always believed that hardship builds character.

As we stand in clusters on and around the docks, I remember with miserable clarity how I felt when, after a brief conversation with Yslet that filled me up with faith the way whisky fills a glass, I had to get back into my boat and return to a village I knew was only going to reject me.

It was useless to tell them what I knew more certainly than ever before: that the gods loved me and would always be with me. Because the blank, gold medallion has always meant "Unblessed" on the island of Fuiscea, and Yslet gave me no explanation to the contrary.

I still wonder at that omission. On the days I find doubt and resentment rapping hard on my heart, trying to get in, it is Yslet's silence on the medallion that blows the door open.

When I rowed up to the docks that night, my too-long legs and arms knocking into each other as well as the oars, I wondered for a moment if I could just lie to everyone standing there. If I could somehow keep the anticipation written across their faces from melting into pity and disgust. But the medallion was all I had to show for my trip, and in any case, my conversation with Yslet still burned like a coal in my heart. I knew I could not let her down.

"It's gold," I remember saying in a small voice. "My medallion." A horrible, hollow silence rang all around the docks, threatening to swallow me up—but then conviction rose to my aid. "But I-I don't believe the gods see me as Unblessed. I don't believe they reject any of the people they've made."

The strangest thing about all of it is that I still believe those words, despite the last five years of drudgery, of living as a pariah to everyone but Vira and Gemma. And except for those occasional moments of doubt, I have never blamed Yslet or the gods for my fate.

The monks don't say it, but I know they think I'm daft.

Perhaps I am.

I sigh, looking down the dock toward the unfathomable dark of the sea loch. There has been no sign of Áila for more than three hours, and I'm starting to feel a twinge of anxiety in the pit of my stomach. The sea is rough tonight, and while I don't doubt she's strong, Áila's arms are scrappy, not thick—and those waves could capsize Trem the blacksmith.

I don't notice I'm pacing until one of the monks shoots me a look.

"Have faith," he says, but his tone is more curt than reassuring. I sigh and amble out to the end of the dock to see if I can spot anything through the indigo fog.

The rain has been relentless, and I'm grateful for my hood and woolen plaid pulled up over my head as I peer out over the black waters. The ocean seethes and roars in its ceaseless pushing and pulling, toward and away from the land, its voice a refrain I hear constantly, wherever I am. It is probably the only thing on earth I find perfect, exactly the way it is.

Protect her, Lir, I pray. *Bring her home.*

Somewhere beyond the dock, I think I hear a dog bark. I squint out over the water, pulse jumping in my neck. Then I see movement. The glint of something dark and glossy and solid. Wood.

A boat.

"A boat!" I cry, and I can tell from the gasps of relief that I am not the only one who has been worried.

Oars come into view through the fog, and a moment later Áila herself is visible, pale and grim and haloed in mist. She rows hard another few times, and then lets her arms slacken as the tide pushes her toward the dock instead of away from it. I am shunted backward as her father and brother rush past me to drag her boat down along the dock, to where they may pull her out.

"Áila!" several people cry.

"What does Yslet say?" clamor others.

"Tell us who you are, Áila!"

This is a common refrain on Trial nights—*tell us who you are*—and it always makes me flinch. Why should who we are be determined by how the goddess apprentices us—or doesn't?

I watch Áila climb onto the dock and lean into Matan, while her father bends down to retrieve something from the rowboat. Her mother and sister push forward too, and for a moment they are all too busy hugging each other to spare any attention for the crowd.

Then Áila looks around the dock and onto the shore, where the entire population of Carrighlas waits in eager anticipation to hear how she will fit into its tapestry of crafts and occupations. And as I watch her mud-streaked face, something in it strikes a low, ominous toll inside me that I know too well, even if I don't immediately recognize why. I watch her chest swell as she takes a deep breath, watch her throat bob, and feel suddenly sick with understanding. I scrape my eyes over her whole body, scrutinizing her hands especially, but find no glint of gold anywhere.

Her father straightens up, looking puzzled. He is holding something small, dark, and wriggling in his arms.

"The goddess didn't come," Áila says in a strong, ringing voice. There is pride there, and defiance, and I wonder whether she is defying the people around her, or her own fear. Her strength makes me ache with compassion.

"Unblessed?" someone gasps, and I hear the word repeated in a low murmur all around, echoing like we're in a cave. Áila stands tall, though I know from experience how small she must feel.

"I-I don't know," she says, her voice faltering. "I have no medallion."

I am seized by the irrational compulsion to go to her, to shield her from these people who would inflict upon her the same mistreatment I have known. But there is a growing commotion, a buzz of chatter as the news spreads over the dock, and Áila's fate seems increasingly unclear.

"We must call a council!" shouts someone.

"The LaCail will know!" calls someone else.

"Fáthair Firnan! Where's the priest? Fáthair!"

The crowd pulls apart and I see our chieftain walking swiftly down the docks, Fáthair Firnan hurrying along after him.

"We will consult the ancient laws," says the LaCail, looking anxiously at the cluster of pale, taut LacInises around Áila's boat. "Áila, you will come with us. We must hear exactly what happened."

She turns to her father and takes the squirming bundle into her arms, hoisting it up like a sack of potatoes before following the LaCail and the priest up the dock. As she passes the point where I stand, a few rows back in the crowd, her gaze catches on me as if snagging on wool.

The breath goes still in my chest. I know exactly what she is wondering: if we are the same now, she and I.

Her eyes hold mine for a long moment, and then she looks away. As she goes, I see the thing in her arms is not a bundle at all.

It is a dog.

A dog?

I bite down on the inside of my cheek, fighting desperate curiosity—and then slip through the crowd, following her at a distance.

Chapter Twelve

ÁILA

My body tingles with cold and unease as I follow the LaCail and Fáthair Firnan into the kirk. I hug the damp, warm puppy tight against my chest, even though it has stopped squirming. When I glance down at it—swirling brown coat showing a patchwork of black spots in the lamplight—I see it has gone to sleep.

"Sit down, please, Áila," says the LaCail. He opens one of his broad, brown hands to indicate a leather armchair beside the fire in Fáthair Firnan's office, and I sink into it. The priest has gone to work on his hearth, adding a slab of peat and stoking the embers back to life. I am grateful to sit so near the heat, but even more grateful they are not yet treating me like I'm Unblessed.

Fáthair Firnan pours three drams of whisky and hands them around.

"Drink, lass," says the LaCail in a weary voice. "It'll warm you quicker than the fire will."

I obey. The liquid burns all the way down my throat just as it did before my Trial, except that now it roots me to the chair instead of making me buoyant. It seems to strike a spark deep in my belly, though, and I feel it push some of the sea's chill out of my bones. I exhale.

"Now, please tell us what happened, Miss LacInis," says Fáthair Firnan. He and the LaCail both look grave, sitting forward in a pair of wooden chairs behind the priest's wide desk. They are stiff as chess pieces: the priest a white bishop with his pale complexion and silver hair, and the chieftain a black king, with his broad shoulders, coal-black hair and beard, and rich brown skin.

I glance down at the puppy—still asleep—and hug it a little closer as I begin my story. Its warm weight and deep breathing make me feel less alone. By the time I have finished describing what happened on the island, I find I am stroking the dog's small, floppy ears, which have relaxed outward like speckled dragon wings. I wonder how it can trust me enough to sleep in my arms when we have only just met.

I glance up to find the LaCail and Fáthair Firnan exchanging looks of uncertainty. The sleepiness brought on by the combination of whisky, a fire, and a warm puppy vanishes, and I sit up straighter. My future is theirs to decide. I suddenly feel again like I might throw up.

"I won't pretend this is not an unusual situation, Miss LacInis," the priest says slowly. He is older than the LaCail and has probably seen more Trials than most people in Carrighlas. Before she died, the priest's wife was a celebrated archivist of our histories, so Fáthair Firnan is also well aware of what constitutes an "unusual" Goddess Trial. "Greme and I have some work to do in deciding what this means. We will consult our laws, traditions, and historical records, and determine what is right to do."

With me, I want to finish for him. *You'll decide what is right to do with* me.

Will what is "right" show I belong here, or will I be declared Unblessed? Without a medallion from the gods, who can say where I belong?

Or indeed *if* I belong.

Because people should get medallions when they go and visit Yslet's island. They should get guidance and direction and affirmation. They should get apprenticeships.

They should *not* get dogs.

Anger at the gods stirs in my depths like the embers of the peat fire before me.

"What should I do with . . . with the puppy?" I ask. I glance down at it again, at its speckled pink belly rising and falling with each deep breath. Something strange takes hold of me as I do, a tightness all through my chest, and I realize with both confusion and shock that I already don't want to give this creature up.

The men across from me are also watching the sleeping dog, and their faces are blank and baffled. "We have to assume it was on the island for a reason," says Fáthair Firnan at last. "You must keep it, Miss LacInis. At least until we learn more."

I nod, my relief almost as potent as the whisky—but much more surprising.

"You may go home," says the LaCail. "We'll keep you appraised of what we find."

At this postponement of my sentence, my exhaustion returns and I stifle a yawn. I nod again and get to my feet, careful not to disturb the puppy. As I pull the door quietly open, I glance back and see the LaCail and Fáthair Firnan already deep in conversation, their heads bent together. The idea that I can do nothing to help myself makes me feel like I'm trapped in a collapsed tunnel. I take a deep breath.

Maybe they'll have a solution by morning. I almost pray to Yslet that they will, but I stop short. The goddess is the one who left me in this mess. Why should I think she would help me now?

I ease the door shut behind me, turning toward the nave of the chapel—and gasp, jumping so badly I startle the dog. It wakes with a yelp.

Right in front of me, scrabbling backward along a pew with no place to hide, is the Unblessed boy, Hew. When he realizes the LaCail and Fáthair Firnan aren't behind me, he begins making frantic shushing motions with his hands.

"What are you doing?" I say. "Are you even allowed to be in here?"

He's still flapping his enormous hands, and between his sodden robe and the russet curls plastered like wet yarn to his forehead, he looks a bit demented. I wait for him to calm down. After a moment, he seems to realize I'm not going to shout for the LaCail, and stops gesticulating.

"Were you spying on us?" I say, too tired to be diplomatic.

His gray eyes go wide again, and he jerks his head toward the front doors. "Can we talk outside?" he hisses.

I start to reply, but he's already walking away, tall frame hunched like he's hoping not to be noticed. I follow, torn between irritation and curiosity.

"What were you doing?" I repeat as soon as the heavy doors are shut behind us.

I can hear distant chatter and the lilting strain of someone singing coming from the village, but here on the steps of the kirk, the prevailing sounds are the sleepy calls of gannets and the roar of the sea. Pale starlight glimmers between clouds, mingling with the dim, colored light shed by the chapel's stained glass windows. The Unblessed boy sighs and pulls a long hand through his hair. Wet curls stand up on one side of his head, making him look like a disheveled little boy.

"I just . . . wanted to know what happened," he says. "On the island."

I expected him to lie, I realize. To say that he wasn't eavesdropping, or that he had come for a word with the priest and ended up listening by mistake. His obvious honesty pulls me up short.

"It's Hew, isn't it?" I ask. "Hew LacElla?"

"LacEllan," he says. He sounds apologetic, like he's sorry to correct me.

"Were you hoping I'd be Unblessed too?"

I don't bother to disguise the bitterness I feel, but his face is earnest when he meets my eyes. "No," he says. "I've been praying you won't be."

Again, this is not the answer I expected, and I feel wrong-footed by it. "You're kind," I say in surprise. "Genuinely kind. That's . . . well, it's . . . not what I expected from someone . . . in your place."

"And are *you* now in my place too?"

He has no right to ask, but somehow I don't blame him for wanting to know. I shake my head. "I'm not sure yet."

Hew chews his lip and stares down at his feet for a long moment while I adjust my grip on the puppy. It isn't squirming, but it's sitting up, watching him with interest. After a few more moments of silence, he gestures to it, a silent request for permission to pet it. I nod.

"It's a bonny dog," he murmurs as he strokes the dog's head. "Yslet must have something special in mind for you both."

I choke back a laugh, and a confused look flashes across Hew's face. "Sorry," I say. "I just . . . I guess I was feeling the opposite."

He nods seriously. "The gods don't always do what we expect. But I believe they have good reasons for it. Sometimes, we just have to wait a bit to find out what they are."

I smile at him. The words themselves are a little pious, but he's so obviously sincere that it's hard to feel offended. Especially since he has as much reason to be angry at the gods as I do.

"Thank you," I say. "Well . . . good night."

The dog twists in my arms to watch him as I turn and walk down the steps, striding back up the road toward the village. I am no longer sure what to pray, or to whom, but I offer one desperate plea to the heavens anyway, clutching the dog tight as I hurry on my way: *Please have good reasons for this*, I pray. *Whatever they are, let them be worth it.*

Chapter Thirteen

ORAIL

lights
    dark
    smells
    salt, still, but also
        fish
          earth
          wish
          humans, humans, humans.

hands, Hers
    hands, his

he is good
        because
          he
        smells of
    Hope.

I watch
    Her,
        wonder,
          try

        try
        try

> to fly
> backward, See

what am
> what was

who am

why am?
> but that
>> is
>>> plain:

Her.

Áila.

> I am for

Her.

I smell,
> wonder,
> try to tell,

see

what is
> She
> wants,

how to
> make

happy

Her?

Chapter Fourteen

ÁILA

The puppy wakes before I do. It is her short, high bark that jolts me out of the sluggish depths of sleep.

I know four things about this dog: She is female, she is young, she is peculiar-looking. And she refuses to be separated from me.

My mother has never allowed any pets on our beds, saying that fleas are the foot soldiers of Dhuos the Deathkeeper—yet even she seemed to realize it would be futile to try and drag this animal out of my room. And as I pulled off my muddy Trial dress last night and climbed beneath my blankets, I realized I was grateful. Grateful not to be alone. Grateful to keep the steadying warmth of the puppy's body against mine.

Now, however, as her barking subsides into a persistent growl, I am tempted to dump her in the yard with the chickens.

But then I hear voices, and I sit up.

Men, speaking quietly in the front room.

The LaCail.

I am out of bed and pulling open my trunk before I remember that laundry day is tomorrow—and all my clothes are filthy. While the puppy watches with eyes that seem to laugh, I yank out a pair of patched trousers and an oversized sark: not traditionally what you'd wear for a meeting with your clan chief, but these are not traditional times. I'm halfway out the door when the puppy gives a yip behind me, and I turn to find her pawing and wriggling at the edge of bed. She is afraid to jump.

Wishing she weren't so small and helpless, I swivel back to grab her—only to stop short. Before my eyes, the puppy *doubles in size* and leaps easily from the bed to the floor. I stare at her, mind stuttering over itself as her canine mouth cracks into a wide, toothy grin.

I could swear she knows exactly what I'm thinking.

"How did you do that?" I demand in a hushed whisper.

She looks up at me, still grinning, but doesn't answer. With a jolt of shock, I realize I almost *expected* her to. Wondering if I'm losing my mind, I scoop up the dog, who is a good deal heavier than before, and hurry down the hall.

The LaCail is pacing in front of the hearth with his hands behind his back, his face gray-tinged with exhaustion. Da sits in the shabbiest chair—his favorite—leaning forward onto his crutch, and as I enter, Mother bustles in from the kitchen. She is carrying a tea tray stacked high with mugs and biscuits. Fáthair Firnan is nowhere to be seen.

"Thank you, Genivieve," says the LaCail with a small bow to my mother as she begins to pour tea. She has barely spoken two words since my Trial last night, and I don't know whether she's angry or scared—though surely regretting her choice to let me go to the island.

"Áila." The LaCail nods to me as I take a seat beside Da. My parents both give me swift, worried looks; Mother's hands tremble as she hands me a mug.

"You were saying you'd decided, Greme?" Da urges, gripping his tea without seeming to notice it. "You and the priest?"

"Aye." The LaCail rubs his eyes wearily. "Firnan and I have been all night at the records and the histories."

"Did you find anything?" I ask, my voice hoarse. On my lap, the dog is sitting up, watching us closely. I can't quite repress the feeling she understands what we are saying.

The LaCail clears his throat, looking strained. "Only a few

cases, I'm afraid," he says, "where Yslet could not be found on her island during a Trial. And none at all where there was a dog instead." He looks at the puppy with obvious curiosity, and she stares back at him, unblinking.

"What happened to those people?" I say, knowing my parents are afraid to ask.

The LaCail shoots a glance at Da, who has clenched his jaw so tight the muscles are jumping. "They were tested further," says the LaCail. "A series of Ordeals, that together would indicate whether the gods had rejected them—making them Unblessed—or favored them. If the latter, they would be sent to Yslet's island for a second Goddess Trial. If the former . . . well. We know what happens to the Unblessed."

His face is grave, but not without hope. I nod.

"But you have a choice, Áila," he says, glancing quickly between my parents. "If you don't want to undertake the Ordeals—which I must tell you will not be easy—you are fully within your rights to leave Carrighlas and start a new life elsewhere. We can book you passage on a ship and recommend you into the temporary care of a priory until you find work."

The same right they give those who come back from the island with the gold medallion.

"But if you decide to stay," the LaCail continues, "you must leave your parents' home today. You will spend the entirety of the five Ordeals, which will each be one week apart, living in isolation in a small cottage near the monastery. You will not interact with anyone—including your family—without the presence of a designated chaperone, who will make sure you are given no outside help or guidance." He pauses, as if summoning courage. "At the beginning of every Ordeal, you will be given the option to make a sacrifice in place of the Ordeal itself, each as costly as the task you would have undertaken. You must pass all five in order to win another chance at the Goddess Trial, and each one will test you in a way that requires the gods' intervention for you to succeed. What is your choice?"

I stare at him, absorbing the enormity of his words. I have never lived without my parents, much less completely alone. I have never had every action and word scrutinized or observed. And I certainly have never undergone any impossible tests to try and prove I am accepted by the gods.

But I want to stay in Carrighlas with the people I love. And I want to be apprenticed, to have a meaningful way to work and contribute. To understand who I am.

For a moment, the choice stretches before me, twin corridors of dark unknowns. Either choice could be terrible, and either could lead to a satisfying life.

But only one of them can lead to the life I *want*.

I intend to say I'll do the Ordeals. But when I open my mouth, something else comes out. A question: "Can I keep the dog with me?"

The puppy turns its head and fixes me with one gold eye, and any lingering doubts as to whether she understands me vanish like smoke in a high wind. I can't decide whether this is terrifying or thrilling.

The LaCail considers us both for a moment. "Aye," he says finally. "I think so."

I nod twice: once for the LaCail, and once for myself. "Then I'll do the Ordeals." I look at my parents. They are both rigid and tight-lipped. Mother nods stiffly, but Da doesn't move.

"In that case," says the LaCail, "I will need you to pack your things and say goodbye to your family and friends. You have until the end of the day. The monks will ready your new home, and at sunset I will return to collect you."

He bows to my mother, nods to my father. Then he gives me a long, searching look before turning for the door and striding out into the lightening morning.

Chapter Fifteen

HEW

Two hours from dawn, I hurl off my blankets with a roar of frustration and swing my feet onto the cold stone floor.

I have not slept at all.

Not even a minute of the six endless hours I have been lying in bed.

For a moment, I stare at the paints scattered across my desk and contemplate sitting down to work on my icons. It is a practice that has often settled my thoughts when they're in a jumble—the calming precision of tiny brushstrokes on small squares of wood—but this morning, I doubt even that will help. Instead, I reach for my clothes.

My robe and plaid still feel as if they've just washed up on the beach, so I yank on my stained work breeks and shirt before pulling my woolen blanket over myself and stalking out of the monastery into the misty early morning. Usually, it would nettle me to put on dirty clothes—not to mention part of my own bedding—but today I hardly consider it. I walk the cliff path out to the promontory that has been my prayer spot for the last five years and sink onto the stone bench half-hidden in sea sedge.

What in the name of Wise Ecna am I going to do?

I was so sure of myself, so certain of my decision before that—*damnable* Trial. I felt confident, relieved at the thought of leaving Carrighlas; believed I might use this very morning to visit the shipyards and see how much gold I needed for passage to the mainland. I'd planned to sell my medallion, go to Vira and tell her of my decision, and maybe embark on a new life by week's end.

One that might grant me a theological education, a life as a priest.

And then last night wrecked me like a ship caught in the Carrivrack whirlpool.

"Damn!" I shout into the mist rising above the sea, and then cringe, guilt churning through me like the waves below. I never swear. There are so many other words to use, and the foul ones are an insult to them and a degradation of one's self-control.

But paint me a liar if I don't want to go shouting every last one I know.

Because how can I leave someone standing on the precipice of a new life that might leave them Unblessed, when I know perfectly well I can offer what I never had, and what I always longed for?

Help. Solidarity. Comfort.

The aid of my own experience.

As if your experience would be of any use or comfort to anybody, sneers the voice in my head.

I sigh, too tired to contradict it.

But my thoughts resume their weary plod. Because whatever I can or can't offer, why should I sacrifice my plan for a better life in order to help someone in a village that has never once helped me? Áila LacInis might be facing a life of Unblessing, or she might not, but either way her fate is not my responsibility. I don't owe her—or Carrighlas—*anything.*

I clench my jaw.

To the shipyards, therefore, I will still go.

Won't I?

But I find I don't know. I've been tracing and retracing these same arguments all night.

While the gulls dip and dive, crying out in chorus across

the waves, I watch the rising sun paint the water silver-blue and gold, relieved when my mind goes quiet at last. I am just starting to notice the growling of my stomach when I hear a shout from somewhere behind me.

"LacEllan! Is that you?"

I turn, as surprised as if Yslet herself were calling. No one ever looks for me; I have often doubted whether anyone would notice if I died.

Coming up the east cliffside path in an eye-watering halo of yellow sunlight is Bráthair Wellam. His deep-black skin glows like burnished wood, and his dark eyes are hooded in a frown.

"Wellam?"

"What're you doing out here? I've been looking for you an hour at least. Fáthair Firnan wants to speak to you."

"Me?"

"No, the *other* Unblessed LacEllan." He glares at me. "What's wrong with you? You look like you've been sitting up here all night."

"Not exactly," I mumble, clambering to my feet and falling into step beside him. "Just this morning. I've had . . . a lot on my mind."

Wellam snorts.

"Why does Firnan want to see me?"

"No idea," he says. "Something about the LacInis girl, probably."

My limbs go suddenly cold. Did Áila tell the priest she caught me eavesdropping outside his office? What punishment would an Unblessed receive for such an offense?

"She's all anyone's talking about," Wellam continues as he trudges up the path. "What in the name of all the gods do you do with someone who doesn't even *meet* Yslet during her Trial?"

I grunt and nod in agreement, but I barely hear him. By the time we reach the monastery, I'm not even pretending to listen to Wellam's monologue about procedures for dealing with Trial anomalies. Every part of me is icy and shaky with dread. Wellam shoots me a look of mixed irritation and concern as he opens the door to the Illumination Hall and nods me inside, and I swallow hard before walking past him.

The room is long, full of bright morning light from the floor-to-ceiling windows at the far end. Stretching down the middle is a single narrow, wooden table, drawn up with benches, where the monks often sit with their calligraphy brushes and paints. The walls are covered in square cubbies, which are in turn full to bursting with parchment scrolls: all carefully hand-painted icons of the gods or illuminations of holy texts. No one is painting today, though. Fáthair Firnan is the only person in the room, and he isn't even sitting; he's standing at the end of the hall, hands clasped behind his back as he gazes up at the enormous stained glass window.

I walk slowly toward him, heart thwacking in my throat.

"LacEllan," says the priest without looking at me. "I have a job for you."

I wait for him to turn away from the stained glass, but he doesn't, so I look up at it too. It's a narrative window, telling the story of how Yslet founded our island many thousands of years ago. A story I have heard told countless times, most often by my mother, who both taught me to read and filled my childhood with tales of the gods. I suddenly think of the last time I spoke with Fáthair Firnan, when he told me I could use the library for my studies: books written in a language he knew I could not interpret.

Some of my anxiety fizzles out in a wave of anger.

"What job?" I say, forcing brightness into my voice.

He turns to me, but his pale eyes are distant, unfocused. He blinks, and his expression becomes more purposeful; but even so, I can tell he still doesn't really see *me*. He sees only an Unblessed, a tool to be used for whatever needs he might have.

My decision hardens inside of me for what is, I hope, the last time.

I will leave Áila LacInis to her fate. By this time tomorrow, I will have bought passage off this island, and soon Fáthair Firnan will be just one more piece of Carrighlas I'll never have to see again.

"As I'm sure you've heard by now, there was a Goddess Trial last night that did not go the way anyone expected. A young woman went to the island and did not meet Yslet anywhere at all. Not even a gold medallion to show for her troubles. We have offered her the chance of an ancient series of tests, to spare her the shame of being Unblessed, but she will live in isolation during the weeks she undergoes the Ordeals. We need someone to act as her servant, messenger, and chaperone during that period. Someone who could neither help her with nor distract her from the tests. Someone unimportant, uneducated. Someone Unblessed. And you are the youngest, most physically capable Unblessed we have, LacEllan."

I blink at him, mind careening between the many offensive things he has said. I think that, beneath all the insults and unkindness, Fáthair Firnan is asking me to be Áila LacInis's only human confidant for the immediate future.

"Naturally, you'll have to leave off your peat cutting duties, but the other Unblessed can do without you for a while. And you will have to work hard when it's all done, to get the village supply back up."

I stare at him, my tired mind as slow as a dull shovel through clay. But after several moments, something makes itself very plain to me: the gods are either giving me the clearest direction I've ever had, or they have a decidedly sick sense of humor.

My longing to leave this place pulls at me, desperate as my niece Gemma when she wants to read another story. But stronger than that pull is the compulsion that has been with me as long as I can remember—for as long, I suspect, as I have been able to think coherent thoughts.

The compulsion to know—and then *do*—what is right.

How could you *know what's right?* says the voice that would be rolling its eyes if it had a physical body. *You can't even read the holy texts.*

For once I long to heed that voice, because it seems to support my desire to leave Carrighlas. But suddenly I am back in front of the kirk in the salty air of the gloaming, light from the windows catching glints from Áila's eyes as she watches me. I can hear her voice, resonant as violin strings, and smell the flowers woven into her dark hair.

Most of all, I can feel the fear rolling off her as she looked at me and wondered if my fate was about to become her own.

A defeated breath leaks out of me as the reason I have been awake all night distills itself into a single, simple, life-altering question: How can I leave this place if there is even one person here who truly needs my help?

Fáthair Firnan watches me with narrowed eyes, as if wondering what could possibly be taking me so long to answer.

"If that's what the gods would have me do, Fáthair," I say with a sigh, "I will of course obey."

The priest studies me a moment longer. Then his gaze drifts away from me, back to more important things, like the window. "Good. Thank you, LacEllan. I will tell the LaCail it's all arranged. Meet me in the entryway at dusk. I will apprise you of your new duties then. You may go."

I am heavy as iron. But as I leave the Illumination Hall, I remind myself it is only temporary. As soon as Áila's Ordeals are finished, I will be on my way.

No one but the gods themselves can stop me.

Part Two

STONE

Chapter Sixteen

ÁILA

By sunset, my family has gathered to see me off. Matan masks his worry with raucous joke-telling; Mother fusses over my bags; Deirdre is a pillar of fury at my side; and Da has lured my dog across the room with some kippers in an attempt to teach it to sit. A crowd of spouses and children ebb and flow through my parents' cottage like kelp on a drifting tide, and I feel someone's hands on me almost at all times. Despite this, I feel disconnected from my body.

"I've failed you, lass," Da says thickly when I cross the room to hug him. "It's my job to protect you. I should never have pushed you to do the Trial."

But I shake my head. "I *chose* this, Da. I have to find my place. That's not something you can protect me from."

When Matan shouts that he sees the LaCail coming, Deirdre takes me by the shoulders and squeezes them hard. "You are *not* Unblessed, Áila," she says. Her dark green eyes sparkle with angry tears. "No matter what happens. I will fight the gods myself if they don't get you out of this."

I almost say, *I'm not sure the gods care very much*, but the words sound bitter and angry inside my head. I force a smile instead and kiss her cheek. "I'll work harder than I've ever worked," I tell her. "I promise."

Fear writhes in my belly, though. What if hard work isn't enough to get me through the Ordeals? What if the gods really *have* rejected me?

Everyone falls silent when the LaCail walks through the door. He looks more uncomfortable than I've ever seen him, and he does not meet Deirdre's eyes. Not that I blame him—she's not the sort of person you want to get on the wrong side of—but she *is* his daughter-in-law. He'll have to talk to her eventually.

Gods help him.

I hug everyone a final time and kiss my mother, who is crying. The LaCail is gracious enough to scoop up all of my bags—one for clothes, and three bulging with the food my family has heaped on me—so that all I have to carry is the puppy. She settles in my arms like I'm home to her. I take a deep breath, wave to my family, and follow the chieftain into the gathering dusk.

Into my solitude.

He doesn't speak, and neither do I.

We walk down the dirt road, exchanging houses for shops and pubs, and the steady sound of the water mill for the evening chatter of folk making their way home. As we cross through the village square, people ogle like I'm headless, and I hold the dog tighter, aching, aching, aching. All through my body, aching. To feel in Carrighlas like I do with my family.

Like this dog seems to feel with me: at home.

We turn left at the kirk, and I am beset by visions of last night. Leaving the chapel full of hope. Rowing to the island. Telling the village I didn't meet Yslet. Whisky bearing me up and dragging me down. The conversation with Hew LacEllan.

We carry on walking up the long, heather-bordered path that leads to the monastery. It's a path I have run countless times, along the cliffs. Always to clear my head, to feel alive.

I do not feel alive now.

We pass the monastery. The path splits, and we follow the cliffs along a very winding, narrow lane. Rolling hills of sedge and fairy flax rise to the left, and the rock cuts sheer to black ocean roaring on the right. White stars glitter amid clouds above us, and I gaze at them as we climb a steep rise and emerge before a wide stretch of heath at the top of the cliffs.

In the starlight, a pale structure takes shape. A small cottage.

I have lived in Carrighlas since I was nearly seven, and I never knew this cottage was here. Never ran far enough to find it.

I'm already lonely.

"Here we are," says the LaCail, his voice unnaturally chipper. He pushes open an old oak door and bows me inside.

It's a one-room stone cottage, bleached white with limewash. There are two windows with shutters to keep out the wind, and thick beams supporting the roof. The thatch smells fresh—replaced, perhaps, this very afternoon—and the floor is worn flagstone. A single lantern on the table has been lit, throwing flickering light against the walls. The place is clean enough, but the contents are meager: a narrow bed against one wall, a wooden chair and small table against another, a fireplace, and a cupboard with a single rusty pot inside. I can't imagine anyone has lived here in at least a century. My stomach sinks into my feet as I realize there is not even a kettle, let alone a cup to put tea in.

"Cozy, isn't it?" says the LaCail, setting down my bags and clapping his big hands together.

I think of my parents' house, which I have always considered spare. The paintings and heirlooms on the walls. The bookshelf. The warm blankets, armchairs, and rugs. The *plates*.

There is none of that here. I realize there's not even a pillow on the bed.

"Aye," I say slowly. "Very cozy."

"Well," the LaCail says, swinging his arms. "Just a few last things before I leave you to get settled. Fáthair Firnan and I will soon have the Ordeals arranged, at which point we will send word so that you may prepare. We would like you to remain in isolation, but after the first Ordeal, you may visit the kirk to pray.

From now on, you must speak to no one without your personal attendant present. He will escort you to the kirk when necessary, as well as tend to your needs here: food, water, and peat to burn. Though I believe there is a well nearby . . ." He squints at a back window.

"Personal attendant?" I say, suddenly remembering the promise of a designated chaperone. Assuming this person comes at least once a day to check I'm still alive, I won't be *entirely* alone . . .

"Aye!" says the LaCail, seizing on the topic. "I think you'll find him very satisfactory. The lad's a hard worker too, I have it on Firnan's authority. He should be here any moment." The chieftain sidesteps through the front door, peering back the way we came. "Ah, yes! Here he comes now!"

I'm a little flustered that this attendant is a "he," but then I think of Matan—perhaps he was saving the news as a surprise—and even, with a thrill that flushes my cheeks, of Morgen LaCree, whom the priest knows well. My heart trips with eagerness, and I step toward the door.

Fáthair Firnan comes through it. And Hew LacEllan follows right behind.

The former smiles. The latter grimaces.

And my heart sinks with irrational, crushing disappointment.

Chapter Seventeen

HEW

The priest is saying something inane about how nice this bare little cottage looks, but I don't hear much of it. I'm too focused on Áila's expression, which went from wide-eyed to something pinched and rather painful-looking and is now working itself into a polite smile. I am struck by the conviction my appointment as her chaperone has disappointed her.

Which, I suppose, is something we have in common.

"This Unblessed boy," Firnan is saying to Áila, "is yours to command. He will come twice a day and bring whatever you need. When you visit the kirk, he will accompany you, to ensure no one assists you in preparing for the Ordeals. He will deliver any letters you might wish to write to your family—though they will not be allowed to reply for the same reason—and if you ever need to speak to Greme or me, this boy will let us know."

Áila nods vaguely. She darts a glance at me, but her smile falters as her dark brows knit together. I can tell she's puzzled by something, but she doesn't speak.

She is holding that dog, just like last night, and in the dim lantern light I can see that it's an odd-looking black-and-brown creature, its coat the color of mud swirled through with toffee and covered with black spots of every size and shape. Its eyes are striking gold, and they fix on me with intelligent interest. I've never in my life seen a dog like this one, all mismatched speckles and short fur, and I suddenly realize it is bigger—much bigger—than it was last night. I stare, wondering if it could possibly be a different dog.

"Bring in some peat for Miss LacInis, LacEllan," says Firnan. To Áila, he adds, "We'll leave you to settle in, but anything you need, you just tell LacEllan, and he'll take care of it."

I almost laugh at the absurdity of the offer, presented as if Áila were being entertained in a palace suite brimming with comforts. I imagine that for her, accustomed to a normal life in the village, "anything she thinks of" might make a fairly long list in a sparse, gloomy bothy like this one. And as for me taking care of it, I can only assume Firnan means with my own ingenuity and resources, because he's given me no gold or supplies.

Heaving a stack of dried peats out of the wagon I myself loaded and hauled up from the village, I stagger back toward the door, fumbling out of the way again when I realize Firnan and the LaCail are on their way out.

Leaving me to my duties, and Áila to her doom.

I walk back inside, where Áila stands in the middle of the room looking like she doesn't know where to go or what to do. Sure of one small way to help, I crouch in front of her hearth and begin the process of lighting the fire. By the time I get the kindling burning and lay on the peats, Áila has perched herself on the single wooden chair and put her dog down to explore. She's watching me work, and I flush slightly, unused to being noticed at all—let alone scrutinized.

"I brought something for you, Miss LacInis," I say, sitting back on my heels. I clear my throat, feeling self-conscious, and draw a small tangle of twine out from my pocket. "It's an icon of Ona. Lir and Yslet's daughter."

"The one who died?" says Áila, brows drifting upward.

"For comfort in your sufferings," I explain. "Ona was a goddess of laughter and light, but she knew great hardship. Her spirit is as much a part of Fuiscea as her parents', so I hope it gives you courage in these Ordeals."

I swiped it off my desk in last-minute inspiration before I left the monastery tonight, thinking it would be nice to offer Áila some encouragement. Of the finished icons I had to choose from, Ona seemed the best choice for someone in such a confusing position with the gods, but now I'm doubting the choice. Perhaps it was morbid or discouraging to give her an icon of a dead goddess.

Áila nods slowly, but reaches to take the icon from me. She sweeps a thumb gently over the gilded surface of the small, wooden pendant, and a smile touches one corner of her mouth. "She's beautiful," she says. "Thank you, Hew."

I nod in relief as she passes the loop of twine over her head and lays the pendant against her sternum.

"Anything else I can do for you, Miss LacInis?" I sweep my eyes over the small, empty cottage, taking in its many inadequacies.

"Aye," she says with a small laugh. "You can call me Áila, for a start. And then . . . I wouldn't mind hearing how you wound up with this task. Is it because you're Unblessed?"

I blink, taken aback. People rarely ask me questions about myself at all, let alone with this kind of candor.

"I suppose so," I say slowly. "Fáthair Firnan said he needed someone unimportant, who wouldn't help with the Ordeals or distract you."

A crease appears between Áila's brows, and something about her changes, becoming more remote. Her eyes take on that glazed quality again, and I realize she's lost in her own thoughts, somewhere far away. But then she comes back to herself, green-ringed pupils focusing as they look into mine.

"Is that why the priest didn't introduce you? Because he thinks you're not important?"

I sigh, shrugging, and Áila frowns, but not at me. I imagine she's realizing that if she doesn't perform well during her Ordeals, she, too, will be declared not important. And just like last night, I'm seized by a desire to spare her pain and anxiety. "*You* won't be, though," I assure her. "You won't be Unblessed. The gods will see you through this."

She doesn't look convinced, but she gives me a wan smile. She reaches a hand down to pet the dog, now sitting beside her chair, and smothers a yawn. "Thank you for your help, Hew. If you don't mind, I think I'll go to bed."

I nod and turn for the door. When I am halfway through it, she says my name again, and I swivel back toward her.

Her eyes are bright and hard. "I don't think you're unimportant," she says.

I nod again, and smile at her as I close the creaky old door. I keep smiling, too, and my footsteps feel light as I start down the path that leads to the monastery.

I don't think you're unimportant.

The moonlight falls silver on the pebbles and heath, and while it is not the gilding of the golden hour, I think for once that it is flawless, exactly the way it is.

Chapter Eighteen

ORAIL

More.
> There is much,
>> much
> more here than
> I
> thought.

Salt, yes, mud, yes,
> fish and love and life, yes,
> but Sadness also.

I can smell it on Her.

And something more, that
> *I* was?
>> Hoof and horn,
>>> feather and claw.
>> But I am neither-nor
> now.

Now paws,
> now tail that moves when I am
> moved.
>> Now belly that looks and looks
> for food.

74

Now nose
and smells.
Smells forever
and ever
and ever
that can't be quelled.

I am this now.
But I am more, still.

I wish I knew what.

Wish!

A bell clangs deep
with memory,
with yes.

I look to Her,
to Áila,
for her wish.

The sadness I smell
is more than I can bear.
Any sadness in Her
would rip me, tear
me. I will smell for Her

wishes as I hunt for my
Self.

This new body stirs,
twinges,

urges:
        I squat near the wall.

"No!" She says.

My head lifts,
        ears fall.
        Shame hits
        like a hand.

"No," She says, but soft.
        "Outside," She says, and lifts
        me,
        takes me
        into the night.

"Good dog," She says, and I
        have never felt such love,
        such life,
        never been so sure of anything

in all my forms

as I am of Her.

I smell deep, find her wishes:

        Teapot and kettle,
            blanket and pillow,
                plate and mug and spoon
    and rug.

        Light.

I do not know the shapes of
these names,
but I smell harder,
do what I can with what I smell.

I leap at Áila,
lick her cheek,
taste salt wind,

hope She is pleased.

Chapter Nineteen

ÁILA

I lead the dog back toward our sad little cottage, trying not to slosh the water I pulled from the well while we were out. She leaps at me, then does a manic lap around the meadow behind the house. In the moonlight she is a blur of panting shadow, and I smile at her energy.

"Not too far!" I call, thinking of the cliffs. "Dog!" I frown, realizing she needs a name. "Dog, come here!"

Even nameless, she comes bounding out of the darkness. Her gold eyes are twin moons.

I push open the door and follow her into the cottage. It's a moment before I realize what is different: soft yellow light fills the space, flickering from the flames of an oil lamp and a dozen beeswax tapers. I crinkle my brow, and then notice the rest of it.

A pillow and two blankets, stacked on the bed. A kettle and some dishes on the table. Another blanket spread across the floor like a rug. I stare at them for a full minute.

Could Hew have brought them? We surely weren't gone long enough for him to light all the candles, let alone set out the rest and leave again. I glance at the dog. She is gazing up at me with a wide grin, pink tongue lolling. I realize her eyes are slightly crossed.

"Do you know how all this got here?" I ask her.

She raises one speckled, batlike ear and warbles, "*Ooooaauurr.*" I have to assume this means something, but I have no idea what.

I cross to the table and examine the dishes. They are similar to what my family use: rough and rustic, handmade from clay, and lightly brushed with a pale, sea-green glaze. I find two of everything. Each pair is more or less identical, except the mugs: one of them has a thin line of gold script running around the bottom, as if it has been written there with a quill dipped in sunlight. I tilt it toward the candlelight to read what it says:

Golden light and thistle, O! Golden light and thistle, O! The pipe and drum begin tae hum of golden light and thistle, O.

My eyes spike with sudden tears, and I have to swallow to dislodge the lump in my throat. I turn back to the dog.

Two gold orbs meet my gaze, intense and unnerving.

"Where did this come from?" I whisper hoarsely.

She doesn't even blink.

I cradle the mug to my chest as carefully as I would a corn-crake's egg and let its familiar words welcome me to this strange new home. The memory of singing them in harmony with my parents and siblings the day we moved out of my uncle's house and into our own cottage is sharp in my memory. It was the first moment I felt things were coming to rights after all the hurt of leaving Learchlas. It was also the first time we had sung together since arriving in our new village.

After a few moments, I place the mug and other dishes in the cabinet and turn back to the dog. She is still watching me. "You need a name," I say. "What shall I call you?"

I tap my lip in thought.

Orail flits across my mind.

I shake the word away. It's not a name I've ever heard before, and I have no idea why it would occur now.

Driftwood?

Toffee?

Peat?

Orail.

I look back at the dog. She has not moved a single millimeter; she is staring me down like we're having a contest and I'm losing.

"What about Apprenticeship?" I say with a humorless snort.

Orail.

"Birch? Alder? Rowan?"

Orail.

"Yslet?" I want to laugh at this one, but it just makes me feel hollow inside.

The dog growls, low and short.

Orail.

I squint at her. She still hasn't so much as blinked. I feel her eyes boring into me, and wonder if somehow Orail is *her* idea. She gives a soft, almost inaudible whine.

I try to think where I've heard the word before. We had some brief tutelage in languages at school, and this is a word in the old tongue, I think. Orail . . . Orail . . . Something to do with metal? Precious metals?

And then I remember.

Golden one.

I meet the dog's eyes again, her intense, gold eyes—as fathomless as Hew's medallion.

Golden one. I shiver.

"Orail?" I say, almost nervously.

She doesn't break eye contact, but her canine mouth splits once more into a wide grin. "Right," I say. "Right." I am shaking slightly, sure now the name *was* her idea. Again, I can't decide whether I feel unnerved or excited by this. "Orail. Well, I don't know about you, Orail, but I'm ready for bed."

I take a shallow bowl from the cupboard and fill it with water for her. Then I unpack my bags: enough food for a month and a small stash of clothes and possessions. I glance around, wishing for a trunk, and find one I hadn't noticed before at the foot of the bed.

Too tired to puzzle out the mystery, I load my things into it, strip down to my shift, and climb under the covers. It's a narrow bed, and I expect Orail to curl up on the ground. But a moment later she's leaping up and turning tight circles at my feet. Before I can protest, she has tucked herself into an impossibly small ball in the crook of my legs.

I sigh, but I am grateful for her presence on this chilly spring night at the edge of nowhere.

"Goodnight, Orail," I whisper.

She groans contentedly.

I wake to find that only a quarter of the small bed is still mine.

Orail is sprawled across it, her back pressed against my legs. She is gradually inching me toward the edge of the mattress.

It isn't yet dawn, but the light creeping in has a faintly morning quality to it. Flinching at the cold, I swing my feet onto the flagstones and wish I had thought to pack my dressing gown. What a fool I was for thinking this place would be well stocked. I turn to pull one of the blankets out from under Orail, but my eyes catch on a familiar brown wool, hanging over the end of the bed.

My dressing gown.

Which I am *entirely* certain I did not pack.

I glance at Orail as I pull it on, but she is still asleep. I think of her unblinking gaze, the moments I have been sure she understands me. The way pillows and blankets and dishes appeared out of nowhere last night. The way I couldn't shake myself of her name, even though I barely knew the word.

The mug.

Fear shoots through my limbs.

What *is* this creature I have taken in? Is she responsible for these things—or are the gods?

Shivering at more than just the cold, I make my way to the

smoored fire and encourage it back to life beneath the kettle. When I have my tea—a sad cup, since I have no milk—I leave Orail snoring and walk out to the bluff.

In daylight, this little patch of the world looks much friend-lier. Where last night I saw hostile cliffs and a shabby stone bothy, I now see dazzling vistas before a quaint cottage, sof-tened by early spring blooms across the heath. The cliffs are not sheer either, as I thought. I am able to sit near the edge without risking my life.

I cradle my precious new mug in my hands, staring across the silver water. If I squint, I can just make out Yslet's island: a black dot on the horizon. For a moment, I try to imagine what it would have been like to actually meet her. Perhaps she would have appeared through the trees where I found Orail, and instead of a muddy puppy, I would have found a tall, flame-haired woman in green, with a silvery unicorn at her side. She would have held out a medallion to me, and my life's path would be clear, my acceptance secured. And if she had given me the blank gold medallion . . . ?

Well. Legend says if you capture a unicorn, it will grant you a wish. Maybe I could have simply seized hold of Cire and wished for an apprenticeship.

But, of course, I never even had *that* chance.

Anger surges in me, hot and volatile. I want to unleash it on Yslet, see her defend herself. Hear her excuse for what she did to me. But anger isn't even the worst of what I feel, which is why I focus on it, dangerous though it seems. It is still better than feeling the ache, the hurt.

The anguish of wondering *why* Yslet chose not to come.

I've never doubted the gods' existence before now—have never had a reason to. But my Trial has carved a yawning hole into my center, and I find myself asking new questions. Questions that have never occurred to me before.

Has everyone been lying about meeting Yslet on the island? Or is the woman they met merely a mortal woman perpetuating a hoax—and no goddess at all? Do any gods exist, or are we mere accidents of nature, alone beneath the broad, cruel plane of the heavens?

I've believed in you all my life, I think. *Give me one good reason to keep believing.*

Then I sigh, because I have my reason already: If I become an apostate, and the gods *do* exist, they will surely reject me through the Ordeals. And I will have no chance at a medallion.

A mad idea occurs to me, and before I can think better of it, I act: *Get me through these tests*, I pray to all the gods at once, stomach churning at my own reckless daring, *and I promise I'll believe in you—all of you—forever. But make me Unblessed, and I'll be done with you. Forever.*

I stare out at the sea, feeling like I've committed heresy. Bargaining with the gods is rarely considered wise.

But it's not like they left me with much choice.

"Áila?"

I jump, spilling my tea. Twisting around, I find Hew LacEllan standing behind me on the path. His copper curls are limned with gold from the sun, and he is smiling tentatively beneath a constellation of freckles. In his long hands is a pitcher of milk.

"I come bearing news," he says.

Chapter Twenty

HEW

It wasn't what I meant to say, and I am disappointed—but not surprised—when I botch both the sentence and its delivery.

I bring news of your Ordeals, I was going to say, after announcing my presence with a subtle clearing of the throat. Áila was going to hear me coming and turn in anticipation and welcome as I approached, and then I was going to reassure her of her capabilities with a gentle delivery of the LaCail's instructions. She was going to feel equal to the Ordeals looming before her, and I was going to be convinced I had done the right thing in staying to help her.

Instead, I forget to clear my throat, and Áila nearly falls off the cliff at the sound of my voice. Then I hold up the milk pitcher and say *I come bearing news*, as if the milk is the news. My voice is more squeaky than reassuring, and Áila looks alarmed to see me, rather than grateful.

You're a colossal fool, you know, groans the voice inside me.

I don't bother arguing, because I agree completely. I wouldn't blame Áila at all if she simply turned back to the ocean and pretended I wasn't there. But she doesn't. She stands up, brushes grass from her dressing gown, and says, "Tea?"

"Aye," I say ruefully. "I brought milk."

Obviously, the voice snickers.

I follow her up the flower-lined walk and into the cottage—where she stops so suddenly I bump against her, sloshing milk onto her shoulder. She doesn't notice.

"Orail!" she gasps.

I look past her. Inside, the brown-speckled dog is doing something I have never seen a dog do before: it's standing with its back legs on the wooden chair and its front legs braced against the cupboard, long, muscular neck craned to push its nose into the lower shelf of the pantry. I think it is already bigger than it was last night.

At Áila's voice, the dog jerks around, ears going flat against its head and all four paws dropping down onto the chair. Sagging from its mouth is a loaf of bread, half-eaten. The dog cowers, but there is something rascally in its gold eyes just the same. The look reminds me of Vira when she was a lass: always getting into some mischief or other, and always caught between sorrow for her crimes and determination to keep committing them.

"What are you doing?" Áila demands. She sounds incredulous, like the dog has confounded her every idea of its moral character. The creature dismounts the chair awkwardly, creeping across the stone floor before rolling sideways, paws limp in the air and head upside-down as it worms its way across the flags. Its tail thumps tentatively, a slow, strong, speckled whip.

A laugh chokes its way up my throat.

Áila sinks down onto the floor, pulling the dog's head into her lap. "Orail," she sighs, and I register the dog's name as well as its sex. "Do not do that again, or I will tan your hide."

Orail seems to detect forgiveness in this threat, because she quivers with sudden energy. Áila cringes away just as the creature leaps up and gallops once around the cottage, then scrambles to her feet to fling the door open. Momentum building like a sailboat catching the wind, the dog races through it in a blur of brown and black, disappearing into the misty morning.

Áila turns back as if nothing unusual has happened. "Did you say you had news?"

"I do," I say, nodding and trying to remember all the things

I was sent to tell her. The LaCail was with Firnan very late last night, working out the details, and they summoned me early this morning to tell me what to relay to Áila. I clear my throat. "Your Ordeals will test the five parts of you that comprise the whole: Body, mind, soul, heart, and life. You will be told what to expect for each one when you have completed the one before it, and will have the intervening days to prepare as well as you can. Except, erm," I say, coughing a little as I remember the most important detail, "for the first Ordeal. Which will be tonight."

Áila whirls away from the hearth, teapot in hand. "Tonight?" she yelps. Steaming tea sloshes over the flagstones at her feet, but she doesn't seem to notice.

Buffoon, says the voice in my head. *You could have mentioned that sooner.*

"What is it?" Áila gasps. "What's the Ordeal?"

"Ph-physical," I stammer. "It's the trial of your body." I grimace at her. "The LaCail will come to fetch you at sundown, and you must stand waist-deep in the sea all night, with your arms outstretched to the gods for their assistance."

Áila stares at me for a long moment. Then her whole body seems to relax as she breathes in and out—and then, incredibly, *smiles.*

I stare at her. "Aren't you worried? I think it sounds very difficult. And . . . *cold.*"

"It does," she agrees, placing the teapot on the table. "But it's physical. And physical challenges are the kind I know best. Years on a fishing boat, see?"

I want to ask her if she's lost her mind, but at that moment a blaring, yodeling sound erupts somewhere outside, as if someone is trying to strangle a bagpipe. Áila sprints for the door, disappearing through it just as I realize the sound is Orail, and that she's either barking or howling—or both.

Which has to mean that something—or someone—is here.

I hurry after Áila, sudden panic spiking my pulse. My job is to chaperone her interactions, and I'm already failing at it.

By the time I reach the end of the garden path, Áila is halfway to the rise, near the track that leads back down to the monastery: the direction Orail's yodeling seems to be coming from. Cursing my gangly legs, I blunder through the sedge and arrow grass after her, tripping over shrubs until at last I crest the rise myself and spot her again.

She has reached Orail at the edge of a copse of pines. The dog has backed two people up against a tree and is showing every appearance of wanting to disembowel them: the scribe Morgen LaCree and his sister, Flora.

"Orail!" Áila shrieks. "Orail, *no!*"

I lope toward the group, trying not to trip over my too-large feet.

Flora looks relieved at our appearance, but her brother is motionless beside her, eyes pinned to the snarling dog. Áila skids on the pebbly path as she reaches Orail and lurches for her, muttering under her breath—and suddenly I have to blink hard to convince myself I am not seeing things, because she seizes hold of a two-inch-wide length of leather buckled around the dog's neck that was definitely not there a few seconds ago.

I lose track of everything else for a moment. But the collar is as solid as Orail herself, because it is succeeding in keeping her from murdering the LaCrees. I pull my eyes back to Áila, who is dragging Orail away and gasping, "I'm so sorry! Salt and scales. I don't know what got into her!"

Morgen and Flora seem too focused on Orail's teeth to notice anything odd about her neck, and both offer Áila shaky smiles as the dog finally yields to Áila's commands and sits, panting and hacking, beside her.

"We never had dogs," says Morgen, turning to make sure his sister is all right, "so I don't know much about managing them. I think I surprised her when we came over the ridge, and I waved my arms to try and scare her off."

"It didn't work," says Flora dryly, pushing a heap of black curls out of her face. Darker than her brother, her skin is a luminous copper, though her eyes are a striking hazel.

"Yes, well, it wouldn't," I put in. "The more threatening you look, the more a dog will want to protect its human from you."

Morgen looks embarrassed. "I'm a bit skittish of dogs," he murmurs.

"And I think they can sense that," says Flora, patting her brother on the arm. "Anyway, thank you for coming to our rescue, Miss LacInis. Any chance we could trouble you for a cup of tea? We brought scones."

I frown, my usual impulse to blend into the background vanishing at this first, suspicious whiff of cheating.

"I think," I say, stepping forward, "that Miss LacInis should be preparing for the first Ordeal this morning, not entertaining guests over breakfast."

"*Hew*," Áila mutters, flushing.

"You're not allowed to—" I begin.

"*Visit the village*, the LaCail said. But he didn't say anything about visitors to my cottage, so long as you're here to chaperone."

I open my mouth to retort, but she's right. So instead I lower my voice, angling my shoulders away from the LaCrees. "But your Ordeal is *today*. They mustn't try and help you."

"You just said the Ordeal is physical. How are they supposed to help with that?"

She has me yet again, but I still feel like the LaCrees are requesting a flagrant violation of the rules. I give them both a hard look, hoping they'll understand I think they should wait until another day, but Morgen merely smiles.

"Tea?" says Áila, beaming at him. She pulls Orail back up

the path and leads the way to her cottage, Morgen and Flora close behind her while I bring up the rear.

"To what do I owe the honor?" asks Áila, holding open the door as if she's a laird welcoming foreign dignitaries into her estate home. I don't miss the warm glances she keeps throwing Morgen, and I want to shake her by the shoulders and remind her she has more important things to think about. If all it takes to tempt her to break the rules is a handsome face, I'll be better off—not to mention happier—leaving her to her fate and sailing to the mainland.

"Well," says Morgen, clearing his throat. "I'd hoped we might arrive at this point in the conversation a little more naturally, but here we are." He laughs, giving Áila a look every bit as charged as the ones she's been giving him, and I roll my eyes. "The truth is your situation is remarkable and rare, and, well, it affords us a great opportunity to gain insight into the ways of the gods. I would love the chance to speak with you regularly throughout these Ordeals, Áila, as research for my book."

"Oh!" Áila says, handing around the teapot. She looks a little disappointed, but not, I suspect, for the same reasons I am.

"Mr. LaCree," I interject firmly, "these Ordeals are meant to be—"

"All chaperoned, of course," says Morgen smoothly, cutting across me.

I frown at him. "I don't know that the LaCail or Fáthair Firnan would agree to this. I'll need to speak with them about it."

"Oh, don't worry, LacEllan," says Morgen with a dismissive wave and another genial smile. "I've already spoken to Firnan, and he doesn't mind at all. He's very supportive of the work we're doing."

I am quite used to being ignored, dismissed, and generally disregarded, so I am surprised at how indignant Morgen's flippancy makes me feel. I want to keep arguing with him until he sees I am right, but Áila takes hold of the conversation before I have the chance.

"Are you helping him with the book, Flora?" she asks.

Flora gives a wry smirk. "I'm no scholar," she says, nudging one slender shoulder up in a shrug. "But I *have* been living the last few weeks in a monastery with only monks for companions. Female conversation sounds wonderful."

Áila laughs. Then, without so much as a glance at me for approval, she says, "Of course. I'd be glad to help."

Morgen claps his hands together. "Excellent! Perhaps in the next few days?"

"Perhaps," I interject, my chest going tight as I fight to keep my tone civil. I shoot a glare at Áila, then cross to open the door. "But for now, I think Miss LacInis needs some privacy to prepare for tonight's Ordeal."

The LaCrees have barely touched their tea, and the basket of scones lies unopened on the table. Indeed, we are all still standing, though I notice with another stab of confusion that there are now four chairs where before I would swear there was only one. But Morgen and Flora seem to scent defeat, because they each give Áila a commiserating look before crossing to the door.

"Until tonight, then," says Morgen.

He pulls the door shut behind him, and the click of the latch resounds through the quiet cottage. I turn to Áila—and find her glowering at me.

"What was that about?" she hisses, stepping close—presumably so the LaCrees won't hear her through the open window. "They weren't doing anything wrong."

"No?" Heat rises in my cheeks as I lean toward her. "What about coming to your cottage without permission from the laird? What about requesting private chats with you during a period of time you're supposed to be highly supervised and solitary?"

"The priest gave them permission."

"Says *them*. Don't you think we ought to at least verify their story before we agree to cheat?"

"It's not *cheating*, Hew. Salt and scales, are you always this controlling?"

I open my mouth to reply, but for some reason I can't quite locate the words I want to say. I'm suddenly aware of how close Áila is standing; another inch and we would be chest to chest.

"I don't know," I mumble, feeling hazy.

She steps away, shaking her head, and starts pulling clothing out of her trunk.

"What are you doing?" I say.

"Exactly what you keep telling me to do. I'm going to prepare for the Ordeal, and the best way I know is to run the cliffs. Do you need to come along and supervise me there too?"

I shudder at the thought of running for any reason other than survival. "No, thank you. I'll go now."

"Thank you."

I stride toward the door, still irritated but already second-guessing myself—then catch sight of Orail. She is lying across Áila's bed, and the lazy grin on her face pulls me up short.

"What?" says Áila.

I meet her narrowed stare. "It's just . . . I was wondering . . ." I swallow. "Was Orail wearing a collar before the LaCrees arrived?"

All the hostility drops out of Áila's face as a wary, knowing expression takes its place. Whatever strange things have happened around this dog, I am now sure Áila is every bit as aware of—and baffled by—them as me. She shakes her head. I glance once more at Orail, but her features have become doggish and inscrutable.

Something changes between Áila and me as I return my gaze to hers, and the argument over the LaCrees suddenly seems much less important. I feel certain that whatever mischief is afoot, we three in this small, cliffside cottage are the only living souls who are aware of it.

"See you this evening, then," she says with a shrug and a smile.

I chuckle, sidestepping a chair on my way to the door. "Be careful out there. And in here. The furniture is multiplying."

Her laughter follows me out into the morning and down the hill.

Chapter Twenty-One

ÁILA

Orail accompanies me as I race along the cliffs, which gives me the chance to test my theories about the wishes I've had granted since arriving at the cottage. It's an apt time to try, because I am always full of longing when I run. Longing for stronger muscles, faster legs. Longing for the beauty hanging, tantalizing, on the horizon—always just out of reach.

And now I will see if Orail is able to answer those longings.

As my body stretches and resists the movement, I think through the odd things that have happened since I found this creature. My failure to meet Yslet and receive an apprenticeship. The moment Orail seemed to grow before my eyes. The sudden appearance of candles, blankets, and dishes in the cottage. Her name. My dressing gown. The mugs. The collar. The chairs.

Each one seemed to answer some kind of need; even Orail's name came to me only when I was trying to find it. They all followed an unspoken want, or a wish.

The unspoken part makes me shiver.

It could be the cottage's doing—or the gods'—but somehow I suspect not.

I glance sideways at the dog, running beside me along the cliffside path as if she has no greater joy in the world. I brace myself a little inside my mind, then think her name.

Orail.

Her head jerks toward me, and she nearly trips over her enormous front paws.

I *do* trip.

My momentum sends me rolling a few times, and dust rises around me in a cloud. I scuff my knees and scrape my palms, but hardly feel either.

She *heard* me.

Orail wheels about on the path. She trots back, head cocked in concern, but doesn't stop when she reaches me. She just keeps walking, right into my lap. Her great paws tread on my legs, my hands, my feet, and her nose and tongue are frantic as they batter my face.

"Ouch!" I cry. "Orail, stop, I'm fine!"

I push her off and sit back, watching her warily. She *acts* like a dog—albeit a strange one. The same could be said for her looks. But she can't be merely a dog if she can hear my thoughts and grant my wishes.

Can she grant my wishes?

There is one way to be sure.

I wish I had a cup of water, I think.

The sandy dirt shifts beside my hand, and I look down to see a clay cup, full of water.

I'm grateful to be sitting, because I feel suddenly like the earth is tilting on its axis. I swallow hard.

"What are the rules?" I whisper to Orail. It strikes me that in fairy stories, magic is never boundless; it always comes with limits. "What can you do?"

She stares at me with those unblinking gold eyes, but I hear no reply. I take a deep breath. If she can't reply, I will have to test the limits myself. I've seen her answer unspoken wishes, so now to see about spoken ones.

"I wish I had another cup of water," I say aloud, and a second cup appears in the dirt beside the first one.

I breathe in and out, taking in the fact I have a wish-granting dog. *I have a wish-granting dog.* I repeat this sentence silently to myself until I stop feeling faint. Then I try and focus again on puzzling out how it works.

Everything so far has been fairly straightforward; all small-ish, material wishes. But what happens if I wish for something less tangible?

"I wish I were the fastest runner on earth," I say.

Orail blinks at me. I feel no change in my body, but still stand up to test it. After a brief stretch, I break into a gentle jog, and build to a sprint. Orail keeps up with me easily, and I feel no faster than I did before.

I slow to a walk and consider the dog again. Perhaps intangible wishes only work with thoughts?

I wish I were the fastest runner on earth, I think, and repeat the process. But nothing has changed. Except Orail, who seems to think we're playing a game. A very exciting one, based on the way she's leaping and grinning.

I skid to a halt. Perhaps wish-granting only works with material wishes that don't impact the human body. But what about emotional ones?

Could I wish someone to like me, or love me? I think of Morgen and shiver. Even if Orail could do such a thing, I doubt I could ever wish for it.

But . . . what about time? Could I wish my way through the Ordeals?

"Orail," I say, very carefully, "I wish the Ordeals were over. I wish to be perfectly successful at them, and to secure a medallion and an apprenticeship."

Again, she only blinks at me. Then she yawns and looks off toward the ocean as if I'm boring her. Since I'm still standing here on the cliffside trail, I can only assume that wish was useless too.

So perhaps she can only grant small wishes, of a material nature.

Which is certainly not nothing.

I push myself back into a jog, nodding, thinking. It might go without saying, but the LaCail *didn't* say magic was forbidden during the five tests.

"Orail," I say, feeling suddenly very close to laughter, "I think you and I are going to do quite well in these Ordeals."

Chapter Twenty-Two

ORAIL

I search, search,
       still,
       for my soul's voice,
       its poetry,
       its *Form*.

It bothers me not to know.
       Like I don't know
       who I am,
       what I was,
       why I was,
       why I am.

I will try them on,
though. The Forms I sense making
up the world, making

up language, poems.
Like I tried on so many
lives, bodies, before

this one. This one that
wags, leaps, wriggles, smells, licks, loves.
This one for Áila.

I begin to sense
the magic in me, power
to grant, to give, to

bring things. Things are all
I can bring now, but I sense
this will change as I

Change. For I know that
too, now. That I will change. Grow.
Learn. Remember. Know.

It is something to
do with the gods, with their ire.
With their wrath and fire.

But I do not know
how. This Form fits poorly, wrong,
like a jumper on a

dog. I am a dog.
But also I am not. I
am a wish granter.

What am I called? What
is my name? Orail, yes, that
seemed attached to this

body, clear as spots.
But not all I am.
What is the Other?

The First? I shake off,
shake away thoughts of Form and
First, Name and Being,

Return to the Now.
To Áila and her Ordeal.
She needs me, needs my

help, my magic, my
wits. No one, I am sure, can
do for her what I

can do. Not even
the boy who smells of Hope,
who sees what could be,

and tries to bring it
Close. His love for rightness and
rules make him my foil,

yet I cannot help
admiring him for it. He
has nothing to hide.

Hew is his Name. He
is nearly as beautiful
as Áila. I like

Him. He will help me
make her happy. Chase away
the Sadness I smell.

But what of the two
Others who came today? What
will I make of them?

Their thoughts are less loud,
more protected, and their scents
are mixed. Fear and doubt,

yes, but also calm,
curiosity, courage,
and sharp empathy.

This Form is wrong, all
wrong, wrong, seven syllables
Wrong. I shed it like

a winter coat,
            breathe,
            smell,
            search.

I will find mine
            in time.

Chapter Twenty-Three

ÁILA

When the sun begins to dip toward the horizon, I do what I can to prepare for the first Ordeal. I layer wool trews beneath my dress for warmth, fill my belly with hot stew, and do my best to quiet my mind. When the LaCail knocks on my door, I am ready.

The chieftain walks a few paces in front of Orail and me as we make our long way down the cliffside path: past the monastery, down the heather-clad hillside, into the village. I hadn't thought to expect a crowd, so my stomach jolts when I hear the low roar of voices coming from the beach.

"Will folk watch?" I ask, my voice coming out a little shrill.

"Many will watch beginning and end," says the LaCail. He glances over his shoulder at me, black beard bristling around a sympathetic frown. "But few will stay all night, I think."

We turn toward the sea before we have even reached the kirk. I realize we are making our way to the beach that runs below the cliffs, south of the docks. Soon I see the crowd, a mass of moving shapes in the dusk. They fall quiet as we cut a path to the water's edge.

Fáthair Firnan waits there, my family clustered nearby. They are pale and anxious-looking. Their features relax when they spot me, but relief is short-lived. Deirdre catches my eye and holds it, her gaze flinty. I can practically hear her thoughts: *You can do this. You can show them. I believe in you.*

I wish I could tell her about Orail—and as I catch myself

wishing, look to the dog. Her gold eyes flash to mine, but they are narrowed. I understand this to mean my wish is useless.

"Stand here, please, Miss LacInis," says the LaCail, pointing me to face the crowd. Many of the faces peering back at me are lost in shadow, but near the front I catch a pair of bracing smiles. Morgen and Flora LaCree look less worried than my family, but certainly not at ease. I spend a moment searching for Hew—but then I remember he is Unblessed. If he's allowed to be here at all, he will be restricted to the back.

As will I, if I fail this Ordeal.

"We are here tonight," the LaCail declares to the crowd in his booming voice, "as a result of the Goddess Trial we witnessed two nights ago, when Miss Áila LacInis returned from Yslet's island having had no sight of the goddess at all. Miss LacInis has agreed to undergo five Ordeals over the next five weeks, which will test the parts of her being: body, mind, spirit, heart, and life. Her performance in these Ordeals will reveal to us the gods' pleasure—or displeasure—so that by the end we will know whether she may revisit Yslet's island, or whether she will henceforth be called Unblessed.

"Miss LacInis," he says, turning to me, "at the start of each Ordeal, you will be given the option to forego the test by sacrificing something to the gods that is part of the facet of your being that is to be tested. So tonight, you may forego the physical trial only by sacrificing a part of your physical body, permanently, to the gods."

The LaCail warned me of this option before I agreed to the Ordeals, but my stomach still roils at his words. On the priest's other side, I hear my mother gasp in horror.

"No, thank you," I say at once. Resolve hardens in me like a stone. I am suddenly more determined than ever to master this Ordeal—with all my body parts intact.

"Very well," says the chieftain. "Firnan?"

The priest clears his throat and turns to face me. "In order to merit a second visit to Yslet's island, you must pass each of the five Ordeals. If the gods favor you, they will provide the knowledge, sustenance, and abilities you need to succeed, so trust in that." He raises his voice a little, so that it carries over the assembled crowd. "For this first Ordeal, Miss LacInis, here is your task: When the sun disappears below the horizon, you will wade into the sea until it has reached your waist. Facing the beach, you will raise your arms parallel to the water, palms uplifted in a gesture of supplication to the gods whose favor has been withheld from you, and keep them straight all night. If at any point they fall to your sides, the Ordeal will be considered a failure. Once the sun has reappeared in the morning, you will walk out of the water, face the rising sun, and do thirty prostrations—kneeling with your arms outstretched and your face to the sand—to thank the gods for their kindness to you. Then the Ordeal will be complete and you will be given what information you need to prepare for the second test."

I nod to the priest, but don't speak. My focus has already left him, going deep inside me to brace for the challenge. I breathe steady, deep, preparing myself. I am strong from my years working on Da's boat, but that will not be enough on its own. My will must be harder than steel.

Orail, stay on the beach, I think.

She whines, and I know she has understood.

"Please remove your boots," says Fáthair Firnan.

I bend, untie the laces, toss my boots up the beach. Then I straighten and watch the sky.

The sun is a red sliver on the horizon. It melts like copper in a forge, then dissolves, leaving only pink haze.

I move my bare feet across the sand and walk down into the icy sea.

Chapter Twenty-Four

HEW

From my position at the back of the crowd with a few elderly Unblessed, I crane and stretch and peer, trying to keep Áila in sight. I am still thanking the gods that she didn't agree to the LaCail's offer of a physical sacrifice, but my stomach rocks with horror every time I think of it. Would she have been allowed to choose which limb or digit? Or would the clan leaders have taken a whole hand, foot, or arm as they saw fit? I cannot imagine that would have pleased any god I know—but, as I am often reminded, I am not anything near a priest.

The crowd begins to thin, so I move forward a bit and find a boulder to stand on, which affords me a better view. Áila has now been in the water for two hours, and she is astonishingly stable for someone who must be aching with cold and fatigue. It's hard to be sure from this distance, but it looks as though her jaw is set and her eyes are closed. I can detect no movement in her outstretched arms.

She wasn't wrong about her physical strength, but even she can't go all night like this.

I pace back and forth on my perch, trying to think of how I might help her. Yet even if I weren't opposed to rule breaking, I can't fathom a way to ease her burden without everyone noticing. So I do what I know how to do: I pray. I pray and pray and pray, incessantly and to every god we have. To Yslet, our goddess, who rules the beasts of the earth and the birds of the sky; to Ecna, the goddess of wisdom, who governs the mind; to Atobion, god of the skies and storms; to Birgid, goddess of fire and forges, and her husband Credne, the great goldsmith; to Bréseh, compassionate god of the earth and harvests; to Belaine, the goddess of healing; to Gaelan, the mother, goddess of fertility and life.

And—I lift a hand almost unconsciously to the icon around my neck—to Lir, god of the sea.

There are only two I leave out: Arial, the trickster, and Dhuos, the deathkeeper. Neither would help Áila, and she wouldn't want their help if they did.

I feel the gods' gentle replies in wordless warmth and the soothing of my ever-rampant anxiety. They do not tell me what will happen, but I feel certain of their control all the same. Of their care. Since my mother died, it is a care I have only ever experienced with the gods.

Time stretches out with the rising moon. I give Atobion thanks for a clear night, but wonder if a little fog might not go amiss; surely Áila could rest her arms then. I can see her shaking now, either from cold or exhaustion, and I have to fight down the impulse to splash my way out to her and hold up her arms myself. I have moved much closer now, and I can see her sister, Deirdre, battling the exact same compulsion; I know it's the same because her brother is restraining her.

As the moon makes its way across the sky, Áila shakes and shakes. Everyone has gone home now except the LaCail and Fáthair Firnan, the LaCree siblings, Áila's family, and me. She has performed incredibly well, but there are hours still to go, and I cannot imagine how she will finish.

She gives a very visible shudder, her arms dipping for the first time—and I gasp aloud. If she drops her arms, she has failed the Ordeal.

But then I feel a strange tickling sensation on my scalp, like the lightest touch of fingertips. I jump in alarm, twisting to look around—and hear several voices cry out on the beach. There is no one behind me, and as I spin back about I realize my hair has fallen in front of my eyes, obscuring my vision.

Which is impossible, because I never let my hair grow longer than my eyebrows.

I push it away—and feel a wave of shock.

Hair shoots down past my chin, curling against my neck, my collar, my chest, my shoulders, and at the same time, a prickling on my chin and jaw announces fresh facial hair spilling down my front. I am fending off a jungle of my own curls while farther down the beach I hear everyone shouting and shrieking in alarm.

"My hair!" someone bellows, and I can only assume they are experiencing the same freakish overgrowth. I bat and paw at the stuff, feeling like I'm being smothered by a sheep, finally managing to push it all out of my face by parting it in two long curtains. Yet even now, new hairs spring from my scalp and drift down over my eyes; I blow air up my nose in a desperate attempt to keep my vision clear.

In the surf, I can see that Áila is still standing. In fact, she looks much sturdier than before, though I can't place anything about her that could be different. Her arms are perhaps slightly less rigid than they were a moment ago, but that could easily be attributed to the moment of rest she must have stolen while we were all distracted. On the shore, the LaCail and Firnan are still battling their hair and beards—which have reached epic lengths—shouting alternately at each other and at Áila, warning her not to move.

She doesn't, nor does she reply; she remains resolute, standing with her eyes closed. When at last everyone has their hair under control, silence falls over the beach again, and I can tell the chieftain and the priest are amazed to see Áila standing just where she was before. They mutter to each other, then turn to witness the incredible lengths of hair now adorning every one of us present—everyone but Áila herself. I steal a glance at Áila's family and see a variety of expressions on their faces, ranging from shocked to gleeful.

I find that my own feelings are somewhere in between, because unless Arial the trickster has escaped her cell in the Halls of Bone and decided to interfere—unlikely, as the legend says she has been imprisoned there since Ona's death—this does not feel like the work of the gods, however in control they may be.

There is something here I am missing; I can feel it deep in my body.

I look at Áila again, and this time I'm sure she's more relaxed.

She is the only person whose hair was spared sudden growth, and I study the dark locks, lifting in the gentle night breeze. But no; Áila couldn't have caused this. If she had any magical powers or special access to the gods' intervention, she wouldn't be in this mess of Ordeals in the first place.

A sudden movement on the beach catches my eye: a dark shape rising from the sand and stretching itself. Walking off down the beach to squat in the surf.

Orail.

As I think her name, she turns her head toward me, and I see the flash of her golden eyes. Cold chills sweep down my neck and over my shoulders.

Damn me to Dhuos if those eyes aren't laughing.

Chapter Twenty-Five

ORAIL

The wish magic is mine, yes,
        but it is not the oldest magic I
possess.
        That magic is all mine, all me,
        and, I seem to recall,
        the reason I am here at all.

I sigh through my nose as I find it,
        remember it,
        and find an outlet for it.

That magic has a name:

Mischief, it is called, and

it is blood in my veins,
        marrow in my bones,
        regardless of the veins,
        regardless of the bones.

I reach for new language,
        a new Form
        to try as I smell Áila's wishes
        and give them a home:

She stands, she is tall in the sea,
        but arms, they both shake and they
heave.
        She aches, she cries out
        to me, silent shouts
        to blind, please, to not let them see.

My soul, it replies, it revives,
        awakes to the call, and it flies
        thrumming, the hair;
        humming, oh beware,
        for I am awake, a beehive

of tricks, of mischief, and of spite—
        But oh! Not of spite, that is not quite
        the right feeling now.
        I'm changed, now, somehow:
        I thaw, I am warmed by her light.

So I do my trick, but carefully hold back
        what will only hurt, inflict cracks.
        I grow the hair down
        until it hits ground
        then pivot to give what she lacks.

She droops, needs support, and I yield …
        A thing I have seen in the fields
        that scares away crows
        will thwart undertow:
        planted, under dress is concealed.

But now she needs warmth, and no fire
        can breathe beneath sea; will expire.

My soul smirks, cackles
calls out, unshackles
a herd, shaggy heads from
their byre.

They plod, amble down into sea;
I push, make sure each wants to pee.
I hear Áila hiss
as sea fills with piss
then I loose a wild bark, set
cows free.

Chaos reigns. I am home, I am joy.
She laughs. The priest yells. Cows
destroy
the dunes as they stomp
away, up to chomp
someone's garden, greens to enjoy.

I shake off this Form,
limerick-born.
It is not mine, not right, not me,
but closer than before.
I will keep searching.

Áila is still laughing, and she is warm now,

and dawn is coming, is near, is almost here.

Chapter Twenty-Six

ÁILA

Exhaustion and shock make me delirious with laughter. I am doubly grateful for Orail's scarecrow crossbar beneath my dress now: it holds me upright while I heave and gasp, choke and snort with glee. Her solutions to my problems were not at all what I expected, but gods, have they saved my Ordeal!

An entire *herd* of shaggy Highland cattle just wandered into the ocean to relieve themselves beside me. I am disgusted. I am horrified.

I am so much warmer than before.

I don't know what it is, but something is different in Orail. I watch her from the water, rambling unnoticed around my family on the beach, and realize she has changed since we left the cottage. There is a new bounce in her stride, and I can feel slight traces of her thoughts emerging in my head. Even the way she grants wishes has altered. It feels more complex than just making cups of water.

And I feel the question pressing down on me, demanding an answer: What *is* she?

Dawn is very near. I lean into the scarecrow pole as the chaos on the beach subsides with the last of the cows ambling toward the village. Hew seems to have been instructed to go with them, no doubt to return them to their owner. Near the water, the LaCail and Fáthair Firnan are having a loud argument, gesturing expansively. I lapse into helpless laughter again as I watch them struggle against hair and beards that trail into the sand.

They look like a pair of ancient hermits, emerging from years of living alone in their caves.

A few paces behind them, Morgen and Flora seem to be explaining recent events to the spectators, who are now filtering back to the beach after their short night's sleep. But the siblings are as wildly overgrown as the clan leaders, and the newcomers stare at them in alarm.

My family have not fared any better. Everyone has hair—and beards, in two cases—almost to their feet. Deirdre has been braiding back these epic tresses so that none of them have to wage the war the LaCail and Fáthair Firnan are currently fighting, and I suspect she has withheld help from her father-in-law out of revenge.

My eyes fall once more on the dark, canine shape sitting between these hairy groups. She is looking from right to left with a wide grin, white teeth gleaming. And despite my curiosity to know what sort of creature she is, I can't quite fear her power, though I know I should.

All I feel is relief at her help, hilarity at her methods—and a building dread for the last stage of this Ordeal.

When I catch my first glimpse of the sun, I think, *Orail, I wish you to take away these supports.*

For one mortifying second, my dress vanishes along with the scarecrow stand and I plunge like a puffin into the water. *Orail, my clothes!* I scream inside my mind as my body shakes with cold and fatigue. *I need my clothes back! My dress! I wish for my dress back!* I feel it return and go limp with relief. On the shore, Orail cocks her head at me. Not malicious, just confused, dog-brained bewilderment over why clothes are so important.

I am trembling all over. From exhaustion, from laughter. From cold. From panic. But I still have to manage thirty prostrations.

Gooseflesh rippling over my skin, I struggle up through the surf, wet sand and grit clinging to my dress. The LaCail and the priest don't even look around as I make my way up the beach toward them and stop a few paces away.

Too tired to worry about their argument, I drop into the sand in front of them and face the rising sun. I sit up on my knees, lower my trunk to the ground, and place my forehead onto the sand. My neck and shoulders scream in cramped agony.

"One," I say.

Above me, the arguing stops, but I don't look up.

"Two," I say, completing another.

After I have done twelve, I think thirty may be impossible. Every one of my muscles is seizing up.

But I was not lying when I told Hew physical challenges are where I feel most adept. They are where my stubbornness finds a home.

"Twenty," I gasp.

"Miss LacInis," begins Fáthair Firnan above me, "if you are responsible for the mayhem we have all witnessed toni—"

"Hush, man!" barks the LaCail. "Let the lass finish!"

I drill my focus into the task before me.

"Twenty-three."

Salt and scales, what I wouldn't give for a drink of water.

A clay cup appears on the sand beside me. My heart jolts, and with an erratic prostration, I throw myself over it.

Orail! The cup! I wish it gone!

Gods. Dog-brained indeed. I'll have to be more careful.

"What was that?" demands the priest.

But when I push myself up again, the cup is gone. From nearby, I hear Deirdre's icy voice. "Fáthair, it sounds as if you'd like my sister to be guilty of *something* here tonight. Might I remind you she's been standing in the cold ocean all night long, where every one of us can see her? That she has done, and is *still doing* the impossible task you set her? If you expect the gods to help her, don't be shocked when they do."

The priest splutters something indistinct, and the LaCail growls at him to stay quiet.

"Twenty-eight."

I think I might faint.

Or possibly die.

From the babble of voices, I can tell more villagers have returned to watch me finish the Ordeal. My wrung-out brain wonders whether Hew has found the owner of the cows yet, and I almost lose myself in another wave of giggles.

"Twenty-nine."

Just one more, says a voice in my head.

But it's not my voice. Not my thoughts.

All the breath goes out of me as I turn my head to the left, toward the ocean.

The water glitters like a sheet of gold in the dawn. Gold, to match the eyes now on a level with my own, half a pace away. Set in a dark face with ears like bat wings.

Orail's voice. In my mind.

Just one more, she says again. Her voice is rough and wild. Wind through a hollow log. Rocks groaning underfoot. Waves battering the cliffs.

I turn away from her and prostrate myself one more time toward the east. Offering thanks to the gods.

But I don't thank them for getting me through the Ordeal, because they haven't done that.

Orail has.

Instead, I thank them for the dog that has now proven infinitely more useful to me than they ever have.

"Thirty," I whisper, pushing myself back up.

I glance left. Orail's sharp, toothy smile breaks like the dawn.

Chapter Twenty-Seven

HEW

For the second time in three days, Áila LacInis has set the whole village buzzing. I long to sleep, but I'm kept busy all morning, running errands for the LaCail and Fáthair Firnan inside the monastery. The two are sequestered in Firnan's study, hashing out the legality of Áila's Ordeal in such loud voices, I can hear them arguing two corridors away. Every time I interrupt to bring in some book or record they requested, they round on me as if *I* were the one who invited forty-two Highland cows onto the beach and enchanted everyone's hair to grow past their waist. Of the three of us, I am the only one who hasn't yet had a haircut, and my knee-length auburn curls and patchy ginger facial hair evoke gales of laughter everywhere I go—because the overall effect has been to make me look rather like a long-haired, orange goat.

Bráthair Gibrat cries with amusement when I hurry into the library to retrieve yet another book for the priest to consult, bleating at me and offering to braid my locks. I ignore him, but I long to find a pair of shears and a few quiet moments to use them. I'd even say yes to a pair of gardening shears; as long as they do the job, I don't care where they come from.

Or . . . I *almost* don't care. Morgen LaCree, roguishly handsome with his fresh-trimmed black waves and rugged stubble, offers his scissors on the way into the dining hall for lunch, and I find myself hesitating. I can't quite forgive him for bringing what still seems to me a request for Áila to cheat on the very first morning of her isolation. For a fleeting moment, I think I might rather spend the rest of my life looking like a goat than accept a favor from this young man who charms people so effortlessly—and yet treats their rules and traditions like black pudding: good to have available, but ultimately a matter of taste.

He raises his brows, and common sense returns to me. I grunt my thanks and accept the shears, hurrying away to find a mirror.

When I return to the hall, clean-shaven and hair cropped as evenly as I could manage, I look around for Morgen and find him seated at the end of the room, with nearly all the monks clustered around him as they bend over bowls of stew or sip mugs of ale. I scoop stew into my own bowl before finding a chair at the edge of the group, not quite following what Morgen is saying as he gesticulates, tawny hands expansive above the rough wood of the table. Until suddenly I realize: it's about the Usurper Prince.

Fuiscea is a small island and gets few visitors from the Ilbhan mainland, so news comes to Carrighlas slowly, if at all. We usually have to rely on traders, letters, and broadsheets to fuel our island gossip—but Morgen was on the mainland during the Aenlandish prince's recent uprising against our kingdom and has firsthand news of what happened there. I settle in to listen and discover—somewhat grudgingly—that the monks' attention has been well-earned: Morgen LaCree is a talented storyteller.

"The eldest son of King Porrl will inherit the Aenlandish crown, of course," he says, leaning forward to brace his forearms on the table. He looks from face to face, smiling a little as he seems to parse through memories. "Prince Herry will have little more than the average courtier, which could never be enough for a man of such ambition. And like any zealous son, he wants to prove himself to his brothers and show his father what he can achieve. So he set his sights on Ilbha—and gave it all the formidable force of his will. The tension on the mainland was thicker than fog during his campaign, such was his influence over the people he met—both for and against him."

"Did you see him, then?" asks one of the younger monks. "When you were on the mainland?"

Morgen nods slowly, dark eyes glittering. "Aye, I saw him. Saw him after he lost the fight for Ellisburgh, after his campaign collapsed and left blood-drenched fields and countless dead behind. King Fireld paraded him through the streets like a common criminal, shackled hand and foot, before sending him back to his father and brothers in Aenland. He wanted the people of Ellisburgh to know that the Usurper was defeated, and that anyone who fought on his side would be brought to justice."

"And was it a close battle for Ellisburgh?" demands another monk.

Morgen shakes his head. "The Usurper could never have won. Ilbha is too strong, and all he had on his side was a few thousand soldiers. He'd need proper magic—or the aid of the gods—to overthrow a kingdom as mighty as Ilbha."

"Aye," growls one of the monks, his eyes flashing with ferocious pride. A few others around him call out their own agreement.

Morgen nods, and I watch him with new curiosity. I had expected him to be fervent about the gods and enthusiastic toward his work as a scribe, but this passion for Ilbha comes as a bit of a surprise. When the monks stand up and begin clearing away their dishes, I step forward and hand the shears back to him.

"Thank you," I say. "And thank you for sharing your tale. I didn't realize you had such a keen interest in politics."

Morgen inclines his head and gives me a wry smile. "Do you consider political awareness incompatible with the work of a scribe?"

"Not incompatible, no," I say slowly. "But perhaps far enough from the lives of ordinary people as to be a little disconnected from the interests of the gods."

"And what happens when someone like the Usurper Prince wins, and ordinary people are caught in the maelstrom? When the traditions and songs and cultures—and even the gods—of Ilbha are swallowed up by those brought in by the conqueror? Do you think that is disconnected from the interests of the gods?"

I stare at Morgen. His eyes have lost their teasing warmth and have gone hard and fervent. "Do you think the Usurper would have done that to Ilbha?" I ask. "To such an extent as would reach us here on Fuiscea?"

He nods. "Ilbha's traditions are nothing more than barbaric ritual and superstition to Prince Herry. He would see it all mown down and made over anew."

I shiver, imagining our village in the grip of the Aenlandish prince. "Well, then," I say, thinking once more of my plans to pursue a priestly education on the mainland. "Let us give thanks to the gods that his efforts were squashed."

"Indeed," Morgen says. "Indeed."

I leave him in the dining hall, my head buzzing. Because while his tale has made me grateful for Ilbha's triumph over the Usurper, our conversation has given me other, more pressing insights to consider. Because it could not be plainer to me that Morgen LaCree is an Ilbhan nationalist—and no one is keener to break rules for the greater good than a political radical.

I will have to watch him closely.

"One more thing, LacEllan," the priest croaks as I turn to leave his office that evening, his voice sounding as tired as I feel. "I'd like you to deliver this note to Miss LacInis. It contains the results of her first Ordeal. Once she has read it, we will make the news known to the rest of Carrighlas. You may tell her as much."

"Aye, Fáthair."

I leave the monastery, trudging up the cliffside path and trying not to wander over the brink out of sheer exhaustion. But when I reach Áila's cottage, I find the door closed and the windows shuttered. As I stare blearily at the house, I realize what should have been obvious before I even left the monastery: Áila is free to do what I've been longing for since the Ordeal ended. She is free to sleep, and surely has been for most of the day.

I should wake her; she will want to read the letter as soon as she can. But I sink down on the front stoop first, for a brief rest. I am vaguely tempted to open the priest's note, but even my curiosity and worry are dulled by fatigue. The sun is sinking in the west—weren't we just watching it go down on the beach before Áila's Ordeal?—and I wonder what would happen if I laid my head on the step, just for a moment.

I am barely aware of giving in to the impulse before I jerk awake again.

It feels like only a moment has passed, but the sun is gone and a chilly night mist has crept up over the cliffs from the sea. I also realize I am not alone.

I fling myself to my feet and jump away from the step, upon which sits a large, dark shape.

A hulking animal, shadowed by the night.

It lifts its head—and relief makes me weak all over.

Orail.

She is bigger than yesterday. How she got out of the house is beyond my ability to conceive, because the door and windows are as firmly shut as before, and Áila is nowhere about. It seems increasingly unlikely she could be an ordinary dog, but whatever Orail is, it's still less terrifying than the long list of beasts she isn't.

I hope.

"Hi there, girl," I say, sagging back onto the stoop beside her.

She watches me, eyes bright in the foggy dusk. She still has the gangly limbs and overlarge paws of a puppy, but she is closer to the size of a full-grown dog, even though Áila brought her back just three days ago—as a small, snuggling creature—from the island. I squint at her, wondering why no one has remarked on this incredible change. But a heartbeat later, I realize the answer—and with it, the genius of the gods in giving Áila a gift like Orail.

Because obviously, there has been far too much going on for anyone to pay any attention to something as commonplace and insignificant as a dog. It strikes me too that the LaCail and Fáthair Firnan are fools if they don't include this animal in their estimations, because whatever she is, I am certain she is not here by accident.

Orail is still watching me with those eerie eyes, and I reach out to pet her speckled head. "What are you, then, beastie?" I ask. "Just a dog, or something more?"

Orail leans into my hand for a moment, and then stands up and shakes before moving languidly down the steps and out into the deepening night. I watch her vanish into the shadows, wondering how best to wake Áila—but a sound behind me makes me jump, and I turn to find Áila herself shouldering open the front door with a candle in one hand and the other raised to shelter the flame from the draft. Her face is pale, and she is moving very slowly, as if each step pains her. Which, I realize, it probably does.

"Áila," I say, clambering to my feet. "I'm so sorry to disturb. Did I wake you?"

She shakes her head as if still battling sleep, looking around. "Where is Orail?"

I gesture out into the dark garden, and Áila nods, frowning. "Can I help?" I say. "You look a bit . . . sore."

A husk of a laugh blows through her lips, and she groans. "You could say that."

But her eyes clear as she looks at me, and she seems to realize why I have come at the same moment I remember the letter in my pocket. Wordlessly, I draw it out and offer it to her.

But she shakes her head, grimacing. "You read it," she whispers, passing me her candle.

I nod. Hands trembling slightly, I break the wax and unfold the parchment.

"Dear Miss LacInis," I read aloud, "after much consideration and consulting of the historical texts, the chieftain and I have agreed to rule your first Ordeal a pass." I pause, relief surging through my body, and hear Áila exhale. "The unusual events we experienced last evening can only be attributed to the work of the gods, so we must assume they have assisted you to success. Congratulations, and may they continue to favor you.

"In six days' time, you will undergo the second Ordeal, which will test your mind. You may prepare for this test in whatever way you see fit, but we would like to remind you that you may solicit no outside help. You may visit the kirk, but only with supervision from Hew LacEllan.

"Wishing you continuing success, Fáthair Rab Firnan and Greme LaCail."

I finish reading and Áila gives a wide, weary smile. "Help me sit down?"

I grip her beneath the elbow as she lowers herself onto the step, and while she gasps a bit, she makes no other sound. When I sit gingerly beside her, the voice in my head pipes up to remind me that only Vira and Gemma would want to sit so close to an Unblessed—but before it can hit its stride, Áila loops her arm through mine and leans her head against my shoulder.

The voice is struck dumb—and a baffling, tingling heat spreads along the entire left side of my body.

"I can't believe I passed," she breathes.

"I can," I say, fighting the strange, heady sensation that is filling my limbs with air. "You were inspiring."

She laughs. I want to ask her about the hair and the cows, but her forehead is warm against my jaw, and I can't quite summon the words. So for a few moments we just sit, cool night air blowing wisps of her dark hair across the back of my neck. Then she pushes herself upright again, turning on the stoop. Orail has returned, and Áila wraps both arms around the dog's neck—who tries to wriggle free, like she has better things to do than let her mistress hug her.

"We made it, you fool," Áila says quietly to the dog. "One down. Four to go."

It's an innocent enough thing to say, but there is something in Áila's tone that prods at my suspicions . . . as if she is talking to someone who understands her.

As if she *knows* the dog understands her.

The words are all but falling off my tongue—*Is that a magic dog you have there?*—when I realize how ludicrous they will sound, and so swallow them down. I help Áila stand again, then bid her and Orail goodnight before making my way back to the monastery. As I stumble downstairs to my room, I decide that tomorrow I will make use of Fáthair Firnan's gift to me after all: I will use the library to research what kinds of creatures walk this earth under magical guises. Theology might be written in the old speech, but I know from today's experience ferrying books to the priest that the others are not.

Whatever Orail is—or isn't—I am determined to work it out.

Chapter Twenty-Eight

ÁILA

Sometime in the very early hours of the morning, nearly a full day after the first Ordeal, I wake and no longer feel the urge to stay in bed. I cannot remember ever sleeping so many hours at a time, but my body feels better for it—much better than it did last night when I rose to hear the results of my Ordeal. Even so, I groan and gasp as I push myself to sitting. I can't decide what hurts the most: my arms from being held out beside me, my legs from standing on the shifting seabed all night, or my stomach from my thirty prostrations. I wonder if it's possible for every muscle in my body to be knotted at once.

Then I wonder if I'm crazy for feeling so alive.

I grin across the room at Orail—and remember.

Remember *everything*.

My grin slips away.

I sit still in my bed, watching her in the slowly lightening cottage. Though she turned briefly when I sat up, she has now gone back to watching out the window with slightly lifted ears, sniffing and listening like any dog might.

But I know she is not *any dog*.

"Orail?" I say, quiet and tentative.

She turns again, looking at me with her head on one side. I feel suddenly uncertain; did I perhaps dream it all?

I think, *I wish I had a lovely full breakfast and a pot of tea.*

It materializes on a tray on my lap: breakfast fit for a queen. There are poached eggs and sausages, black puddings, tomatoes, beans, and a thick slice of rich, buttered bread. Steam curls from the spout of a floral-painted porcelain teapot, and milk sits in a little silver pitcher beside the mug.

"Orail," I say, my voice slow and measured. "We need to talk. You *can* talk, can't you."

She ambles across the flagstones to the bed, then sits down and stares up at me, eyes round and searching. She is bigger today than she was at the Ordeal. I shake my head. "No, let me eat first. Have you had any food yet?"

I'm braced for it, but it is still a bone-deep shock when her voice rumbles through my mind: *I have not.*

"Can . . . can you not get things for yourself?"

I cannot.

I feel a pang of guilt, remembering the loaf of bread I scolded her for yesterday. I divide the food into two portions, setting Orail's down on the floor on one of the plates. She eats like a starving wolf, devouring her portion before I have begun to cut into mine. I frown at her.

"Orail, I wish for . . . well, what do you like best?"

She cocks her head again, not understanding, and I try and remember what Matan feeds his wolfhound. Raw meat, probably, but I can't stomach the sight of blood so early in the morning. "I wish for a large mutton steak, please," I say, and another plate appears, steaming and fragrant. I give that to Orail too and start into my own breakfast.

When we have both finished and I am nursing my second cup of tea, I put the tray down on the ground and pat the bed beside me. Orail leaps up and lays at the foot, head up and ears alert, watching me.

I look at her, long and searching. At her brown-and-tan body, speckled all over like she's been sprayed with chocolate and cream. At her russet face, with a large black patch covering her right eye and spots dusted over her nose. At her bat ears and glittering eyes. At her short, soft fur, her long, whippy tail, and her great, long-toed paws. She is strange from whiskers to toenails, but she is also marvelous: a marriage of chaos and beauty. I am baffled by her magic and the mystery of what she is, but as I think about last night, I realize something startling: I already trust her. Fully.

As I think this, something in her golden gaze softens. She inches slightly closer and lays her head across my ankles.

My heart aches with a new feeling, a terrifying one. A desire to protect and care for this creature who trusts me with her words and her otherworldly gifts. Who has guarded me from physical harm, and who has become my friend and ally.

I've never had my own dog before, so I am surprised by how quickly it has come—but I think the feeling is love.

I place a hand on Orail's head, stroke the bony ridge of her skull, and scratch behind her ears. For a moment my nagging curiosity returns—what could she *be*?—but then I realize something that both disappoints and comforts me: knowing the answer would change nothing. Whether Orail is a gift from the gods or curse from Dhuos, I will still keep her, care for her, and love her. There's nothing I could learn about her that would change my mind about that.

A tension I didn't know I was carrying bleeds out of my body. I find I can breathe deeply again.

"Will you explain it to me?" I say after I have finished my tea. "How all this works?"

She considers me for a moment, whiskers sharp with definition in the morning light. Then she says, *I do not yet know it all. But I will tell you what I can.*

I nod.

I can sense what you want, she says slowly. *For a while I could only smell it, but now I can hear it in your thoughts too. When you want something, I want to give it to you. And I can.*

Straightforward, really. And how like a dog—how simple and painfully beautiful—to want to grant all your desires.

"And do you have to?" I ask. "Or can you pick and choose?"

I have to when you ask aloud. When anyone asks aloud. Spoken wishes are beyond my ability to ignore. If it's inside your head, I can choose. But I will choose your wish if it will make you happy.

"Can you hear inside everyone's head?"

Only yours, and sometimes the gangly boy who comes here. His thoughts are very loud. But I think with a little time I could learn to hear other people—if they are willing to let me in.

"I didn't let you in, did I?"

When you want to know what I think, you let me in.

I mull this over, laughing a little at her description of Hew. Then I realize I'll have to watch her around other people, in case someone makes an idle wish aloud.

"What about the things you can't do?" I say. "Yesterday, on the cliffs, I asked to be faster, and I asked for the Ordeals to be over, but nothing happened."

Orail squints, and her gold eyes seem a little distant. Finally, she says, *I think I am still growing, but there will always be limits. I can sense them, if I push at the boundaries. And the closer to the boundaries a wish is, the more it costs me.*

"Costs you?"

Effort, she says. *Energy. The cows were not far from the beach, so they didn't cost much to summon.*

"What about things you make, instead of summoning?"

She looks confused. *Make?*

"Like the breakfast. The hair."

She lets out a whuff of a breath—a laugh, I realize. *I did not make those. I cannot make. I can only bring things that already exist, or change what already is.*

I glance, bewildered, at the now-empty breakfast tray. "So where did that come from?

The chieftain's home, says Orail matter-of-factly. There is neither laughter nor shame in her tone, and I goggle at her, torn between hilarity and horror that I have just eaten the LaCail's breakfast.

"So you were able to change the length of everyone's hair because some of it already existed? And the urine? Did you change that too?"

No need, says Orail, and this time I do hear a smile in her voice. *Cows are always full of pee.*

The absurdity, the wonder of it all crashes over me like a sudden downpour, and I am breathless with laughter as I fall back on my bed and recall the details of last night's Ordeal. I laugh until my stomach aches and my jaw hurts.

When I catch my breath, I find Orail watching me with light dancing in her gold eyes.

"Do you know—" I begin. "Did Yslet send you to me?"

There is a brooding pause, in which Orail gazes out the window. *I don't know,* she says at last, and I can hear worry in her tone.

I wrap my arms around her speckled neck, wanting to forget about the gods who may or may not be involved—who may or may not even exist at all.

"Orail," I say, "we deserve a rest. I wish for a comfortable armchair, a pile of soft blankets, another pot of tea, and a good book. What would you like?"

I wouldn't say no to another of those steaks.

I wish for that as well, then walk the few steps across the room to the new armchair in front of the hearth. It has silky, brocade upholstery, and the blankets stacked upon it are a finer wool than I've ever felt.

I settle into it with my new book and fresh tea in my now-beloved sea-green mug, laughing again as I imagine the LaCail asking his wife where their breakfast and furniture have run off to.

Chapter Twenty-Nine

HEW

The day is half-spent by the time I make my way up the stairs from my cloister, still groggy despite having slept away the morning and part of the afternoon. I am starting to formulate a plan for the week—perhaps I'll ask Áila what books she might like from the monastery library to prepare for the next Ordeal—when I nearly run into Bráthair Gibrat near the double front doors.

"LacEllan," he says, sliding out of my way with a smug smile. "I've been looking for you. Fáthair Firnan would like to see you in his study. As a matter of urgency."

I frown at him. "I'm just leaving to go tend to Miss LacInis. Surely that's the only matter of urgency I have."

"Ah, yes, I was hoping you'd mention that," he says, smile widening. "You see, Firnan has passed off your duties to Morgen and Flora LaCree today. It would seem they've requested some time with Miss LacInis to hear about her Ordeal firsthand—for LaCree's book, you know. Your services won't be required again until tomorrow." He smirks. "Never fear, *mallacht*. You're perfectly replaceable. Now run along."

Fury—at his words, his tone, his flaccid, oily smile—make me tremble all over, and I turn away from him before I can say or do anything I might regret. I stalk back down the corridors, barely seeing the monks passing in the opposite direction.

"Ah, LacEllan, good," says Firnan when I appear in his study doorway. I can feel anger flushing my cheeks and tightening my muscles as I move to stand across from where the priest sits at his desk—and as furious as I am with Gibrat for being a pompous ass, LaCree for being a handsome charmer, and Firnan for calling me to heel like a chained hound, I'm angrier with myself for failing to bring all these negative feelings to order. If there's one thing I hate, it's losing control.

"You requested me, Fáthair?" I say, trying to force my voice into some semblance of obedience and calm.

Firnan barely glances up as he scribbles something on a piece of parchment. It looks like he's reviewing foreign broadsheets before they're filed away in the archives; a mundane task that still appears to be vastly more important than me. "Yes, I'd like you to go into town and collect several orders for the cook. I've asked him to keep our meals at the highest standard while we're entertaining guests, and that seems to require more frequent trips to the village for fresh meat."

I'm grateful for the priest's distraction, because I am unable to repress the flush of hot fury that washes over my cheeks and down my neck like scalding water. *This* is the task he's called me to do instead of chaperoning Áila, *as a matter of urgency?*

"Doesn't the cook have an errand lad for tasks like that?" I say through gritted teeth. "I'm meant to be chaperoning Miss LacInis."

Firnan shrugs. "The cook's lad is sick today. I was looking for someone who could spare a few hours, and Bráthair Gibrat suggested you, since Miss LacInis already had an appointment with Morgen and Flora LaCree. Mr. LaCree and his sister have proven themselves trustworthy on every account, and I am not concerned about their conversations with the girl going unchaperoned. The work they are doing is a great one, and deserves whatever aid we can give it."

My blood leaps back to a rolling boil, and I can't decide what makes me the most irate: the fact the priest trusts a pair of Cheltlander strangers above anyone else on our island, the way he's ready to compromise his own strict rules for the sake of Morgen's writing project . . . or learning who put my name in for errand boy of the day. "Gibrat?" I hear myself repeat in a low growl.

Firnan looks up. "Aye," he says, his brows creasing. He passes me the parchment he's been writing on, and I glance down to find an extensive grocery list. "And it strikes me, LacEllan, that Bráthair Gibrat is an ordained monk of the Order of Bréseh with every right to give me his opinion, whereas you are nothing but an Unblessed orphan whom we have housed and fed for *years* out of charitable service to the gods. Which of course means that not only are your opinions irrelevant, they are also best kept inside the obscurity of your own head. You are dismissed."

I am through the door before he has even pronounced the final syllable of the word *dismissed*, striding back down the corridor with fire licking at my heels as I look for anything at all that I might hit. I don't find it until I'm outside again, and the poor alder tree that takes the brunt of my fists doesn't deserve my violence. When I have finished pummeling the trunk, and my knuckles are bleeding, I lean my forehead against the rough bark and breathe in and out until my heart has calmed and my breathing is steady. The pendants around my neck swing free of my collar and bounce against my chin, golden medallion and painted icon the perfect paradox to sum up my existence.

"Why have you let that man be a priest?" I whisper against the trunk, wishing with all my heart that Lir would leave his ocean dwelling and come talk to me here, face-to-face. Come explain why the gods allow fools to claim piety and service to them when in fact their service is to themselves. Or explain why a man like Gibrat, whose greatest delight comes from tormenting people with less power than himself, was allowed to be ordained in service to the goddess of *compassion*.

But Lir doesn't come, and there's nothing I can do to make him. Yes, his waves crash against the cliffs—forever beating out his grief for the loss of his daughter—and the vast expanse of his ocean roars and glitters beneath the horizon while Yslet's cormorants cry out above it. But the god himself stays hidden, as usual.

Sometimes I can delude myself into thinking I have some measure of command over the world around me. Other times, it is painfully clear I don't have *any*.

I sigh and start off for the village, praying as I go. It is the best way I know to combat the bitterness that pushes into my heart when my knuckles are bloody and my soul is sore—and it is the only way I know to bring *something* back under my control, even if it's only my own feelings. By the time I reach the butcher's shop, I once more feel the familiar, strange comfort of the gods' love lacing through me, and I am able to brace myself for the usual unkindness I receive in the village.

Which is why I am startled when the first thing I hear upon opening the butcher's door is an excited voice crying my name.

"Uncle Hew!"

A wide smile cracks my face as Gemma, my three-year-old niece, pelts across the shop toward me and throws herself at my knees. I catch her up in my arms and swing her around, taking care not to knock her against the haunches of meat strung up around the shop. "Gems!" I say, squeezing her in a tight hug. "Doing some errands? You've got very grown up to be doing the shopping on your own!"

She giggles into my shoulder, and I look over her head to Vira, taking a wrapped parcel from the butcher. "Hew!" she says with a smile, settling the meat inside the basket over her arm. "We haven't seen you in more than a week!"

I shift Gemma onto my hip and grimace. "I'm sorry. I've been . . . reassigned."

"I heard," Vira says, raising thin, auburn brows. "Chaperone to Áila LacInis, the poor and mysterious subject of the gods' indecision."

"I don't know that the gods are ever *indecisive*, Vira," I say, narrowing my eyes at her.

She laughs and hugs me on the side I'm not holding Gemma. "Well, then, do you think they'd let you off some evening to come have dinner with us? Gemma's going to forget what you look like."

"That doesn't seem likely," I say as tiny fingers probe my nostrils and Gemma erupts in raucous laughter. "But yes, of course. I'll ask the priest for an evening I might come and then send you a note."

"Good," says Vira. "Gemma has a new book she's been dying to show you."

"A new book?" I say, swinging Gemma around to face me. She shrieks as I dip her backward and flip her over to land on her feet. While I'm loathe to interact with Vira's husband Colm, I never turn down time with Vira and Gemma, especially now that Gemma's old enough to enjoy some of the myths and fairy stories I loved when I was a boy.

She is already clinging to my legs again, so I hike her back onto my hip to walk my sister out of the shop. "I don't want you to leave!" Gemma wails when I tell her goodbye, so I do what I always do to assure her we'll meet again: I sing a song.

"*O'er the heath where hurcheouns sleep, all cradled by the solum,*" I begin in my terrible, tuneless croon, "*the westly winds arise and pen a tune both bright and solemn, O.*"

The voice in my head begins its well-worn tirade about the quality of my voice, but Gemma's delight drowns it out. This song, to her, has always meant what songs mean to so many in our village—and I suspect, in Ilbha generally. That she has a home wherever it is sung, that someone loves her, that all will be well.

She joins me in the chorus, and even though her three-year-old voice is better at finding the notes than my eighteen-year-old one, I belt out the words.

"*Golden light and thistle, O! Golden light and thistle, O! The pipe and drum begin tae hum of golden light and thistle, O.*"

The song does for me what I only intended it to do for Gemma, and when I turn back to my cart and my errands, I find that my heart is lighter.

Chapter Thirty

ÁILA

I am halfway through the book Orail magicked up for me, and the day is half gone, when there is a knock at the door. "Come in," I call, since it can only be Hew. But Orail's sudden growl makes me start.

"I'll wait out here," calls back a deep, pleasant baritone that is completely unlike Hew's husky tenor. I sit up straight, the book falling into my lap. I know that voice.

I scramble out of the armchair, blanching as I realize I'm still in my dressing gown. "Just a moment!" I call. Then I throw open my trunk and dig for a clean dress. A few minutes later, with Orail firmly instructed to neither growl nor bite, I hurry out of the cottage, tying off my freshly braided hair.

Morgen LaCree stands a few paces down the garden path, smiling uncertainly. His fear of Orail does nothing to diminish the ruggedness of his good looks: even his blue monastic robe and brown wool cloak look more like the clothes of a knight or a prince on his muscular frame than they do the garb of a scribe. I return his smile but feel a little tongue-tied.

"Miss LacInis," he says, inclining his head. "I hope you'll forgive the intrusion, but Fáthair Firnan has given my sister and me permission to host you at the monastery today, while you give us your account of the first Ordeal. Is that acceptable to you?"

"Oh!" I dart a glance at Orail, hoping she might help unfluster me, but she's sniffing through the foxglove and seems to be ignoring our conversation. "What about Hew?"

"The priest thought Flora and I would suffice for chaperones today. He needed LacEllan for some other tasks."

I nod, unsure whether to feel excited at the prospect of an afternoon alone with Morgen and his sister, nervous about recounting my perspective on the first Ordeal, or concerned that Hew has been so easily reassigned. But if Hew were here, he would probably object to Morgen's proposal anyway. I smile again. "Sounds lovely."

Morgen's teeth flash white, and we start off together. It's a classic Fuiscean summer day—windy and rainy with occasional outbreaks of sunshine—and I hug my knit shawl tight about my neck to keep the rain out as we take the steep path down the cliffs. Inside the monastery, the entry hall is cold and damp, lit only by a pair of torches in brackets on either side of the double doors. As soon as we cross the threshold, Orail shakes, spraying a fine mist all over a group of monks passing through. One of them—a short, pale monk with dark hair—glares at me.

"No animals in the cloister, the dormitories, or the chapel," he says, more to Morgen than to me. "The beast will have to join the dogs in the inner yard."

Morgen opens his mouth to protest—for my sake alone, I know—but I lay a hand on his arm. "She'll prefer to be outside, I'm sure," I say, noting Orail's look of distaste at all the cold stone.

After I settle Orail with the other dogs, hemming her in with wishes to prevent her from fighting, damaging any property, or eating any chickens, I follow Morgen through dimly lit corridors that are occasionally brightened by the odd stained glass window or oculus. Finally, he stops before a carved wooden door and holds it open for me.

"Áila!" Flora rushes to meet me, and as she presses my hands I glance around the room. It is a handsome study with wall-to-wall bookshelves, a plush settee, several leather armchairs, and a large window overlooking the bluff. There is a stone fireplace against one wall, lit with merry flames, and a low table set for tea. A welcome sight after the rainy walk.

"Please sit down. Let me take your wet things."

She steers me into a chair before the fire as if I'm an honored guest, peeling off my damp shawl and offering me a towel for my hair. I fidget under the attention, but Flora fusses and motions for me to stay seated every time I try to help. Soon she and Morgen are settling into chairs across from me and pouring out tea, Morgen with notebook and quill in hand.

"So," he says with a smile that warms my bones far more thoroughly than the fire has. "The first Ordeal. Evidence of the gods' intervention if ever I've seen it. Tell us what you experienced."

I laugh, and the sound is high and nervous to my ears. Trying to seem casual, I take a sip of tea, but my pulse taps in my throat as I think of all the things I shouldn't mention. "Well . . . I suppose it wasn't the easiest night of my life. But I had years of physical training on my side, from working on my da's fishing boat."

With a little encouragement from Morgen, I recount the whole Ordeal as I experienced it, leaving out only the most important parts. When I come to the bit with the cows and the hair, I shrug as if I'm baffled like everyone else, and say the gods must have decided to intervene.

"Remarkable," Morgen says. His dark eyes are warm and encouraging, and they make me feel safe, seen, welcomed. "In all my travels, I've never heard of such divine meddling. You must be very special indeed, Áila."

Heat creeps up my neck, but his eyes hold mine, and I can't look away. When he drops his gaze, I feel like the sun has gone behind a cloud.

"Is divine intervention your primary area of research?" I ask, wanting to call his attention back again.

"Not exactly," he says, but he is scribbling something in his notebook and doesn't look up. "It's more regional faith customs, generally. But divine intervention is fascinating to any scribe." He meets my eyes again, and I feel weak with relief to have earned his interest once more.

"And of course, Fuiscea has a history of divine intervention that is quite unique in Ilbha," says Flora. I pull my eyes from her brother to look at her, but she, too, is watching Morgen. "No other region has a Goddess Trial, even if they do claim to have a deity dwelling nearby."

Morgen turns to her, suddenly frowning.

"The practice of going to meet Yslet, for instance . . ." Flora continues, raising her dark brows.

"No, Flora," Morgen says.

"Well, why not?" She gives an airy laugh. "Why not ask her?"

"Ask me what?" I tilt forward, looking between them.

"She won't betray our trust." Flora winks at me. "It's the grumpy young monk you have to watch out for."

"Hew?" I chortle. "He's not a monk, he's—"

But Morgen isn't listening, and he interrupts me with a groan. "It's not fair to ask something like that of her," he says into his hands. "Not when she has so much to worry about already."

"What do you want to ask me? Please, I want to help."

Indeed, as I watch Morgen wrestle with his conscience, I feel an almost unbearable longing to assist him. To do whatever I can to bring back the welcoming warmth of his gaze, so different from the hollow unbelonging I've felt since my failed Goddess Trial.

"Yslet," Flora says when Morgen still does not speak. "He wants to meet Yslet.'"

Morgen goes still, head still in his hands, and for a moment there is silence between us.

"What?" I say at last, completely baffled.

"Tell her, Morgen," says Flora.

At last Morgen lifts his head, and his face is creased with worry—worry, I suspect, that his sister has just betrayed something that might ruin all his work. "Fine," he says tersely. "Fine. I—well, I'd love a chance to see Yslet herself. I've never seen a god or goddess before, and that sort of experience would make my book invaluable to the histories of our people."

I blink at him. "But . . . how?"

"Well . . ." He sounds sheepish. "If I already knew she was going to be somewhere, then I could make sure to be there too . . ."

"You mean . . ." I say in a hushed voice, "the *island*? At the end of my Ordeals?"

He gives the tiniest of nods, his eyes hooded with anxiety.

"But what if I don't make it through them? What if I don't earn a second Trial at all?"

I hold back the question that makes my stomach feel like it's made of lead: *And what if Yslet doesn't appear even then?*

Morgen glances toward his sister, but she has crossed to the window and is twisting a black curl around her finger as she gazes out on the iron clouds. He leans toward me instead, eyes beseeching. "That's why we're here, Áila," he says. "That's why we came to Carrighlas. To try to meet the goddess your island claims to know so well. Hearing about your Ordeals—well, it could be useful to my book, but not half as useful as seeing the goddess herself. So Flora and I want to help you." He throws one more glance at Flora, who finally turns and meets his eyes. She gives a very small nod, and Morgen says, "We want to do whatever we can to help you pass the Ordeals."

I stare at him, fear and shock pulsing through me with every heartbeat. The one thing that has been made very clear to me is that I am not to have any help in these Ordeals. Hew has been diligent in ensuring I am never left alone with anyone, and it feels slightly unreal that the first moment he is called away—by Fáthair Firnan, of all people—I receive an offer of assistance.

Morgen watches me with tension straining every line of his face. He must know I have the power to ruin his entire effort with a word if I want to.

But I *don't* want to.

What I want is another chance at my Goddess Trial. A medallion. A place of my own in Carrighlas. And whenever possible, the delicious warmth of Morgen LaCree's eyes on mine.

No one follows the rules more closely than Hew—and no one is more repulsed in this village than he is. But what might bending the rules a little grant a person? For though Morgen is an outsider, there is no one in Carrighlas who doesn't love him. If I help him, could I secure my own share of that love and belonging?

"I accept," I say. "If helping me will help you, I accept."

Morgen's brow lifts and his expression clears like a storm breaking apart. "We won't let you down, Áila," he says, leaning forward to fold my hands into his broad ones. A shiver runs up my arms at his touch. "Now, let's get to work. We have limited time before your next Ordeal."

His smile returns at last, heating me to the tips of my fingers.

Chapter Thirty-One

HEW

Late in the afternoon, I make my way back to the monastery, my old peat cart heaped high with meat, fish, yeast, salt, whisky, and a crate of expensive chocolate truffles. I'm thankful the monastery grows all its own produce and brews its own beer, or I would probably not be strong enough to pull the cart. As I crest the hill where the path turns toward the monastery, I see several figures coming out of the front door.

It's Áila and Orail, followed by Morgen and Flora. The LaCrees stand on the front steps and wave as Áila makes her way across the lawn and Orail bolts away in her typical arrow-shot-from-a-bow method of leaving a building. I hesitate, hoping to avoid notice by hiding behind the same alder I recently delivered a beating to, and for a moment I think it will work: Áila begins cutting her way across the hill to meet the path as it continues up the cliffs and the LaCrees disappear back inside the monastery. But Orail discovers me.

As her arrowlike flight seems to reach its peak, she swerves in a broad arc, mouth opening wide as she gallops away from Áila—and straight toward me. I brace myself for the impact of her body, but it still nearly knocks me off my feet, and I bend double with my hands up to defend my teeth from being accidentally bashed in as she begins her muscular, destructive whirlwind around me and my cart.

"Hew!" says Áila, jogging into view. "I'm so glad it's you! Orail, leave him alone."

She does, turning her attention—and her nose—to the variety of fragrant wrapped parcels in my cart.

"How was your morning?" I ask, trying and failing to keep the awkwardness out of my voice. All I can think is how easily Fáthair Firnan replaced me with Morgen and Flora, and how the very person I most worry about has now had an entirely unchaperoned afternoon with Áila.

"It was fine." Áila looks a little awkward too, and I am suddenly prickly with suspicion. Was I right? Has Morgen offered to help her prepare for the Ordeals? Or perhaps they shared more than conversation in his study, and she is now embarrassed to think I might guess the truth. But I want to shake myself for caring at all. *Why* do *I care?* I cast the question around in a wild, silent arc, willing anyone to answer me: the gods, perhaps, or the grass at my feet, or the strange canine now nosing through the fruits of my labors.

A split second later, a voice speaks inside my head. But it is not *the* voice inside my head, the one that is always cruel and critical. This is a different voice: a wild voice, a strange voice. And it comes just as Orail looks up to fix her golden eyes on me.

Why do you think, fool pup?

I gape at her, jaw flapping open like an oystercatcher's beak. Then I turn back to Áila for any sign she heard the voice as well. She gives me a blank look, and I wheel back to Orail, whose eyes are sparkling with something like delight.

Did you . . . did you just talk to me? I think inside my head.

You wanted my opinion, the wild voice replies, sounding for all the world like it's shrugging. *And I'm giving it. You care because you care about everything. You want the whole world to be right and good, to be perfect, the way you think it could be—or even should be. You care because you can't help caring, the way I can't help sniffing this meat. The way I can't help eating it, if I can ever find my way through this paper.*

I sway on my feet, feeling weak and dizzy and a little nauseous, and I can't decide whether it's because Orail is speaking to me or because somehow a dog has understood the inner workings of my soul better than I have. I turn slowly back to Áila, my mouth still sagging open.

"Hew?" she says. "What's wrong?"

I make a vague noise in the back of my throat and try to gesture at Orail. A glance back shows she has succeeded in working a haunch of lamb free of its paper, but I hardly care. Suddenly I feel Áila's hands in mine, steadying me, and I look down into her face. She has followed the direction of my gaze, and her eyes are urgent.

"She spoke to you!" she whispers. "Didn't she?"

I feel my head nod, and Áila laughs, gripping my hands tight as she ducks her head to muffle her laughter. Orail is trying to dislodge another parcel of meat from its paper, and I stare at her, dumb as a startled rabbit.

"Orail!" cries Áila between snorts of laughter. "Stop!" The dog obeys, licking its lips as it ambles off to squat in the grass.

"She speaks," I say, not sure whether I'm offering a question or a statement, and Áila's head bobs a clear yes while she squeezes my hands again. I try to clear my throat. "Has she always?"

"Not always," she says, releasing me. I feel colder without her touch, and have the strange impulse to reach for her again. "It started the day of the first Ordeal."

Orail comes back to sit between Áila and me, looking up at us with her usual uncanny impression of awareness. Only now I know it's never been merely an *impression*. She is as aware as I am.

"Can she hear all my thoughts?" The idea chills me; I have never shared the whole contents of my scathing, imperfect mind with anyone.

"You'd have to ask her," Áila says. "She can hear all of *mine*."

I look at Orail, dreading the answer, and her face cracks into a grin again. *You invited me in, pup. I didn't ask for full access.*

My head swims, and I sit down on the grass. Áila follows, and together we face the creature she brought back from Yslet's island. "What is she?" I say in a hollow whisper. "Is she truly a dog?"

"She seems to be," says Áila, though I can sense her doubts. "But she obviously has magic of some kind."

Áila bites her lip, and another revelation clubs me over the head. "The beach!" I gasp. "Was it *her*?"

"Oh, Hew, please don't tell the priest," Áila begs. "I'm sure he wouldn't understand."

I think of Fáthair Firnan telling me my opinions don't matter, saying Morgen LaCree is as trustworthy a chaperone for Áila as I am, and shake my head. "I won't tell him," I say firmly. "Anyway, the gods gave Orail to you, so it's only fair she should help. But how? How did she do it?"

Áila watches Orail roll onto her back and begin working her way across the grass, paws in the air and tongue lolling. It has started to drizzle again, but neither girl nor dog seems to care. "She grants wishes," says Áila. "Mostly material, but her powers are still immature. I don't know what she'll be capable of when she's fully grown."

I try to absorb this. "So the hair? The cows?"

"Her doing," Áila says. "She furnished my cottage too. You have to be careful what you think and say around her."

I nod seriously, imagining how disastrous it could be to have a creature like her among hapless people. Orail flips onto her belly again and gives a loud snort of satisfaction.

"What *are* you?" I say to Orail.

The dog gazes at me, and I squirm where I sit, feeling like she's boring into my very soul. For all I know, she *is*.

At last, her voice comes again: *I can't remember.*

Not "I don't know," but "I can't remember," which implies a past to be recollected. I swallow.

"Are you a god?" I scour my mind, trying to remember whether any of the gods sometimes take the form of a dog—but then stop, because what god would fail to remember who they are? Even Arial has never been said to take beast form or suffer amnesia, as far as I am aware.

The dog scoffs. I can hear it inside my head, a sound like rocks crumbling. *I am no god*, Orail says with something like scorn.

"And you obviously don't care for them either," I say, my pulse quickening. A being who doesn't remember what she is, who isn't a god and has no liking for them. Cold creeps over my skin. Could she be one of the deamhain, a servant of Dhuos?

No, she says, and I shiver at her awareness of my thoughts. *The deamhain are as dull as the gods. Always picking the same side, always keeping to the rules.*

Chaotic, then, but Arial isn't the only mischief-maker in the cosmos.

I look sidelong at Áila, wondering if she has heard both sides of this exchange, and she shakes her head. "I can't hear what she says to you. Just to me."

Orail stretches and stands, apparently bored with our conversation, and her lanky, overlong limbs remind me how young she is in this body—even if not in others. Áila climbs to her feet after her. "I'm so glad she talked to you," she says, offering me a hand up off the grass. "It's been awful, trying to keep this to myself."

I shake my head, still a little overwhelmed. "See you tomorrow?" I say, pushing a damp curl out of my eyes as I look down into her mist-speckled face. "I'll be happy to escort you to the kirk to pray, if you'd like."

Several water droplets are suspended on her dark lashes, and as she smiles at me, one of them breaks loose and lands on her cheek. I watch it go, a little spellbound, and shake myself as she says, "Tomorrow." With a small wave, she turns and jogs off toward the cliffside path, whistling for Orail.

I watch them a moment before returning to my cart. I have no responsibilities this evening, and I now know exactly how I will be spending my time. Because while my search didn't yield much the last time I tried, I also had much less information then than I do now.

Wish granter. Mind reader. Growing at a remarkable rate . . .

Orail is not getting less mysterious, but I am growing closer to uncovering what she might be.

To the library, therefore, I will go.

Chapter Thirty-Two

ORAIL

The Mischief in me is
      hard to quiet.

We live days together,
      Áila and me,
      and sometimes the boy who smells of Hope.
      And other times the Smiling Slug
who fears me, and his sister—
      the pair of them as veiled as Hew
is open.
      Mostly, I keep myself

Tame.

Tame for Áila, tame to make her happy.

But I am restless, anxious
      to know who, what I am;
      restless to find my Form,
      my language.
      And so the Mischief needles,
      nettles, prods, and pokes, makes
      me want to

Act.

I try on a new Form,
            one which belongs to this Land,

and

when Áila takes me into town,
where smells are ripe and all around,
I fight to keep my Mischief down
but find I fail.
Temptations pull me, threat to drown,
grab me by tail.

I fly from her, pull sharp away
through fisher's legs, race up the quay.
Knock some to sea, while others sway.
Teeth grab, seize fish;
dodging hands, I kick, grit sprays.
This is my wish.

I veer up roads packed hard by feet
and head for chapel, Yslet's seat.
I tear off scales, fins, scatter meat
on her altar:
not to bless, and not to entreat,
But to fault her.

I start in spite but end in glee,
the bliss of rolling, smells set free.
I lose myself, and so the knee
I see above
strikes me frozen, scares, shocks me.
Its snarl lacks love.

But then comes Áila, close behind;
Her face is stern, though voice is kind.
She tells the priest she does not mind
cleaning my mess.
His eyes blaze hot, his molars grind;
he bows his *yes*.

She cleans, I watch; she scrubs, I sit;
she asks why did I do it.
I try to answer, to acquit
who and what I
Am. But the pieces still don't fit.
I don't know why.

There is still something that I lack;
a memory I must call back.
Áila's still: she has a knack—
Sensing? Smelling?
all the things I can't unpack.
She smiles, quelling

The fear I have at not knowing.
"Let's go home," she says, throwing
a glance at the priest's door, there showing
her own deep doubts.
We hurry out, sunlight slowing
down our breakout.

"Don't go defying the goddess
again," she laughs, strides incautious
Away, up the path—

And

I

stop.

Form breaks, but it is not mine
         anyway.

Her words drag, dredge, carve
         something up in me.
         Something
         so close I can almost *smell* it.

Don't go defying the goddess again.

Who I am.
         Why I am.

And my Form.

I have almost found it. If
         I hurry, I might catch it.

I rear my head, electric energy
         running through me like a bolt
         like a strike
         like light and fire and wind.

I tuck into myself, reach out of myself
         body bunching
         toes gripping
         muscles stretching and pulling and
     pushing and flying

And I am off, up, away—

and Áila is flying behind.

She laughs,
        and so do I.

Chapter Thirty-Three

ÁILA

A week between Ordeals hadn't sounded like much time, but I am still shocked by how quickly I find myself staring down the last sunset before my second Ordeal. Despite the help the LaCree siblings have given—slipping up to my cottage after dark most nights with books borrowed from Fáthair Firnan's own study, which they come back to return again before dawn—I am more nervous for this test than the first. For one thing, it's the Mind Ordeal, and I have never been particularly academic. But for another, the last time I saw Fáthair Firnan, Orail was shredding fish guts on Yslet's altar, and I can't help worrying that might make him look less kindly on my efforts.

I am pacing the garden in the fading light, trying to remember a series of dates Morgen and Flora helped me memorize, when Orail flashes past me in a blur of black and brown. She goes haring down the hill in the tucked-up way she has of running, like her body is trying to outrun itself, and I cringe for whoever she has spotted. Not for the first time, I marvel that a creature with the intelligence to communicate and grant wishes should have no more self-control than an avalanche.

To my relief, however, it is Hew, whose curly, auburn head appears over the ridge.

"I brought chocolates," he says, holding up a small box in one hand while he fends off Orail with the other. "To toast your next Ordeal. Firnan ordered them to impress the LaCrees, but it turns out Morgen can't eat the stuff. Makes him sick." He grins. "Which happily is not the case for me. You?"

"I've don't know," I admit. "My family never had money for extravagances."

"Well, that makes two of us. But there are perks to living in a monastery, especially when the priest has guests he wants to indulge."

I can't help feeling Hew is more pleased by Morgen's inability to eat the chocolate than by our inheriting it, but I don't point this out. I try not to draw his attention to the LaCrees any more than necessary.

"Want to sit?" I ask, nodding at the cliffside bench Orail summoned a few days ago. It faces southwest and is nestled between tall patches of cotton grass and clumps of purple heather, so that when the sun goes down over the ocean, you almost feel you're a part of the landscape.

Hew follows me to the bench, and Orail plops down beside him with a dirt-encrusted bone I decide it's best not to ask about. I do, however, ask her to furnish us with drinks.

A bottle of pale gold liquid appears on the seat beside me, with two glasses that glitter in the waning sunlight. I fill them both while Hew opens the chocolates.

"Cider?"

"Thank you," he says. "And thank *you*, good lady," he adds to the dog, now rolling in the grass with her bone held aloft in her long front paws. She lets out a low, protracted *rowl*.

Comfortable silence settles over us as the sun dips toward the western edge of the sky, painting the ocean blush-pink and lilac. The chocolate is delicious, and I feel a rush of pity for Morgen. Then I wonder—for the thousandth time—if I have doomed myself by accepting his help. When I am with him, I always feel I have made the right choice; but somehow being with Hew tends to make me doubt again.

"Did you have apprenticeship aspirations?" I ask him suddenly. "Before your Goddess Trial?"

He blinks as he turns to me. "Aye," he says, sounding surprised. "I did. I still do. I-I want to be a priest."

He shifts back toward the ocean, and I can't tell if the rosy tint on his pale skin is embarrassment or merely the reflection of the sunset. Then I see a muscle jump in his jaw and realize he's clenching his teeth. I wonder if he's bracing himself to be ridiculed.

"You'd make a much better priest than Fáthair Firnan," I tell him. "I'm still waiting for him to justify Yslet's absence during my Goddess Trial."

He laughs, shoulders relaxing. "I won't do our priest the disrespect of agreeing with you, but I will thank you for the compliment."

I raise my cider glass to him, though when it is halfway to my mouth, I realize something. "But . . . you said you *still do*. You can't become a priest here, can you?"

He shakes his head.

I stare at him. "Then why have you stayed?"

His expression is conflicted as he meets my eyes, but he only holds them a moment before turning back to gaze out over the fuchsia-and-indigo-streaked sea. "The last five years, I've stayed for my sister Vira and her daughter, Gemma. But I think they can do without me now." He turns to look at me again. Somehow the roaring of the waves seems louder as his eyes take hold of mine, catching me up in the tumult I can see raging there. I don't know what he's thinking, but there is something in his face I haven't seen before; a gravity that strips his youth away and makes him seem strong and stern and certain.

"I'm planning to leave," he says. "As soon as your Ordeals are finished and you're safely on your way to an apprenticeship."

I find myself nodding, but a strange emptiness opens up

inside of me as I do. I barely knew Hew LacEllan a week ago, but it seems to me now that Carrighlas will be a much sadder place without him.

Tell him that, says a quiet, gravelly voice in my head. Orail's speckled ears swivel like twin periscopes beyond Hew, barely visible through the tall grass.

Don't be ridiculous, I say. *I'm not going to hold him back from what he wants.*

"I should get to bed," I tell Hew after another few minutes, standing up and stretching. The sun has disappeared, and the sky is a smoky blue-lavender above the glittering black sea. "Thank you for the chocolate."

"Keep it," he says, smiling as he hands the box to me. "You can celebrate again tomorrow after you've passed the second Ordeal."

I nod, tension lacing through me at the thought of the Ordeal, and click my fingers for Orail. Then I turn toward my cottage and resume my rehearsal of the dates I memorized.

But my last thoughts before I drift off to sleep are not of the books I've been scouring every night for the past week. They are of Hew LacEllan somewhere on the mainland, studying to become a priest. Curiosity to see more of the world prickles like an unscratched itch as the fog of sleep swims over me, and in the nonsensical way of dreams, I imagine myself with Hew: exploring wide streets, meeting new people, tasting strange food.

Orail is there with us, I realize, as the dream changes and folds me up in its heavy embrace. And beside me on the bed, she groans and stretches, pushing against the backs of my legs.

Not a bad plan, she yawns. *But you'd make a terrible priest.*

Chapter Thirty-Four

ÁILA

Unlike the first Ordeal, the second is to take place in the morning, so I am just finishing my porridge and tea when the LaCail arrives at my door, ready to escort me down to the kirk. The last bite of porridge sticks like paste to my throat, and I swallow repeatedly as I follow him out into a misty morning. Orail stays close at my heels, ears rotating with interest and tail wagging as if there is nothing to be worried about.

I scowl, resenting her calm.

The kirk is full of people, all quiet and solemn. Orail and I enter behind the laird, and he leads us up the main aisle to the altar of the chapel, where Fáthair Firnan stands waiting, a sheaf of parchment in his hands.

"The Mind Ordeal," begins the LaCail, "is designed to test the faculties of your thought, Miss LacInis. It may examine any area of your mental acuity, but the primary focus will be on divine history, since these Ordeals are an assessment of your standing with the gods. Some of the questions are obscure, but if you have their approval, the gods will give you the answers you need."

I nod. This is what Morgen guessed would happen, so the facts and dates he and Flora helped me memorize were largely to do with the gods—and all gleaned from the books Firnan had on his desk.

"As before, we will now allow you to make a sacrifice in place of this Ordeal, if you so wish," says Fáthair Firnan. "An appropriate substitute, we have determined, would be to offer a portion of your memories to the gods. If that is your choice, we will conduct that ritual here this morning. What is your preference, Miss LacInis?"

It takes an effort not to gape at the priest. A ritual to sacrifice some of my memories? Can the gods *do* something like take memories away?

They're the gods, Orail's voice growls as she stands beside me. *They can do whatever they want.*

For a moment I am tempted by the offer, because I'm still not convinced I believe in the gods at all. But like the last time I flirted with apostasy, I am drawn up short by worrying logic: if I am wrong, I could lose memories that are precious to me.

"I will undergo the Ordeal," I say.

The priest nods. "Very good. Then let us begin."

The questions are simple at first, and I answer them without much trouble. I resist throwing the occasional smile at Morgen and Flora, who are seated in the second pew from the front and surely recognize the questions as easily as me. Next to me, though, I can feel Orail growing restless. It's impossible not to think about the last time I was here, cleaning up the fish entrails she spread so thoroughly over the very altar I am now standing in front of. If the direction of her gaze is any indication, she's thinking about it too.

"What was the goddess Belaine's greatest triumph?" Fáthair Firnan asks.

I stare at him, my mind utterly blank. This was not a topic Morgen and Flora brought up at all. As I scour my brain for some scrap of memory about the healing goddess's victories, the only thing I can think of is her creation of the chamomile plant, which is commonly used to treat wounds. But that seems like an unlikely answer.

Beside me, Orail bristles with energy.

What was it, Orail? Do you know?

Yes, comes her immediate reply, crackling with passion. *Belaine's greatest triumph was her decision to let Yslet's daughter die when she was attacked by the wolf, instead of healing her.*

I know the story of Ona, of course. It is the same story my father recited on the boat only a few weeks ago, the story that leads to the tale of Fuiscea's creation. As I have always heard it, the healing goddess Belaine arrived too late after Arial set the wolves on Ona—at which point the child was beyond saving. The story I know says Belaine determined to speed Ona toward death as the kindest option, not that she chose to let her die when there was still a chance to heal her.

This must be what Orail means.

"Belaine's greatest triumph," I say with as much confidence as I can, "was her decision to let Ona die instead of healing her."

Firnan freezes at my words, mouth half-open. For a moment, silence stretches out across the chapel, deafening and terrible. Then the priest whispers, "That is very near to blasphemy, Miss LacInis."

I glance, panicking, to Orail, whose intense gold eyes are trained on Yslet's altar. Then my gaze snags on the LaCail, who is staring at me as if I have just expressed an interest in eating human babies.

"I didn't mean it like *that*—" I fumble, heat climbing my neck and swallowing my cheeks. "I only meant, she must have had great . . . *fortitude* and . . . *compassion* to make a choice like that, when the child was so gravely injured . . . and would plainly suffer from any efforts to heal her, and, erm . . . and . . . surely nothing could be a greater triumph than that kind of courage . . ."

I look around, hoping upon hope that I am striking somewhere near the truth. But when I catch sight of Hew standing in the back doorway, pale with wide, horrified eyes, I realized how far off the mark I have shot.

157

I stop short, blushing furiously.

Firnan lets out a long breath and exchanges a look with the LaCail. "We will overlook your blasphemy, Miss LacInis," he says in a measured voice, "since it is clear your answer is largely drawn from your own wild imagination and not from any knowledge of divine history. But we cannot count your answer as anything other than false."

Why did you tell me to say that? I shoot at Orail, burying my shaking hands in the folds of my skirt.

Because it's the truth, she replies, and only then do I realize the tenor of her bristling energy is vengeful rather than excited. I can taste the bitter flavor of her words, feel their corrosive acidity. Furious that she would give me such a gravely wrong answer out of her own inscrutable rancor, I determine to ask for her help no more during the Ordeal.

I turn my mind resolutely away from her.

"With whose help did Yslet first raise the isle of Fuiscea from the sea?" the priest asks next.

I am gripping the fabric of my skirt in both fists, trying not to let panic overwhelm me. But my thoughts flail like lapwings in a thunderstorm. I know I read that story this week, and I before I can stop myself, I find myself wishing I could glance over Firnan's book again.

Horror seizes me—

But it is too late to take the wish back.

A heavy, leather tome appears out of thin air between me and the clan leaders. For one unending moment it hangs there, solid and improbable, before it drops into my hands—which I raise helplessly to catch it.

Behind me, the entire village seems to gasp as one. The priest's eyes look as though they might pop out of his head. My face burns as the kirk buzzes with murmurs of fear and shock, and though I do not look at Orail, I bellow at her from the safety of my own head.

What are you doing? Do you want to be found out? Do you want me to fail this test?

"Miss LacInis," says Fáthair Firnan, sounding quite beside himself, "are you practicing magic during this Ordeal?" I can hear the unspoken second half of his question: *Were you practicing magic during the first Ordeal too, when our hair grew long and the cows came down into the sea?*

"No, Fáthair," I say earnestly.

"Do you know how that book came to you?" he says, each word like a hammer striking steel.

But no matter how hurt I feel by Orail's carelessness, I will not betray her. "No."

The priest's nostrils flare. "Very well," he grounds out. "Give me the book. We continue."

But I am so focused on not wishing anything, I can barely hear the questions he sets me. I answer five in a row without being aware of what I say, and two of my answers are wildly incorrect. Trying to focus, I shut my eyes as the priest reads the next question:

"What is the historic paternal and maternal lineage of our king, Fireld the Third?"

My brain feels like a wrung rag. I beg it to drag forth the answer, wish desperately that someone here would just tell me the names I need—

No!

I gasp, wheeling to Orail, but too late.

From the back of the chapel, a man's voice breaks out, loud and shocked-sounding, "Ranald the First, who wed Gretchen LacLinty of the northern islands; their daughter, Breven the First, who wed Sir Ciran LaKine—"

"What is this?" cries Firnan, looking like he might come apart at the edges. "Silence, man!"

But when that man claps a hand over his mouth, someone else speaks up, sounding just as stunned as the first. The priest and the LaCail screech out warnings like a pair of angry ravens, but people continue to proclaim all the names of the lineage until it is finished. When silence finally falls, ringing around the room with deafening finality, I squeeze my eyes shut. My skin burns so hot, I think I might die right there at the front of the kirk, burnt to ash by my own humiliation.

Yet there is something even more painful searing a path through my insides: the terrible conviction that Orail could have withheld all this chaos—if only she had wanted to help me.

Fáthair Firnan clears his throat. I swallow my agony and look up at him. He is red-faced and fuming, and I brace for his sentence, sure it will mean my failure, my doom, my Unblessing.

But then another voice speaks out from the pews behind me. It's a strong voice, deep and calm.

"If I may, Fáthair?"

Morgen LaCree.

The priest and the LaCail both turn toward him, though I can only watch their faces. The LaCail nods, and Morgen continues in that same calm, reassuring voice: "These Ordeals are meant to test not only Miss LacInis and her aptitude in bearing up under various types of strain, but also the gods' opinion of her. Doesn't it stand to reason that these . . . *extraordinary* events are evidence of the gods' favor? How else could you explain such things as we have witnessed here today as anything but the gods' desire for Miss LacInis to succeed?"

Both clan leaders look a little surprised by Morgen's question, and I can see Fáthair Firnan wrestling with it as he might contend with a painful bout of trapped gas. But the LaCail seems to relax as he takes in the idea, and he turns to raise his eyebrows at Firnan. I suddenly remember Hew's comments about Firnan wanting to impress the LaCree siblings, and feel a rush of knee-weakening gratitude toward Morgen for taking such a chance and coming to my aid. Already I can see the priest's anger fizzling, and he is starting to look even a little abashed—as if he should have thought of this himself.

Of course, I know exactly how to explain the things we've witnessed here today, and it is not by the miraculous favor of the gods. Their interference, I imagine, would be much less disruptive than Orail's.

Firnan nods, clears his throat, and nods again. He exchanges a silent look with the LaCail, then nods a third time. "Let us finish the questions."

Buoyed by Morgen's support—and my own powerful relief—I keep hold of my wits through the last five questions and manage to scrape correct answers to all of them. It helps that they are drawn from a book the LaCrees brought me only two nights ago, and when I have answered the final question, I feel so limp I have to dig my fingernails into my palms to keep from sinking onto the floor.

"Miss LacInis," Firnan says, looking almost as weary as I feel, "the gods have favored you. You will proceed to the third Ordeal—the Heart Ordeal—in a week's time. Meanwhile, get some rest and do what you can to prepare for the next test. You are dismissed."

I bow and stride out of the kirk ahead of everyone else. For once I am grateful for my enforced solitude, because right now I need it badly—need to be away from every last one of these people in order to process what has happened.

What Orail has done.

I lead her up the trail to the cliffs, past the monastery, and all the way to our cottage in white-hot silence. Behind me, she says nothing; she merely follows with her batlike ears pressed against her head and her tail low. When we reach the door of the house, I shove her inside ahead of me. Then I throw off my dress, pull on breeks and a shirt, braid back my hair.

Then I command her to stay, to *stay*, if she has any shred of respect for me at all in that dog-brained skull. Threaten to cast her out forever if she disobeys.

I hurl myself onto the cliffside path, trying to outrun my shame, my anger—and above all, my crushing sense that Orail has betrayed me.

Chapter Thirty-Five

ORAIL

I listen, smell
        Her simmering anger as
        She leaves, snarls
        at me to stay.

I obey,
        but simmer too—
        so close, so close to
        Understanding, to remembering,
        and my proximity
        to the truth makes
        me
        quiver,

        pace,

        rage.

It is Yslet's doing, I am sure
        at least
        of that.

I prowl the flagstones,
        roam the cottage,

sniff for something
to eat, to destroy:
vengeance for my captivity—

but which captivity?
Which captor? I
hardly know.

Fury at Yslet burns in my blood,
and though I know Áila is not to
blame,
not really to blame,
she is easier to punish than Yslet,
so I look for a way.

I could eat,
chew,
ruin her things.
But there is something
here that smells better,
entices,
lures me away from blankets and
shoes.

In the cabinet, not too high with
the chair nearby, I strain,
reach, nudge the door aside, lunge
to knock the box free,
the box that came with the boy who
smells of Hope.

I topple to the ground, but the fall does not
bother me like it does the box—

                    all splinters now, its contents
            scattered
                    like dark gems across the floor.

I sniff, eat
            one,
            two,
            three,
            five,
            fifteen,
            All.

Dark, smooth, explosions of bliss on
            my tongue, waking my brain, my
        being—

at last!—

my *Form*.

The language of my soul is not five, seven,
        five.
                    It is neither limerick
                    nor Burns verse—
                    But *Bard* verse.

Before, I was but half-awake, half-formed;
All body, half of mind, and without soul.
All impulse, lacking nuance, depth. My
        swarmed
Memory a hive beneath the bees, whole
Dwarfed by the smaller, less critical parts.
But now my soul opens its eyes, and now

The whole embraces all its parts, heart starts;
The woken captain returns to the prow.
I know at last, remember who I am:
Traitor and trickster, cursed, damned and
        condemned;
Shapeshifter, wish-granter, crow, stag, cat,
        ram.
And now dog. Faithful. Earnest. Loving.
        Friend.
What I've been and what I am no longer
Agree. And I feel—jarringly—stronger.

I know why I am here, what Yslet wants
From me: That which I could not accomplish
In any other body yet. It haunts
Me, plagues me to think I might abolish
My own prophecy: that in no body
Will I ever become what they want me
To be, will I ever wear their gaudy
Adornments: love and generosity.
I am fortunate the dog's body seems
To love mischief as much as I do. That
She is as willing to hunt down my dreams
Of chaos as I am, mayhem down pat.
Every hope I have in thwarting Yslet
Now rests in the dog's chaotic roulette.

My thoughts break from gods, Form, and
        betrayal
As my body jerks, shivers, drops like stone.
Muscles seize; something in me cries, *Fatal!*
And I writhe on the floor, mouth
        pouring foam.

My eyes roll to the box, lying fractured
In pieces. Were the dark bites of heaven
A trap, cold poison bound up in rapture?
They've spread death through this body like
     leaven
Through bread. I buck at the senselessness of
Finding myself just before losing me
Again. What will I be next? Hawk? Lynx?
     Dove?
But I freeze, stilled by bleak epiphany:
In a new body the curse is prolonged,
For Áila will cease to be where I belong.

Chapter Thirty-Six

HEW

If Áila's first Ordeal sparked a buzz of excitement throughout Carrighlas, her second has created a positive roar of amazed speculation. Most of the village stayed in the kirkyard for a solid hour after the test finished, eager to talk over what happened and debate whether it was the intervention of the gods or some other mystical miracle. None of the theories I chance to overhear come anywhere near the truth, though—which I am certain only Áila and I know.

I stay with the priest and the laird for half the afternoon, performing small tasks as they finalize the details around Áila's pass of the Ordeal. When I am dismissed, I leave at once for Áila's cottage, anxious to see how she is coping—and to hear Orail's explanation for her behavior.

The day is cold and misty, and by the time I arrive at the cottage I'm damp through and hoping tea and a warm fire will be waiting inside. But Áila's windows are dark and quiet, and when I knock at the door, there is no answer.

I sigh. She's off running the cliffs, no doubt, and I wouldn't be surprised if she stays out for hours. I'm just turning back toward the monastery when I hear something from inside the cottage—a scraping sound drifting through one of the windows.

"Áila?" I say, my heart missing a beat. "Orail?"

There is no answer, but I hear the sound again. It's a faint thumping, followed by something like a small object being scratched over stone. Indecision briefly freezes my limbs—but concern takes me by the throat. I plunge through pink sea thrift and yellow saxifrage to the window and heave myself up onto the wooden sill, knocking the shutters wide with my shoulders.

The cottage is dark, deserted—except for a large form lying across the flags, four legs splayed in front of it like fallen limbs. The figure is deathly still except for some faint twitching in its back legs, long-toed paws scraping faintly over the stone. There is a puddle of something whitish at its mouth.

Orail.

I am barely aware of my body as I scramble through the window and drop to the floor, crossing to the dog in three long strides. I crouch beside her, pulling her head into my lap, panic clouding my brain as I register the whites of her eyes, her dangling tongue, the saliva spreading through my trouser legs like seawater. She is jerking feebly, and beneath my hand pressed hard into her chest I can feel the frantic, weakening beats of her heart. I rake my eyes over the cottage for some clue as to what has happened—and I see broken wood fragments scattered over the floor.

They are pale, unstained, and rough, and one piece bears part of the seal of the village baker, whose chocolates Fáthair Firnan is so partial to.

My stomach plunges.

There had to have been twenty pieces left, at least—and it's a fine, dark chocolate, made with cocoa imported from across the sea. I know from listening to Firnan talk at length that while delicious, chocolate is also toxic to many animals.

Including dogs.

"Orail!" I gasp, shaking her heavy shoulders. "Orail, can you hear me? Stay with me! I wish you'd stay with me!" The haze of terror clogging my brain like morning fog clears as I register my own word: *wish*. "Orail!" I all but bellow. "I wish the chocolate was out of your body! Every last speck!"

She convulses in my arms, neck arching as she opens her mouth—and vomits. Glutinous brown liquid pours from her throat in a flood, running over my leg, the flagstones, and the rug. I gag at the sight and the smell, but hold on to her as she jerks against me. She vomits half a dozen times, shaking and coughing, and I wish for charcoal, which I know to be absorbent enough to stop some poisons.

"Eat this," I say when the black clumps appear beside me, and she hesitates only a moment before obeying.

Unwilling to do anything that might cost her more energy, I refrain from wishing the mess away. Instead I drag her back from the chocolate lake, wiping her snout and front legs clean with a rag, and begin to search for a bucket to fill at the well. But before I have found one, the cottage door opens, and Áila steps through it, head down, wet to the skin, and looking like a thunderstorm.

"Áila," I say.

Her head snaps up and I watch her green eyes widen as she takes in Orail lying on the floor, the rag in my hand, the flagstones covered with wood fragments and chocolate vomit.

"Orail!" she cries in a strangled voice. She darts to the dog's side, kneeling beside her and sweeping her hands lightly over the speckled body as if checking for broken bones. "Are you hurt? What happened? Hew, what happened?"

"The chocolates," I say, gesturing to the box shards. "She ate them. I was outside and heard her . . . struggling. So I climbed in through the window, wished the chocolate out of her body, and made her eat some charcoal. I think . . . I think she'll be okay." As the adrenaline and fear leak out of me, weak relief pushes in to take their place.

Áila is now sobbing, a stream of apologies and regrets pouring out as she buries her face in Orail's neck. "I never should have left you," she chokes. "Oh, but why did you eat the chocolates, of all things? Orail, you stupid, *stupid* creature!"

Orail is looking more subdued than I have ever seen her. Her usual glinting eyes are watery and pale, and her ears are laid back against her head. A submissive, embarrassed smile pulls at her mouth, and her tail thumps weakly against the floor. Áila has not stopped hugging her, but she now gives only the occasional, watery hiccup as she strokes Orail's dark, speckled coat.

Suddenly, she pushes herself to her feet. "Hew," she says, floods returning to her eyes. "She would have died if you hadn't come."

I hold out a hand to stop her—my breeks are wet with vomit—but she flings her arms around my neck anyway, hugging me fiercely. Her clothes are soaked from the rain, and I can feel water seeping into my shirt . . . but suddenly that doesn't seem very important.

Death was lurking in the shadows of this cottage mere moments ago, and now it has fled. Life seems all the more fragile—and precious—in its wake.

I wrap my arms around her and hug her back.

For a few minutes we stay that way, the only sound our mingled breathing and the distant drone of the waves against the cliffs. Áila's tear-dampened cheek is hot against my neck, and her wet hair smells like rain, lavender, and sea salt. I breathe her in—and all at once it is not merely *life* I am holding on to but the warm, flesh-and-bone body of a person I am coming to care very much about.

I take a sudden step back, breath short. Under the pretense of checking the weather, I cross to the window. "Still raining," I say casually, even while a cold breeze pulls the heat from my skin and calms my blood.

If this is what's going to happen anytime a girl hugs you, the voice in my head observes dryly, *it's probably for the best you're Unblessed and undesirable.*

This thought is more effective than cold ocean air and sobers me at once. Today's adrenaline and high emotion have obviously made both Áila and me a little more volatile than usual—and I need to be careful not to let it get the better of me.

"Good," Áila says behind me. If she is suspicious of my behavior, she doesn't show it. "That means we can do this."

I turn in time to watch her sweep the rug—on which more than half the vomit landed—over the flecks and puddles of chocolate foam dotting the flagstones. Then she gathers it into a soggy bundle and stands up.

"Would you mind drawing some water from the well?" she asks. "I'm going to lay this over the line so the rain can take care of it."

I can't decide whether to gag or laugh at her methods, but I am happy to obey. When I return, Áila has produced a small pile of rags and is busy scrubbing vomit out of Orail's speckled coat. I go to work on the flagstones themselves, which I quickly realize have years—or perhaps even centuries—of dirt on them already.

"When she's feeling better," I say, surveying my already-filthy rag, "you might ask Orail to procure you a new rug. It'll be easier than trying to find the floor."

She laughs, and I am dismayed when the sound warms me like a hot toddy, leaving me equally lightheaded.

A few minutes later she puts her rag down with a sigh. "What am I going to do with her?"

Orail's gaze is trained on her, even though the dog's eyelids are drooping with weariness. Áila stoops to help the dog up off the floor, then leads her to the bed, which Orail struggles onto even with a boost to her hindquarters. Áila settles herself cross-legged on the quilt beside her and begins to scratch the dark fur of her head. In seconds, Orail's golden eyes drift shut and her breathing grows deep and steady.

"I should have failed today," says Áila quietly, as I draw a chair close to the bed. "Would have done, if Morgen hadn't intervened."

I nod, but a prickle of irritation needles me. Morgen the rule-bender. I wish someone else would have come to Áila's aid during the Ordeal.

Sorry, pup, says a weary voice inside my head. *I can't change the past.*

I almost laugh aloud as one gold eye cracks open to twinkle at me before sliding shut again. I can suddenly see how easy it must have been for Áila's Ordeal to go wrong.

I have searched for an indication as to what sort of creature Orail is, but so far I have turned up nothing useful. It doesn't help that Bráthair Gibrat scrutinizes the books I take out like a hunter looking for tracks, determined—for his own unfathomable reasons—to work out what I'm looking for. I have begun taking out a wider variety of titles each time, just to throw him off the scent, but even the few promising volumes I've managed to scour so far have yielded nothing of use. *A Natural History of Ilbha's Creatures* included no magic species at all, and *Enchanted Beasts of the World* turned out to be a work of pure mythology. The only mention I found of wish-granters was something called a Gen, which seem to live inside vases or bottles, and looks roughly human in form. Whatever Orail is, it's not broadly catalogued as either fact or fiction.

"Probably better leave her locked up somewhere during the next one if I don't want another disaster like today," Áila says, pulling me out of my thoughts. "With supervision, of course." She gives a weary smile, and I suddenly remember what she said last night, about how Firnan has yet to make sense of her strange trip to Yslet's island.

"You do love her, though," I say.

If Áila is confused by the abruptness of this assertion, she doesn't show it. "Yes," she sighs. "I do."

"So if the gods are responsible for giving her to you instead of a medallion . . ." I say slowly. "Well, what I mean to say is that it may seem like part curse, but it's also a blessing."

She peers at me, frowning. "Tell me, future priest," she says. "Do the gods ever give us just blessings? Or do they always come with curses as well?"

Maybe it's the fact she used the words *future priest* without any sarcasm or scorn, or maybe it's that I feel iron certainty rising to my aid, but I don't give the voice inside of me an opening before I speak again. "I think life comes with curses," I say, "but I don't think the gods give them to us. It's my opinion the things that come from the gods that look like curses are just blessings we haven't yet understood."

She raises her eyebrows. "Is that what your Unblessing is, then? Not a curse, but a blessing you haven't yet understood?"

From anyone else, the question might sound like mockery.

I shrug, but feel one side of my mouth curve upward. "I don't know yet. If not, then it's simply one of the curses that come with life. The kind people make for each other and for themselves."

Her eyes hold mine for a moment, and in the overcast light from the window, they look stormy as the hills in a downpour. The more moods I catch in those green eyes, the more beautiful they seem to me—and the more I want to see the full scope of their expressions. Even as I think this, Áila's features soften, and the sun comes out over the storm-tossed peaks. Warmth spreads through my body—and with it, a powerful urge to scoot my chair closer to her.

Or better yet, climb onto the bed and pull her against me.

I get to my feet instead, needing a little more sea air and a lot more sanity. "Goodnight, Áila."

I throw another peat on her fire and leave her snuggled up with Orail. As I shut the door behind me and step out into the misty evening, I hear her begin to sing.

"*O'er the heath, where hurcheouns sleep, all cradled by the solum, O, the westly winds arise and pen a tune both bright and solemn, O; the pipe and drum first creaky hum, I turn to hear the whistle, O; lyke night hae daw, ilk freeze hae thaw, an golden light and thistle, O.*"

The song is a lullaby for Orail, but it follows me down the hill like carrying birdsong. By the time I reach the monastery, I feel almost as if I have arrived at home—a name I have not given to any place since I was thirteen.

Chapter Thirty-Seven

ÁILA

"This one could be tricky," Morgen LaCree says to me the day after the Mind Ordeal. We are once more in his study inside the monastery, and I feel a little flushed, because for the moment we are alone. Flora went into town to post several letters, and Orail is in the yard with the other dogs.

She was less willing to go this time.

They call this cheating, Áila, she rumbled. *If you're going to break the rules, at least do it where everyone can see, like I do. And don't leave me out of it.*

I ignored her, but each step closer to Morgen's rooms added another drop of guilt to my squirming stomach. *Orail simply doesn't understand,* I told myself. *Even if I am cheating, it's more to help Morgen and Flora than to help myself.*

"I've spoken with Firnan," Morgen continues, calling me back to the issue at hand, "and from what I can tell, the Heart Ordeal will be more a matter of making choices than knowing facts. I'll have to visit his study tonight for more clues."

I nod, nerves bunching as I try to imagine what sorts of choices I might have to make. But then Morgen seats himself beside me and anxiety morphs into heady exhilaration.

"I thought we could do some practice choices," he says, his voice low and his eyes welcoming. His arm is inches from my own, and I am more aware of the space separating us than I have ever been of any gap. "Know thyself, right? So. If you had to choose, what would be your choice? Sea or land?"

My mouth falls open. "How can I possibly—?"

"Don't hesitate," Morgen interrupts. "Trust yourself. *Know* yourself."

"Land," I say. "I can't run on the sea."

"Good." Morgen nods, smiling. "Reading or writing?"

"Reading."

"Dogs or cats?"

I snort. "Dogs."

"Talking or singing?"

"Singing."

"Mother or father?"

"You can't expect me to choose—"

"*Mother or father?*"

"Father," I whisper, horrified at myself.

Morgen's broad hand closes over mine. "Know yourself," he murmurs, soft as a late-summer breeze. "Once you do, nothing will be beyond your reach."

Heat courses up my arm and down into my belly. I raise my eyes to Morgen's.

"Hew LacEllan, " he whispers, ". . . or me?"

I am frozen, paralyzed, suspended in time as he holds my gaze. Slowly and very gently, he lifts a hand to brush his fingertips over my earlobe and down my neck. My skin shivers—

And the door of the study swings open.

I jump away from him. Flora strides in, looking cross about something, but stops dead as she catches sight of us on the settee. Morgen is still sitting very close to me, and my cheeks and neck are boiling.

"That's probably enough for today, Áila," Morgen says, and I feel myself flush still deeper at the sudden carelessness in his voice. "I'll check the priest's office tonight and see if I can learn anything more. Come again tomorrow?"

I am off-balance as I leave, as if someone has struck me in

the side of the head. I long for more time with Morgen—to discover what he meant by that last question.

But when I return in the morning, I find Morgen has learned nothing helpful in his search of Firnan's study, and failure has made him moody. He is too busy pacing the floor to give me so much as a smile, even when I try to catch his eyes. Flora seems anxious to soothe Morgen's worry, and the gathering anxiety makes the air in the room feel suffocating. I leave early and spend the rest of the day baking bannocks over my cottage fire with Hew, trying not to think about Morgen.

The next day I come to find only Flora waiting for me. "He gets like this when he's worried," she says with a reassuring squeeze to my arm. "My brother, I mean. Goes off on his own, avoids what's bothering him. But he'll come back around. Fancy a walk?"

"Good idea," I say, ignoring the disappointment plunging through my gut. At least I can bring Orail with us if we leave.

Ten minutes later we are striking out across the moors behind the monastery, Orail bounding ahead of us like a hare. But we are barely over the first hill when a voice rings out behind us.

"Áila! Orail! Wait!"

I turn to find Hew jogging to catch up, his lanky arms swinging at his sides. There will be no talking openly about the Heart Ordeal if Hew joins us, but I don't know how to stop him. He frowns at Flora as he reaches us, disapproval and dislike written all over his face, and I want to kick him in the shins.

"Hello," Flora says in a voice that could freeze the sea, and Hew gives her a curt nod.

"What are you all doing?" Hew asks.

"Going to find a soothsayer," Flora replies, "so we can find out what the next Ordeal will contain." She levels her eyes at him, pursing her lips. "What does it look like? We're going for a walk."

"Unchaperoned, I notice," he says, bristling. "Áila, you know I have to come with you when you go places."

"But Firnan gave Flora and Morgen permission to act as chaperones too," I remind him, wishing he would calm down about the LaCrees.

I can't change the way someone thinks or feels, Orail says from ahead.

"Not outside the monastery," Hew argues, before I can snipe a reply at Orail.

"Did the priest tell you that?" says Flora. "Or did you just decide those were the rules you wanted?"

Anxiety over the Ordeal rakes at my thoughts, but Hew's, Flora's, and Orail's relentless voices echo overloud through my skull. "Oh, I wish you would all just shut up!" I whisper under my breath.

There is sudden silence as Hew's voice snaps off mid-word. I look up at him to find his eyes wide, his mouth clamped shut. A glance at Flora shows a similar expression, and I turn with horror to Orail, who is still trotting ahead of us, tail swaying jauntily over her back.

"Oh holy Bréseh."

Flora is already following my gaze to Orail, no doubt drawing her own conclusions.

Orail! I shout in my head. *Let them speak! I wish you would let them speak!*

Hew blurts out the second half of the word he was just forced to swallow, and Flora gasps, raising a hand to her mouth. She turns toward me, her dark eyes very wide.

"Good to see you both," I say abruptly. "I need to go prepare for the Ordeal." And with a sharp whistle for Orail, I break into a jog and cut back through the heath toward my cottage.

As soon as the door shuts behind us, I turn on Orail.

"*This* is why I need the LaCrees," I hiss at her. "Because I can't trust you! Where would I be in these tests right now without them? If it were down to you, the Mind Ordeal would have been my last!"

It was a strange day, she says. *I was trying to help you, but something inside me was off. I'm better now. I know myself.*

"So there, on the moor—was that you knowing yourself? Was that you *helping* me?"

She huffs, and I can feel her exasperation with language. But I also sense a reluctance to tell me even that which she knows. It feels like a barrier between us, and it makes me seriously question bringing her to the next Ordeal.

I know the rules now, she says at last. *All of them. And when you do too, you'll understand why I answered your wish on the moor.*

I glare at her. "The rules of your magic?"

Yes.

"And how do you know them? Did someone tell you?"

I remembered them.

I sit on the floor in front of her, folding my arms. Her eyes bore into mine, and even though I am used to it now, I have to work hard not to look away.

The things I told you before, she says, *about summoning or changing, are still true: I cannot create things, I can only move or alter what is. But now I have more strength, and I can summon from farther or change more drastically without becoming too tired. And there are restrictions I am certain of now: I cannot change the way a person thinks or feels, I cannot move a person in space or time, and I cannot take a life by magic except at the cost of my own.*

"Strange rules," I observe, shivering slightly at the last one. "Who made them?"

Whoever made me, I would think.

"And are you finished . . . growing? Is your magic complete?"

She blinks, briefly shuttering those gold eyes. *It is. But there is one last piece to it. A rule you invoked without knowing it today. You alone may bind me to a wish.*

"Bind you?" I repeat. "I don't like the sound of that."

Since you are my mistress, any wish you speak aloud is my highest order until it's fulfilled. Nothing anyone else wishes can override it before it is accomplished. When you wish silently, I am free to ignore it, but spoken wishes are binding. If you are concerned about the next Ordeal, bind me before we go.

I sit, chewing on this information. Finally I say, "Orail, what do you mean, you *remembered*? Do you know what you are? Where you came from? Is that why you remembered?"

I am afraid to ask the last question that burns in me: *"Have you existed before now, in some other body, in some other place, with some other master?"* If Orail hears it inside my head, she doesn't reply.

For a long time, we simply stare at each other. Then, *I am Orail*, she says at last. *That is what I remembered, and with it, the things I can do. Nothing more.*

And I know the choice to trust her—or not—has been laid at my feet.

The first week I knew her, I decided Orail's true identity made no difference to me. But if she knows what she is and hasn't told me . . . ? A new kind of unease claws into me. Such a silence could mean only one of two things: Either Orail doesn't trust *me* with the truth, or she knows I won't like it.

And yet, I have almost never felt surer of any creature's devotion than I do hers.

I nod. "You are Orail," I agree. "My Orail. And I trust you."

She bobs her head once in agreement. *And so I can come with you to the Heart Ordeal?*

"Aye," I say, getting to my feet and going to the cupboard for some supper. "But I *am* going to take your advice and bind you."

I glance down at her, and it strikes me that she could be in some danger from a trial that is meant to test my heart. Regardless of what she is or isn't, I do love her.

And gods help me, I will do what I must to protect her. Whatever the cost.

She hears my thoughts. *There are some costs I will never let you pay.* In the strange, gravelly voice that has become so familiar, I detect a strain of something fierce and steely, something impenetrable. As I meet her unflinching gaze, I realize she will do anything to protect me.

Just as I feel I would do for her.

So what happens, I wonder with foreboding, *when those wills are at odds with each other?*

I will win, snorts Orail.

Chapter Thirty-Eight

ÁILA

The next three days blur past. There are new rumors the Usurper Prince has escaped Ilbhan justice and is loose on the mainland, and they thread tension through our village. I don't see Morgen at all, and Flora invites me into the monastery each day with a new litany of questions designed to help me search my feelings. To know my heart.

What do I fear? What do I long for? What do I love?

I am not sure the questions work. I am not even sure I answer them honestly.

The night of the Heart Ordeal, the LaCail leads me all the way out of the village, past the peat bogs, into a wood that stretches across the eastern side of the island. Orail stays close to my side, pressing her warmth into my legs, but I am still cold with fear. Of the Ordeals I have faced so far, I feel the least prepared for this one—and also the most dread over what it might demand.

We walk an hour in taut silence before I see lights and hear voices ahead. Then the LaCail slows his pace and picks his way toward a stone-lined path. Following close on his heels, I duck into a ring of stately rowans, boughs heavy with white flowers. A dozen braziers are planted around the circle, and in the center stands the largest rowan of all, its canopy towering over the rest, its once-silvery bark covered in shining copper coins that have been hammered into the wood.

My heart sticks in my throat as I realize what it is: a Wish Tree.

With half a glance at Orail, I step farther into the grove, where I see Fáthair Firnan standing behind a trestle table set with something lumpy. In between and behind the trees surrounding me, I hear the rustle of garments and the low murmur of voices: villagers, gathered to watch the Ordeal. My family are behind and a little to the right of the priest, their faces drawn and strained. Morgen and Flora are not far from his other side, and Hew stands on the opposite side of the glade, gnawing on a thumbnail.

"Come forward, Miss LacInis," says the LaCail in his deep, authoritative voice.

I walk toward the trestle table, hands shaking.

"As before," he says, "you have the opportunity to offer a sacrifice to the gods in lieu of tonight's Ordeal. Since this trial is a test of your heart, acceptable sacrifices would include the severing of a beloved relationship, the giving up of an important goal, or the death of a creature or pet that is close to your heart." His eyes flicker to Orail, and I suddenly feel like I might be sick. Fury burns in my heart at the suggestion that taking a life—deliberately ending any good and pure thing—might please the gods.

"No," I say, firm and cold. "I will not make a sacrifice."

"Very well," says the chieftain. "Please approach the table."

I do as he says, Orail at my side. Fáthair Firnan lifts a linen sheet lying atop the uneven shapes spaced across the trestle table, and I suck in a breath.

Beneath are . . . my own things.

There's an embroidery hoop framing a beautiful floral rendering of my initials, lovingly and expertly stitched by my sister Deirdre for my tenth birthday. There's a book Morgen gifted me last week, inscribed with a note I have now memorized. There is a silver brooch that belonged to my grandmother, which my father entrusted to me when I turned sixteen. There is—I startle at the sight of it—the icon necklace Hew painted for me, which I took off last night before bed.

And there is a simple clay mug, sea green, its glaze dripping from the rim as if the potter had melted verdant limestone over it. Flickering at the bottom, running all around the base of the cup, is a line of tiny text I doubt I would notice if I didn't already know it was there: *Golden light and thistle, O! Golden light and thistle, O! The pipe and drum begin tae hum of golden light and thistle, O.*

My throat is tight when I raise my face to the priest to see what he will say.

"These things," he says in his usual, impassive voice, "are all precious to you. The gods have revealed to us what objects we might secure to perform this test of your heart, and these are the possessions they directed us to."

I glare at him, then rake my eyes over the objects again. I doubt the gods have told them any such thing, but I can't deny I feel a powerful desire to protect each one from harm. How could Firnan have known what even I can't comprehend?

"It will be a lesser sacrifice, to be sure," he continues, "but the first part of tonight's Ordeal is a sacrifice nonetheless. You must make a votive offering to the gods, of whatever object here is most precious to you. You will take the offering through those trees there, to the bluff, and you will throw it into the sea. If you are honest, and choose that which is most valuable, the gods will accept it and you will not see it again—and you will pass the Ordeal. If you are false, however, the gods will send the gift back to you by washing it upon the shores of Carrighlas tomorrow, and you will fail the Ordeal. Do you understand?"

I stare back at the priest, clenching my jaw. What kind of god would require a person to throw away something beloved—something that brings them joy or comfort—just to prove how devout they are? I glance back down at the table, but I can't imagine how I could possibly throw any of these objects into the sea. Every one is tethered to my heart, not by its beauty or value, but by the person—or indeed dog—who gave it to me. And yet I have not even been asked to throw away the one that matters *least*; I've been told to sacrifice the one I love most.

My eyes find Deirdre's, almost lost in the shadows behind the LaCail. She's pale as salt, but her eyes are sharp, and she nods her head minutely when I look at her. I know what she's thinking: *Throw away mine. I don't mind, and neither will the gods. I'll make you another.*

I turn my gaze to my father, who looks like he's in pain. I can easily guess his thoughts as well: *Don't worry, Áila lass. Whatever you choose will be all right. Even if it's your nan's pin.*

I glance to Orail, the wish-granter, who could surely produce a new mug to replace this one if I threw it into the sea. But I remember what she told me, that she can only summon what already is; she can't create. I doubt there is another cup in all of Ilbha with these words painted upon it. And besides, this mug and its inscription arrived when I needed it most, and it is the first gift Orail ever gave me.

My heart aches. The brooch is precious, but I hardly remember my nan. And while Deirdre's handiwork is also very dear to me, I know she is right: she could reproduce it easily. I pass by Morgen's book without too much doubt; the note is lovely, but I've learned it by heart already. And Hew's icon . . . I pause, surprised by the strength of my feelings toward it. I have worn it every day since he gave it to me, and there is something about the simple, gilded portrait of the dead goddess Ona that brings me comfort. When I reach to my throat to touch it, I remember I am not the first to suffer at Yslet's hands.

If she even exists at all.

And if she doesn't? Does it matter which of these things I choose?

The gods are not trees falling in a forest, Orail says gently. *Their existence does not depend on your belief.*

I turn from the icon back to the mug, and my vision blurs. Such a simple, mundane thing, but it has brought me comfort, given me hope. When I imagine tossing the others into the sea, I feel varying degrees of fury and guilt. But the mug is the only one that has made me cry.

You'll have to choose that one, then, comes Orail's voice in my mind, soft as the breeze through the rowan boughs.

Will the gods really care? I ask her. It is my last thread of hope.

They will notice, she says. *I can't say whether they'll care, but you can be sure they will notice.*

Orail believes in the gods, I have begun to realize, which makes my own doubt harder to sustain. Yet again, I find my options blocked, not by what is, but by what I fear might be.

I nod, blinking back new tears, and reach to hook my finger through the handle. I don't look to Da or Deirdre or anyone else, I simply turn and walk through the trees in the direction the priest indicated. My boots crunch over leaves and bracken until the forest thins and the muted sounds of the ocean sharpen into booming clarity.

There is a promontory ahead, jutting out over the bay as though created for this purpose. I walk slow and tall to its point, Orail still beside me, and glance briefly to meet her molten eyes before raising the mug and tossing it in a low arc out over the lip of the rock. The gold script along the bottom glitters briefly in the starlight before it disappears into darkness and hissing foam.

I turn back to the crowd that has followed me, teeth set and eyes brimming. The LaCail watches me with a worried expression, but as usual the priest is stoic.

"Very good," says Fáthair Firnan briskly, leading me back through the trees to the rowan grove. "The second piece of tonight's ceremony should be less difficult. Because the heart is defined as much by its longings as by its losses, you must conclude the Ordeal by hammering a coin into the wish tree. You needn't shout your wish for the whole glade to hear, but I will come close enough to be sure you have uttered one."

The priest offers me a benign smile, as if to reassure me the worst is over—but inside my chest, my heart has tripped into a furious sprint. Make a wish? Aloud?

I glance again at Orail, who has gone very still. She has done beautifully tonight, but we both know she has no power to ignore a wish that is spoken aloud—certainly not from me. And it's common enough knowledge that wishes don't actually come true at the wishing tree. So I must think—quickly—of a wish she will have no power to grant.

As Firnan hands me hammer, nail, and copper coin, ushering me to the thick, coin-studded trunk in the middle of the glade, I plunder my brain. But panic has wiped my thoughts blank. There must be *something* I could wish that won't spark another magical disturbance, but everything that occurs to me is in some way material. An apprenticeship medallion, food to assuage the midnight gnawing in my belly, wealth, a new mug . . . Each of these would be glaringly obvious if they dropped out of the sky in front of me.

Think abstract! I tell myself. And then it comes to me, and I release a trembling breath of relief.

I approach the tree and hold up my coin. Firnan follows, hands clasped in front of him. "I wish Orail would be with me always," I say quietly, my throat going unexpectedly tight. I cut my eyes to her to confirm she can't make anything outrageous of that wish, and find her frozen where she stands, staring at me in apparent surprise. I give a small smile, relief softening my limbs, then place the coin against the bark of the tree.

And behind me, the glade explodes with noise.

Chapter Thirty-Nine

HEW

At first, I have no idea what is happening—though I was braced for *something*. Of all the things Áila's Ordeal could include, a Wish Tree is probably the worst one I can think of. I watched her lips move as she approached the tree, exhaled my relief when there was no immediate consequence—and then sucked in another breath as she touched the bark. Which was the moment everything seemed to happen at once.

Now it's as if the sky has opened up to pour blessings from the gods. Coins and chickens, sheep and grain, as well as piles of thrashing fish and mountains of cabbage, turnips, and potatoes rain down upon the rowan grove in a violent torrent that sends everyone running for cover. Fáthair Firnan runs out from beneath the Wish Tree only to scramble right back under it again, and even the LaCail ducks close to the trunk of a large rowan, narrowly avoiding a dairy cow as it stumbles and staggers upon landing. I still don't understand what's happened, but what I do know is enough to make me scour the scene for Orail.

I find her several paces from the Wish Tree. Áila is still working furiously to hammer her coin into the trunk, but the dog is curled on the ground as though being crushed by an enormous weight. I charge through the copse, weaving through piles of crops and squawking hens, and drop to my knees beside her.

"Orail!" I cry, bending across her to shield her head from falling turnips. "I wish you to stop this! Stop granting these wishes!"

She whimpers, but the bounty continues to fall from the sky. *The tree*, she says weakly.

I turn to look back at Áila, resolutely hammering, perhaps thinking she must complete her Ordeal to make the downpour stop—and an idea hits me like a potato to the head. I spring toward her, catching her by the arm she has just raised to pound the nail in another time, and pull her back a single pace. Her hands come away from the trunk—and the torrent of crops, animals, and coins stutters to a halt.

"Leave it!" I tell her, and spin back toward Orail, still lying in a heap on the ground.

As Áila gapes around the glade, I scoop the great speckled dog into my arms and begin to walk as fast as I can toward the edge of the grove still roaring with chaos. "Áila!" I shout.

She follows at a trot, shaking her head like she's fighting off bog midges. "What happened?" she says as soon as we reach the cover of the forest.

But before I can answer, Orail speaks—to both of us, I think. She sounds exhausted. *The wishes. All those wishes. I could ignore them before . . . before you touched the tree.*

Áila's eyes are as round as the coins hammered into the Wish Tree's trunk. "*All* those wishes?" she repeats. "*Centuries* of wishes? Salt and scales, Orail. Are you all right?"

Tired, says the dog. *I can't stand.*

"You should leave," I tell Orail, "before anyone works out what happened." I look at Áila. "There've been enough strange happenings around your Ordeals as it is, and if anyone saw Orail on the ground, they might start putting it together."

"How?" says Áila. "I can't go anywhere, and you can't carry her back to the village on your own."

I stare at the large shadow on the ground that is Orail. "We'll have to make a pallet of some kind."

"Can I help?"

We both spin around at the new voice, and I feel immediately on guard at the sight of Flora LaCree standing a few paces behind us, looking hesitant.

"You can trust me," says Flora, stepping toward us. "I . . . I know she's special."

"You do?" says Áila, sounding shocked. "How?"

"When we were out on the moor a few days ago . . ." Flora looks apologetic, but Áila's shoulders slump in obvious relief.

"I guess you couldn't have failed to notice she stopped you from talking."

She shakes her head. "What sort of magic . . . ?"

"Wish-granting—" Áila begins, but I cut across her in horror.

"Don't tell her that! We don't even know her!"

Áila turns on me in exasperation. "*You* may not know her, Hew, but she's my friend and I trust her." I clench my jaw as she pivots back to Flora. "We need to get Orail back to my cottage. Can you help us find something to drag her on?"

"I can do better," says Flora. "I saw a wheelbarrow back in the glade. Must've fallen with all the rest of that stuff."

"Perfect."

Flora turns at once and disappears, and a sticky silence creeps between Áila and me. But I can't hold my frustration in for long.

"What are you thinking?" I hiss. "Do you know what people would do for a wish-granting dog? What if she tells someone?"

"Only a madman would want *this* wish-granting dog," says Áila, rolling her eyes. "Calm down, Hew. Flora can keep a secret."

"I don't trust her," I say, crossing my arms.

Áila sighs. "Because anyone who does things differently from you is untrustworthy?"

"She and Morgen ignore the rules!"

Áila starts to reply, but Flora reappears before she can, jogging behind a wooden barrow.

"I'll take it from here," I tell Flora, lifting Orail again and laying her gently in the makeshift trundle. "If you want to help, you can do all you can to keep people from remembering Áila came with a dog."

"Thank you, Hew," says Áila, laying a hand on my arm. Her voice is soft now, and I release a heavy breath, frustrated at myself as I feel all my anger leak away. A mad urge to gather her into my arms, hold her against my chest, seizes me—and I bend to lift the wheelbarrow before the temptation can win out.

"Go on," I mumble. "You still need to convince them you're innocent."

Áila kisses Orail's head, then hurries away from me, back toward the glade. I start to push the barrow through the trees, in the direction of the village, but a craggy voice in my head pulls me up short.

Don't be stupid, she says, sounding weary. *We're not going anywhere until we hear a verdict.*

"But you can't stay—"

I have a wheelbarrow now, and someone to push it. So let's find a place we can watch and hear without being seen, and we'll leave when we're sure Áila is safe.

I can't argue, because I want to hear the results as much as she does. So I push her through the woods to the other, empty side of the grove, and crouch down in the shadows beside the barrow.

In the glade, it looks like the LaCail and Firnan have finally organized the chaos enough to confer with each other. The watching villagers have all come out of the trees, and are either talking in animated voices, helping those of their number who were injured by falling wishes, or furtively gathering spoils. Áila stands on the fringes, and almost as soon as Orail and I are in place, the LaCail spots her and calls her forward.

The onlookers fall silent.

"Miss LacInis," he says, "your Ordeals have been memorable, and this one was no different. But you did what we asked you to, and we can find no reason to blame you for this . . . spectacle. However, we must abide by our own rules. The gods will judge your votive offering, not us. If it washes ashore tomorrow, broken or intact, you will fail."

Áila is small and silent before this sentence, but Flora pipes up with a question that makes me feel less hostility toward her.

"Is there nothing more she can do, Laird?"

I strain my ears to hear his answer, but it is the priest who answers. "She can pray, Miss LaCree. As always, she can pray."

Before the crowd has time to disperse, I hurry Orail's wheelbarrow back through the trees, pushing her as quickly as I can toward the village. The dog is silent and brooding, but I don't want any conversation. I ignore the voice in my head—wondering loudly what I might have done differently during the Ordeal to help Áila—and do the only thing that can still help her. The thing Áila might hesitate to do for herself.

I pray.

Chapter Forty

ORAIL

My heart is changing, softening in me,
Like fruit set out too long, it starts to leak.
Have I become what they want me to be?
But gods are not the ones who set to wreak
This havoc on my soul; it is Áila.
So I stand by and let her enact their
Vengeance, heedless of what she does, while a
Storm rages inside of me like warfare.
Do I try to thwart Yslet, dig in claws
And maintain my life as an enemy
To gods and men, or give all that I was
To the melting power of this alchemy?
For I cannot do both. My resistance
Must propel the end of love's existence.

The choice is an agony inside me,
Twisting guts, a predator I perceive.
This long-held feud with the gods is my key
To victory, the last trick up my sleeve
In a gamble where they hold all the cards.
If I convince them they're wrong, that love
    has
No sway over me, they'll call off the guards,
Perhaps, give up, let me go free. Whereas
If I show them I can love, I may keep

Áila, but lose the only thing I have
Left of myself, though it's bruised and asleep:
My pride. Yet there's a loss that has no salve.
Yslet has held my chains through forms and
      years
But the loss of Áila now drives my fears.

Chapter Forty-One

ÁILA

The next morning, Orail sleeps off the effects of the Wish Tree, but I am sick with suspense. I spend the first few hours filling and refilling my remaining mug with tea and wishing it had golden lyrics painted upon it.

"*Golden light and thistle, O, golden light and thistle, O,*" I sing quietly to the sea from my cliffside bench. Still, the worry does not dissipate.

Hew comes and sits with me from midday to late afternoon, but we hardly exchange three words. When he leaves, he does so with hunched shoulders, and I wonder if he is even more nervous than me.

At dusk, the LaCail arrives. As if sensing his presence, Orail comes out of the cottage, and together we stand on the front porch and await my sentence.

The LaCail spreads his hands. They are empty.

"Congratulations," he says with a smile. "You've passed the third Ordeal. Only two more to go."

A wild, whooping sound comes from beyond the rise, and we both turn to see Hew galloping up the path, as ungainly as a newborn colt. He is grinning broadly, and I can't help smiling back as the LaCail chuckles.

"You've earned a bit of celebration," he says, winking.

But Hew's celebrations aren't the only ones I have to look forward to. The next morning, Flora almost knocks down my cottage door with an enthusiastic invitation to a beach picnic-supper with her and Morgen, already sanctioned by Fáthair Firnan. I know I should spend the day preparing for the Soul Ordeal, but I am too excited about time with Morgen to think about anything else.

When sunset finally arrives, I run alongside Orail—recovered at last—in my prettiest dress, and don't even try to hide my smile as we meet Morgen and Flora on the cliffside. Morgen smiles back, and I feel weightless as a seabird.

"So," he says as we pick our way down the steep, rocky path toward the cove where we are to have our picnic. "Flora tells me your dog is even more unique than we realized."

I toss a glance at Orail, two paces ahead of me. The only indication she's listening is her lifted right ear, swiveled halfway back toward us.

"I think that's an accurate description," I say. He beams at me, and I am briefly lost in the dazzling flash of his teeth and the strong, stubble-covered lines of his jaw. I wonder what it would be like to run my fingers along it, and my stomach swoops like I've just jumped off the cliffs.

"She answers any wish you might have?" he asks.

"Not any," I tell him. "There are limits."

Careful, Orail says, an edge behind her words. *I agree with Hew. I don't trust them.*

I give her tail a light tug. *You don't trust anyone who doesn't like dogs,* I remind her. *That doesn't mean they're bad.*

Doesn't it? she says darkly.

"Would you care to demonstrate?" Morgen says. His excitement is palpable—like a child who's spotted a plate of cakes fresh from the oven.

I honestly don't see the harm, I tell Orail. And then I say, "Orail, I wish you'd take all this stuff and set it up on the beach for us."

In a blink, our arms are emptied of the loads we carry, and there is a magnificent picnic spread out on the beach below us.

Flora laughs. "That would have been handy about an hour ago," she says, lurching across the sand to give me a gentle poke in the ribs.

Morgen laughs too, but it's a crow of delight. "That's a handy skill. I suppose there's no end to her uses."

I feel a stab of annoyance. He talks like Orail is a tool to be used, rather than a creature with thoughts and feelings—and indeed, my dearest friend. But I do my best to pardon him; a man who doesn't like dogs can't be expected to think about them as I do.

We sit down to eat, and Morgen chooses a spot near me. I find myself leaning toward him as he recounts my Ordeals anew, now with the missing piece of information—that Orail was responsible for all the mayhem. He laughs good-naturedly, like it's all some marvelous joke, and every time he catches my eyes I feel like he's taken physical hold of me. We move on to dessert, and the conversation shifts as easily as the wind. Flora asks what medallion I'd most like to have, and when I can't make up my mind between the fishers' sea glass and potters' glazed clay, I turn the question back around on her.

She looks taken aback, but after a moment a small smile plays at the corner of her mouth. "Do you know," she says, sounding a little distant, "I think I would quite enjoy baking. My mother and I used to cook together when I was small, and I, um . . . well." She stops abruptly, blushing, and looks at Morgen. "I miss it," she finishes quietly.

"What happened to her?" I ask, suddenly aware of the hard set to Morgen's jaw, where a muscle is jumping in and out of view. "Your mother?"

"She died," he answers a little roughly, but his gaze is still set on his sister. I wonder if he is angry with her for bringing up something that causes him pain, and scramble for something to redirect the conversation.

"What medallion would *you* choose, Morgen?"

"Whatever they give to the scribes," he says, lighthearted again.

"So you've always wanted to serve the gods?" I think of Hew and his longing to be a priest. "How do the people of Cheltland decide on their work?"

Morgen throws another glance at Flora, but she is still solemn, eyes on her lap. "Our parents choose for us, generally," he says slowly. "But my—*our*—father would have had me follow in his footsteps and become an overbearing landowner who does nothing but sit in his fine house and order other people around. So I left."

"Does your father not see value in serving the gods?" I ask, trying to reconcile this aristocratic image of Morgen's childhood with the self-sacrificing life of a cleric.

Morgen shrugs. "He just wants me to be like him, I think. But no, religion never impressed him much—and certainly not the academic work of a scribe."

I look at Flora, to see what she makes of this assessment of her father. She is leaning back on her hands now, head tipped up to the sky as it swirls and blurs with color. "And you, Flora?" I ask. "What does your father want you to do?"

She laughs, still gazing upward. "He doesn't think of me much at all, to be honest. I'm not sure he cares what I do, which is why I went with Morgen."

"I'm sure your brother is very grateful for you," I tell her.

Morgen turns to look at Flora, his eyes warming again. "I am," he says, and Flora gives him a faint smile. She looks as if she is about to answer when suddenly Orail growls deep in her throat and leaps to her feet beside me.

All three of us swivel to look at her. Her body is still as carved stone, and she is staring up the beach while the fur on her back rises in a long ridge from her neck to her tail. My skin prickles at the sight, and I squint in the direction she is staring—half-obscured by the shadow of the cliffs in the setting sun.

And then I see it: two low, dark shapes, moving fast along the beach toward us. I watch them come, trying to work out what they are—too small to be horses, too big and too fast to be sheep—and for a moment I wonder if they are dogs.

Then Morgen says urgently, "Wolves."

I surge to my feet. Flora leaps up as well, while Morgen seizes a knife and a heavy bottle from our picnic spread, stepping in front of us. I look around for Orail—and my heart stutters.

She is a blur of black and brown, kicking up sand as she speeds toward the wolves.

I scream for her to stop, but it is already too late. She meets the attackers head-on, and a terrible cacophony of growls, yips, and snarls echo off the cliffs. Flora takes hold of my wrist, but I yank it free and start forward—just as Morgen puts his arm out, catching me hard across the chest. I shove him off with a roar—*how dare he hold me back from helping Orail?*—and at the same moment, one of the two wolves breaks free from the skirmish and lopes toward us.

There is a ghastly sound from up the beach, a cry of bone-wrenching pain. Terror washes through me in a cold rush. I dart past Morgen, heedless of the wolf already halfway to us, and start toward Orail. I don't know what I will do when I reach her, only that I cannot stand back and watch her die.

"Áila!" Flora screams.

But I stop, because one of the creatures up the beach has broken free from the other—leaving it in a motionless heap—and veers back toward us with breathtaking speed. The second wolf is nearly upon me, its open mouth red and gleaming white in the dusk, but it never reaches me. Because the animal now racing back down the beach is Orail, and she is moving faster than I have ever seen anything move. She overtakes the second wolf, and a heartbeat later it is over.

The two wolves lie dead on the beach, dark blood seeping into the sand, and Orail moves toward me with gold eyes blazing. She is panting hard, her mouth dripping blood and foam. Morgen and Flora stand in shock, staring from Orail to the beasts she killed. I simultaneously feel the urge to be sick and the impulse to hug Orail and never let go.

She meets my eyes, and I remember the impenetrable will I sensed in her before the Heart Ordeal, the realization she would do everything in her power to protect me from harm.

After what feels like lifetimes, Morgen lets out a shaky groan, and Flora crosses the picnic blanket to hug me, trembling with tears. "Are you all right?" she asks.

"I'm fine," I say, still staring at my dog. "She's fine. I'm fine."

Morgen's voice is unsteady when he finally speaks. "Can you blame me for being afraid of dogs?" he says. And then, as Orail walks down to splash herself clean in the surf, he adds quietly, "Gods help anyone who ever tries to come between you and that animal."

Chapter Forty-Two

HEW

I am late for Vira's, and I detest being late.

After the incident with the Wish Tree, I took out a dozen books from the library, and have spent every spare moment searching them for clues about what Orail could be. On the evening I promised Vira I'd join her and Gemma for dinner—an evening Firnan gave the LaCree siblings permission to take Áila on a picnic—I'm so caught up in my reading that it isn't until the monastery bell tolls the hour I realize I'm due at my sister's house *now*.

I throw the book aside and leap up, pulling on my boots. Vira lives halfway across Carrighlas, and by the time I reach her house, I am sweaty and panting.

"I was worried about you!" she says when she opens the door.

"Sorry," I say, guilt pulling at my limbs like iron weights. "I didn't mean to frighten you. I lost track of time."

From the house beyond, I hear her husband call, "Do they not teach Unblessed whelps how to tell time?"

Vira frowns, but ignores him, pulling me into the house. "Gemma will be thrilled," she says, giving me a quick hug. "Gems! Gemma, darling, your uncle's here!"

My niece flies out of the kitchen like a small ginger windstorm, shrieking my name. "Uncle Hew! Are you going to read my new book to me?"

"I am!" I tell her, lifting her above my head and doing my best to ignore Colm's stream of snide comments from the next room. I set Gemma on her feet and she takes off again, a bolt of loose energy. "Gems!" I say. "Get your book and we'll read!"

"Supper will be ready soon," Vira warns, but I give her a wheedling smile.

"Just one quick story before we eat?"

"One, then," she says, rolling her eyes. But her lips twitch.

I settle myself into a chair by the fireplace, its peat burning low in the grate, and Gemma trots toward me with a leather-bound book that's almost as big as she is. My amateur artist's eye wants to linger on the gold scrollwork adorning the cover, but before I can do more than register the title—*Dreachan's Fables*— Gemma has clambered into my lap and heaved open the tome so that it lays across both our legs.

"This one!" she says, pawing at the leaves until they slither apart to a page of pen-and-ink illustration and calligraphy that reads, "The Tale of Kind Callum and the Púcca." Two twisting trees sit one to a page, their branches crowding around the title; and across the binding, at each tree's base, are a shabby-looking boy and a dark, vaguely lupine animal with big eyes. I start to read.

"Once upon a time, there was a poor boy whose family lived in a mud house in the hills because they couldn't afford stone. This boy's name was Callum, and for all his parents' poverty, he was a kind-hearted, hopeful boy who never treated anyone ill. But he had four older brothers, and they were not so kind. In fact, they resented Callum for his easygoing nature and gentle heart, and thought he should be taught a lesson to remind him that life was hard for most folk."

"Oh no," says Gemma gleefully.

"So one day, while their mother was doing the laundry and their father was out minding a rich man's sheep, these four older brothers took poor Callum out to a pond and dangled him above it upside-down by his ankles. Now, Callum couldn't swim, so it wasn't any good trying to wriggle free. And his brothers told him if he'd only be the one to sneak next door and rob the widow of her hens' eggs, they'd let him down. But Callum wouldn't agree, so his mean older brothers, they just left him there to dangle. And all the while, the blood was rushing into his face and his ears and his nose, hurting something horrible, and he didn't know what to do. And that's when—"

"The Púcca came!" Gemma shouts, clapping her hands in delight.

I raise my eyebrows at her. "What's a Púcca, Gems?"

She merely flaps her arms. "Keep reading!"

"Right. So that's when the Púcca came. This Púcca, like all of them, had once been a person—and not a very good person at that. But the gods had given him a chance to redeem himself, if he would only use the magic they gave him to help someone brave and kind and good. And when poor Callum started crying out for help as he dangled there over the pond, the Púcca saw his chance to win his freedom. So he came to Callum and said, 'What can I do for you, young master?'

"Now Callum was a sharp lad, in addition to being kind, so he hesitated a moment before answering.

"'What are ye?' he asked the Púcca. For the creature was strange to behold, and while it looked like a beast, there was something uncanny in its gold eyes that made him think of some people he knew. Its fur was dark as night, and it walked on four legs, its shape like that of a wolf.

"The Púcca smiled at his question. 'I am the Púcca,' it said, 'and I will grant whatever wish you may ask of me.'"

I break off reading, my heart suddenly bouncing around my chest like a bee trapped in a jar. "Whatever wish?" I repeat, staring down at Gemma.

"Yes!" she cries, clapping her hands again.

I feel outside of myself as I continue to pinch the pages of the book between my fingertips, my eyes sliding out of focus. I shake my head and shift Gemma so I can look her in the face.

"Gems, have you read this story before?"

She looks at me like I'm witless. "Of course, Uncle Hew. How else do you think I'd know what a Púcca is?"

"Are there other stories in this book about them? Any other Púcca stories?"

Gemma squints at me in suspicion, but she nods. "Two more. Uncle Hew, are you well?"

"Aye, yes," I say, waving down her concern. "Show me, won't you?"

Gemma fumbles with the thin pages, but eventually directs me to another story, which seems to be about a Púcca in the form of a donkey who helps a group of selfish, ungrateful servants, but eventually tricks them into taking its punishment in its place. At the end of its good service, the Púcca is rewarded with a natural death—a release from the torment of living life as a beast in service to fools. The third story follows a Púcca trapped in the form of a horse, whose wish-granting powers are discovered by someone who wants to use them for her own ends, and who is eventually drowned when the Púcca traps her on its back and dives into a deep loch. At the end, it is reborn as an eagle and made to try its redemption again.

I flip back to the first story, where poor, kind Callum is still dangling over the pond by his feet, trying to work out whether or not he should trust the Púcca. Which Callum does, and as I read, the Púcca helps with panache: teaching a lesson to Callum's sleekit brothers, gifting his parents with wealth and good fortune, and eventually leaving Callum with a beautiful bride, a chest full of gold, and the favor of the king. At the end of the tale, like the donkey Púcca, the beast is rewarded for its service with an ordinary death, at which its soul is given true and proper rest.

I finish the story feeling like I've run the whole length of

Fuiscea. I am breathless, and my heart is pounding harder than Vira's mortar and pestle in the kitchen. I am no longer uncertain what Orail is; she is patently one of these creatures of fairy tale—a Púcca, a wish-granting shapeshifter, a being who was once human and is now being punished in beast form until she can learn decency and kindness . . . or something like that. So will she die when she has finished her service to Áila? And when will that be? Is there some way Áila and I could prevent her death, perhaps by discouraging her from being too good too soon?

Though I have only just arrived at Vira's, I am suddenly desperate to be gone, to find Áila and tell her what I've learned. Every moment could be precious, for the gods only know how much time Orail has left.

"Uncle Hew?" Gemma asks. She has been watching my face closely. "What's wrong?"

I force a smile and lean my forehead against hers. "Can you keep a secret, Gems?"

She nods eagerly.

"I think I might know a Púcca."

Her brown eyes go very round, and she lets out a small gasp. "You *do*?"

"I think so. And I need to go find her, to make sure she's okay. Can you tell your mother I had to go, but I'll be back next week? Tell her I'm sorry?"

Gemma nods, but when I stand up and put her back on her feet, she gasps again. "Uncle Hew!"

"What is it, Gems?"

"Is the Púcca in *trouble*?" Her eyes are suddenly swimming in tears, and I give her shoulders a quick squeeze before planting a kiss on her forehead.

"Not if I can help it," I say. "Pray to the gods that she'll be okay, won't you?"

Gemma nods and puts her little hand inside mine to squeeze my fingers. "I'll pray to Lir," she says. "I know you like him best."

I give her one last smile, and then hurry to the door under cover of Vira's pounding pestle. As I pull the door shut behind me, I glance back—and see Gemma standing with the book of fairy tales clutched tight in her little hands, watching me go.

She smiles, brave as kind Callum, and gives me a watery wink.

I take off up the cobbled street as fast as I can run.

Chapter Forty-Three

ÁILA

After the wolves, the effortless fun of our picnic seems like a thing of the distant past, so we pack up and decide to head to the monastery. This time, I wish our things back so we don't have to carry all the extra food, and Flora gives me a grateful hug. As we hike back up the beach toward the path that leads to the cliffs, Orail stays close beside me with a kind of edgy watchfulness, as if she expects there could be worse yet to come. Morgen hovers close by as well but doesn't say much. He seems lost in his own thoughts.

"Flora, will you go tell Bráthair Gibrat what happened on the beach?" he asks his sister when we are close to the monastery. "He'll want to know."

Her brows contract. "I don't know that we should—" she begins, but he fixes her with a look of such intensity that she breaks off. Pursing her lips, she strides across the lawns in front of the towering stone building and disappears inside.

"Bráthair Gibrat?" I ask, thinking of the cranky monk who works in the library. My interactions with him have not been overly favorable.

"He keeps the records," says Morgen, "and he'll be very interested to hear about the wolves. They haven't been a problem on the island since Yslet's intervention centuries ago, as far as I know."

Since Arial used them to murder Ona, I think with a little shiver of dread. I throw a quick glance at Orail, chills rippling down my arms, until I remember she killed the wolves tonight. If she were some incarnation of the trickster goddess, she surely would have joined them instead of dispatching them.

"I've had a wonderful time with you these last weeks, Áila," Morgen says, his voice low and a little rough as he steps closer to me. His lips pull up into the smile that has become so familiar to me, and my abstraction about wolves and Arial and Bráthair Gibrat evaporates like mist. I have not quite forgiven him for the way he tried to restrain me on the beach, but I'm also ashamed of how violently I reacted when he did.

"You're a remarkable person, Áila," he continues, ducking down a little to catch my eyes as they drift toward my toes. I can't avoid meeting them, and I feel my resentment fizzling as his dark irises envelop me in tingling warmth. He swallows, his jaw working beneath the stubble as if he's nervous. Finally, he whispers, "I've . . . *cherished* . . . the moments we've spent together."

It starts to rain, and the cold drops are a welcome relief on skin that suddenly seems far too hot. His face is close to mine, and it is impossible to keep my eyes from following the beads of rainwater down his cheeks and across his lips.

"Unfortunately, it'll be a few days before I see you again," Morgen says, and now the smile is gone, lost in dreary reluctance. "The monks are conducting a sacred hunt that I must attend to take notes. It is a rare practice—they only do it once every ten years, and I'm lucky to be here when it happens."

"A hunt?" I've never heard of a sacred hunt, but I suppose there are many sacred things I'm unaware of. "How long will you be away?"

"Three days," he says. "I won't be able to help you prepare much for the next Ordeal."

"Oh," I say, trying not to show my disappointment. But he sees it anyway, and moves still closer, eyes roving my face and setting my skin ablaze.

"Can I give you something before I go?" he asks. "For luck?"

"Do scribes believe in luck?" I murmur. Somehow both my hands have found their way into his, and I nod helplessly as he releases one of them and raises his fingers to my cheek. I feel their gentle pull as he brushes the skin of my temple, down to my jaw, drawing me inexorably toward him. And then his mouth is on mine, and I am reduced to rain and wind and salty air as I melt against him. His hand moves to my neck as the other drifts to my hip, and though the cold rain falls on us both, I am like fire in the smith's forge. I think I would do anything keep him, to stay with him.

And then we are forced apart, something hard and sharp dragging down on my arm, my clothing—and I hear her roar breaking through the thunder of my own heart in my ears. Orail, leaping to separate us with her powerful front legs, her lips pulled back in an ivory snarl as she growls at Morgen for the crime of touching me.

I know I'm not the only one thinking of the dead wolves on the beach.

"It's all right!" I gasp. "Orail, it's all right! I wish you would stop!"

She does, abruptly, as if I have muzzled her.

"I'm sorry," I say to Morgen, still gulping for breath and trying to cool the heat raging through me. I turn my face up into the rain, letting it pour over me in icy, calming droplets. I want nothing more than to step back into Morgen's arms, to press my lips once more to his—but he is standing back now, looking wary.

"LaCree!" comes a voice from across the lawn, and I jump.

It's Bráthair Gibrat, hurrying toward us in obvious agitation. For a moment, I think he is offended by our kiss, but then he speaks again. "Clementina is sick!" he says, sounding almost indignant. "Sick, LaCree! She can't retrieve in this state!"

I frown. "Who's Clem—"

But Morgen has already started toward Gibrat. "Sick? Is there anything to be done?"

Gibrat has stopped, however, and is looking at Orail with interest.

"Who's Clementina?" I say.

"We'll have to cancel the hunt," Gibrat says to Morgen. "Unless *you* can find a dead pheasant on the moors in the dark." He sniffs, then strides back toward the monastery without so much as looking at me.

"*Who's—*"

"The monastery's retriever," Morgen groans, turning back to me with a furrowed brow. He glances at Orail, and then rubs his temples with his thumb and forefinger. "If she's ill, the hunt can't proceed. This particular hunt requires specific training, as it is different from all the others, and she's the only dog who's been conditioned to retrieve for it."

"Can't you just wait until she's better?" I say, confused.

"This event is scheduled around the alignment of the stars," says Morgen, sounding utterly defeated. "It is timed to a particular meteor shower that passes once every ten years. There's no point doing it another week."

I stare at him, wondering how I can help . . . and then understanding clunks into place. "Oh," I say, dread seeping dark and heavy into my veins.

"No!" he gasps, following the trail of my thoughts. "Áila, no, I would never ask it of you."

"When do you leave?" I now wish with all my heart I had gone straight home and never heard a word about this wretched hunt—even if it would have cost me that kiss. Orail is still standing between us, but she is now watching me with frozen intensity, as if she can't believe what I'm thinking. I can't believe it either.

"Áila, it's fine. Truly. I'm sure there are plenty of other things I can put into my book. And I'm afraid of your dog, remember?"

I squeeze my eyelids shut, hating myself. But if I loan Orail to Morgen, surely he'll never turn his back on me, whatever might happen in the next two Ordeals. And if I want any kind of future with him, he and Orail had better start learning to get along. "You know as well as I do there's not another dog in the kingdom who could do what Clementina's been trained to do, especially on such short notice," I tell him. "Anyway, I can make her leave you alone. Orail, I wish you wouldn't attack him."

For the first time, I feel something from Orail that is wordless, yet still communication. It's a whirl of panic and resistance and anger—and, above all, a bone-deep fear that makes me shiver when I feel it.

No, she says. *No, no, no. Please don't send me with him.*

I already feel sick with regret, but I can hardly recant my offer immediately after giving it. If I can't give what I have, what right have I to a place with Morgen or anyone else? And besides, it's just three days. Surely Orail and I only feel afraid because we've never been separated that long before.

I think of my spoken wish at the Wish Tree: *I wish Orail would be with me always.* I meant it then and I mean it now, but it is not the only thing I want. And if we are apart for a few days but gain a better future through it, surely that will have been worth it?

I shiver again.

"Thank you," Morgen says, running his thumb lightly down my arm. "It means a great deal to me that you trust me with her." He pours his eyes into mine again, and my breath grows shallow. I am seized by the desire to step toward him, to take his face in my hands—but before I can act, he exhales and turns away.

He squints up at the sky. "We leave at dawn. I suppose I should take her now."

I freeze, feeling Orail's panic swell.

"Now?"

He raises his eyebrows, silently asking why that would be a problem.

"Oh," I say, fumbling for words. All I can think is that I don't want to send Orail now, don't want to spend an extra night in our cliffside cottage without her. But I can also see that objecting would create unnecessary conflict between Morgen and me. And besides, what rational person can't be separated from their pet dog for a few short days? "All right," I hear myself reply, even as inside my head Orail's steady stream of *no* lands like the relentless, pattering rain.

I feel as if I might collapse, so I sink to my knees and put my arms around Orail's neck. "I wish you wouldn't bite him, or anyone else," I whisper into her speckled fur. "I wish you'd go with him, and be good and obedient, unless they ask something of you that's wrong or try to harm you or someone else. Then you may bite all you need to. I love you. I'll see you in a few days."

Orail's gold eyes are wide and terrified, a reflection of my own feelings, and in my head I hear only a few words in reply: *Please don't send me. I want to be with you.*

I feel my heart shatter into irremediable fragments as I watch Morgen lead my strange, spotted friend across the lawn toward the monastery. And when I turn to walk back up the cliffside path I have never once traveled without Orail, I feel those fragments being stomped into dust beneath my own feet, each step taking me farther and farther from her.

Chapter Forty-Four

HEW

I feel a little foolish as I hurry through the village, heading right back where I came from. The voice inside me does nothing to help.

Why do you need to leave before supper? it says, ringing with scorn and disgust. *If Orail has lived this long without evaporating into some kind of newly absolved spirit, why should she be in any immediate danger now?*

I don't have a good answer to this, and for a moment I slow, wondering if I ought to go back to Vira's. Inside the pub, I hear someone singing "Golden Light and Thistle" in a toneless, drunken slur, which reminds me of my own inability to carry a tune, and the way Colm crowed with cruel laughter the first time he heard me sing. The thought of what he might say if I reappear so soon after my late arrival and abrupt departure pushes my feet into motion again, and I soon resume my steady jog, wheezing for breath as I start to climb the cliffside path.

I have always hated running. My limbs are too long and uncoordinated to make it comfortable, and I never learned the graceful fluidity people like Áila seem to find so natural; instead, I jolt along like a stork, every stride a jarring agony to my knees. Nevertheless, I pound my focus into a single thought—*I must hurry for Orail's sake*—so that by the time I arrive at the foot of the lawn that stretches up to the monastery, I am surprised to find it smudged by drizzling twilight; I hardly noticed the rain moving in, let alone the sun setting. Lights wink from the windows and cast stripes of pale gold across the shadowy grass as I slow and gasp for air. Just beyond the reach of one of these stripes, I see something move, and stumble to a halt.

There are three figures standing in the middle of the lawn, beneath the canopy of a large oak tree. My mouth goes dry as I recognize a fourth: a dog, nose to the ground, sniffing casually. The other three must be Áila, Morgen, and Flora. And sure enough, as I squint toward them from the deeper shade of the hill, I recognize Flora's willowy, curly-haired figure as it turns and hurries toward the monastery. Light spills from the doorway, her silhouette disappears, and the light is cut off again.

My breath lodges somewhere in the back of my throat as I stand, irresolute, in the damp darkness beyond Áila and Morgen. I don't want to spy on them, but I also don't want to risk revealing my presence. I have just arrived at the conclusion I must leave quietly and wait for Áila at her cottage when Morgen's tall figure takes a step toward her silhouette and joins their two shadows by taking her hands.

I am frozen in horror, but I can neither move nor look away. Dark and distorted though their figures are, I cannot mistake the kiss Morgen leans in to press against Áila's lips, or her arms that lift to embrace him.

There is a strange ringing in my ears, and for a wild moment I don't know where or even *who* I am. I long to scrub the image of their twined figures from my eyeballs, erase it from my mind forever. I want to hurl rocks into the sea, I want to throw up the meager contents of my stomach—and I want to turn back time and never leave Vira's house again.

Envy and bone-drilling anguish rip through me.

Because, I realize with dizzying shock, *I am in love with Áila LacInis.*

I slip and stumble back down the hill, barely aware of myself, while a roaring within my head deafens me to all other sound.

I walk and I walk, and have no awareness of where my feet are taking me.

Sometime later, I find my feet have led me to the old promontory I often visit when I need to think or pray. I am missing supper in the hall right now, but the hunger growling in my stomach feels distant and inconsequential.

Oh hideous, hideous irony that Morgen should secure Áila's affections at the exact same moment I realize I want them for myself. I feel like a man who has been blundering around with his eyes shut without knowing it. How could I have missed this love growing inside me? I can't even comfort myself by thinking she's making a terrible mistake, because by all accounts she *isn't*. I have suspected Morgen to be a rule-bending political radical, but the only thing I have to recommend me over him is the fact Orail seems to like me better—and that's easily explained by the fact Morgen doesn't like dogs.

Orail. Who is almost certainly a Púcca, and might die at any moment if she achieves whatever level of goodness the gods set out as her marker for redemption. Perhaps I should have interrupted Áila's moment with Morgen to tell her what I've discovered, but I can't imagine how I could have done it. How I could have spoken a single word with the sight of her kissing Morgen searing holes through every part of my being.

How did you let this happen? says the voice inside me. *How have you been so careless with your heart?*

I sit down on the cliffside bench and stare out at the ocean, despair settling through me like a dense, numbing fog. For a long time, I just watch the waves, neither thinking nor praying, nor even feeling much beyond the numbness and the wind. When my backside begins to ache against the wood slats, I move to sit on the rock ledge at the end of the promontory and let my feet dangle toward the ocean. My brown wool robe is hiked up around my thighs, and I have scraped my hands through my hair so often it is both sticking up and plastered down over my eyes in the rain. I am not comforted by the thought that I probably look every bit as bad as I feel.

I reach for the twine around my neck, and grip both icon and medallion at once. "What am I going to do?" I ask Lir in a hoarse whisper.

Far below, the sea roars and seethes, swallowing up the rain. In the distance, I hear a grumble of thunder, and a sudden flash of lightning splits the horizon over the water, making me jump. It's a rare sight on Fuiscea—rare enough I have only seen it once or twice in eighteen years of life here. Either Atobion and Lir are at odds, or one of them is trying to get my attention.

I am on the point of repeating my question, this time directing it to Atobion, when I hear something behind me—a low voice, coming down the cliffside path that crosses just behind the promontory.

"*No*, you filthy cur. Keep up."

The voice is familiar, but also . . . not. There's something different about it, something that keeps me from immediately recognizing who it belongs to. But as another familiar voice joins it, I realize who it is, and why it has changed.

It's Morgen LaCree.

And he's not speaking in the northern Ilbhan accent he usually has; instead, he's using a rounder, more polished accent I have heard only once before, in the shipyards.

An *Aenlandish* accent.

I freeze, listening hard as the second voice—unquestionably Bráthair Gibrat—speaks again. "I brought a rope, Your Majesty," he says. "Here."

Your Majesty?

The confusion clouding my head is as dense as freshly dug peat.

"Must you be so rough?" says yet another voice I know—but it is angry and petulant, unlike the usual, lighthearted way Flora speaks.

"You saw what she did on the beach," snaps Morgen, again in that smooth Aenlandish accent. "Do you want her ripping *your* throat out? Give me the rope, Gibrat. Whatever Áila says, I won't trust the beast until her mouth is tied shut."

Beast? Tied shut?

Áila??

I scramble to my feet, wondering with frantic rapidity what Morgen is doing, why his accent has suddenly changed, and where Áila is.

Although I have a horrible, dawning suspicion about the second one.

They're saying the Usurper Prince escaped justice, and that he's loose in Ilbha and unaccounted for. And Morgen, who only arrived on Fuiscea *after* the failed overthrow concluded, has an Aenlandish accent. Morgen, whom Bráthair Gibrat just called *Your Majesty.*

I keep low as I hurry after the party, trying to stay concealed below the tall seagrass and broom. But I am not careful enough, and send a pebble skittering along the path ahead of me. I crouch and hold my breath, shivering with cold and nerves, but Morgen doesn't seem to have heard me.

Though someone else has.

Hew?

I almost yelp with shock. *Orail!* I return in my mind. *What's happening? Where is Áila? Where are they taking you?*

I scuttle along behind them, desperate to keep Orail within speaking range. Her words come fast and urgent.

Áila is safe, I think. Probably at the cottage by now. This slug tricked her into lending me to him for a hunting trip that will never happen, and I don't know where he's taking me. I can't see into his mind—or any of the others'—and I am afraid, Hew. He knows what I can do. But I'm bound by Áila's wish: unless he tries to harm me or someone else, I can't fight back.

Dread sinks through me like iron plunging into waves. Even if my suspicions about his identity are wrong, Morgen has plainly deceived us all, and should not have access to Orail's powers. And if my hunch is correct . . .

I feel faint at the very idea.

How can I help you? I ask. *Can I wish something? For you to be free?*

Áila wished me into this, she replies. *And her spoken wishes are binding until they're fulfilled. You couldn't contradict them.*

What can I do?

Protect Áila, Orail shoots back. *If anything happens to me . . . to Carrighlas. To Ilbha.*

To Ilbha.

I swallow sour bile, and continue to follow, bent double, as quickly as I can.

It is harder to pursue Morgen's party unobserved once the tall grass of the cliffs gives way to low patches of heather, and eventually to bare rock and moss. I keep as far back as possible without losing sight of them, and when they cut a path into the island's hills, I hike after them. My lower back is in agony from hunching, and I am grateful when the bog gives way to tree-scattered fields and small patches of forest, which grant me better cover and spare me bending over.

I have now realized where we are going, and the revelation brings no comfort. I feel only a kind of irrepressible panic, because I have no idea how I will save Orail when we get there.

Gusts of brine-laced wind make their way into my nostrils first, and then I begin to hear the distant shouts and calls of men. Next come the creaks and thumps of moored ships and shifted cargo, the thunder of boots on the pier, curses, laughter, and jeers—busyness, despite the hour. And then at last, as I creep over a rise, the shipyards unfold below me: a network of stone buildings, sprawling docks, and huge ships, illuminated by countless lanterns as sailors work to load and unload. I am far enough behind Morgen and the others that I can barely make them out at the edge of the crowd.

I scramble down the incline toward the shipyards, afraid of losing them. By the time I reach the cobbled streets on which a line of inns and taverns stand facing the pier, I am panting, but still have the group in sight. I duck around sailors and merchants, so consumed by my chase that I barely notice men shoving my shoulders or swearing at me to get out of the way. Morgen's dark head is all I can focus on.

Until suddenly, I don't see it anymore.

I spin in a furious circle, searching . . .

"Looking for me, monk child?"

I choke on a gasp, staggering back as Morgen looms before me, his usual kind expression replaced by a savage grin. Behind him, Gibrat looks like a carnaptious child eager to see a sibling punished, and Flora is glowering with her arms crossed. Orail thrashes at Morgen's side, snarling, trying to loosen the rope wrapped tight about her snout and neck.

"I'm not a monk," I spit at Morgen, fury boiling through my body at the sight of Orail bound up like a wild animal. "I'm a future priest. And I know who you are. You're the Usurper Prince."

He laughs. "Oh, *well done*, monk child! And have you also worked out what the dog is, or has all your research been in vain?"

I shoot a look of venom at Gibrat, who smirks. "What, no books on Púccas in our library, eh, *mallacht*?" he taunts, as if he's known all along. As if he hasn't spent the last weeks obsessively checking what books I take out, searching for the same information as me—because he wanted to give it to the Aenlandish snake he's been serving this whole time. I lunge at Gibrat, swinging my fist in a wide arc that barely grazes his ear. Morgen catches me by the collar and hurls me backward across the boardwalk planks.

I catch my balance and lurch toward them again, desperate to free Orail, even though I have no chance against Morgen's bulk.

Keep Áila safe, Orail says with palpable urgency. *Tell her I'm sorry. Tell her it's not her fault.*

"Where are you going?" I shout, more to Orail than to Morgen, grasping for some hint of an answer.

Morgen's fist comes out of nowhere, and I see a flash of something pewter-colored before everything goes dark.

Chapter Forty-Five

ORAIL

I was wrong about Morgen: he's no Slug,
Smiling or otherwise. He is a Beast,
All muscular cunning and deceit, smug
In his treachery, white teeth bared to feast.
Made of bile and dust, ashes and rust,
The putrid, wet reek of a week-dead kill,
Old dung in the sun, all baked to a crust,
The bleached glare of bones on top of a hill.
I will open his belly to sky,
I will fracture him like bracken and leaf,
I will leave him out like jerky to dry,
I'll show him my claws and give him my
     teeth.
And he won't know what doom has claimed
     him, what
Horrors await in the Halls of Bone—but—

I am empty and I am full, brimming
With fury and devoid of all defense;
Teeth stolen by Áila's last wish, skimming
The Beast for permission to attack, tense.
Hew is somewhere behind, but he is kind,
Peaceful: become the Boy who smells of *Love*.
He will not free me. I will have to find
Another means, another way out of

This mess. But suddenly we wheel about,
Stalk back the way we came, and I see why,
And my once-hard heart stutters. The Beast's
        shouts
Shock Hew as much as his fist flying high.
I have my reason now. I am released.
I lunge, then iron swings: I join the priest.

Chapter Forty-Six

ÁILA

Without Orail, I do not sleep well.

I wake often during the night, sometimes because I think I hear wolves howling in the hills, other times because I am cold without her warmth curled against my legs. Each time, I sense something is different before I remember what it is, and each time, I clutch my quilts a little tighter to fend off the fear. Even the familiar shapes and shadows in my cottage take on an ominous pall without her golden eyes and wicked smile to keep the night at bay.

I don't feel lonely so much as terribly alone.

When morning finally breaks outside the shuttered windows, I give up trying to sleep. I wrap myself in my old dressing gown, add a few peats to the hearth, then set the kettle to boil. A fresh stab of dismay pricks through me when I reach absentmindedly for the "Golden Light and Thistle" mug and find it gone. I carry my tea back to bed, curling into the blankets with my knees pulled up to my chest. I feel a little ashamed of myself—until I realize this is the first time I have ever slept without another creature nearby for comfort.

Perhaps the monks will let me join their hunt, I think with sudden hope. So long as I bring my own bedding and food—and perhaps Hew, to keep up his job as my chaperone—surely they won't send me home? After all, I did loan them my dog. And who's to say I can't prepare just as well for the fourth Ordeal on the moor as I can in my cottage?

I swing my feet out of bed. It's a thin and deluded hope, but regret is making me desperate. Whatever I feel for Morgen, I should never have loaned him Orail.

Quick as I can, I pull on my most durable dress and lace up my boots. Then I pack a blanket, a waterskin, and some food—I can always wish for anything else when Orail and I are together again—and head down the cliffs toward the monastery. I'll have to find out where they went before I can pursue them, but I doubt it will be hard to get directions. Maybe I can even catch them on the road.

It is still early, so I wander the stone halls of the monastery for a while before I find anyone to ask. The monk I meet is a tall, dark-skinned man with a kind smile, who I have seen with Hew; I think his name is Wellam. He raises his eyebrows at the sight of me.

"Can I help you, Miss LacInis?"

"Yes," I say, giving him my most winning smile. "I was hoping someone could point me in the direction of the sacred hunt? I'd like to join."

Wellam stares at me like I've just spoken a foreign language. "The sacred hunt?" Fear shoots through my body as I search his face for a trace of guile—and find nothing.

"That's what Morgen called it last night, but perhaps you know it as something else? He said it only happens once every decade, that he'd be gone with the monks for three days. He borrowed my dog for it."

The concern spreading over Wellam's face makes me a little dizzy. "I've never heard of such a hunt, Miss LacInis," he says seriously. "Are you sure that's where he was going?"

"Yes," I say, my windpipe tight as a fist. "Bráthair Gibrat said so too."

"Gibrat?" Wellam presses his lips together. "Let's see if we can find them, shall we?"

He sets off down the corridor at a rapid clip, and I have to jog to keep up with his long legs. He takes us first to Morgen's study and knocks hard on the door. When no one answers, he pushes it open and squints into the still darkness. I rush to open the curtains, but daylight offers no more help than the shadows; the room is still empty, with no clues as to where Morgen or Flora might be. Wellam checks both bedrooms—one on each side of the study—but they are vacant, and the beds are cold and neat with no sign anyone has slept in them. What's more, Morgen and Flora both seem to have taken all their things. Nausea churns through my belly; had Morgen said Flora was planning to join them? And why would they take everything they have?

"Bráthair Gibrat?" I ask Wellam, barely able to force out the words.

He nods and leads the way out of the LaCrees' rooms, striding off down the hall at an even faster pace. This time we weave halfway through the monastery before he stops at an upstairs corridor.

"You'll have to wait here," he says.

I nod, and spend the next few minutes pacing the small landing. When Wellam returns, I can see the news on his face.

"Gone," he says. "But no one else is missing, as far as I can tell. We'll need to speak with Fáthair Firnan about this at once."

I am swamped with images of Orail in trouble, in pain—even dead—as I try and comprehend what has happened. And though my mind tries to exonerate Morgen, how can I hope to believe he is innocent if someone like Wellam has never heard of a hunt that should have all the monastery buzzing? I don't realize I've stopped moving until Wellam comes back to put a hand on my arm.

"Are you all right, lass?" he says gently.

I look up into his face, and new hope flares inside of me. "Do you know where I might find Hew LacEllan?"

He nods slowly, as if he doesn't trust me to wander off on my own. "His room is in the cellar," he says. "I'll take you there after we speak with the priest, if you want."

"I—I'd like to go now, if that's all right," I say, my voice wavering.

He sighs but gives me another nod. "This way, then."

I follow him down two flights of stairs to the main level, where he points to another staircase leading down into darkness. "Take those stairs, then follow the hallway to the left. Hew's room is the last one on the right. Meet me here when you're done. I'm going to see the priest."

"Thank you," I say, and hurry to follow his directions. The cellar is dark and chilly, and indignation quickens my steps at the idea of my friend living in this kind of a place. But Hew's Unblessing probably doesn't merit a real room by Firnan's standards, and sure enough, the chamber I find at the end of the hallway is little more than a cupboard. It's furnished with only a shabby cot, a small desk, and a battered trunk. Evidence of Hew is everywhere, though: half-painted icons on the desk, a small basket of paints and brushes, a neat stack of books piled beside the cot, and a damp tartan spread out over his trunk to dry. But Hew himself is not here, and a quick touch of his bed reveals it to be just as cold as the others.

He is gone as well, but not with any premeditated intention of leaving, it would seem.

The flurrying panic inside me hardens into a gnawing dread.

I turn and run back up the stairs, into the corridor where Wellam and I parted. He has not returned, and I don't know whether I can wait for him. It is clear now that something has gone very wrong, and I am desperate to do something—*anything*—to find Orail. Without really thinking, I find myself striding toward the front doors—which suddenly groan and swing inward as someone pushes them open from outside.

My heart shoots into my mouth—could it be Morgen?—and just as quickly falls like a withered cherry pit into my stomach. It is not Morgen; it isn't even Hew. It is several grave-looking clansmen, armed with claymores and smelling strongly of horse. They both look surprised at the sight of me.

"Where's the priest, lass? We need to see him."

I don't have time to fumble for a reply before footsteps sound over the stone behind me. "Here."

"Fáthair," says one of the clansmen. He bows to the priest, who is striding up the corridor with Wellam at his heels. "The LaCail needs you. He's asked us to take you down to the shipyards. There's been some kind of stramash. They're saying it's to do with the Usurper Prince and that scribe. LaCree, wasn't it?"

I blink at the man, my whole body pulsing with sudden, frenetic energy. A disturbance. Something to do with the Usurper Prince . . . and Morgen.

Who has Orail.

For the first time in my life, I do not stop to consider my options. I stride past the two clansmen, push open the double doors, and leap down the steps. I swing myself into the saddle of the horse breathing least heavily, and turn it about with a sharp tug of its rein. Before the men can protest, I squeeze my heels into the horse's sides and it springs forward. The cool morning air rushes over my face as we canter westward across the lawn, toward the shipyards.

Toward Orail, I hope with all my heart.

I kick the horse into a gallop.

Chapter Forty-Seven

HEW

I have never had such a headache in all my life.

When I wake, I don't remember much at all, apart from my name. I have no idea where I am or what on earth has happened to me. My head swims horribly; it feels like my brain is bouncing from one side of my skull to the other, so I keep my neck perfectly still, squinting toward the narrow wooden door across the room. Apart from it, the only other things in the small space are a pile of wooden crates, several empty casks, and a broken chair. A storeroom of some kind.

"Hello?" I call. "Anyone there?"

Footsteps clump on the other side of the door, and it swings open. A thin, bespectacled man peers in at me beneath a shock of white, curly hair.

"Awake, are ye? You can be on your way, then."

I push myself gingerly to my feet. "How'd I get here?"

"Some lads," he tells me with a shrug. "Seemed to think you'd die otherwise, and paid me to let you sleep it off." He turns back to drying mugs, and I realize we're standing behind the bar of a pub. The white-haired man must be its proprietor.

"Thank you," I say, even though it's obvious the man doesn't care much for me or my thanks. I make my way to the door, trying to remember what happened—and then I catch sight of what lies just on the other side of the diamond-paned windows.

A quay.

The shipyards.

I shove the door open and step through it, last night's events pouring over me in a torrent. I sweep my eyes over the busy piers, and despair squeezes the air from my lungs. Orail is surely leagues away by now, and Áila . . .

Oh gods. I put my head in my hands and beg Lir to keep Orail safe, wherever she is. *And give me strength to tell Áila what happened*, I plead. Despite my hatred for Morgen and desire to see him exposed, I dread revealing truths that will only cause Áila pain.

The sound of hooves thudding over the docks startles me out of my prayer, and as I look around I find myself wishing Lir would take a little more time to answer my prayers. For there is Áila herself, windblown, wild-eyed, and desperate-looking as she slides off the back of a horse and stares around the quays. She has not yet spotted me in the shadow of the pub, though I am less than ten feet from her.

I say her name quietly—in part to save my own pounding skull, and in part to avoid startling her.

She startles anyway, whirling around as if I have blown a horn. "Hew!"

Tears spring into her eyes as she hurries to throw her arms around me, and though my blood leaps at her touch, I ache at the agony and confusion in her expression. She must already know something of what I have to tell her.

"I'm sorry, Áila," I say, pulling her in tight and trying my best to ignore the heat humming across my skin. "I'm so sorry."

She pulls back to search my face. "What happened? You know, don't you?"

As succinctly as possible, I tell her everything that happened—everything except the moment I saw her kissing Morgen and realized I was in love with her—from discovering the Púcca story in Gemma's book to waking up in a tavern storage cupboard. When I've finished, Áila has stepped back from me, quiet and very still, her unfocused eyes trained somewhere over my right shoulder. I give her time to process, swallowing as I watch her battle her emotions, which flicker across her face in clear waves. Every time her eyes fill with tears, something fierce and angry hardens her features to drive them away, and I begin to sense she is fighting back grief with fury.

"I have to go after them," she says finally, her voice low and tight. "Now."

For a moment, I am frozen by indecision. Following the Usurper is one of the most dangerous things we could do, and even if we did there would be no guarantee we could find him. And if we *did* find him, what then? I am half tempted to tell Áila she should go back to the village for help, assemble resources and information, and ask for permission from the LaCail and Fáthair Firnan before taking action.

But Morgen has already been gone half the night at least. Even if the clan leaders let her go, it would be days before she could leave. And with Orail in the hands of the Usurper, the gods only know what might happen in that time.

"I'll go with you." I meet her eyes with the most determined look I can muster. "I'll help you, Áila."

She shakes her head. "No. It might be dangerous."

"All the more reason you shouldn't go alone." I swallow, screwing up my nerve. "If you want to stop me, you'll have to resort to Morgen's methods—because as long as I'm conscious, I will follow you."

Her sea glass eyes search mine, pupils darting back and forth in frantic thought. "I don't want to risk your life," she whispers. I can see the fear in her eyes—fear for *me*—and it makes me want to pull her against me and never let go. It makes me want to run and never stop, to climb a mountain or scale a wall or fight a warrior . . .

I have never wanted to do any of those things before.

Love is very strange.

"You're not risking my life," I say, stepping closer to her. "*I* am. And I won't stand by and watch you do this alone."

She nods slowly and grasps both of my hands. I can't tell which of us is trembling. "Thank you, Hew." She takes a deep breath. "The LaCail and Firnan will be here soon, and we need to go before they arrive."

My pulse trips over itself, but I know she's right. I look around, wondering where to start—just as someone calls, "Áila LacInis?"

There is a sailor jogging up the docks toward us. Áila tenses, ready to run. "Who's asking?" she says.

The man gives her a sympathetic smile. "Your brother, lass. This way, if you don't mind."

Chapter Forty-Eight

ÁILA

My stomach drops. I have never been reluctant to see Matan before, but right now a brother's protective interference is the last thing I need. I strain my eyes in the direction the sailor is pointing, where a ship is being loaded with barrels—and freeze.

Barrels of *whisky*. For which Matan will have just been paid. An idea crystalizes in my mind, and I hope Mat loves me enough to forgive me for it.

Before Hew can stop me, I am running, pounding up the docks beneath a bleary yellow sun.

Matan is a few yards away from the whisky ship, his expression wild. "Áila!" He catches me against him as I throw myself into his chest.

"LaCree," he pants. "Áila, Morgen LaCree has your dog. I tried to stop him, but he was too quick. His ship was ready when he got to it. I'm so sorry. I don't know why he would take her."

"Where did he go, Mat?" I ask urgently, pulling back. Hew jogs up beside us, panting, and Matan's eyes widen.

"*You're* the reason I couldn't catch him before he left," he says to Hew. "What did you do to make him try and bash your head in? My men and I lost time begging a safe place to leave you."

"It was you?" Hew says in disbelief. "Thank you—I think you saved my life!"

"I definitely did," says Matan. "That rank scunner was ready to toss you off the dock, and you'd have drowned for sure."

Hew pales, and I tense beneath fresh waves of fury. Morgen's duplicity—his manipulation and betrayal as he wheedled Orail from me with a kiss, his cold-blooded attempt to kill Hew—churns through me until I think I might be sick. But Orail's absence wraps my chest in an iron cuff that tightens until I can hardly breathe.

Like a drowning person flailing for driftwood, I think, *Orail, I wish for a map that shows us where you've gone.* But nothing happens and nothing comes. I step away from Matan to look out across the azure waves. "Orail, I wish you would show me where you've gone," I whisper, hot tears gathering in my eyes. But nothing changes.

She is gone.

Not just borrowed. Stolen.

Not just somewhere on Fuiscea. Across the sea. Beyond the reach of my thoughts and my voice.

I feel dizzy, disoriented, numb. The world is vast, and what if we can't find her? What will I do without her, this creature who has become a part of me? Who has threaded her way into my soul and held me together with her outrageous, unyielding love? I feel like I've lost a limb, some vital part of me I don't know how to live without.

And yet—I know I cannot blame anyone but myself. I am the knife that severed the limb I now grieve. I am the one who told Orail to go with Morgen, despite her resistance.

I sway where I stand, my breath coming in shallow gasps—until a gentle hand against my shoulder brings me back into my body and lends me some of its steady strength.

Hew.

"Where did they go?" he says to Matan.

"To the mainland, most likely," Mat replies, sounding nonplussed. "Most ships here do. But surely you're not thinking of following them."

Though it was my idea, I waver. If I leave Carrighlas now, I forfeit the Ordeals. I condemn myself to the very life I have feared.

But if I don't go, I lose Orail. And possibly leave Ilbha at the mercy of a Usurper Prince with wish-granting magic.

And lose Orail.

My nerves ossify.

I look at Hew and find his stormy eyes hard and resolute. I can't risk Matan guessing what I'm about to do, but I hope Hew can read my expression well enough to stick close.

"Of course not," I say with a hopeless shrug. "How would we ever find them?"

A few yards away, I hear the captain of Matan's whisky ship shouting orders, and the vessel groans as anchors are winched up from the seabed. Sailors draw in the gangway, and I have to clench my fists to keep from running over and begging them to wait. I need them to get underway.

"I'm so sorry, Áila," says Matan again, and his eyes are full of sympathy as he watches me. "I know you loved that dog. She was special."

"Yes," I agree fervently. The whisky ship has raised its mainsails. The hull groans, the water churns, and the ship surges forward.

"I'm sorry too, Mat," I say. Then, "Hew—*now!*" And without a glance back, I hurl myself down the dock after the ship.

"Áila!" my brother cries, but I am already level with the stern and eyeing a bit of rigging that looks within reach. I hope Hew is a better jumper than he is a runner.

I push myself harder—the dock has nearly run out—and leap off the end of the quay.

The side of the ship crashes against my body from shoulders to hips, but I grasp at the sail lines with fingers that are practiced at clinging to ropes as they swing and jerk. A second heavy thump tells me Hew has hit his mark as well, but I can't turn to look at him. I can only focus on pulling myself up.

My muscles protest as I climb, and my feet scrabble for purchase against the wet hull. Compared with the first Ordeal, though, this is nothing at all, and I want to laugh aloud at the thrill of it. I heave myself over the bulwark and tumble onto the deck. A few seconds later, Hew follows, gasping.

I am briefly surprised by his arm strength—he's leaner than a beanstalk—before I remember: he's been cutting peat since he was thirteen.

We collapse against each other, gasping and laughing. But then a sound above us makes me stop, and I bite off my laughter as I lift my head.

The captain stands over us, glowering, hands on his hips.

"Hello," I say with a tentative smile. "We'd like to buy passage to the mainland, if you don't mind."

And, reaching into the pocket of my dress, I draw out a handful of silver coins from Matan's leather purse, which I slipped off his belt when I hugged him.

The man narrows his eyes, then gives a single, curt nod. "Stay out of the way," he says, "or I'll pitch you both overboard. We're due at the Glaisgoah quays three hours after midday."

I feel as though the waves pushing us from the shores of Fuiscea are unmooring me, setting me loose. For the first time in my life, I am leaving this small, blustery island, setting off into waters that speed these familiar coastlines out of both sight and reach. My pulse claps a steady beat in my throat as I get to my feet.

I'm coming, Orail, I think. *Wherever you are, I'm coming.*

Part Three

SONG

Chapter Forty-Nine

ORAIL

There is a merciless irony to
It all, to the fact that I am captive
Now to a man who would strike the land through
    through
With a chaos both cruel and extractive—
The very way I once felt born to live—
And yet suddenly all I want, the one
Thing I long for, the one life I would give
Anything to have is the one who shuns
Pandemonium, the one that makes me
Exactly what I swore I would never
Become: tame, docile, a loving, trusty
Companion; fruit of Yslet's endeavor.
I swore Yslet would not change me, never
Own me. And she won't: I'm Áila's forever.

But Áila is far away, across the
Sea. And I am here with Morgen. The Beast.
The Usurper Prince. He hounds, bombards me
With wishes, and I grant him swords, release
Imprisoned insurrectionists, summon
Feasts, intercept correspondence, equip
Him, in short, for everything a common
Interloper might do now to outstrip
A kingdom that thinks it's invincible.

There are wishes I cannot grant, of course,
And the Beast renders me insensible
With each refusal, strikes without remorse.
I ache and I bleed, muzzled by each rule
That limits my power. For I am a tool.

At night, I lie on the stone cellar floor
Of an ancient manor house whose master
Has fallen beneath the Beast's sway, each door
Around me bolted and guarded. After
The sounds of the house have fallen silent,
I limp to the high sliver of window
Cut into the wall and stare, defiant,
At the dark sky. While the black clouds
        billow,
I wish until my heart is sore, I howl
Until my throat is hoarse, I even pray
Until my soul is scarred. The aching growl
I hear in reply cements my doomsday,
Because it's my own. There is no other
Answer. My ship has been robbed of its
        rudder.

The Beast wishes for fine clothing one day,
And piles of game, casks of wine, platters
Of cheese and fruit and bread. I hear him say
Spare nothing (meaning me), nothing matters
Except success of this gala he's sure
Will place the kingdom at his feet—if he
Can play his cards right. So I'll be the cur
To make him lay them wrong, to guarantee
The kingdom stays as distant from his feet
As Áila is from me. Caged by wishes

In daylight and walls by night, I'm concrete
In my surety there are no bridges
That can reunite us. I draw the knife
Of knowledge: to end him will cost me
     my life.

Chapter Fifty

HEW

During our first two days on the mainland, Áila and I enact the plan we hatched during the passage to Glaisgoah: we speak to a dozen ordinary people who might be easy to overlook—dockworkers, coachmen, fishmongers, and street vendors—and more than half reward us with useful information. Some of them remember a man of Morgen's description; others a brown, merle dog with black spots; and still others have already heard rumors of the Usurper's second rising. When we pass through the blackened bones of a village recently burned, the lone person left in it tells us it was the Usurper's doing six months ago, and that he's at it again, rallying his allies across the kingdom. Over the next few days, we follow this string of information across the lowlands of Ilbha to the capital city of Ellisburgh.

Where our trail runs cold.

"What do you think?" Áila asks as we stand beneath a butcher's awning, waiting for the pouring rain to ease. Between the streets and the buildings, I have never seen so much stone in my life, and I am already homesick for the sound of the ocean, the sight of a green-and-purple moor beneath a navy sky.

I sigh. "We'd better find someplace to stay the night, I think. Then ask around again tomorrow."

She nods, chewing her lip. I can tell the size of the city combined with our lack of success here has made her worry Orail may be impossible to find. *It would help if she had a companion with any real skills*, sneers the voice in my head.

Determined to be useful, I point across the way at a shabby-looking inn. "Shall we try there?"

Áila nods, and though the rain is almost a solid sheet in front of us, she ducks out from under the awning and crosses the street at a brisk walk. I follow, blinking rivulets of water from my eyes as she pushes open the door.

"Two rooms, please, if you have them," she tells the old barkeep, shaking her wet hair back. "And two suppers." She rummages in Matan's purse and slides a few coins toward the man.

"Aye," he grunts, reaching under the bar for a pair of keys. "Right up the stairs—the selkie room and the stag room. Fargus'll bring up yer food."

Once we reach the creaky second-story hallway, Áila hands me the key etched with the word *selkie*, and gives me a half-hearted smile. "See you tomorrow," she says.

I nod, reluctant to be parted from her, and watch her trudge down the hall. It would be scandalous to sleep in the same room, but as I turn to the door with a seal silhouette inexpertly painted on the wood, I can't help wishing we could stay together.

Forever and ever? mocks the voice inside me.

I sigh again and slouch into my dingy bedroom, where a dingy bed sags like a spurned lover in the middle of the room, waiting to receive me.

The next morning, I am dismayed to find that no dazzling plans have formed in my brain overnight—and the inn is driving me to distraction. The bed leans to one side, the window looks as if it's never been cleaned, the rug seems to have been chewed on, and last night's meal was so burnt I can still taste charcoal on my tongue. I am almost twitching to fix what I can; surely I could at least wedge up the bedpost on one side if I shoved something under it?

But Áila rescues me from myself. "Let's go," she says when I open the door at her brisk knock. "I don't want to get fleas."

We find a bakery we can smell a block away and start off into the crisp, new morning with bannocks in hand, the cheery light of day making the world look more hopeful.

"Same as before?" I say.

She nods, polishing off her bannock. "Someone's bound to have seen them . . . *somewhere*."

But not, it turns out, in the carriage house, the milliner's shop, the apothecary, or the pub on the royal mile. Not in the weaver's, either, or the chapel we pass around midday. Every street merchant, hansom driver, and flower lady we stop on the street is either too busy or unable to help us.

When dusk settles over the sky, I see defeat creeping back into Áila's face. I feel possessed by the need to do something about it, to fix what has gone so badly wrong.

"Look, we haven't asked in there yet," I say on a desperate whim, pointing to the pub several doors down from where we stand. "No stone unturned, and all that?"

Her eyes widen. "Hew . . ."

"So it's a little nicer? I bet Morgen has loads of wealthy followers. Maybe the barkeep has heard something?"

She raises an eyebrow.

"Or," I say, shrugging, "we get a really good meal as consolation for the last few days of rotten luck."

Help us, Lir, I think. *This is the best I can do.*

Áila's gloomy expression lifts into a reluctant smile. "All right, then. I'm convinced. And also . . . *really* hungry."

Laughter trips out of my mouth. I may not have found a solution to our problem, but I *have* made Áila smile, and that feels like a mighty deed. I hold out an arm for her to take—as if we are elegant patrons—and lead her inside, where we are shown to a booth with green velvet curtains drawn back.

"In case you should desire privacy," explains the proprietor with a bow.

I flush a little at the thought.

Despite my original idea of asking the barkeep for information, Áila and I sit in weary contentment for a while, first sipping pints of a thick, dark ale, and then savoring fragrant leek and chicken stew. In the next booth over, we can hear another couple growing steadily drunker, and Áila keeps biting down on her knuckles to keep from laughing.

But then a word drifts over the wooden back our booth shares with theirs, and we both freeze.

"Usurper . . ."

Áila's eyes narrow in concentration, and I press my ear against the wood, but we needn't bother. The couple are now so drunk that their next words are perfectly audible to us both— and probably half the pub.

"Can you imagine what it will be like to live on Aenlandish lands?" the woman's voice exclaims. "To get away from all this . . . *squalor*?"

"Aye, he'll be our deliverance," her companion replies eagerly. "Herry'll be like no king we've ever had before."

Herry. Morgen's real name.

I swivel back toward Áila, ready to exchange a look of amazement, but she is sliding out of our booth, already halfway to standing. Hot panic floods my limbs, but she moves quickly, and before I can find my feet she's standing in front of the couple's booth with her fists on her hips.

With a glare that could curdle cream, she hisses, "Hush, now! Do you want the entire city to hear you? You're putting the whole glorious cause at stake with your loud-mouthed blether!"

Chapter Fifty-One

ÁILA

The strangers—a man and a woman just a little older than Hew and me—look up from their booth in obvious shock. In their intoxicated state, they seem to have forgotten anyone else exists around them at all.

"Please join us, if you'd like, but do keep your voices down," I say, waving them toward our booth with my best effort at gracious forgiveness.

I turn to find Hew staring at me with his mouth hanging open. I widen my eyes at him, hoping he'll get a clue and shut it, before shooing him back into our booth. When the couple has followed, sliding onto the bench I just vacated, I unhook the ties on our curtains and slip in after Hew. The heavy green velvet swishes together and encloses us all in warm, shadowy darkness, lit only by the solitary taper on our table.

To my satisfaction, I see the couple has brought their drinks and is continuing to sip them as they watch us with nervous interest.

"I'm Anna LacTalish," I invent quickly, inclining my head to the pair. "And this is my husband, Hamish."

Hew chokes on his ale, and I squeeze his knee under the table, silently urging him to pull himself together.

"Ipona," says the woman in much too loud a voice. She flinches at the sound in our enclosed booth and tries again: "I'm sorry. I'm Ipona, and this is my husband." She is small, with feathery blond hair and an upturned nose, which is currently as red as her rouged cheeks.

"Rupart Cairsmuir," says the man—a square block of a person, with vivid red hair and beard—extending a hand for us to shake. Before we can work out which of us he means to take it first, he retracts it to cover a sudden belch.

"Well," I say, offering them both a warm smile. "It's lovely to meet some fellow, er, *believers* at last." I pause, worried my word choice will set off some kind of alarm bell in their heads, but they are glazed with alcohol and beaming as if I am Morgen himself. I continue. "Hamish and I came up from the Lowlands, to see if there might be any way we could help the Us—er, *Prince* Herry. If we could but see Ilbha ruled like Aenland, we might feel we can bring a child into this world in good conscience."

Beside me, Hew chokes again.

"Oh!" cries Ipona, evidently moved by my story. "I feel just the same! Naturally, I'd love to raise a child in Aenland itself, but not all of Herry's followers will be lucky enough to merit titles there. Only the most loyal." She lapses into thoughtful—or possibly just drunken—silence and lays her head against her husband's shoulder. He jumps, as if he's forgotten she was beside him, and looks down the front of her bodice with interest.

Suddenly afraid they might forget Hew and I are here, I rush on. "We've only been in town a day, but we would love to be connected to whatever work the prince is doing here in Ellisburgh." I try to think of something else that might prompt them to talk, but feel myself losing steam.

"Yes, we want to help in any way possible," Hew cuts in, his presence of mind returning not a moment too soon. "But we haven't had any news since we left home. Can you tell us anything?"

Either Hew has managed to convince them, or the Cairsmuirs are too drunk to be suspicious of our clumsy bid for information. Ipona lifts her head once more and eagerly bobs it up and down.

"Oh yes! We're from Glaisgoah, but we've been here two weeks already, and were part of the reception party that welcomed Prince Herry back from his exile. We'd had advance word, since he'd been planning it for so long, but it was still such a relief to see him in the flesh!"

Rupart giggles under his breath. "Flesh."

Ipona shoots him a bleary look, then turns back to me. "Forgive him," she says, her voice still slightly too loud. "He's had too much."

"You were saying?"

"Oh yes! So we welcomed him back, and there are quite a lot of us, but we're from those Ilbhan families who have *much*"—she smirks and gives a puff of a laugh—"to offer him. I assume that's true of you as well?"

"Of course," I say, hoping she hasn't noticed our shabby, five-day-worn clothes.

"Aye, so he's been preparing as before, gathering allies, gold, supplies—but it's happened so easily it's almost like magic!" She gives another breathy little laugh, and I laugh too—though it takes an effort.

"Goodness, but you must join us!" she says, reaching her hands toward me across the table. "We're constantly in talks with his supporters and doing all we can to help."

"We'd never want to intrude," I say, laying my hands over hers on the tabletop.

Now it's Hew's turn to grip my knee.

But Ipona shakes her head. "You're not intruding at all. Where are you staying? We're in the King Chares, two streets over."

I gasp with all the shock and delight I can muster. "The King Chares? Us too!"

"Well then, tea tomorrow? We'll call on your rooms, shall we?" Ipona turns to give her husband a glowing smile. He returns it with interest, then slides a broad paw around her waist.

"We should go. Good evening," Hew says, and I hope the Cairsmuirs don't hear the panic in his voice. Though even I am not sure whether it's over the lie I just told, or the apparent likelihood of Rupart Cairsmuir ravishing his wife right here.

Ipona tries for an embarrassed smile, but winds up giggling instead, wrapping her arms around Rupart's neck.

"The barkeep can deal with them," I whisper to Hew, torn between amusement and mortification as we hurry through the pub and into the street. "We have an inn to find."

Hew doesn't say much on the way to the King Chares, and I find myself worrying he might be offended or even angry over my claim that we are married. As we climb the steep street toward the inn, I glance sidelong at him. He's biting his lip, watching his feet.

"Sorry about all that," I say. "I shouldn't have lied without asking you first."

He turns suddenly, as if I've startled him. "Which lie?"

"Oh." I laugh, feeling silly. "The, erm, husband one."

A deep red flush creeps up his neck and over his cheeks. I feel my own face growing warm too.

"It's fine," he says, slightly hoarse. He clears his throat. "Honestly. It was a good idea."

We're both still blushing when we approach the innkeeper in the King Chares's opulent lobby. The man bows to us, though he looks dubiously at our clothes, which I make a mental note to replace first thing tomorrow. Matan's purse is still fat enough to cover our costs, and I silently vow to thank him with a tenfold repayment once we have Orail again. Trying to sound flippant and assured, I ask for a pair of rooms under the names Hamish and Anna LacTalish.

"A pair?" the innkeeper repeats, looking confused.

Hew's skin has achieved a shade similar to a fresh beetroot, and I stammer incoherently for a moment as I realize what I have done. If the Cairsmuirs are to call on us here, they will need to find us in the same place.

"One suite, please," I correct myself, hoping I am less red than Hew. And that a suite contains more than one room.

The innkeeper leads us through the lobby and up a wide staircase, down a hall at least a dozen times nicer than the one we found ourselves in last night, and to a polished wooden door with a brass knob and knocker. He ushers us into a well-furnished parlor, and we stand for a moment in stunned silence as he walks around lighting the lamps. He opens a second door and disappears into the bedroom—and I give a tiny sigh of relief.

"A maid will be in shortly to see to your fire," he says. "Will you require supper?"

"No," I manage to say, and then he is gone, leaving Hew and me to struggle through our embarrassment alone. It would be less uncomfortable, I think, if we had not just witnessed Rupart and Ipona Cairsmuir on the point of copulating in the booth at the pub.

"I'll sleep out here," Hew says in a much higher voice than usual. He once more clears his throat, and nods to the settee in front of the hearth. "I'll be quite comfortable."

It's far too short for his long legs, but I don't argue. I suddenly feel that if I stay in this room with him any longer, I might be in danger of becoming reluctant to leave.

"Aye," I say quickly. "Aye, that's good. I'll just—goodnight."

And I hurry into the bedroom and shut the door behind me.

The morning proves to be one of those blessed occasions on which everything is improved by a night of sleep. Hew and I arrive at an unspoken agreement not to mention the awkwardness of last night, and we spend an hour over breakfast talking through our stroke of luck with the same ease of friendship we've always enjoyed.

Then we hurry out into the city to replace our old Fuiscean clothing with some secondhand finery. The Cairsmuirs are unlikely to be drunk every time we see them, and they must continue to believe that we, too, are wealthy landowners.

"You look bonny, husband," I say with a teasing wink as Hew and I make our way back to the King Chares. He's wearing what the men in Ellisburgh seem to prefer: breeches with tall boots, a linen shirt, and a thick, worsted vest, topped with a jacket to keep off the rain. My dress is updated to the latest fashion in daily wear, which really just seems to mean more fabric. I'm drowning in herringbone.

Hew doesn't blush this time. He takes my joke in stride and returns it. "Aye, well, not half as bonny as my new bride. How many sheep do you think gave up their winter warmth so you could walk around in a tent made of wool?"

"At least a dozen," I say seriously, and he laughs.

But I am soon grateful for the fabric, because Ipona arrives at our suite in a dress even more voluminous.

"Sit down, sit down!" she tells us, waving her husband, a maid with a tea tray, and a butler bearing tartlets all inside as if this is her suite and we are her guests. She and Rupart are quite different sober—both sharp-eyed and haughty—and when they smile at us, I am doubly grateful for their inebriation last night.

Ipona waves away the maid and the butler, snaps the door shut behind them, and turns to us with an almost giddy look on her face.

"Time is short," she says, rubbing her hands together. "We have much to discuss. Prince Herry is hosting a gala!"

Chapter Fifty-Two

HEW

Ipona shrieks with delight and runs forward to grasp Áila's hands, and for a moment all I can think is how grateful I am last night's enthusiasm to join forces with us has not been diminished by sleep or sobriety.

"The gala is tonight!" she cries, whirling Áila around the parlor while her husband watches with a bemused smile. "We've been invited—and we want to take you as our guests!"

"Tonight?" I repeat, trying to sound thrilled rather than horrified. This is the opportunity we've been hoping for, but it leaves us almost no time for planning. And if we want to attend an event with Morgen present, we will certainly need a plan.

"It's a banquet," says Rupart, grinning at me. "To raise support for his war. Sit down, won't you? These tartlets are my favorite."

I lower myself into a seat, afraid my limited knowledge of this insurrection will prove suspicious, but it soon becomes clear the topics of apparent import are not what I would have expected.

For Ipona and Áila, it would seem, the subject of formal dress is most pressing. And for Rupart and myself, it is less discussion than a lecture of brain-boring dullness on the financial contributions of each Ilbhan house committed to backing Morgen's war. I listen to him drone for a solid hour, his focus shifting from numbers to worries he and his family have not given enough to be invited into the Usurper Prince's inner circle. Whenever I let my attention drift from this monologue, I hear Ipona quizzing

Áila on fabric selection, the style of her train, and the manner in which she might do her hair.

A quiet storm of panic starts to build in my chest after the first hour bleeds into a second, and I dart occasional glances at Áila; we *must* begin our own planning. Several times, she meets my eyes, but seems no more aware of how to shake off our guests than I am. And Ipona and Rupart are relentless: after dress and finances, the Cairsmuirs turn the conversation to court gossip.

If they don't leave soon, I might fragment into shards of anxiety on the floor.

"Gods!" I declare after another half hour, feigning a shocked look at the carriage clock on the mantlepiece. "Is it already so late? Anna, we must get to the tailor and see about your gown!"

To my relief, the Cairsmuirs gasp in horror at the time, Ipona actually going so far as to leap up and clutch at her bodice. "Rupart! My red gown will need new seed pearls!"

In a whirl of apologies, frettings, and excited promises to call on us at five o'clock sharp with their carriage, they are gone, and Áila and I are left staring at each other across the platter of demolished tartlets.

"We'll have to get more clothes," she says in a tense voice. "Matan's money will be gone before the week is out, at this rate."

"Matan's money?" I repeat, feeling slightly hysterical. "Matan's money is the least of our problems. We'll be dead before tomorrow unless we think of a way to get through this gala without being murdered—and that's not even including finding a way to free Orail. Áila, I don't think we should go unless we can come up with a plan."

A small furrow appears between her dark brows, and she moves away from me, starting to tidy up the parlor. For some reason, this makes me feel angry as well as panicky.

"Did you hear me?" I say, my voice loud in my own ears. "We have to think of *something*. Our plan must be perfect!"

"I heard you," she says sharply, looking up at me with her eyes narrowed. "But I don't have an idea right now, and this is the best chance we have to find Orail. So I'm not going to waste the day fretting over what might go wrong when there's still so much we need to do just to *get* there."

I goggle at her, incredulous. "Fretting?" I repeat. "Áila, the things that might go wrong are all things that could end with us *dead*. I don't think it's a waste of a day trying to work out how to prevent that!"

But there is a stubborn set to Áila's jaw that I have seen before—when she was standing waist-deep in the ocean with her arms held straight during her first Ordeal. "Then put your formidable powers of problem-solving to the task. I'm going to find us something to wear that won't get us *un*invited before we even have a chance to save Orail. Arriving there is my first priority, Hew. Unless something has gone badly wrong, there is a wish-granting dog waiting for us at this gala. That's enough for me."

Áila scoops up Matan's leather purse and stalks out of the suite, leaving me alone with my panic, my self-doubt, and my overwhelming urge to think of a foolproof strategy to get us through tonight.

I spend the afternoon splayed on the settee, thinking through all I know of Orail's magic and all I can guess about Morgen's gala. I recall the rules of the dog's wish-granting, as Áila has explained them:

She cannot move living things, only objects.

She cannot create, but she *can* alter what already is.

She cannot kill by magic.

Áila's spoken wishes are her highest order to fulfill, but she is still bound to grant any spoken wish given by someone else if it does not conflict with Áila's wishes.

So perhaps Áila could wish her to immobilize Morgen? Or wish that Orail would only answer Áila's wishes?

But even if we cut off Morgen's ability to wish or retaliate, we still can't eliminate his guards, or the fact we'll be surrounded by his followers. So our best way forward is likely through stealth, which means we must try to go unnoticed. I seem to recall Rupart saying the prince never appears at these gatherings until dinner, so as to prevent any would-be assassins from stabbing him in a crowd. Surely we could find a place to hide until we locate Orail and wish her out.

But what if Morgen has Orail with him?

And how can I ensure Áila stays safe if we waltz right into the lion's den and try to steal his most-prized—albeit stolen—possession? Cold dread seeps through me every time I imagine something happening to her.

My stomach is growling and I feel like I'm being pummeled by despair when at last I sit up and look at the clock again.

It is four in the afternoon.

The Cairsmuirs' carriage will arrive in one hour.

The door to our suite flies open and Áila strides in, hair damp and windblown, and carrying a stack of parcels. "Here," she says, shoving a few of them at me as she hurries by my settee toward her room. "Get dressed. We're out of time."

I have never before had occasion to fidget in fine clothing, but now I understand why people do: fine clothing is excessively uncomfortable. I try not to grimace as I shrug into my second-hand wool dining jacket and stand before a tall oval mirror in the corner of our suite, mind still turning over my unformed plan.

But the person looking back at me startles me out of my abstraction.

Because he is not a boy. He is not Unblessed. He's not even awkward—though he *is* brooding.

He is a tall, well-dressed young man whose only evident flaw is the shock of auburn hair curling stubbornly across his right eye. Even his liberal smattering of freckles has been transformed into something rakish by the look of intensity he wears. I give him a small nod, and am pleased to see that, for all my worry, he somehow looks confident.

It must be the clothes.

Behind me, Áila's door creaks open, and I turn. The grass-green brocade gown draws out the color of her eyes so that they seem to glow.

Though her dress is also secondhand, she looks every inch a queen. Her dark, wavy hair is pulled loosely back from her face with a white, satin ribbon, a length of which she has also used to restring the icon of Ona I painted. It now hangs just above the hollow of her throat, and I feel a spark of gratification that she has chosen to wear it. Morgen will recognize it, but that's the least of what he will recognize if he catches sight of our faces.

She smiles at me, our earlier disagreement either put aside or forgotten. "You look very nice," she says, and I struggle to push down the voice snidely observing that the young man I so recently admired in the mirror isn't even fit to be her footman.

"As do you," I say with a croak. "Beautiful."

She steps toward me, looking down at her dress and smoothing some of its thick folds. "Fine clothes won't disguise who we are, though," she says quietly, and when she raises her face to mine again, she looks a little rueful. "I'm sorry about earlier. Did you think of anything?"

I swallow, resisting the urge to step closer to her. "The best I have is based on something Rupart said."

She raises an inquisitive brow.

"He said Herry—Morgen, I mean—wouldn't make an appearance until supper. He said the prince keeps out of crowds to avoid traitors, and only sits at the table after all his guests are seated."

"So what does that mean for us?"

"It means we can probably go unobserved until we're inside. Then we can find a place to hide and locate Orail by speaking to her thoughts. Assuming he has her there."

"And if not," she says, "we'll slip away as fast as we can."

I nod. Terror leaps on me again as I imagine all the things that could go wrong, and I feel almost smothered by the impulse to find something better. To bring our safety under my control.

"It's time, Hew."

As we leave our rooms behind and start down the hall, I can hear Ipona's and Rupart's voices drifting up the stairway from the front parlor. I hurry forward, but a light touch on my arm stops me just before the stairs. Áila beckons me back into the shadows of the hall, and I follow, my mind still sifting through plans and ideas.

"Whatever happens," she whispers, leaning close to me, and suddenly I can't remember what I was trying to think about, or why. Áila—her nearness—consumes my thoughts. We've been in Ellisburgh for days, but somehow she still smells of home: salted wind and lavender. "And I mean *whatever* happens, Hew, thank you. For all you've done to help me. And I don't just mean here in Ellisburgh."

I look into her face, and it feels like I'm falling headlong into the ocean from the cliffs beside her stone cottage. "It's been my honor," I say hoarsely.

She is locked to my eyes, searching them, and I feel her fingers tighten on my arm. For a moment we are drowning together, tethered by clutching hand and woven gaze, and I wonder if she is as breathless as me; if she, too, is in danger of either toppling down the stairs or floating up to the rafters.

I break the tether, tear my eyes away—because if I still have a life when all this is over, I'd like to have a heart as well. I reach for the banister, but again, Áila forestalls me.

"Together," she insists, threading her arm through mine. "After all, we *are* married."

I rasp out a laugh, thinking that perhaps my heart is already lost, and lead my lady down the steps, toward the carriage, toward our hope, toward our doom.

Chapter Fifty-Three

ÁILA

I feel discombobulated as I move down the steps arm-in-arm with Hew. I'm sure the reasons are simple: At last, we have arrived at the culmination of all our efforts since we left home, and are heading both toward danger and toward Orail. Anyone would feel off-balance under such circumstances.

But why does the feeling get worse when I look at Hew? Hew and his kind eyes, his earnest heart . . . his new clothes.

He hands me into the carriage after Ipona, talking easily with Rupart. I try to follow Ipona's lighthearted chatter as the men climb in and the carriage rolls forward, but I'm distracted. I feel every bump, every jolt of the road beneath the coach's tires, and I hardly register a word Ipona says. After a few minutes, she feigns crossness.

"For shame, Anna, you are worlds away. Won't you tell me where you've gone so I can bring you back?"

"Oh," I say with a shaky laugh. "Sorry." It doesn't help that being in Ipona's confidence reminds me of my erstwhile friendship with Flora, which makes me ache with confusion and hurt. Will she be at the gala today? "I suppose . . . I must be nervous about meeting Prince Herry. I'll be so disappointed if he doesn't want our help."

Not a complete lie. But guilt bludgeons me, because am I not doing the same thing to Ipona that Flora did to me? Surely no cause, however good, can justify earning and betraying honest trust.

The same kind of trust I betrayed when I handed Orail over to Morgen.

Ipona smiles sympathetically and reaches for my hand. Hers are encased in white gloves—a trend she assures me is *rampant* in Aenland—and I can't help thinking how plain and dated my dress looks compared with hers. She has kindly refrained from mentioning anything of the sort, but I saw the way her eyes traveled over me when Hew and I arrived in the parlor at the inn. I almost wish for criticism; it might ease my guilt over the way we are using her and her husband.

"What a charming necklace," she says, obviously trying to put me at ease. "Is it an icon?"

My hand goes to my throat, fingering the tiny, square pendant I have worn smooth with my relentless fiddling over the last few weeks. I force a smile. "It was a gift from H-Hamish. He gave it to me when we met. He's very devoted to the gods."

Across the carriage, Hew smiles, his ocean-gray eyes kindling with warmth. He moves his foot beneath the petticoats of my dress and presses his ankle gently against mine: a reminder I am not alone. I take a deep breath, feeling steadier.

Ipona resumes her recital of Aenlandish nobility gossip, and it seems mere moments later we are slowing, wheels crunching over small stones as a stately country house appears through the window in the evening light. By all appearances, it is a dinner party for Ilbhan aristocrats: they climb from their carriages as each coach pulls level with the walkway, chatting and laughing and milling about on the steps. Our coach creeps forward, waiting for our turn, and I peer up toward the house.

My blood freezes as if winter has swept into my veins.

Morgen is there. Standing beside the open front door.

Orail is at his side.

It's as though someone has punched me, knocking all the air from my lungs. Hew follows my gaze, going very still as he sees what has distracted me. My mind races, trying to account for the fact Morgen is out in the open, greeting his guests, but all I can think is that our slim shred of a plan has just blown away like a seed puff in a high wind. There will be no hiding from him if we have to grasp his hand and look him in the eye before we cross the threshold.

I should have listened to Hew when he said we needed a foolproof plan.

Beneath the cover of my skirts I press my foot on top of Hew's, hoping he understands what I want to communicate: *Don't try anything!* Then I draw a deep breath through my nostrils, close my eyes, and think, *Orail.*

There is a horrible pause, an eternal moment of silence. And then I hear her familiar, gravelly—precious—voice crash through my head as though borne on the back of a rock fall. *Áila? Áila! What are you doing here? How did you get here? Are you mad? Where are you? How can I help you?*

I bite down on the inside of my cheek to keep from sobbing aloud. All I want is to leap out of the carriage and run to her, wrap my arms around her spotted neck until I'm sure she is unharmed. And then I want to kill Morgen for stealing her from me. But I can do neither of those things without him noticing; at this distance, all I can do is make an unobtrusive wish.

Orail, there's no time, but we're here to get you out—Hew and me. We have to keep Morgen from seeing us until we can work out how. So I need you to do something for me. When we step out of the carriage, I wish for you to do something to Hew and me to make us unrecognizable. Whatever you can and whatever it takes.

I remember her words to me that day she explained what she could do—*I cannot make. I can only bring things that already exist, or change what already is*—and hope it is enough.

She is silent a moment, and then she says, *Yes. I will.*

I nod, still facing the window while tears burn in my eyes.

Then one other thing. The moment we are inside the house, I wish for you to change our clothing. Transform it so the people we're with won't know it's us.

I'll do it, Áila.

"Anna, dear, are you all right?" says Ipona behind me.

"Fine!" I say, forcing too much brightness into my voice. "The man at the top of the steps. Is it him?"

"Oooh!" says Ipona, squeezing forward for a look. "Oh yes, that's him!" She gives an exaggerated, husky sigh. "Gods, isn't he divine?"

I flush, embarrassed and ashamed that, not long ago, I thought something similar. Indeed, the last time I saw him, I was letting him *kiss* me. Now, I think the only divinity he resembles is Dhuos the Deathkeeper. I cut my eyes at Hew, who is watching me closely, then look away again.

These men are too bewildering. I will focus on Orail, my uncomplicated mistress of chaos and loyalty.

But Hew draws my attention back to himself with a cry of dismay. "Anna, we forgot our purse! Prince Herry will need to be assured of our loyalty in more than just words, certainly. Rupart, can we trouble your driver to take us back to the King Chares?"

"No!" I say, much too forcefully as I shoot Hew a look of warning. "No, I have it, Hamish. It's in my skirt pockets."

I can see the fear in the set of his jaw, and I know he wants to escape at once, before Morgen can spot us. But I will not be separated from Orail now I've found her again.

He gives his head a tiny shake, his eyes like granite. "Show me, Anna," he says. "We mustn't present ourselves to the prince without an offering. I won't waste this chance."

"Do you not trust me?" I grind out, hoping Rupart isn't growing suspicious of our conversation. Ipona, at least, is still craning over my shoulder, absorbed by the sight of Morgen on the front steps.

Tell him, Orail, I think, annoyed Hew hasn't thought to reach out to her with his own thoughts.

But Ipona comes unwittingly to my rescue. "Finally!" she cries as our carriage grumbles to a stop in front of the steps.

A footman opens our door, and I thrust my hand at him, using the other to drag Hew after me. Orail must be quick and thorough, or we'll have no chance.

I feel the change as it happens, first to my face and then to my hair: a strange prickling beneath my skin.

I cannot make. I can only bring things that already exist, or change what already is.

Raising my hand as if to dab my brow, I register the changes as certainly as if I am seeing them in a mirror: thinner lips, wider eyes, a longer nose, lower cheekbones, sparser brows. My skin pulls differently in each place, just as my scalp feels strange as the hair growing from it becomes straight rather than wavy.

I swallow, relief and awe slowing my raging blood. Orail has grown powerful indeed.

When Hew steps out behind me, I don't recognize him. Orail has made him handsome—as handsome as Morgen, and more—and I stare at his strong jaw, full mouth, and wavy auburn hair for a split second, registering his own shock at my appearance, before turning back toward the house.

We must hurry, before Ipona and Rupart glimpse our faces. I all but tow Hew toward the steps, handing our improvised calling card to the butler standing at the bottom, waiting to announce us as we approach Morgen.

"Mr. Hamish LacTalish and his lady, Mrs. Anna LacTalish, Your Highness," calls the butler in an unabashedly Aenlandish accent.

I swivel the ribbon at my throat so my Ona icon is hidden beneath my hair as I climb the steps to face Morgen, doing all I can to keep my eyes from straying down to his side, where Orail sits like a speckled statue. I mustn't stare at her and risk drawing his attention. Something flickers in Morgen's eyes as he looks into my face, and for a moment I am frozen by doubt: has he recognized us anyway? But then whatever it is passes like a wisp of drifting cloud. He smiles warmly.

Two weeks ago, that smile had the power to melt all my bones and steal my resolve, but today it makes me want to pull the sword out of his scabbard and run him through.

"I'm pleased to welcome you," he says, his Aenlander accent shocking to my ears.

Hew's hand digs into my lower back as he bows to Morgen, and for a moment I think he is struggling to control his own anger at the Usurper's presence. He nudges me slightly, prompting me toward the house, tension in every line of his body—

And that's when I realize where he's looking, and my eyes, too, fall at last to Morgen's side.

To Orail.

Who is chained by a broad iron cuff bolted tight around her neck.

Whose muzzle, back, and legs bear welts and lacerations—some mostly healed, and others so fresh they still glisten with bright blood. As though she has been beaten as recently as today.

The vivid gold eyes meet mine, and I don't need her words to tell me what she's thinking.

They come anyway, urgent and fierce: *Do nothing yet. Walk away, Áila, before he hurts you too.*

Chapter Fifty-Four

ORAIL

The chain about my neck has changed from
    steel
To light, to air, to nothing, because my
Áila has returned to me. Now I feel
Hope surge anew, and I hasten to try
On a fresh plan, a plan which will restore
Us to the life we had. I no longer
Need die to thwart the Beast; I will look for
Chances Áila might take to wish, conquer
My chains, and spirit us out of this place.
By morning, perhaps, we might be again
In Carrighlas, and the Beast will not chase
Us there, not with a war still yet to win.
The gashes striping my spots cease to sting,
For Áila's arrived to dethrone the false king.

Chapter Fifty-Five

ÁILA

Despite my silent pleading as we walk into the house, clothes changing subtly on our bodies as we do, Orail refuses to tell me any of what has happened to her in the last fortnight. In the absence of terrible fact, I have constructed worse imaginings, and I am drowning in shame. If I had listened to Orail when she begged me not to send her with Morgen . . . if I had seen his kiss for the manipulative trick it was, all of this might have been avoided.

Hew's steady arm braces me; it seems like the only solid thing left in the world. My thoughts wheel back to Morgen and his Aenlandish accent, his charming smiles . . . and something hotter than shame starts to burn inside me. I have never wanted to hurt a person more than I do him. A bubbling, seething current of rage courses beneath my skin, sharpening my focus . . . but giving me new solutions as well.

Hew whispers at my side as we move through the crowd of traitors in the lavish parlor. His words are feverish and fast, and I can only hear half of what he says. He wants to start a brawl, I think, to draw the gathering's attention away and give me a chance to free Orail. But I have begun to wonder why we can't just kill Morgen and be done with it. Even if we manage to steal Orail away, what's to stop him from following us—or indeed, attacking Ilbha with the resources she's already summoned for him?

Orail's voice sounds a warning in my head. *I can't end a life by magic, Áila, and his followers will turn on you if you try to kill him yourself.*

But the hot river of fury inside me churns like a sea storm, and my muscles scream for release. I am desperate to do something, to avenge the wrongs Morgen has inflicted on us.

After what might be minutes or hours of pointless mingling, a tinkling bell sounds at the top of the room. Then a voice—Aenlandish again—calls out, "His Royal Highness invites you all to convene in the dining room for supper."

Murmurs of excitement ripple through the room. Hew and I float with the current of rustling silks and taffetas—out of the parlor and into a high-ceilinged dining room. There is a great wooden table with Morgen at the head, standing like the imposter of a king he is—Orail held close to his side. My stomach jolts as I spot Bráthair Gibrat and Flora a few chairs away from him, both dressed in the latest fashions. I know now Flora's deception was thorough: the Usurper has only brothers. But if she isn't his sister, what *is* she to Morgen? Did she resent me for the time he spent with me, or were they both laughing at me all along? The aches inside of me compound, tender bruises pressing against each other.

Hew and I are seated halfway down the candlelit table, mercifully distant from Ipona and Rupart. The pair of them are looking around with worried expressions, and I feel another spike of guilt for the way we have used them. But then I remember: they are here in support of the man responsible for the glistening blood striping Orail's nose.

Rage returns to eclipse my guilt.

As the rest of the party finds their seats, Hew leans toward me.

"Do exactly as I say," he murmurs. "And do nothing unless I tell you to. When Morgen begins to eat—"

"I have another idea," I interrupt. I can't stop stealing glances at Orail and her wounds, and I feel hot all over. My hands tremble in my lap. "We can end this madness now—"

"Áila, please listen to me. I've thought this through."

"Like you thought through 'going back to get our money'?" I snap. "You didn't trust me, but I had a perfectly sound plan. What makes you think your ideas are the only good ones?"

"When Morgen begins to eat," Hew perseveres doggedly, "you must wish the shackles off of Orail and tell her to make her way under the table and out of the hall. I will start a brawl at this end of the room, and you can—"

But he breaks off, because at the head of the table, Morgen has started to speak. I turn back to face the Usurper, fuming at Hew's unwillingness to listen to me.

"I am grateful you are all here," Morgen says, his eyes as sincere and inviting as they were the night he took Orail. Disgust roils in my gut. "Many of you I have met before, and some are still yet strangers." His gaze flickers across Hew and me. "But all will, I pray, soon be as family to me. The gods have smiled upon me, and I can assure you all that this cause is their cause. They have blessed me with good fortune and will see me through to the throne. Even now, I have an army ready to march as soon as I give the word. If you join with me, if you follow me and support this quest to turn Ilbha over into my hands—my *gods-given* care—you will be blessed beyond your wildest imaginations. Lands, titles, prestige, rule, and my lasting gratitude. Tonight is but a taste of the blessings to come. Now, shall we eat?"

He smiles as titters ripple over the table, followed by a smattering of soft applause. I imagine Ipona is ready to rush out and order the wallpaper for her Aenlandish estate as soon as she leaves.

"Long live King Herry!" someone calls out, and Morgen's smile widens.

I clench my trembling hands in my lap, hating every

manipulative line of his face. I barely even *believe* in the gods, and even I am offended by his invocation of their blessing. On top of everything he's done—seducing our village, seducing *me,* taking Orail, attacking Hew, trying to overthrow the Ilbhan monarchy—he now claims that the gods *want* him to do it. When the source of his so-called blessings is a stolen Púcca—if Hew's theory is correct—which he took by force and trickery, and has been abusing ever since.

This seems to me the final evidence there are no gods at all. If they did exist, how could they stand by and let this madman claim he's doing their work? Do they even *care* if people believe in them?

Blood pounds in my skull.

I don't notice I'm moving to stand until Hew reaches over, surreptitiously putting his arm across my lap.

Restraining me.

I am back on the beach the night of the wolves, desperate to help Orail, with Morgen's arm flung across my chest. Keeping me apart from her, just as he does now.

There has always been a dam inside of me, holding things back. My anger, my impulsiveness, my fear of conflict. Suddenly it breaks, and the flood pours through—

At the same moment Morgen, apparently distracted by something Orail has said or done, turns to strike her forcibly across the nose, making her yelp with pain.

Blinding, red rage erupts through my veins. I am ready to tear Morgen's eyes out with just my fingers. But then I remember my plate was set with a pewter knife.

I shove Hew away, slip the knife from my napkin, and stand. At least a dozen black-and-white-clad servants with platters are now serving food up and down the table, but I push my way through them, toward the front of the room.

Áila, sit down, I hear Orail bark urgently through my head.

I ignore her. Once I have saved her—saved us all—she will thank me.

As I pass the place where Ipona and Rupart are sitting, Ipona glances up and catches my gaze. I see her eyes drop, slightly, to my throat.

My hand flies to it, and I realize too late that the icon of Ona around my neck has fallen forward. Orail did not change it when she changed my clothes, because she couldn't see me while she did it. Ipona's mouth sags open as she drops her fork with a clatter.

"Witch!" she shrieks, pointing at me. "That woman has changed her face!"

The room falls shockingly silent as every eye turns to me—including Flora's—and panic explodes inside my chest. I act without thinking, and bind Orail with a wish.

"Orail," I shout, "I wish you would make everyone here look like the Usurper!"

Screams erupt through the high-ceilinged room as a ripple of distorted shape and color tears down the length of the table. I spare it only a glance, but the sight is like a hall of mirrors: dozens of Morgens now line the table, leaping up, crying out, and staring at each other in wide-eyed horror.

As I intended, Orail has not excluded me from this transformation, and I use my new body to push forward with increased strength and speed. I have almost reached the head of the table, and I knock a plate of fragrant roasted ham out of one servant's hands as I brandish my knife and lunge at the true Morgen, who still has Orail trapped at his side.

He is surprised, at least; surprised enough that my blade catches him, though it doesn't find its intended mark in his heart. He knocks the knife away with a reflexive hand, and I gouge deep into his forearm as I fall toward him.

Orail leaps to her feet between us, shoving me, hard, away

from Morgen with her body so that I overbalance and crash against the wall. She barks a loud warning as I fumble to get up, and I see Morgen reach lightning-quick for the dirk at his belt.

From my awkward half-crouch, I reach for the duplicate of that same dirk in my own belt, but Morgen is too quick for me. His blade flashes as he rips it loose, and I suddenly realize just how stupid this impulse was. Dozens of copies of Morgen's voice bellow all over the room—one of them Hew's, for I hear Orail's name shouted above everything—but the real Morgen is silent and sneering before me. He raises his dirk high, flipping the handle deftly as he draws it back to throw.

I am paralyzed where I sit, unable even to close my eyes against the impact.

Out of nowhere, I think of the wolf on the beach, remember Orail's otherworldly speed. I think of her iron will, and the day I asked what would happen if our mutual desires to protect each other were ever at odds.

I would win, she said.

Something worse than the fear of death seizes my heart.

Orail springs up like a pheasant taking wing, lunging at Morgen's throat. His eyes go wide, and I am suddenly sure that there is one thing he has not lied about: he is truly afraid of dogs.

His arm comes down hard—

I hear the dirk hit with a sick thud—

I think I hear my heart fracture too—

And Orail crashes onto the rug at my feet, mouth wide in a garish grin of triumph as blood stains her speckled chest and seeps out around her in a terrible, glistening pool.

Chapter Fifty-Six

ORAIL

Áila's voice fills my head, she is screaming
In her broken silence a different wish
With every heartbeat, and tears are streaming
Over her cheeks, silver as scales of fish.
She wants me to mend the wound, but I don't
Have time, not if I am to honor Hew's
Wish too. And his wish is mine, so I won't
Ignore it. I will see them out, into
Hiding, because without me they'll never
Leave this house alive. Without me, my lass
Will die by the Beast's hand, and I'd sever
My soul before I let that come to pass.
Hew leaps to his feet, close to the wall like
I tell him, and I raise another wall
From the floor: a long, narrow, groaning spike
That severs rug and ceiling, shooting tall,
But also severs *us*. She is safe now
With Hew—the only parting I will allow.

I can hear her sobbing as he lifts her,
Drags her out, and my remaining moments
Are few, but I use the last beats of my Cur-
Heart to tell her the things burning potent
Inside me: *Áila. Please do not regret*
This day. Do not fail to see the great gift

It is to me to save you, to upset
The efforts of that Beast-man and to shift
The balance of his war hard against him.
She is almost out of the house now, Hew's
Strength straining, his heart sore, soul dark,
    mind grim.
I hurry on, desperate not to lose
My chance to say what matters most: *Áila,*
Nothing in the world's as bright as your smile.

I gasp and shake, blood leaving me, empty
        and even my Form begins to unravel.
        How to choose words when there is
    still plenty
        left to say . . . ?

My Form quakes, shudders
        leaves me.

Áila, I growl with all
        my last effort,
        my last hope,
        my last being,

You are my whole world.
        You have made me whole.
        I have never felt at home
        anywhere the way I have
        with You.

The Beast looms over me,
        I grin at him.

He

yanks

out

his

blade

and I am—

Chapter Fifty-Seven

HEW

Orail is gone. I feel her thoughts slip out of my head like beads of glass from a jar, and I gasp at their sudden absence. It feels different from when Morgen kidnapped her, when she seemed to only grow more and more remote. Now her voice leaves a yawning emptiness in its wake, a chasm that makes me dizzy to try and examine.

I cannot comprehend it, somehow. Death has visited my family three times before, but I was young those times, and both Da and Auntie Denna were already lost to me—one to whisky and one to my Unblessing—when they went. I did not feel their deaths the way I do Orail's.

A creature I cared about—loved, even—here one moment, her voice ringing strong through my head, and the next . . . simply gone. Cut off.

I have always trusted the gods, always believed in their care. But where have they taken Orail? Has she been unmade? Or is she still herself, somewhere beyond all this conflict and pain? Was her courage and sacrifice enough to deliver her soul from the imprisoning reincarnation of her Púcca life? I push it down, all of it, the messy thoughts I can neither explain nor organize, the uncontrolled chaos I will never perfect.

I focus on what I *can* make right.

"Áila, up. You have to get onto the horse, now."

She shifted back into her own, unaltered body again the same moment I felt Orail slip away, and she is almost limp in my arms, wracked by great, gasping sobs. I pull her against me as I hook one foot into the stirrups and haul us both over the back of the horse Orail summoned for our escape. The things the dog summoned have not gone, it would seem, though the things she's changed have. Which means our barrier has vanished, pursuit is certainly imminent, and none of the weapons, resources, or money Morgen used her to obtain will have disappeared. It is enough to make me weak with despair. Still, I rouse myself.

Áila sags over the front of the saddle, and I grip her waist tight as I kick the horse into a trot. We bounce like rag dolls until we have cleared the narrow garden paths, then I urge the horse into a smoother canter, settling Áila's back against me as we pound down the road, away from the house that holds both dead dog and living monster. Soon we have moved into a gallop, and I cannot tell Áila's shaking sobs from the horse's movements, so I cling hard to both and shut my mind to a maelstrom so wild within me, it silences my critical companion and keeps me even from praying.

We ride for nearly an hour. No one catches us, and we meet no one on the road until we have left the countryside behind and arrive among the towering stone buildings and twisting cobbled streets of Ellisburgh. Night has fallen, and the streets are empty of all but revelers and travelers. We clop down the cobblestones behind a hackney coach, and I feel dreadfully exposed, expecting an army of Morgen's followers to appear at any moment.

Áila has stopped crying, but I sense she has retreated deep into herself.

I steer the horse into a wide gap between two buildings, trying to appear purposeful rather than paranoid, and continue weaving through the damp alleys until I am thoroughly lost. Then I pull the horse to a halt, slip out of the saddle, and reach to help Áila down.

She peers at me through deadened eyes. Ignoring my raised

hands, she drags her leg over the saddle and slides down onto the cobbles without assistance. I begin to pace before her, determined to fix the disaster we find ourselves in.

"We need a new plan," I say, and I feel strange as the words trip off my tongue, like I am speaking things that have not yet crossed through my brain—because my brain is still shuttered against the raging storm. Yet words are ready to pour out of me: words that will fix, mend, right the impossible wrongs of this night.

"We should go from here to the castle and speak to the guards at the gate. They will know who needs to be informed. Morgen will be weakened now, and the king must strike while he can. It would be foolish to wait long, when the Usurper has lost his greatest asset."

I hear my own voice as a bubbling, chattering stream, and I marvel that I am able to speak without being hindered by my exacting self-criticism. I feel I am voice without encumbrance, without broken heart or self-doubting mind to stand in the way of perfection.

I can make this right.

I can fix everything.

"We know where he is, and the names and faces of many of his supporters. We can dismantle this uprising before it has time to properly begin. You saw that burned village—soon all of Ilbha could look like that. With loyal supporters of the king, we can attack Morgen directly, take his legs out from under him before he can regroup."

"Hew."

I break off, startled by the knife-sharp edge of Áila's voice. I have missed, perhaps, the darkening of her eyes and the hardening of her face in my haste to find the next step.

"Orail is dead."

My heart is caught in a mangle, and I struggle to breathe

until I have pushed all thoughts of Orail firmly out again. I rush on. "You should stay behind. You need rest after tonight, but I can easily lead the army to Morgen."

"She is dead, she is not an asset, and YOU DON'T EVEN CARE," bellows Áila, tears cutting furrows down her cheeks. I think inexplicably of the peat bog, of the rows of scars I used to leave in the earth after a long day's cutting. I blink at her, my words stoppered like whisky in a cask.

"I had a plan!" she screams. "I knew we couldn't steal Orail and expect Morgen to just turn tail and leave—he's grown too powerful, and killing him was the *only* way forward. But would you listen to me? Even enough to *hear* my plan? No! No, because you're so determined to control an uncontrollable situation, to control *me*, that you wouldn't even acknowledge someone else might have a better plan! If you'd listened to me instead of trying to *hold me back*, if you had helped instead of trying to get in my way, Orail might still be alive!"

She doubles over onto herself, roaring grief and fury into the heels of her hands. "You don't have all the answers, Hew," she sobs through her fingers.

I stare at her as her words pound me like hailstones. I can feel the hairline cracks they leave behind, and I wonder when those cracks will overlap enough to shatter me.

She stands again, her beautiful face a wreck of deep grooves, tears, and blotchy red patches. She spears me with the cold ferocity of her eyes. "You'll never fix the world by trying to control everything in it. So stop."

She turns her back on me and walks away, and the spidery cracks spreading thick over my heart suddenly give way.

There is nothing I can say in reply. I watch her go like the impotent scarecrow I am, and sag against the building behind me, hearing her words echo through my broken parts over and over again, harsher and truer than anything I have ever said to myself.

Beneath my fancy clothing, I feel cold metal against my aching skin.

The gold medallion that first made me Unblessed.

I have never deserved it more.

Chapter Fifty-Eight

ÁILA

I leave Hew standing in the alley, struck dumb by my attack. But he deserves it. Everything I said was true and justified, and if he had acted differently, Orail might not have died. I repeat this to myself until I am almost shouting inside my head to keep believing it. I walk quickly and aimlessly, blind to my surroundings as I flee my thoughts, more afraid of them than I could ever be of the dark streets of Ellisburgh.

But they catch up to me anyway.

It's not Hew's fault, they whisper, dark jaws nipping at my heels. *It's yours.*

I come out of a narrow alley, looking for somewhere to run, and the creak of hinges draws my eyes. A sign swings faintly in the breeze over the door of a whitewashed stone inn. The illustration is ghastly, and I stare with my mouth slightly ajar.

For the first time in months, I am struck by the conviction that the gods *do* truly exist—who else could indict me with such awful, inescapable poetry?

The inn's sign bears the image of a severed dog's head, lying in a pool of blood. Beneath it, the words *The Slaughtered Hound* are painted in ornate red letters. I feel all the fight go out of me as I look at it, and stop struggling against the monster trying to drag me down into the depths. I submit to my drowning guilt and walk slowly through the door into the tavern's common room.

It is dingy and sparsely populated. There are a few people

seated around the candlelit room, most of them nursing lonely pints of ale and looking as miserable as I feel. Despite the warmth of the summer evening, a fire burns hot in the hearth, making me sweat in my heavy finery. A middle-aged woman carrying several empty tankards on a tray stops when she sees me and makes her way across the creaky wooden floorboards.

Her eyes widen as she takes me in. I want to laugh at the thought of how I must look, with my fashionable gown, wind-snarled hair, and tear-splotched face. But I can't quite manage it.

"Can I help you, dear?" she asks, and her wholesome Ilbhan accent is balm to my stinging soul after an evening with treacherous Aenlanders. My face must show some relief, because her gaze softens. "Has something happened to you, lass? If you have any coin at all, I'll see you to a room where you can sleep safe."

"I do," I choke out, feeling smothered by a kindness I know I do not deserve.

I dig into Matan's purse for a few coppers—trembling at the shame of leaving Hew without a penny—and hand them to the woman. She nods, sets down her tray, and leads the way upstairs. She turns left down a hallway, then unlocks a door with a set of skeleton keys she pulls from her pocket.

"My man and me are the proprietors here," she says, ushering me inside. She lights the lamps and turns back the threadbare quilt. "Anything you need, just let us know."

"Thank you."

She bustles out of the room again, and I almost beg her to stay. But I remember the sign above her inn, and know I cannot escape what waits for me here in this room. When the door clicks shut, I squeeze my eyes closed and hug myself, wishing Orail were here to hold, to talk to.

It is the unanswered wish that breaks me. I find myself on the ground, knees folded to my chest and arms trembling as I press my face into my kneecaps and choke back a scream. I am captive to that unshed scream; it presses against my insides and rattles through my skull until I put my fist in my mouth and bite down, trying to quench it. If only I could strip off these awful clothes and run the cliffs, my beloved cliffs, with my beloved dog.

I can do only one of those things, so I do it as quickly as possible. I lurch to my feet and start clawing at the laces of my gown, my corset, my petticoats. The stiff fabric falls off me in swathes and panels, sometimes hanging on like a broken branch until I can find and yank free whatever thread or ribbon is tethering it to me. At last I have shed the gown, and I stand in its wreckage like the figurehead of a ship, held aloft by the same broken hull that is sinking beneath the waves.

Trembling with the need to move, to escape myself, I stride across the small, musty room in my shift, slapping the walls when I meet them, trying to release the terrible fury and guilt I feel pushing at my insides.

But it is fury at myself, and it has nowhere else to go.

Because Orail's death was *my* fault.

I know it—and I ache, ache, ache. I think I will die of the ache. If not for my relentless desire to prove myself, to earn a place by what I do, might not Orail be alive? And not only alive, but still safe with me in Carrighlas, with no welts or cuts marring her glorious, speckled coat, and no memory of betrayal or abuse?

Because I know quite well it was that very desire that prompted me to lend Orail to Morgen in the first place. I thought that by helping him, I might prove myself worth loving, worth accepting. Worth belonging. I thought I could earn a place by his side.

But all I did was give him my best friend, whose love and acceptance I already had.

Damn me.

Damn *Yslet*.

I round on her in a last, savage hope for my redemption. This is *her* fault. If she had just given me a medallion, an apprenticeship, I would have been content, and none of this would ever have happened—

But I stop, stricken by the obvious counterpoint.

If Yslet had given me an apprenticeship, she surely would not have given me Orail.

I sink, defeated, onto the moth-eaten quilt. As the reality of Orail's death—of her nonexistence—sweeps over me, I find I cannot quite keep myself up anymore. There is no one to hold; no warm, breathing assurance of life to draw comfort from. Orail is dead, and Hew is somewhere in the dark labyrinth of this city, fending for himself—or perhaps crumbling beneath the weight of the cruel things I said to him.

I curl onto my side, cold and empty, and hold nothing.

And then I wish, though there is no one left to grant it, that Morgen's dirk had pierced me instead.

As it was meant to do.

When I wake in the morning, I wonder if the rest of my life will feel this empty.

The kind innkeeper brings me a simple breakfast, and after some persuasion, gives me a plain, homespun dress in exchange for my fine, brocade one. I eat and dress quickly, then head out into Ellisburgh and begin looking for Hew.

I search an hour in the bustling city before I lose heart. But I remember the horse Orail summoned for us last night, which Hew still had when I left him. Perhaps he rode it to the coast and sold it in exchange for passage home. Unless he decided to alert King Fireld's guards after all. But the city would be in an uproar if he had convinced the king Ilbha was under threat. And by now

Morgen will have relocated himself and his followers, so there would be no point taking guards to the manor house.

The house where Orail died. Is her body still there, or did someone bury it?

Grief rocks through me again, and I do the only thing I have energy for: I hail a coach and spend most of Matan's remaining coin on transport to the western coast. I suppose I will have to work for passage to Fuiscea, and while I'm sure the thought should worry me, I can't bring myself to care. I'm not sure I will ever care about anything again.

I spend the hours-long journey trying to imagine what life will be like when I return to Carrighlas, but it feels like imagining how I might fit into a garment I've outgrown. My Ordeals will have been forfeited in my absence, which is just as well. I can't imagine trying to make any kind of effort at them now. The LaCail's words float back to me from weeks ago, that now feel like years: *At the beginning of each Ordeal, you will be given the option to make a sacrifice in place of the Ordeal itself, each as costly as the task you would have undertaken.*

The last of the five tests was called the Life Ordeal. So it stands to reason I would have been given the opportunity to sacrifice a life in place of taking it.

Before I know what's hit me, I am breathless with sobs, furious at the gods all over again for their cruel, merciless irony. Alone in the carriage, I weep tears I wasn't aware I still had left to cry. I weep until I am limp and exhausted against the window, watching the purple heather drift by outside like a relic from a beautiful world that has long since vanished.

At midday, the carriage stops to change horses at a roadside inn. I climb out of the carriage, exhausted, and for a moment I merely stare dully across the packed dirt road, my surroundings a pointless blur of shape and color. But gradually I become aware I am looking at the scorched remains of a village Morgen and his people attacked during the last rising—a village Hew and I passed on our way to Ellisburgh. My gaze sharpens, and my blood courses faster. When we were here before, the place felt like a monument, a tragedy. Today, it seems like a prophecy.

Once there were houses and shops, roads, trees, and flowers. There is now only ash and slag. Skeletal, black beams rise against the sky like a decaying whale carcass. Not even the woman we met before is there now; there are no voices raised in laughter or song, no children playing games in the square, no kirk bells calling the village to prayer.

At first, all I can think is how much I hate Morgen for doing this. For *all* he has done. But then another thought breaks through the haze of my anger.

Carrighlas.

If Morgen is not stopped, if this second rising is not thwarted, what's to prevent him from doing the same thing to our village? I imagine the quays, the village square, the monastery, even my own little cottage on the cliffs reduced to spears of charcoal piercing the salty, indigo skies of the island, their inhabitants dead.

The LaCail.

My family.

Hew.

My pulse pounds in my ears, and I suddenly find that I *do* care about something beyond the loss of Orail.

Someone must tell the king. And if Hew hasn't, who else can?

I am moving back toward the carriage, body running quite ahead of my thoughts, before I remember I don't have any idea where Morgen and his followers are now. Without some kind of proof or instruction, how will the king's guard believe me if I tell them the Usurper is back?

I sag where I stand, overwhelmed by the impossibility of such a mammoth undertaking even if I *wasn't* alone. Hew would be daunted by the prospect as well, but I know he would be willing to help me. To try.

I wish I could tell him how sorry I am.

My eyes drift to the destroyed village again, and I see a man picking his way through the burnt corpses of buildings. A monk, by his plain robes, quite clearly praying. As I watch, he lifts up the icon strung around his neck as he offers a blessing to the clouds before the skeleton of what may once have been the village kirk.

And suddenly I know where in Ellisburgh I will find Hew.

Chapter Fifty-Nine

HEW

It is no surprise to me when, as the dawn breaks rosy and lemon-hued over Ellisburgh, I find myself outside the tall, wooden doors of the cathedral. Somehow, kirks always seem to find me, regardless of whether I am allowed inside.

I have not slept. After Áila left, I wandered for a while, leading our stolen horse by the bridle and wondering what to do. I walked first toward the castle, but the longer I walked, the more turned around I became, until I realized Morgen and his supporters had surely packed up and moved their headquarters elsewhere. So I stopped at an inn and asked if they would buy my horse, since I knew he must be as hungry, thirsty, and weary as I was.

I used some of the gold to buy myself a plate of hot beef and turnips, then resumed my aimless walk through Ellisburgh's streets, pursued every step by Áila's words. Until I arrived at the doors of the cathedral.

As I cross into the dark, cool stone of the sanctuary, lit only by stained glass, I feel my muscles slow and sigh, anticipating rest at last. A monk clad in deep green robes offers a kind smile as he goes about his duties, and I return it. Even after weeks of being treated as a normal person, the experience is newly strange in a cathedral, which feels so like the monastery back home. To be regarded without derision in a place of worship is an unlooked-for blessing, which, at the moment, I feel I do not deserve.

I slide into a pew directly in front of a glittering aqua and cerulean window and look up at the familiar icon depicted there.

Lir.

It is a well-known scene: Lir, head bowed toward his open palms, face wracked with grief as his waves churn up a tempest around him. It is the moment the god learns that his daughter, Ona, has been killed by a wolf; the moment he realizes his choice to stay behind and shepherd his seas while Yslet took Ona across Fuiscea to drive out the wolves was a terrible mistake.

For if he had been there, if he had acted differently, his daughter might not have died.

For the first time since I felt her voice slip out of my head forever, I allow grief for Orail to claim my full attention. Tears fall in scalding drops onto my hands, clasped tight in my lap. If *I* had acted differently, if I had helped Áila as she said, perhaps Orail would not have died. But like Lir, I was focused elsewhere; I was bent on controlling our circumstances, on keeping us alive even at the expense of what might have been a viable solution to our problems.

As a result, I missed what was critical: Áila's urgency to bring Orail to safety and ensure it by Morgen's death. It was her feelings I should have noticed, smoldering beneath her words.

I do not realize I have bent to mirror Lir until I push my face against my open palms, to both hide and catch the tears as they fall.

I have never had much, and when I became Unblessed I had even less. My urge to follow the rules, to control myself and the things closest to me, was all I had to call my own, and before my whisky-loving father died, the only way to protect my sister and myself. With the exceptions of my mother, Vira, and eventually Gemma, few have cared for me—certainly after I became Unblessed.

Until Áila and Orail.

But I couldn't bring myself to relinquish control, and in the end it cost me dearly: my relationship with one, and the life of another.

I do not know how long I sit like that, face pressed into my hands, but after a long while I begin to feel peculiar, light, almost as though there is water lapping around my legs. I think of how strange it is to have been away from the sea for so long, away from the sound of it—and even as I think of the ocean, I begin to hear it. The hiss of the waves as they pull away from the cliffs; the seething tumble of the breakers against the sand; the roar of the vast ocean at night, wending its way into my soul as I sleep.

I am seized by the impulse to sit up, but equally strong is the impression I should wait a moment longer, remain in the whirl and weightlessness.

And then I hear a voice as clearly as though someone has spoken from the seat beside me. "Hew."

I know who it is. I would know his voice anywhere, even though I have never heard it before.

Lir.

I feel his smile like sunlight on my face, but I keep my head bowed into the rocking comfort of his waves.

"What is it that you want, Hew?" he says.

I think about the question, letting the water swirl and eddy around me. At last I answer, silently, *To fix what I have broken. To be less broken. To stop failing. To be without fault or flaw.*

"And what do you think that would give you?"

I am ashamed of my answers, but they come quickly. *Worthiness. Acceptance. Safety. A place at a seminary. A priest's robe. Áila's love.* I swallow hard, but I have never been able to lie to Lir. *Your love.*

"Do you think you do not have it already?" he asks gently.

Tears slip through the cracks between my fingers. *But I don't deserve it. If I can be perfect, I will deserve your love.*

"Hew." Lir's arms fold around me, large as if I am a child. "You can never be good enough to deserve the love of a god. But you have it, and there is nothing you can do to lose it."

I exhale, and the breath going out of me feels like poison being drawn from my veins. I wonder what it would be like to live without all this *striving*. Without the never-ending criticism, worry, and effort to manage everything.

The sound of the sea is gone, I realize, and I raise my head. No one is sitting beside me; there is no trace of saltwater anywhere. I am alone with Lir's window and his grief.

But somehow, my own grief feels lighter.

After a while, I stand and wander the cathedral, stopping before each of the tall, stained glass windows, one for every god and goddess. I stay the longest with Yslet, gazing up at her merry face, her red hair, her green dress dancing above bare feet. I wonder that the builders of this cathedral chose to show Lir in his grief for Ona, but depicted Yslet joyful and light, no trace of sadness about her. But perhaps they merely wanted to remind us that even the gods are defined by more than one event—no matter how tragic. I feel the cold weight of my medallion against my sternum again, and think of the day Yslet gave it to me.

I smile, remembering the playfulness in her face, the freckles dusting her nose, the amber depths of her ancient eyes. This window has captured her well. She seemed both young and impossibly old as she handed me the gold medallion and told me to use it well.

I think of the only other thing she said to me that day: "I love you. You are precious to me."

My heart twists, but this time it is a sweet sort of ache. I think I am finally beginning to believe that it's true.

I leave the sanctuary and wander the corridors of the adjoining monastery, where monks in a variety of robe colors are tracing purposeful paths through the stone halls. At last I find an elderly man wearing a blue robe and a purple stole like the one Fáthair Firnan usually has draped around his neck. A priest. He is walking with an enormous leather tome tucked under his arm and talking quietly with a young monk. As I approach, their conversation seems to end, and the older man spots me.

"Greetings, child," he says lightly. "I don't believe I've seen you here before. Are you from the city?"

"Er, no," I say, feeling awkward. "I'm from Carrighlas—on Fuiscea—but I got a little lost on my way back." I stop, wondering what on earth I hoped to ask this man. A place in his monastery? A sponsorship to attend seminary?

"Fuiscea?" repeats the priest in surprise. "We don't often meet with islanders here. I hope you know you are welcome. Do you need a place to stay?"

Despite the many hours since I last slept, a bed is still not what I want. "No, Fáthair," I say. "Or at least, not yet. I think I need a place to work."

A place to practice imperfection.

His white brows go up, but he does not comment. "Indeed? Well, we have plenty of work here. What are you best suited to?"

"Labor," I say. "Physical labor." It isn't what I want to tell him—and it's certainly not the work I want to give my life to—but for now it is the truth. He could hardly ask for a more experienced peat cutter. And even better, after nearly a month away from the bog, my muscles will be a long way from their best.

"Then I shall send you to the gardens. How are you with a spade?"

I almost laugh. "I know my way around one."

The priest's eyes twinkle. "Then follow me."

He leads me out into the gardens to a greenhouse, and asks if I know how to prune and deadhead. Then he leaves me to my work.

Hours amble by, and I fill my basket more times than I can

count with spent blossoms and clipped branches. I am sweating from my labor, stiff muscles loosening and soul unwinding, when I catch sight of a young woman striding up the garden path in the afternoon light.

She is wiry and slight, beautiful, with long dark hair and tanned skin. My breath gets snarled up in my throat as I watch her coming, but she doesn't notice me.

She hurries toward the doors of the cathedral—has nearly passed me by—

I find my voice.

"Áila?"

Chapter Sixty

ÁILA

I jump so badly I nearly tumble into the hedge.

"Hew?" I say, stunned. "What . . . what are you doing?"

He is a few feet away, knee-deep in a row of rosebushes. With a pair of shears in one hand, a basket of clippings in the other, and a lopsided straw hat on his head, he looks like a cathedral fixture; a gardening monk.

"Er," he says with an awkward shrug. "Deadheading the roses."

For a moment, we stand facing each other over the rosebushes, our last conversation as prickly as the thorns separating us. I have spent the better part of the day traveling—first away from, and then back to Ellisburgh—fighting despair, and thinking often of Hew. Of his gray eyes, his earnest face with its many freckles. His bright smile and his grave anxiety, and the warm strength of his hands. The way he is both immovably sure of himself and crippled by self-doubt. Of his gentle kindness, even after years of rejection in Carrighlas,

Of the way he didn't deserve *any* of the things I said to him last night.

"I should never have left you—" I say, at the same moment he bursts out, "I didn't know where you'd gone—"

We break off in unison, and Hew gestures for me to continue, his face very pink. I clear my throat, my own cheeks reddening. "I just . . . wanted to say that I should never have left you in that alley," I say, throat tight. "And I should never have said those things to you. They were cruel and untrue. It wasn't your fault, Hew, it was mine. Orail's death was—entirely—my fault. I'm so sorry for what I said. For leaving you alone, without any money or . . . or anything."

"I wanted to go after you," he says quietly, his eyes over-bright, "but I was afraid and ashamed. So I came here instead. I'm sorry as well, Áila. I should have listened to you. I should have trusted you." His gaze is open and earnest as always, but there is something different about the way he holds himself. His tendency to cringe after he speaks has vanished; the usual self-protective hunch of his shoulders has given way to a straight-backed ease. It makes it difficult to avoid noticing the way his copper hair catches fire in the light of the sinking sun, or the impossibly gentle expression softening his face.

"Hew," I say, feeling suddenly flustered. "You were right last night. We should have gone to the castle and tried to tell the king where Morgen was. It will be harder now, but . . . well, I think we still should."

His auburn brows lift, but a hardness settles into his jaw. "For Orail," he says in a low voice.

I nod, eyes burning with sudden tears. "And for our home. If Morgen succeeds, if he conquers Ilbha . . ." I trail away.

"He would come for Carrighlas first," he says, expression distant and grim as he imagines it. "Everyone we know and love would be made to pay for our little rebellion against him."

"He took Orail," I say quietly. "I won't let him take everything else."

Hew nods, light sparking in his eyes. "Agreed. So we need to work out where he's gone, find some proof of it, and go to the castle to tell the king?"

"That's about as far as I've thought too," I admit. "Not much of a plan."

Hew smiles, but there is something rueful in it. "Not much

of a plan is just right for me," he says, and before I can ask what he means, he says, "Let me go inside and tell the priest goodbye. I'll be back in a moment."

I watch him go, basket swinging and straw hat flapping with every step, and smile to myself. If this is what Hew would be like as a priest, then the world is being deprived of something beautiful.

When Hew reappears ten minutes later, the sun has all but set, leaving the cathedral gardens in a smoky haze of scarlet-tinged indigo. As he hurries toward me, I can tell he is carrying something.

"What's that?" I ask, and he hands over a stack of parchment and leads the way out to the cobbled street.

"Broadsheets," he says. "Monks have always been the keepers of history, and even in Carrighlas we archive things from all over the world, in case the records should be lost to war or disaster. Broadsheets and wedding bans and birth records and funeral announcements. We have whole rooms full of them, and Ellisburgh is no different."

I turn the stack over to find a sketch of Morgen on the top page, illustrated in full military regalia with a look of impudence on his face. At the top, in bold letters, is the headline, WANTED BY HIS MAJESTY, PORRL, KING OF AENLAND, FOR CRIMES AGAINST ILBHA AND AENLAND. THE CROWN WILL PERSONALLY REWARD FOR PRINCE HERRY'S CAPTURE AND RETURN.

I stare at it for a long moment, then turn back to look at Hew.

"I asked the priest for a few of them," he says as we stride up the street. "Saw them on his desk and thought they might be useful. Did you know King Porrl was opposed to his son's attacks on Ilbha?"

"No," I say in surprise, thinking of Ipona and her desperate hopes of being given crown-sanctioned lands in Aenland. "I thought his father was behind him. So perhaps some of his Ilbhan followers are also ignorant of that fact?"

"Indeed," Hew agrees, and he divides the small stack in two and hands me half. "In case we're separated."

I fold up my half and tuck them into my bodice, then look back at Hew. He is staring up the high street toward a building whose windows glow gold in the dusk. The King Chares Inn.

It's been barely over a day since the last time we were there, but it feels like years. It would be incredibly dangerous to go back, yet it seems our best chance of finding where Morgen and his followers might have gone.

Hew meets my eyes in the darkness of a shopfront awning, where we have stopped. When I nod, he nods back: crisp, grim, and certain.

"We'll be careful," he mutters, offering me his arm as we start off once again.

The hilly streets are less busy now than they were a few hours ago, though still peppered with carriages. We keep close to the buildings lining the road as we walk, safe in their shadows.

"Morgen might be expecting us to return," Hew says, still squinting toward the inn. "Ipona and Rupart will obviously have told him everything about us."

"We could sneak around back? Find a groom or someone who might be persuaded to ask questions for us."

"Bribed, you mean," says Hew dismally, as we pass in front of an alley. "You have to have money in order to bribe someone."

"What else can we do?"

"You can rethink this plan altogether," says a new voice, coming from the dark mouth of the alley we have just passed.

I whirl around, my skin trying to jump off my body while Hew fumbles for his dirk. The person stepping out from the shadows is tall and slender, wearing a long cloak and hood so that their face is hidden. They step toward us and pull back the hood—and all the breath leaves my lungs as if it has been sucked clean out of me.

It is Flora LaCree.

Chapter Sixty-One

HEW

"Stay back!" I cry, putting a hand out to stop Flora—though of course if she has any kind of weapon, I'll be easy enough to dispatch. All I have is an ornamental dirk and very little practical knowledge of how to use it.

Flora holds up her hands to show that they're empty, save for a shuttered lantern. "I'm not here to hurt you," she says. Her eyes are beseeching, and they're fixed on Áila.

Áila looks like a sapling wavering in Fuiscean winds, and I rest a hand between her shoulder blades to steady her. She is watching Flora just as intently as Flora is watching her, but her expression couldn't be more different. Áila's eyes are wide, her jaw is set, and her nostrils are flaring. I suspect either tears or shouting might be imminent.

"What *are* you here for, then?" I spit at Flora, as much to spare Áila as anything else. "Haven't you and your 'brother' done enough to us?"

She looks at me at last, her gaze withering. "Herry sent me to find you on the Cairsmuirs' information. He trusts me still, you see." Her face hardens and she turns back to Áila. "But I'm sorry for what he did—what *we* did—to you. It was wrong. It was all wrong."

"Aye," says Áila, her voice hard as the cliffs of Carrighlas. "It was."

Flora swallows. "I-I want to help you."

There is a long silence. Áila is staring at Flora like she doesn't trust a word she says. After a moment, Flora goes on, "Herry's people are searching the King Chares for you, as well as a number of pubs and inns around the city. If I were you, I'd keep out of sight and leave the city as quickly as possible. Don't go back to Carrighlas. Start over somewhere else, or he will find you when this is all over and make you pay."

"And where is he?" asks Áila.

Flora's eyes widen. "Why? You can't be thinking of revenge. Áila, you'd stand no chance. None at all. He has an army at his command."

"If you want us to believe that all this"—Áila waves a hand at Flora—"is sincere, and you really do want to help, then give up his location and tell us what he's planning next."

Flora stares at her, dark eyes inscrutable. Then she nods. "Fine. He's at Redbrook House, just south of Feldkraich. They're planning to attack the city at dawn and move in a circuit from there, taking towns and villages until Ellisburgh is surrounded."

Áila watches her for a long moment, perhaps looking for some evidence of honesty or deceit. She crosses her arms over her chest. "Prove yourself," she says, her voice taut. "Tell me something you wouldn't give up if you were still helping Morgen."

Flora looks helpless, like she doesn't know how to answer. But then her expression hardens. "The wolves," she says quietly. "That night on the beach. They were Morgen's idea—he had them brought in, half-starved, from the mainland. He wanted to test Orail's powers, and to determine whether he could just steal her or if he needed to convince you to give her up. When I went into the monastery afterward, it was to tell Gibrat to go out and plant the lie about the monastery dog."

I see Áila shiver slightly. She uncrosses her arms and turns to me. "Dawn. That doesn't give us much time."

My heartbeat is starting to pound in my throat. "What are you thinking of doing, Áila? Are you telling me you trust her word?"

"I'm not sure. But whatever side she's on, she *will* lead me back to Morgen eventually. I'm not going anywhere without her."

I stare at her, still not following.

"You just said we might have to separate, and you were right." She taps the front of her bodice, where she has tucked the Aenlandish broadsheets. "You must go to the castle and convince them to ride to Feldkraich and stop Morgen. And I'll go to Redbrook House and try and thwart his war. If he isn't there, I'll find a way to hold Flora until the king's soldiers arrive, and they can drag Morgen's location out of her."

"Thwart his war?" I yelp, just as Flora says, "Áila, that's madness!"

But she shakes her head, slow and stubborn, and I think I see a glint of canine gold in her eyes.

"Flora," she continues, "will take me there. Hew, you must do all you can to raise the king before dawn."

"Please," says Flora, and there is real fear in her voice. "Please, Áila. Don't put yourself in Herry's way. He's a monster. I know what he can do."

But this seems to have the opposite impact Flora intended; Áila breathes a hiss of fury through her nose and leans in toward her. Flora's eyes widen as she absorbs Áila's expression, which I imagine must give her some clue as to how much rage Áila is holding back.

"I do too," Áila says. "Which is exactly why I'm going to stop him."

"Let me go to Redbrook," I interrupt. "Flora's right. Trying to stop this war on our own is suicide."

"I'm not going to be reckless," says Áila impatiently. "I just want to steal his plans. Then, when the king's army arrives, they'll be able to rout the turncoats from all the places they've planned to be, without Morgen's army getting the better of them. Besides, if this rising is to be stopped, the king will need to know which of his people are traitors, and that means stealing the evidence before anyone knows it's at risk. So I'll meet you and the king's army on the road outside of Feldkraich with as many of Morgen's private plans and papers as I can steal. Get him there before dawn, Hew." She looks at Flora. "I suppose you know where Morgen would keep such information?"

Flora nods slowly. "If you succeed, will you vouch for me to the king? Secure my pardon?"

"I will."

Unshuttering her lantern, Flora points it into the alley she appeared from. It is empty but for a black horse, saddled and bridled a few feet away. "Then let's go."

"Good," says Áila.

She turns back to me, and for a moment her bravado falters. She is transparent before me, all fierce courage, broken heart, and windblown hair, and I can see the trust we have forged mirrored in her eyes. I want to tell her I am grateful for it, that her friendship means more to me than I can say, and that I will do all I can to help her, to protect her, to save our kingdom from Morgen. Even more than that, I want to tell her that I love her. That if we make it through this, there is nothing I want more than to spend the rest of my days with her, if by any wild chance she will have me.

But instead I just squeeze her hand. "Be safe," I whisper.

Her throat bobs and she squeezes back, fingers laced tight through mine. "You too."

She turns to follow Flora into the alley. I watch them mount up with my heart throbbing, Flora in front, Áila behind, and then step back as they break into a trot, clopping out onto the streets of Ellisburgh. They are briefly visible as a tall, dark shadow passing between stone buildings before they turn and disappear from view.

Watch over her, Lir, I plead and set off, directing my steps toward Ellisburgh Castle.

Chapter Sixty-Two

ÁILA

Flora and I ride at a steady canter to conserve the horse's energy, settling into a rhythm that soon mesmerizes my tired mind. I cling to Flora's waist, relieved not to feel any weapons concealed in her bodice, but wonder all the same what I would do if she actually tried to attack me. While I think I am right—she will lead me to Morgen—I am only half sure she's taking me toward Feldkraich. If she lied about his location, she could easily take me there instead, and Hew would never find me again, with or without the king's army.

But somehow I don't think she will betray me. There was real fear in her face when she spoke of Morgen, and I suspect she has suffered at his hands too. And in any case, this is the best hope we have of capturing him before it's too late.

After several hours, when the moon is high in the cloud-streaked sky, we pass a dilapidated signpost on the side of the dirt road bearing the worn word *Feldkraich*. I am weak with relief.

"We're close," Flora murmurs. "But the turnoff to the estate is easy to miss in the dark."

I squint up the road, picking out a mass of hulking dark shapes on the horizon: the sleeping city that has been marked as Morgen's first target. There is no sign of fire, no sounds of shouting or screaming. No glint of steel in the moonlight. We still have time before dawn.

Flora studies the road just ahead of us. Then she steers the mare off to the right, cutting into the countryside where the grass is slightly trampled. A private, little-used path created by farmers or landowners, most likely.

We ride another fifteen minutes before I hear men's voices—lots of them—speaking low and calm, intermixed with the clink of steel and the soft whinny of horses. Flora steers our horse into the gorse and we both dismount a little stiffly.

"Keep close behind me," she says. "I can get us in, but the moment someone suspects you, it's all over. I'm going to take you through the servants' corridor to the war room, where Herry's plans and papers are. Hopefully, by now he'll be out on the field preparing for the battle, but I don't know that for certain. Be ready for anything."

I nod, adrenaline and fear making my throat dry.

"Let's disguise you a bit first," Flora says, striking out across the moonlit fields. "This way."

We stride through grass already drenched with dew toward a shadowy house rising above us on a low hill. The rumble of voices we heard from the road grows steadily more distant as we do. I suppose they must belong to the foot soldiers Morgen has amassed, waiting in the fields between the house and Feldkraich. The house is dark ahead of us, but every now and then I catch a glimmer of light through a window; I realize they must all be covered or curtained to prolong the surprise of the attack. Flora does not make straight for the house, however. She leads me first into a barn.

"Here," she whispers, rummaging through a cupboard and pulling out an apron, cap, and pail. Nearby, I hear the sounds of cows shifting and lowing, ready to be milked. I tie on the apron and cap and follow Flora back outside, keen to avoid the real milkmaids who are sure to arrive soon.

We cut straight toward the house. Flora nods to the guards standing on either side of the double front doors, and they incline their heads but don't speak. I keep my own head down and stay close to her heels, gripping my pail.

As we cross the threshold and the doors swing shut behind us, I don't know whether to whoop with triumph or beg to be let out again. The foyer is vast, dark, and empty, and for a moment we stand still beneath a darkened chandelier, staring at each other.

"This way," Flora breathes. "When we get there, I'll go first to check that it's empty. If something goes wrong, follow the servants' corridor all the way to the end of the house and find someplace to hide until the battle starts. Then leave."

She pushes a wall panel behind a tall, spiral staircase, and a door slides open, revealing a gloomy hallway beyond.

"Flora? Is that you?"

Flora shoots me a look of alarm. Then she shoves me through the door. Before I can turn back toward her, the door slides shut again, hiding me from view. I press my ear to the panel and listen, and the voice I hear makes me feel cold all over. It is Bráthair Gibrat, who certainly would have recognized me.

"Where have you been? You've been gone for hours. Come, the prince is waiting to hear your report."

Their footsteps retreat, leaving silence behind, and I stand frozen in the servants' corridor, wondering whether I should take Flora's advice and hide. But then I realize there is nothing to keep me from doing alone exactly what we planned to do together, so I start down the dark hallway in search of the war room.

It is dim and dingy, too narrow for more than one person to walk abreast. I keep to the shadowy wall as I run, soft-footed, along it. Doors are spaced every ten or fifteen feet, and occasionally another tiny corridor branches off the main one, providing discreet access to other rooms. Anxiety tingles beneath my skin, but I meet no one. Behind one of these doors are Morgen's plans, and I must be cautious as I search. But which to try first?

There is a sound up ahead—footsteps and the creaky wheels of a cart—and my heart almost jumps out of my mouth.

I open the door on my immediate left as silently as I can, sliding into a room that is mercifully—and terrifyingly—dark. A tea parlor, I think, judging by the humped shapes of chairs and settees spaced throughout it. Gilt frames glisten in the trace moonlight slipping in through cracked curtains, and I stand for a moment, letting my eyes adjust. An elegant pianoforte stands halfway across the room, superfluous in a house surrounded by soldiers. I have almost decided to venture back into the servants' corridor when I hear a sound that turns me as still as marble, rolling through the room like the sighing of wind.

Breathing.

Ice shoots up my spine. I feel like my skin is an unfurled map that has just been released, rolling up my body in one great curl. I want to scream, but I bite it back, straining to locate where the sound is coming from.

Who it's coming from.

A moment later I spot the dark form of a man lying on one of the settees. And then, as though the first one has lifted a film from my eyes, I see a second man, and a third, all sound asleep on the fine furniture. Polished leather boots shine at the ends of their legs, and I see the sharp cut of jacket lapels—military uniforms whose dull red is visible even in this darkness. Aenlandish soldiers.

I hold my breath and back toward the servant's door, grateful when I find the latch almost at once. I slip back through it, thinking that meeting an unsuspecting servant would be far better than waking any of those men.

Deep breaths, I tell myself, resuming my walk back down the corridor. *Deep breaths*.

What I wouldn't give for a nice cup of tea.

The next time I hear footsteps coming down the hall, they are behind me. I accelerate to a quiet run until I find a narrow side corridor to duck down.

And that's when I hear it.

A very familiar voice, speaking with loud confidence through the hidden door in the wall beside me.

My heart roars in my temples as I press my ear to the wall and listen to Morgen talk about how many men are currently stationed outside of Feldkraich and how many more will be arriving soon. As he calculates how quickly they will be able to dispatch Feldkraich itself and where they will attack next. As he parcels out village after village, city after city, like my country is a pie he's deciding how thinly to slice.

Then I hear Bráthair Gibrat's voice, though I can't make out what he says. And Morgen says, "Well, Flora? What have you found?"

"Nothing," comes Flora's brittle reply. "They've left the country, for all I can tell."

"Well, that's interesting," Morgen says, his voice so low I have to actually hold my breath to hear him. "Because one of my men was in Ellisburgh this evening, and he says he saw you talking with a young woman and a young man on the street. He says the young woman left with you, on your horse."

I am so absorbed by their conversation that I don't realize I'm leaning against the hidden door. It gives a low squeal, like a loose floorboard, and I gasp and jump back. Blood thunders in my ears—I am torn between fleeing and staying to hear more—but no one opens the door, and in a moment I can hear talking again.

"Sounds like your men have been drinking on the job again," says Flora in a bored voice. "Seeing double. I rode back alone, and only spoke with people I thought might have information."

"We shall see," says Morgen.

And then there is silence. I lay my ear carefully against the crack in the wall, trying to hear what's happening—but it's as if everyone has vacated the room without making a sound. I frown, wondering how that could be possible, and then—

Flora's voice cries suddenly, "Run, Áila!"—

Just as the door swings fast away from me, and I fall into the room, straight into a pair of thick, hairy arms that stink of sweat and sour ale.

"Ah," says Morgen's voice from somewhere nearby. "Áila LacInis. Welcome to my war council."

Chapter Sixty-Three

HEW

Ellisburgh Castle is a mammoth structure, built on a mighty hill in the middle of the city. The hillsides are sheer as cliffs in places, and there is only one way to approach the gates: by following the single road that climbs up toward the fortress. This I do, as quickly as I can, and by the time I reach the iron gates, which are flanked by a dozen armed guards, I am gasping for breath and clutching a stitch in my side. I think of Áila's habit of running the cliffside path, and shake my head at the kind of insanity that would drive a person to inflict such misery upon themselves.

The soldiers at the gates give me looks of bland curiosity.

"The Usurper Prince!" I wheeze out. "He's marshaling an army at Redbrook House, near Feldkraich. He's going to attack the city at dawn."

The guards exchange glances, their expressions barely changing. One of them steps toward me—a tall, rangy man with a scar running the length of his jaw—and says, "What's your proof of this claim? Who are you?"

I try not to deflate at this question; my answer has no chance of impressing them. "I'm Hew LacEllan, of Carrighlas on Fuiscea. The Usurper spent the last month in our village, disguised as a scribe, and just returned to Ellisburgh. He has resources beyond anything he had before. I believe he'll be at least detrimental—if not successful—if he isn't stopped."

Again, the guards exchange mild looks. The one with the scar sighs and repeats, "What is your proof, lad?"

"I . . . I don't have any," I say, my shoulders sagging. "Only my word."

There are snickers from the men behind him, but the scarred fellow gives me a pitying look. "The word of an island peasant won't be enough to justify interrupting the king's sleep, I'm afraid," he says.

Desperation and anger fill me up like a tempest as I think of Áila, putting herself in harm's way in order to aid these soldiers when they reach Feldkraich. I am helpless against such men, but I still feel the mad urge to run at them, to shake them, to make them believe me. *Lir!* I pray. *Help me!*

"The king isn't asleep," says a voice from behind me. "Not yet, anyway. Not until he's said his prayers to the icons I bring, as he does every week."

I whirl around. The elderly priest of Ellisburgh Cathedral is climbing the hill to the gates behind me, carrying a basket of painted icons.

"Fáthair!" I cry, gaping. He dips his head to me, and then addresses the guard with the scar.

"Tell me," he says, "why you won't convey this young man's message to the king."

The guard looks only slightly less surprised than I feel, and he glances side to side at his men for support. "He has no proof to back up his claims, Fáthair, and we don't know who he is. We can't ferry every message that wanders in off the street, can we?"

"Then let me vouch for him," says the priest. "He is an honorable young man. If he has requested something be conveyed to the king, I think you ought to do it."

I feel again the way I felt in Lir's presence in the cathedral: small, and utterly undeserving of the kindness I am being shown. But something nudges me not to shrink away from these feelings, or the gifts they were brought on by. So I do my best to accept the priest's generosity without squirming: I incline my head to him, thanking him with my eyes, and he smiles.

The guard is still looking like he doesn't know what to do, but at a nod from the priest, he sighs.

"Very well. Mr. LacEllan, was it? Fáthair. Come with me."

He turns and leads the way through a small door to the left of the gate. I pass beneath it after him, trying not to gape at the spikes of the portcullis.

Ahead of me, the guard beckons to another soldier just inside. "Take them upstairs," he says to the man. "They need an audience with the king."

Chapter Sixty-Four

ÁILA

The door bangs into the wall with a crash that draws every eye in the room. And it is a large room, full to the brim with eyes. The man who catches hold of me is a giant, seven feet tall at least, and intercepts my empty milk pail easily as I make a wild swing at his head. He wrenches it away from me and stands me on my feet.

Like the last place I saw Morgen, I'm in a vast dining room, but this time there are no mouth-watering dishes, crystal goblets, or pewter cutlery. Instead of being laced with the scents of hon-eyed ham, roasted garlic, and floral perfumes, this room feels like walking into a solid wall of body odor, gunpowder, and whisky fumes. I gasp as the reek hits me. The table is spread thick with maps and scribbled notes, and on one end there is a pile of steel blades. Other weapons line the deep-burgundy walls—swords, knives, axes, cudgels, and pistols—in piles and rows wherever there are not already barrels or chairs. And there are lots of chairs, both wooden and upholstered, most of them occupied by men in varying states of uniform and undress. Morgen himself stands over the table in a crisp, red Aenlandish military jacket, with his hands splayed across a map spaced with chess pieces.

No one moves as the shock of my appearance registers in every face. Every face, that is, except Morgen's. His smile is languid, as if he had been expecting—or even hoping for—my arrival.

I wonder if he will kill me like he killed Orail.

"Listen to me!" I cry suddenly, a wild idea possessing

me—my last flickering hope of salvation. "You have all sworn your armies, your support, your very lives to a man whose promises are empty and who can give you nothing! All the wealth and titles he's promised you in Aenland are not his to give. His father, King Porrl, has disowned him, and promised a ransom for his return. I have proof!" And I pull the broadsheets from my bodice, waving the drawing of Morgen and his ransom like a banner over my head. "Stop this madness," I say. "Beg forgiveness from King Fireld, and send this lying usurper back where he came from!"

Silence follows my pronouncement, so profound that for a moment I think I have done it: sprung such surprising news on Morgen's followers that they will all disown him here and now, before a single drop of Ilbhan blood can be spilled. Several men exchange wide-eyed looks, and then, as unexpected triumph swells in my chest—

Laughter.

Faint and snickering at first, and then growing into such a raucous tumult of hilarity that I gape around the room in dismay. Even Morgen is chuckling, I realize, bent over his maps and leaning on his hands as he grins back and forth at the men beside him.

The hand clutching the broadsheets falls limp at my side.

Finally, the laughing ebbs to a feeble trickle. The man standing directly to Morgen's right clears his throat and smiles at me. "Sorry, lass," he says. "No offense meant, but those wee broadsheets are hardly news to us. You seem to think we're here because we want *Aenlandish* lands and titles."

Someone across the room laughs while another man scoffs and spits on the floor.

"We don't want Aenlandish shite," barks the man who spat—his accent is Ilbhan. "Our king holds back. We want what we're owed *here*. In our own land."

"You see, Áila," says Morgen, smiling at me with the same hesitating earnestness he used to employ in Carrighlas, "I never promised anyone Aenland. I promised to give them what should already be theirs. I promised them the wealth of Ilbha."

I glare at him, thinking of poor, deluded Ipona and her visions of Aenlandish lands and titles. "The wealth of Ilbha," I snarl, "is not yours to give."

"Not yet," he counters, still smiling.

I want to slap the smile off his face—and perhaps he can tell, because he barks out an order to the man holding my arm: "Restrain her."

The giant seizes my other forearm and jerks me, none too gently, toward Morgen.

"Careful!" comes Morgen's directive again, this time with a snap of anger. "We treat this young woman like the lady and guest she is. Do not hurt her."

"Why do you care?" I throw at him. "You've already hurt me more than these brutes ever could!"

Morgen's brow contracts as if my words have actually caused him pain, and he stands away from his maps and notes to come around the table toward me. He takes hold of my elbow, guiding me through clumps of staring men to a pair of double doors at the front of the room.

But then he stops, and I see Flora—half hidden behind several tall men before us—watching me with a tormented expression.

"Liar," Morgen says calmly, and slaps her, hard, across the face.

And he pulls me through the doors, into an opulent hallway.

My heart beats a frantic rhythm inside my chest. We are alone now, and I have no idea what he will do to me. But he merely looks down into my face with a slight pucker between his brows.

"I know you're angry with me," he says, as if I'm a petulant child—or worse, a jealous wife. "But I hope you know I never wanted to hurt you. I meant what I told you that last night on Fuiscea. I think you're wonderful. And I did regret having to do what I did."

I gape at him. If I doubted he was a madman before, this is enough to banish my uncertainty. "Which was *what*, exactly?"

"Take your dog," he says, looking confused. "I had intended to steal the goddess's unicorn once you secured another Trial, but infinite wishes are much preferable to a single wish. You understand that, of course?"

I stare at him. For a long moment, his words hang in the air between us—stunning me, enraging me—and then I erupt. I am no longer thinking of stealing his battle plans or stopping his war. I'm not thinking of anything except the burning hatred I feel toward this monster of a man who seems to believe, some-how, he has cared for me in any authentic way. "And what about the rest of it?" I shout. "What about lying to everyone in my village about who you are and what you wanted? Pretending to condemn the Usurper Prince! What about trying to get close to me so that you could, what, *steal Yslet's unicorn* and make a wish? What about trying to conquer the kingdom I live in? What about trying to kill Hew, and what about *beating* my dog—and then *m-murdering* her in front of me?" I'm all but shrieking at him now, and I can feel the wet heat of tears coursing down my face.

Morgen is staring at me like he can't believe the charges I'm leveling against him. Like I'm completely irrational—an emo-tional madwoman—and need to have a good sleep and a cup of tea to sort myself out. Losing all control, I lunge at him with my fingernails—the only weapons I have—and try to gouge out his eyes.

He catches me by the wrists like he might a toddler throwing a tantrum and wrestles me down until my arms are twisted behind my back.

"I hope you'll learn to see all this differently, Áila," he grunts. "I really do care for you. I stopped my affair with Flora for you. But this rising is what I was born for, and I could hardly give it all up for a *girl*—even one as pretty as you."

I am amazed to find that there's room for more anger inside of me. I feel like a feral mountain cat, full of spitting, tearing rage, and all I want to do is shred Morgen's handsome, arrogant features until his face is mere ribbons of flesh clinging to bone. I wish with all my heart my blade had not missed its mark at the gala. And then, as I catch myself wishing, I think of Orail and feel like I am collapsing from the inside out.

I would give back all the wishes she ever granted me—every last one—if it meant I could have *her* back.

Morgen hauls me into the war room again, where his councillors stand waiting with neutral expressions, as if they haven't just heard every word I screamed. Morgen passes me to the giant who had hold of me before.

"Tie her up," he says, "but leave her legs free. I want her to watch the battle. She must learn proper respect."

The man nods and muscles me across the room, where he takes a coil of long, prickly rope and ties my hands together behind my back. When my fury cools slightly, I remember my last hope is to delay these baboons, so I try shouting out dire warnings, threats, and even lies in my efforts to pull the attention of the room from its goal. But each attempt earns me a slap from the giant, and after the third blow sets my ears ringing, I give up. For ages, it seems, I sit and watch the treacherous Ilbhan clan leaders, battle chieftains, and landowners prepare themselves for battle. They pull on jackets, strap pistols to their chests, and buckle scabbards with claymores to their hips to rest alongside their dirks. They tie back greasy hair, swig the dregs of old whisky, and lace up boots. Then they and their Aenlandish counterparts clomp out of the room with a clattering of weapons. The giant pulls me out of my chair to follow.

Morgen has not looked back at me once.

I drag my feet, creating as much resistance as I can, but my captor is so strong it hardly matters. As we leave the house behind and file out into fields now lightening in the pre-dawn, I glance over my shoulder, trying to find Flora. But she has disappeared. Whatever has happened to her, I am now alone.

And powerless.

And without any idea of what to do next.

Chapter Sixty-Five

HEW

I follow the soldier up a flight of stone steps, the priest keeping pace behind me. We wind through increasingly opulent corridors, carpeted with thick green and purple rugs and adorned with fine tapestries, lit by flickering torches in brackets. I blink at the splendor around me, a wealthier version of the monastery back in Carrighlas. I suppose the castle is just as old, or older, and the familiarity of the stone puts me slightly at ease.

Until we reach the king's apartments.

Stone they may be, but that is where their resemblance to the monastery stops. The sitting room we are led into is crowded with furniture, from plush chairs upholstered in red-and-gold jacquard to polished mahogany tables with intricately carved legs to ornate woven rugs and oil paintings. Flames leap behind an iron grate in a fireplace as tall as I am, burning logs. If it has ever so much as *seen* a block of peat, I'll eat my own boots.

The soldier passes us off to another pair of guards, who in turn leave us in the care of the king's attendants. One of them seats us before the fire, and another disappears into an adjacent room. Then King Fireld himself appears, pulling on a heavy, green velvet robe over plain shirtsleeves and trousers. I can tell it's him because the servant who went to fetch him is hurrying along behind holding a large gold crown and trying to hand it to him.

"Put it away," says the king impatiently, waving the servant down like he's an eager hound with a stick. The image strikes me with all the force of Orail greeting me at the top of the cliffside path, and reminds me why I am here.

I get to my feet and offer the king a low bow.

His scraggly gray brows disappear into scraggly gray hair. "Who is this, Fáthair?"

"His name is Hew LacEllan, Your Majesty," says the priest. "He has news of the Usurper Prince that I believe you would do well to hear. Your prayers, I think, can wait."

"Hm." The king's eyes sharpen as they swivel to me. "Go on then, boy. I'm listening."

I clear my throat. "Time is very short," I say. "But here is what I know."

When I finish my tale, the king is no longer watching me. He is pacing up and down the sitting room, velvet robe dragging along the ground behind him and catching on the corner of a tufted runner rug.

"Dawn, you say?" he keeps repeating. "Feldkraich? That's not far, not far at all."

"He means to surround this city, Your Majesty," I say again, shifting from foot to foot behind the armchair I sat so briefly in. "But if your men can reach him before dawn, you can stop him before he starts. My friend has gone ahead to try and steal his plans and records. If she succeeds, the information could help you end the Usurper's efforts once and for all."

He rubs his chin, paces a few more steps, then swivels toward the fireplace. "What say you, priest?"

The priest has not spoken a word, though he has followed the conversation with keen eyes.

"I say the gods have given you a boon," he says after a pause. "And if you act now, we may be spared much bloodshed and grief."

King Fireld rubs his chin again, then clears his throat decisively. "Then I will mobilize my army," he says. "If we act now, we might reach Feldkraich by midday."

I grip the back of my armchair. "*Midday?*"

"Midday will give us ample time to cut him off," says the king, frowning at me. "But you are neither a councillor nor my captain of the guard. So you may go, Mr. LacEllan, and I thank you for your service to Ilbha. I will see you rewarded."

"Midday is too late!" I protest, alarm making me forget who I'm addressing. "People will die before then!"

Áila will die.

The king pins me with a look. "Can *you* mobilize fifteen thousand soldiers and get them to Feldkraich in the next"—he pauses to glance out the window at the sky—"five hours, Mr. LacEllan? If so, I give you full leave to lead my army there by dawn. If not, I will lead them myself, sometime after midday, and you may find some other employment for your talents while you wait for justice to be dealt."

I swallow hard, screwing up my courage. I hope King Fireld does not have a quick temper, or I may soon be without a head. "Then might I request my reward now?"

The king's eyes bulge, and even the priest goes pale.

"A horse," I say quickly, "with Your Majesty's leave. I wish to save my friend. She will be waiting for us at dawn, and if we are not there, I fear she will die."

The indignation purpling the king's face subsides, and he suddenly looks a little too understanding. He releases a breath. "Very well," he growls. "Go with him, Fáthair, and see he gets his horse. And LacEllan?"

I turn, halfway to the door, and remember I have forgotten to bow. But as I bend at the waist, flushing again, he says, "I hope you win your lass."

Chapter Sixty-Six

ÁILA

The fields separating Feldkraich and Redbrook House are mostly flat, with a slight roll to them—a landscape I imagine might be good for a battle. However, my impression is that the rebels don't expect to wage their battle here in the fields, for they are attacking the city before dawn. I imagine cottages of sleeping Ilbhans—many with small children—which will soon be set upon by swords and guns. Nausea rolls through my belly.

As we draw nearer, I realize Feldkraich is less of a city and more of a village in both size and structure. The houses and buildings are jarringly familiar, the same blackstone and thatch we have at home in Carrighlas, and even a few paler ones that look limewashed like my own little cottage on the cliffs. The closer we draw to the edge of the town, the rawer my heart seems to become, until I almost feel as if we are approaching Carrighlas itself. I can see a mill wheel rising beside the river, and a kirk spire in the middle of town. The rest is a shadowy tangle of low buildings, but I can easily imagine what they must be: bakers, smithies, milliners, butchers, schoolhouses, pubs. I imagine market stalls on the high street in summer, storehouses stocked with canned and dried preserves in winter. And year round, hot cups of tea before peat fires in homes while families sit together and exchange tales, eat meals, laugh, cry, live.

I can see mothers like my mother, brothers like Matan, sisters like Deirdre. I can see fathers like my da, leaders like the

LaCail, even priests like Fáthair Firnan. I can see tall, earnest young men like Hew, eyes bright and full of hope.

I can see fey-eyed cur dogs, half wild with mischief as they break from exasperated owners to scatter a flock of sheep or upset a basket of fish.

I can see home, a place of belonging.

The world seems to rock beneath me as I realize it. Though I don't know a single person inside the sleeping village sprawled at my feet, I do know one thing about each one of them: they *belong* there.

I can hardly breathe for the revelation. The man dragging me forward tugs me slightly, and I almost fall on my face.

As I imagined Feldkraich, I didn't see medallions or apprenticeships or people who had failed to earn their keep. I didn't see people who *might* justify staying there if only they would work a craft or give a bit more to the welfare of the village. And as Feldkraich turned to Carrighlas in my mind's eye, I still didn't see those things. Because, I realize, those are not the things that amount to belonging.

Across the fields, I hear Morgen's men shouting orders to their foot soldiers. Most of them are Ilbhan, but there are clusters of Aenlandish soldiers here and there as well. The closest group to where I stand is a group of Ilbhan fighting men under the command of a stocky, red-faced fellow who looks as if he has spent his entire life sitting on a velvet cushion eating truffles and drinking whisky. I see stony obedience in the faces of his soldiers as they watch him totter about barking orders, but not respect.

The seed of an idea drops into the soil of my mind.

My captor has a flock of soldiers to direct too, so we continue forward through the assembling lines of Ilbhans until we have come about midway through the army. Then the giant holding my tether stops and begins to shout his commands to the men who serve him. Again, I see resigned subservience in their faces, but not much in the way of conviction.

I rake my eyes over them, trying to understand what my gut already seems to know: that these soldiers are *not* eager to attack Feldkraich. Their clothes tend toward shabby and their faces are careworn, but that could easily be the result of travel, hunger, and bad accommodations. They span a range of ages, and of course all are armed with at least sword, dirk, and targe, if not pistols, but some hold these with more confidence than others. There are even some who—

I gasp as it hits me. There are even some who *look like they'd be more at home with a pitchfork than a sword*. These men lack conviction because this battle isn't theirs. It's their chieftains' and lairds'—the men in the war room to whom Morgen has promised the "riches of Ilbha."

Yet all those men are landowners, with tenants and farmers who owe them allegiance—just like at home. I remember my mother saying that if the LaCail told the people of Carrighlas to follow him into battle, we would all have to do it, or risk losing our homes or our lives—because he is the leader who owns our lands, to whom we have sworn fealty. Just as these soldiers have sworn fealty to men who betrayed their king in order to serve Morgen.

It doesn't matter to their chieftains whether these soldiers believe in the Usurper's cause, because they all have families and livelihoods that can be threatened if they prove reluctant to fight. Which has to mean that many—*most?*—of these soldiers have been brought to this field without any shred of belief in the thing they are fighting for.

Hope takes root in me as a very slender shoot.

I think suddenly of Hew, who for all his Unblessing was still defended by my brother and his distillers on the quays of Fuiscea when an outsider threatened to kill him. It strikes me

322

like a hammer blow that even *he* can claim more belonging in Carrighlas, where he is called Unblessed, than Morgen can in the kingdom where his own father has offered a reward for his capture and imprisonment.

Morgen, a man who has toiled and striven and worked to the point of domination for a place to call his own.

But of course you *can't* strive to belong. Because belonging doesn't come on the back of hard work; it comes as a result of being loved.

I feel simultaneously like I am falling and soaring high into the predawn sky. Because I have just realized that what I long for most in the whole world is not an apprenticeship or a medallion. What I want most is to have Orail back, because I knew the warmth of belonging with her.

Not because I did anything whatsoever to deserve it. But merely because she loved me.

Despite my flaws. Despite my stupidity.

Just like I loved her, and gave her belonging with me.

I almost laugh aloud as I realize how futile my efforts have been to merit a place for myself in a village I already had every right to claim as my own. While all along I was loving and claiming a dog whose every chaotic action should have, by my rubric, made her less deserving of a home with me.

Inexplicably, I think of the mug she summoned for me that first night in the white cliffside cottage, the mug I threw over the cliffs as a votive offering to the gods.

And suddenly I know what to do.

Chapter Sixty-Seven

HEW

My gifted horse came equipped with both sword and pistol, but I was not made for fighting. Even so, as soon as I finish my headlong gallop to Feldkraich, I realize I am going to have do some amount of it if I am to find Áila. For though it is still a little before dawn, she is not waiting on the road for me, as she said she would be—which must mean she is still in the house.

My years cutting peat have made me strong enough to hold my own against an opponent, but as I grapple with the lone guard standing sentry outside Redbrook House, I realize my heart isn't really in it. And will probably never be. Because I don't want to hurt this man, no matter who he is or what he's done. I just want to walk peaceably past him to go help the girl I love. And so I grunt out a plea for a truce even as I duck beneath his fist and dodge his whistling sword.

"Please!" I gasp. "I'm trying to save Ilbha! Aren't you Ilbhan too?"

"Piss off," he snarls, and his Aenlandish accent answers my question.

I grunt, ducking around another punch. I have somehow managed to kick his sword out of his hand, and for the moment, all his supplementary weapons are out of his reach. "Surely you don't want to be here, if you're from Aenland," I try again. "Do you really want to follow a man your king has rejected?"

But the Aenlandish guard is not one for conversation. He lunges at me, trying to hook an arm around my neck, and I dodge him again, kicking open the door to the manor house and hurtling through it. The Aenlander follows, growling obscenities into the cavernous foyer as he does.

We have more room to maneuver inside, which is to his advantage, and in quick succession I take a hard blow across the jaw and a jab to my nose, which lands with a nauseating crunch. The metallic taste of blood fills my mouth as I cough and stumble backward, looking around for some defense.

There is a door to my right, and I lurch toward it. As I stumble into the dark room, I register a small desk, on which sits a ceramic water pitcher and basin. Without pausing to think, I seize the pitcher and raise it, bringing it down hard onto the guard's head as he charges through the door after me.

It shatters, water and pottery shards raining down onto us both—and the man drops like a felled oak.

For a moment I stand there with a broken handle clutched in my fist, breathing hard and watching the man to make sure he isn't about to spring up and attack me again. When he continues to lie still on the floor, I drag him a little farther into the room, check his pulse to make sure I haven't killed him, and walk out again, pulling the door shut behind me.

The hall is still deserted, and I start down it as quietly as I can, listening for sounds of pursuit or approach. I pass closed doors every few feet, and stop to push my ear against them, listening for voices. I hear none, and those that are already open reveal only dark emptiness. I start to walk faster, taking less time listening at doors, and eventually I start throwing them all open, dismayed when one after another reveals a deserted room. The house smells of sweaty men, old liquor, and sharp, acrid smoke—a scent I recognize as freshly extinguished candlewicks.

"Áila!" I cry, abandoning caution. "Áila, are you here?"

No one answers. The house echoes around me, deafening in its empty quiet.

I tear into the main hall, terrified to discover she has gone—or worse.

"Áila! *Áila!*"

A door opens halfway down the hall, and someone walks through it. A short someone, with thinning, black hair. He turns at the sound of my voice, and an incredulous smile stretches his face.

"Lost your charge, have you, LacEllan?" says Bráthair Gibrat.

The anger I am always so careful to control rears unchecked inside my chest. "I only want to hear one thing from you, Gibrat," I snarl, striding forward with clenched fists. "And that is where your Aenlandish snake has taken Áila."

Gibrat's eyes skim over the veins popping out from my forearms, my height, and the blood still trickling down my face and staining my shirt. He raises his hands, palms out toward me. "Peace, *mallacht*," he says—but the word *mallacht* snaps my remaining self-control like it's a piece of worn twine. Before he can say anything more—to help or hinder—I let my fist swing hard and fast at his face. I didn't want to hurt the Aenlandish guard . . . but I do want to hurt Gibrat.

My knuckles connect with a crack and a crunch, and for a moment I don't know whether I've broken his cheek or my hand. Gibrat's head snaps around and he topples to the floor with a grunt while I gasp at the fire pulsing through my knuckles and up my arm. I'm briefly afraid I've killed him—until he lifts a shaking hand to his face.

"The gods will never forgive you for striking a man of faith," he grinds out.

I stand over him, rage pounding through my limbs. "You're not a man of faith, Gibrat. Maybe you should be more worried about whether the gods will forgive *that*."

And I turn and stride up the hall, leaving Gibrat to the mercy of whatever god might still care to claim him.

I search every remaining room in the house, throwing doors wide and calling for anyone else who might be able to help me. I find empty glasses, dirty plates, and spilled candle wax in almost every room, often alongside rumpled blankets on floors or couches. The odor of unwashed men is so powerful, I am certain there has recently been a large number of soldiers in these very rooms, but no one is here now. Even the servants seem to have left.

At last I come to a dining room on the very northern end of the house that has obviously been repurposed into a strategic headquarters for Morgen's advisors. I stride to the far side of the room and tear back one of the heavy, purple drapes. Outside, the sky is beginning to lighten, and I see countless figures moving across the fields toward Feldkraich, small as a swarm of black ants.

They are starting to move on the town.

A cry of despair bubbles up in my throat. I look around for some clue to Áila's presence, some indication of where she has gone, and my eyes fall on any number of the things she came here to steal: maps with notes and plans; correspondence; lists of clans and their pledged swords . . . My eyes skate over them all, and as they do, I catch sight of a single piece of parchment lying, a little crumpled, on one end of the table.

I snatch it up. It is a broadsheet—identical to the ones I still carry, folded up in my pocket. One of Áila's, I am sure.

Which means she has been here. Likely in Morgen's presence.

I dither on the spot, desperate to know where she has gone. Her safety is out of my hands, and my helplessness at this knowledge feels smothering.

Suddenly, I remember Lir's words to me in the Ellisburgh Cathedral: *What is it that you want, Hew?*

To save Áila, I think at once. *To keep her safe. To prevent any bad thing from happening to her.*

And if you cannot?

I hear the underlying question: *If you cannot control the outcome, if you cannot ensure a perfect ending, what will you do then?*

"I will stand at her side. I will die with her," I say aloud, aware that there could not be a less perfect plan in the world.

As I speak the words, the panic inside of me quiets as abruptly and completely as if I have stepped inside and out of a storm. Somehow, I feel lighter. And suddenly I realize the snide voice inside of me has nothing to say; I do not even feel his scrutiny anymore.

I wheel around, back to the window. Bráthair Gibrat is now hurrying across the fields, toward the army, where it seems every soul in this house has already gone.

Every soul.

I sprint out of the room, down the hall, toward the massive front doors—which I push open before jumping the front steps three at a time and pelting off into the hazy dawn, toward Feldkraich.

Where Morgen is.

And Áila, I think, if she's still alive.

As I run, I pray to every god in the heavens that she is.

Chapter Sixty-Eight

ÁILA

Across the foggy fields before Feldkraich, Morgen's advisors and generals are shouting orders, organizing their troops into the formations they plotted out in that reeking dining room at Redbrook House. I can barely see all of them through the mist, let alone hope to be heard by them all, but nevertheless I clear my throat.

At first, my voice is a little weak, a little tremulous, but I think of Orail, her blazing gold eyes, her reckless courage, and the wild, triumphant grin she wore as she died. I force out the first line of the song I have loved so long:

"O'er the heath where hurcheouns sleep, all cradled by the solum, O!"

In front of me, the giant man holding my tether turns to look at me as if I am a dog on a rope that has just started to sing. I think of the first time I heard Orail's voice in my head and almost laugh aloud. I push out the second line, my voice marginally stronger:

"The westly winds arise and pen a tune both bright and solemn, O!"

"Shut *up*, you mad, wee beastie!" cries the man, incredulous. "Have you lost your bloody wits?" He yanks hard on my tether, and I jerk forward, stumbling briefly to my knees before I scramble up again. But I am singing almost before I am upright, as loud as I can manage.

"The pipe and drum first creaky hum, I turn to hear the whistle, O."

The man holding my rope looks like he might have an apoplexy; his face is turning purple and his eyes are popping beneath his wool bonnet. But behind him his soldiers have all begun to watch me with curious, almost wondering expressions. One of the men at the front of the line—a lad about Matan's age, with curly black hair and umber skin—meets my eyes and actually smiles. And when I belt out the next line, he opens his mouth and sings with me in a vibrant, rich tenor:

"Lyk night hae daw, ilk freeze hae thaw, an' golden light and thistle, O!"

His voice alongside mine does what I could never have accomplished alone, and amplifies the sound over many of the shouting lairds and commanders nearby. My skin shivers as the song skims along the morning mist, as though the two are old friends.

Perhaps they are.

A stunned silence ripples over the formations of soldiers nearest to us. I can see their breath coming out in silver puffs against the indigo morning. But when the next line of the song comes, there are at least three more men singing it. The chilly air feels suddenly charged, connecting me to those whose voices have lifted up to join mine: music forging a bond between those who sing together.

"Golden light and thistle, O! Golden light and thistle—"

The giant jerks me forward again, obviously intent on taking my rebellion into his own hands. But the young soldier who sang with me first reacts so quickly I almost don't see him move: he swings his claymore in a hard arc and severs the rope so that only a foot or so dangles below my bound hands, leaving his own chieftain with a fistful of disconnected tether. The giant turns in bulging-eyed vengeance on his soldier, but the man steps back into his formation. Around him, the whole line of plaid-wrapped soldiers—all of them now singing—raise shining iron swords against their chief.

"Here!" I say to the soldiers, tearing a broadsheet from the front of my bodice and handing it to the nearest man. "This is who you're being made to fight for! Even his own king stands against him!"

Trembling with the gravity of what I have done, I turn and sprint, flinging broadsheets at soldiers as I go. I run and run and run, boots sluicing through dewy heath, dodging the occasional sword or bellowing laird—but I am lighter and quicker than any of them. The song follows me as I go, born on the rosy morning sky, and it swells as it gains a life of its own. I sing with it, until at last I have reached the very front of this enormous tide of Ilbhan soldiers gathered to attack their own people. More voices join with every stanza, crying the words of a song that is less than the sum of our kingdom, and also so much more.

It's a simple song, with no care for kings or armies or politics. And yet it claims exactly the land I want to belong to—exactly the land I *do* belong to: a land of kinship and misty hills, peat fires and whisky, purple swathes of heather, brooding seas, warm taverns, enigmatic gods, and people with callused hands and gentle hearts.

"*. . . she dawns a robe of Ilbhan rose, an' golden light and thistle, O!*"

A sea of faces—frightened boys with smooth cheeks, stubborn old cottars with skin wrinkled by wind and sun, and flinty-eyed lads with squared shoulders and set jaws—stare back at me as I face the army and sing for all I'm worth. Many of them have joined me now, and some of their ranks are in chaos—iron ringing through the morning as they fight each other or their leaders. It is more than I imagined, and it overwhelms me with fear, with hope. I sing on, and then I see a small figure moving fast, weaving through the army as it runs from the direction of Redbrook House.

Its arms swing madly, a galloping colt.

My voice catches and my legs feel weak. *Hew.*

He does not stop, not even when one of Morgen's generals

takes a swing at him. He darts through the armies like a homing pigeon trained to return to my hand, and soon he is panting as he slows to a stop beside me, face shining with perspiration. At once, he starts unknotting the rope still binding my hands together. Tears burn and gather in my eyes as I watch him, and for a moment my throat is too tight to sing. But the song is almost finished, and more than half the soldiers on the field are now belting it out in deep-voiced harmony:

"In the rest o' the zephyr's breath, the swallow takes the tune, O!
Then chorus formed, an aeriform organ sings and croons, O!"

Hew is all but tone-deaf, but he sings too. I lace my fingers through his callused ones and we stand hand in hand between the army and sleepy Feldkraich, seal pups before a tidal wave. But the army has started to unravel like a torn tapestry, neat rows of soldiers disintegrating into shouting clusters as each faces its commander in whatever way it must.

And then they begin to rush forward, toward Hew and me.

At first, it's just ones and twos, running with plaids streaming and boots pounding to stand beside us, facing not Feldkraich but Morgen and his army. But then the groups grow larger—whole squadrons at a time, swords and targes clattering—and soon more men are defending Feldkraich than standing ready to attack it. Finally, I hear Morgen's voice above the rest, bellowing for his men to capture me, to silence me, to kill me. Many of his commanders have already been overcome by their own soldiers, and either lie dead on the field or tied and gagged by those who will soon bring them to justice.

Morgen is charging toward us now, this strange, armed choir singing in roaring chorus before the very village they were summoned to attack. His face is flushed with wrath, all charm and charisma gone, and he has drawn both sword and dirk, boots churning up mud as he runs. Weaponless though I am, I brace myself, knowing I will be his first target. But when he is a dozen yards away, someone steps out from the confused chaos of his supporters, levels a sword at the Usurper's belly, and braces herself for the impact.

Morgen tries to stop, but cannot. With a squelch of mud and a hideous thud, he is impaled on Flora LaCree's sword, and he sinks with a gasp and a groan onto the dew-wet fields that will now be spared nearly all blood but his own. Flora staggers a few feet away and falls to her knees, weeping into her hands as the man who was once her lover, her false brother, and presumably her king, slowly bleeds to death in the grass.

I let out a shaky, choking breath, overwhelmed by all I have lost, all I have gained.

And then, with wavering voice, I lead Morgen's army of simple, land-working Ilbhans in the last chorus of the song that has saved us:

"Golden light and thistle, O! Golden light and thistle, O! The flowers tell of warmer spells an' golden light and thistle, O."

Chapter Sixty-Nine

HEW

The deck of the ship sways beneath my feet as I make my way across to the starboard railing. Beyond the gently pitching bulwarks, the afternoon sky is fathomless, azure with sunlight. Only a distant darkening on the horizon warns of any rain at all, and we will be in Carrighlas long before those clouds break.

I can hardly believe we are going back.

The events following the stillborn battle outside of Feldkraich still seem tinged with unreality, even days later. As promised, King Fireld arrived with his army a little after midday, by which point Prince Herry's surviving men had been brought back inside Redbrook House, tied up, and locked in Morgen's war room to await judgment.

The king insisted on seeing Áila and me at once. We met with him in the gardens of the manor house, clutching hot cups of tea and staring at him in disbelief as he insisted that anything we wanted as reward for our service to Ilbha would be ours, if we would only speak the word. Then he said he would arrange a ship home for us in Glaisgoah's harbor in three days' time, and that we should spend the intervening time resting and being waited upon at the King Chares Inn in Ellisburgh, where he had rooms prepared for us.

Separate rooms this time.

Over the next two days, I learned that Redbrook House had been surrendered to King Fireld by the nobleman who owned it, and that all of Morgen's supporters had been arrested and taken to the Ellisburgh Castle dungeons to await trial—all except Flora, who seemed to have won her redemption by aiding us. I also heard that Morgen's body had been returned to Aenland, and that King Fireld himself had gone with it in hopes of forging a new peace with King Porrl—and that he publicly attributed Ilbha's freedom from the Usurper's poison to a pair of young Fuisceans who had risked their lives to stop his rising.

I wanted to talk to Áila about it all: to laugh with her over the absurdity of our becoming national heroes, to cry with her over the deaths we witnessed on the field, to marvel with her that a folk song could save an entire village from slaughter. Above all, I wanted to tell her that I loved her; to ask whether there was any chance she loved me back; if there was a future we might forge together, she and I. But for those first two days, I barely saw her; every time I went to her room, one maid or other informed me she was sleeping and had asked not to be disturbed.

The third day, the day of our departure home, she finally answered my knock herself. She smiled to see me, but her eyes were creased and shadowed, as if the sleep she had been getting had not yet chased the ghosts from her mind. I wondered suddenly if Morgen's death had been a heavier blow to her than she anticipated, and all the things I had been longing to say to her froze on my tongue.

"Ready to go home?" she said.

I nodded, though all at once I was much less certain.

But now, with the shores of Fuiscea appearing like smudges on the horizon, I realize I must speak—or risk the unspoken words withering my heart. Áila stands alone at the edge of the deck, and I step close as she grips the bow railing.

"Are you all right?" I ask her quietly.

She turns her face toward mine, and I am dismayed to see a sheen of tears glittering over her eyes. "I'm . . . not really sure."

I don't know whether the tears are for Morgen or Orail, but

I swallow my fear of the one and draw on my compassion for the other. Orail was not my dog, and I didn't know her the way Áila did—but I certainly loved her.

"I'm sorry," I say. "We stopped Morgen, but we still lost Orail. It seems . . ."

Áila nods, and a pair of tears chase each other in a silver trail down her cheek. "Unfair," she whispers.

It does, I tell Lir. *But . . . maybe death always is? Your cliffs seem to say as much.*

Áila can't hear my prayers, but she still leans her head against my shoulder as if something of my thoughts has reached her and given her comfort. I wrap an arm slowly, tentatively around her, and for a long time we stand like that, looking out together over the vivid, jade ocean. But my pulse is anything but tranquil with Áila pressed against my side, and the words I have been keeping restrained burst free of their bonds.

"I think I love you, Áila," I say, and my face flames, because even I can hear how abrupt the words sound. "I-I'm sorry, I know this isn't the right time. But I care about you—deeply—and I-I want to be with you, if you'll have me. I mean, if you want . . . if you think . . ."

Beneath my arm, she is stiffening. Mortification creeps through my body, inexorable as magma, and I almost can't bring myself to turn and look into her face. But despite all my horror and fear, I remember my new conviction: to release my need for control, to allow—even embrace—imperfection.

I have given myself a monumental opportunity to practice.

Áila's face crumples. "I'm sorry, Hew," she says as I pull my arm away. "I'm sorry. I don't—I don't know anything right now."

She bends over the railing, dark hair falling down in a wavy curtain to cover her face, and it feels like a door has swung shut between us. My whole body feels hollow as I step away, barely hearing myself as I mutter, "Of course, I understand."

I can hardly retreat belowdecks fast enough. Life, I decide, was safer, easier, and infinitely less painful before Áila and Orail stepped out of the rowboat and into my life that night of her Trial.

When the ship's captain whistles sharply and calls to the crew to prepare to berth the vessel, I find my way back to Áila, determined to show her my words were not empty—even if she can't reciprocate them. She is hollow-eyed and silent: sure signs that she barely knows I'm present. Nevertheless, when the gangplank is lowered, I accompany her down onto the quay and up the docks in the direction of the inn where her brother once left me to recover from Morgen's attack.

But when we leave the shipping berths behind and turn onto the rickety planks of the main quay, we both stop short. There, ahead of us in a large cluster, stands a group of people who erupt into cheers, applause, and bellows of delight at the sight of us: The LaCail and his family; Fáthair Firnan and a number of monks, including my friend, Wellam; Áila's parents and siblings and the whole expanse of her nieces and nephews; Vira with Gemma and Colm; and a slew of other familiar faces from the village. All waiting to welcome us home.

They surge toward us.

"We heard what happened!" cries Áila's sister, pelting ahead of the pack to swoop Áila into her arms. "We heard how you saved us, and all of Ilbha, you mad, beautiful creatures!"

"A messenger came yesterday, just to tell us all!" says Matan, looking flabbergasted that news could ever travel so fast.

We are bustled down the quays in a flurry of hugs, shoulder claps, and chatter—and it is not only my sister, Gemma, and Wellam who embrace me as a hero, but the whole group, even

Colm and Fáthair Firnan. I am just beginning to wonder if it's all some bizarre dream in which my Unblessing has been forgotten when the LaCail speaks out over everyone in his deep, booming voice.

"The priest and I have been talking," he says, "and it would seem to us that the gods have given clear ruling on the lives of Áila LacInis and Hew LacEllan. From this day forth, they are to be given whatever apprenticeships they choose. They will no more be called Unblessed in this village."

I'm so stunned I can't even croak out a reply.

And then the crowd shunts me into a carriage with my family, a few monks, and the blacksmith, all of them beaming at me like I've saved the world.

"If only I'd known," I say wonderingly as the carriage door swings shut and we trundle into motion, "that all I had to do to get an apprenticeship was run away to Ellisburgh and try to stop an uprising, I'd have done it years ago."

My companions laugh, and I do too—but only because I don't know how else to hide the yawning void opening inside of me.

Áila has joined her family inside another carriage—joined them without so much as a glance back at me—and as the road forks and bears us apart, to different homes and different lives, I can't help fearing that our paths have split forever, and that it happened too quickly for me to do anything about it at all.

Chapter Seventy

ORAIL

I am and I am not. Outside of form
And beyond it, but still not prevented
From claiming Form, this shape that calms the storm
Inside me. And so I do, cemented
To myself by a structure that keeps me
Me, regardless of the body that holds
My soul. And for once I find myself free,
No creature-form wrapping me in its folds.
I am as I was, at the beginning
Of things, and beside me my mother sits,
Watching. I watch her too, my soul spinning
To think how far we've come since that deep split.
Inside me, the creatures clamber and leap.
I tell all but one to go back to sleep.

"You can be free now, child, if you would like,"
Says Mother, gentle, careful, like she thinks
I might startle, beast that I've been. Doglike,
I put my head on one side and I blink,
As I oft did with Her, then contract
My brows. "I didn't want to become what
You wanted me to be," I say, voice cracked
From long neglect. "I wanted to win. But
I saw to win against you was to shove
away all that I loved. You knew that ruse

Didn't you? Because you knew that to love
Is to lose, and to win is also to lose,
Because it is to miss out on loving.
I never knew you could be so cunning."

"'Cunning' was never my objective, child.
All I wanted was you to understand
That loving *is* winning, however wild
Or painful, glorious, aching, or grand.
That it's always better than the hatred
You wore before in the name of chaos."
I let out a breath. We have both waited
Many lifetimes for her grace, my pathos.
Both have arrived, but the result is not
What I expected. "You are Arial
No longer," she says. "That life is now fraught."
"Neither am I Ona. A burial
Tends to end a name," I say. But her eyes show
Compassion, not pain. She smiles. "Yes, child, I know."

"So who am I?" I ask, desperate to hear
The answer. I have been so many things:
Horse, stag, cat, goat, crow. Dog. Each one a sneer
To the first form I wore: lithe with bright wings,
One part sea, one part joy, all parts divine,
Child of two gods, who should never have died.
Yet god-babes will die when mothers resign
Them to fate amongst wolves, leave them to bide
While they seek the welfare of others. "You
Know I never meant to leave you," she says,
Reading my thoughts. She can. It is her due.
I shrug, "Neither of us can change what is."

But now she laughs, the sound soft and bright. She says,
"We can't change what *was*. We can both change what is."

She is right. So I repeat my question,
Anxious for the first time in my lifetimes
To hear, to know my mother's suggestion:
"Who am I now? Beneath stanzas and rhymes?"
Her smile is gentle, like somehow she
Knows, like it isn't a puzzle at all.
"You're a child of earth and a child of sea,
Girl who was trickster and beast who could maul.
You're the sum of these things, and you are more,
You are fire and frost, you're shelter and gale,
You're gold that comes from the heating of ore.
Be at peace, golden one: you are Orail."
I smile at last, relief that I'm freed.
If I am Orail, I know what I need.

My mother hears my choice, and her eyes glint.
"For how long?" she asks, and I see her fierce
Consent. "For as long as she is." I squint:
"Can that be done?" My mother's smile could pierce
Iron, and it pierces me now, like sun
Striking snow. "It can," she says, "But I'll not
Send you back as a Púcca again. One
Sentence is all your wrongdoings had wrought."
"How then?" I ask. Her brows contract, eyes' light
Dims. "There is only one way," she says. "You
May go as an earth creature, with its might
And its weaknesses, gains and lacks. Eschew
Power, divinity all your days there.
I nod: The exchange is both just and fair.

"A dog," I tell her. "Amber-brown and merle,
Black, speckled all over like cream-flecked tea."
"You will have no speech," she warns. "You may curl
On the rug to sleep and share hide with fleas."
"But will I be with her?" It's less question
Than answer, and she nods, understanding.
"I'm proud of you, daughter. This regression
Of shape is progress of soul, expanding
The bounds of your heart. And since love begets
Love, you may yet come to love *me* again."
She twinkles, but I smell her masked regret.
Yet—my heart is not so hard to retrain.
"I love you already," I say, earnest.
"You took me rusted and left me burnished."

Chapter Seventy-One

ÁILA

The first night back in Carrighlas, I sleep in my old bed, at my parents' little stone house beside the distillery. I am fitful and sleepless, though, so the next day I tell Mother and Da I want to spend time with Deirdre. My sister welcomes me with crushing enthusiasm, offering everything she can think of for my comfort, from hot baths and soft dressing gowns to my favorite foods and drinks made by her cook. She offers her ear if I should want to talk, her silent presence if I don't, and everything else her home and family have to offer.

But I feel aimless and distracted. The weight of death still hangs heavy around me, like a dense fog that muddies my thoughts and feelings. I know they will sharpen later—both the joys and the griefs—but for now they merely feel oppressive, exhausting. As soon as I have stepped out of bed, I find myself wishing I were back in it.

And yet my body is restless. My muscles itch to move. Questions hammer at my brain.

After two days with Deirdre I realize that, much as I love her, she isn't really the person I want to talk to. So I pack my meager things again, and when darkness falls, I walk the familiar path back down the main road, past the shops and the pub and the kirk, and up the rocky track that leads to the cliffs.

Summer is stretching out to its languid climax, and the air blowing in off the sea is the warmest it will be all year. The salt tang in my nostrils is as familiar to me as my own family, and I breathe it in as I crest the clifftop path. Tall sedge ripples in the wind, stars blaze in the black sky overhead, and the white-capped waves throw themselves against the cliffs with abandon. By the time I reach my cottage, I am swallowing back tears, because I have still only been here without Orail one time before—the night I gave her to Morgen.

The cottage is almost exactly as I left it. I shouldn't be surprised, since Hew and I were gone only two weeks, but it feels like years. I make my way through the small space, lighting candles, taking note of what disappeared and what stayed after Orail and her magic died. Most of the things she gave me in answer to my wishes were summoned rather than changed, because she was still growing into her powers. She could never have changed my face or raised a wall from the floorboards in those early days.

I sit down on the edge of my cold bed and pull the blanket up around my shoulders, thinking of gods and dogs, wishes and bargains. And I remember the last prayer I prayed, weeks ago, before my first Ordeal: *Get me through these tests, and I will believe in you forever.*

Well, it would seem that the gods did. But I am heavy as I think of the cost of that bargain, and the weight of my promise. I curl onto my side in the cold, empty bed and stare at the candles until they gutter and die, and I am left alone in the darkness.

The next day I wake with a reflexive urge to talk to Hew. I miss him, and it strikes me that he might have answers to some of the questions that have been piling up and weighing on my heart since Orail died. But a breath later I remember—

He loves me.

I have barely allowed myself to think about that conversation since I stepped onto the docks of Carrighlas. Have barely allowed myself even to think about *Hew*. When I do, I feel like I can't breathe, and the sensation is so bewildering on top of everything else that it makes me want to run, fast as I can, away from it.

Because Orail is dead—and what grief steps lightly aside for thoughts of earnest gray eyes above a freckled nose, strong, callused fingers, or a tall silhouette with hair copper-bright in the setting sun? What mourning heart is cheered by hopeful, if tentative, love? Besides, wasn't it only a few weeks ago I thought myself besotted with Morgen? Can what I feel for Hew be any more trustworthy—even if *he* is?

No, I cannot talk to Hew.

So I decide to try and talk to Yslet instead.

I wait until night has fallen and make my way down the cliffs as the still-warm air flirts with the fresh breezes arriving from across the sea. The night smells of rose blossoms and evergreen, and I think with pinching heart of "Golden Light and Thistle"—of the way it saved Ilbha, and the way it saved me. I wonder if Yslet knows the song.

On the docks, I find a sturdy-looking rowboat and push it down the launch into the waves, jumping in as it catches the tide.

"O'er the heath where hurcheouns sleep, all cradled by the solum" I sing softly as I begin to row, *"the westly winds arise and pen a tune both bright and solemn, O."*

There is no accompanying harmony from Yslet or any other god, but I feel the heavy pressure around my heart loosen slightly as I sing. I row for much less time than I remember rowing before—because the sea is gentler, perhaps, or because my mind is busy—and climb carefully out onto the moonlit, muddy banks of Yslet's island.

"Nigh the ledge, the water's edge, is found a willow bower, O, all branches twined, and there I'll find my true love crowned with flowers, O. Clear and bright, though meek and slight, we watch as

day will bristle, O; and as it stirs, the smell of firs and golden light and thistle, O."

As before, the peat cutter is planted high on the bank, its grubby lantern swinging vaguely in the breeze. It is not lit, however, because of course there is no Goddess Trial tonight. I struggle up the bank, powerful memories breaking over me. My despair when I found the island deserted. My frustration with the muddy creature who tried to scrabble up my legs as I ran. My fury when she knocked me face-first into the muck and made every effort to lick my cheeks.

What I wouldn't give to have her pushing me into the mud now.

I begin my walk across the island, slow and unexpectant. Half of me still wonders whether Yslet truly exists, and the other half wonders, if she does, whether I'm out of my mind to think she would meet me here now—when she couldn't even be bothered to show up for my Trial. All the while, under my breath, I continue to sing my song.

And then, as I duck beneath the shelter of the towering oaks clustered on the middle of the island, I hear a sound: whistling, faint and thin. I walk a little farther and realize with a jolt that it is the melody of "Golden Light and Thistle." And that it's whistling in time with my quiet singing.

I walk faster, my heart starting to pound. Through the trees ahead, I see a glimmer of light.

And then I stop, my mouth falling open.

In the middle of a clearing there is a small, stone cottage, windows blazing with light. It is weathered, with a roof of old thatch and smoke-smudged windowpanes, and I goggle at it for more than a minute, remembering both my childhood fancy—that Yslet must live on this island—and the reality that the last time I was here there had certainly, definitely, been no house on it anywhere at all.

I step toward the house, from which the sound of gentle whistling is still coming, and approach the door—which stands open. With my heart thumping in my skull, I step through it.

Inside are two shabby plush chairs standing before a peat fire. Herbs and dried flowers hang from the ceiling beams above a scrubbed wooden table, and on the fire, a suspended kettle is beginning to blow steam. A very ordinary cottage—the sort you might find anywhere in the village.

But in one of the chairs is a person I have never seen in the village—or anywhere else. She is tall and red-haired, like my siblings said she would be, but she is wearing a plain brown dress instead of a fine green one, and she looks tired and the slightest bit sad as she gazes at me from her seat in front of the fire. Beside her chair, lying on the rug, is a small, silvery gray horse about the size of a goat, with a two-foot glittering gold horn extending from the middle of its forehead, and a tufted tail like a lion's. Cire.

"Áila," says Yslet, as if she has been expecting me. "Good. I've just made tea. Would you care to sit?"

Chapter Seventy-Two

HEW

In my old cellar chamber, I pace back and forth before my narrow bed, on which lies my open rucksack, packed with nearly every possession I can claim as my own. I didn't have a chance to pack for my first trip away from Carrighlas, but this time I have plenty of time to prepare.

Too much time.

The last four days at the monastery have been some of the worst I can remember. When we arrived back, I insisted on keeping my old room, despite Fáthair Firnan's incessant claims that I deserved better now. Firnan has been the worst of everyone, though some of the monks have proved almost as insufferable. Only Wellam has continued to treat me just as he did before, because he was the only person who ever treated me decently. Now that I am a hero of Ilbha, everyone seems to think I suddenly deserve to be shown kindness, welcome, and generosity.

No one seems to understand I am still more or less the same person they thought *didn't* deserve those things only a few weeks ago.

And so I have split the last four days between Vira's house and the solitude of my chamber, though Firnan has pursued me even here, asking me to join him for private dinners or discussions of village governance. I have not obliged him once, though I have done my best to decline without hostility.

Colm, too, has been different toward me now that I'm a

hero, but in a much more palatable way. Instead of making him sycophantic, my change in status seems to have intimidated him, and he has barely spoken two words to me since I arrived home. Indeed, when we are in the same room, he keeps his eyes averted and leaves as soon as he can.

I will miss my sister, and Gemma perhaps even more, but I am not sorry to be leaving Carrighlas.

Almost as soon I arrived, I went back to the shipyards to book passage with the next vessel carrying passengers to the mainland. It would be another few days, they said, due to the storms currently ravaging the channels between Fuiscea and Glaisgoah. I agreed, and then paid an obscene amount of the gold given to me at Redbrook House to have the ship collect me from the beach near the monastery. The shipyard clerk looked at me like I was daft when I requested it, but said it could be done with a little extra time and effort expended from the crew if I was willing to pay for their trouble. I handed over the money without explaining myself, and he took it without asking.

And now, on the eve of my departure, I am more grateful than ever to have made the arrangement. Because it will mean I won't have to risk seeing Áila again before I go.

My heart feels jagged inside my chest. The thought of her is enough to make me want to curl up and sleep forever, just to escape the love I think I may never stop feeling.

I have not seen her since we parted on the quays the day we returned, or had any message from her. I can only assume this silence is affirmation of the reply she gave me on the ship home, and that she is trying to spare me pain by staying away.

It is a small kindness, and I hope one day I can be grateful for it. For now, like most things, it just makes me ache.

Still, I find that I cannot leave without imparting a few last things—though I will not subject her to another clumsy speech. After I finish packing my bag, I get out a sheet of parchment, a quill, and ink, and sit down at the small desk in my chamber to write.

Dear Áila,

I don't quite know where to begin, but I do know where I must end—so perhaps I will start with that: I think I shall always love you. But I don't blame you for your answer to me. We cannot help who we don't love, any more than we can help who we do.

Please believe me when I say I don't regret a single day, a single hour of the time I spent with you—and Orail. I am forever thankful to have known such an extraordinary creature, to have loved her, even if her time here was far too brief. I know you regret her final moments, but I will never cease to be grateful that she used the last of her power to save you.

I also want you to know that I have decided to leave Carrighlas. By the time you read this, I will have departed already; I don't want you to feel any obligation to meet with me or say anything you may not mean. If you'd like to write to me, I believe letters will find me at Ellisburgh Cathedral. I am grateful to say I shall finally begin my study to become a priest—if King Fireld will sanction my education.

Which brings me back to the place I started, the place I will now end: I shall always love you, Áila LacInis. Thank you for being a friend to me when I had none, and for showing me kindness when everyone said I didn't deserve it. Thank you for seeing past my Unblessing to the human being beneath.

I wish you all the best, now and for always.

Hew

By the time I am finished, the clock on the wall says it is well past midnight, and I am due to meet the ship's dinghy a little after dawn. I fold the letter carefully, seal it with a bit of wax from my candle, and write Áila's name carefully on the front. I will give it to Wellam to deliver in the morning, before I go.

Packing up my writing implements, I extinguish my candles, stretch out on my cot, and stare up at the dark ceiling, praying that Lir will honor my choice to leave and give me peace.

When I wake a few short hours later and light the lamps again, I am so groggy I can barely locate my clothing. But at last I manage to dress for the journey, pulling on the fine clothes I traveled home in as a last tribute to the brief life I led as a spy, an investigator, a nobleman, a husband, and a defender of Ilbha. Beneath my shirt, my gold medallion still hangs alongside the icon I painted of Lir, and I straighten them both, each as much a part of me as the other. Then I pick up my rucksack and turn back to my desk to collect the letter I must now leave with Wellam.

But my hand stops in midair, hovering pointlessly over the surface of the desk.

Because the letter is gone.

Chapter Seventy-Three

ÁILA

For a moment I stand, staring at the goddess I have waited my entire life to meet: the goddess who failed to show up the last time I was on this island, the goddess who has ignored my prayers, the goddess who gave me the greatest gift of my entire life and then took it ruthlessly away. Even though I came here hoping to find her, I have the mad impulse to turn my back on her, to leave the island without saying a word. To see how she likes it.

Yslet's eyes are keen and intelligent—a deep amber brown—and I suddenly know without being told that she hears my thoughts as plainly as if I were speaking each one aloud. I let out a small sigh and walk toward her. Even my revenge is useless against her.

"Milk?" asks Yslet, as though this is a long-standing arrangement we have to sit together and drink tea in her cottage. I nod once, tight and silent. She begins to pour tea from a ceramic floral pot—easily the nicest thing in the whole cottage—into a pair of mugs I recognize with a jolt as my own: the two clay mugs glazed with sea green, which Orail summoned for me.

One of them bears a thin line of scripted gold across its base.

I gape like a fish on land, and Yslet turns with her auburn brows raised.

"My mug!"

"Indeed," she says. She hands it across to me, steaming with hot tea. "Which you gifted to the gods, if I remember correctly, during your third Ordeal."

I take it in numb hands and sink slowly down into the chair beside hers. "I threw it off a cliff. There's no way it could've survived the fall."

"Not even if there was a god waiting in the sea to catch it?" she asks with a little glint of mischief in her eyes. "My husband was always very skilled at catch."

All the air goes out of me. I melt back into the armchair with my mug clutched between my hands, staring into the glowing peat fire. After a while Yslet says, very gently, "I know you thought we weren't there. That you were alone. I'm sorry for that, child."

I turn to face her, desperation and anger vying for dominance over my retort. "What was I supposed to think? The last time I was on this island, you didn't turn up."

"I was here," she says quietly. "But I was not the one you needed to find."

My throat constricts so suddenly, I have a hard time swallowing the tea I have just sipped. When I can speak again, I say, "But that's another thing. You gave her to me and then—and then—" But I have to break off, because my eyes are burning and my throat cinches tight. I struggle a moment, then push the words out, despite the way they halt and squeak: "And then . . . y-you took . . . her . . . away."

Tears slide down both my cheeks. I sit gasping for breath, trying to get a grip on myself, trying to comprehend the enormity of life and death. Trying and failing to understand why the gods would allow any creature to come for such a short time to this strange, brutal, beautiful world we inhabit.

"Don't do her such a disservice," says Yslet, and there is an edge to her voice for the first time since I arrived. I look up, blinking, and find that the goddess's face is grooved with deep sadness. "Orail chose her end, and it was the greatest act of love she has ever performed. Do not rob her of her choice by believing it was mine."

I stare at Yslet for several long moments, steam curling up from my mug and dampening the bottom of my chin. I am perplexed to find her as moved by the thought of Orail as I am. "Hew thought she was a Púcca," I say slowly. "Was that true?"

Yslet's sorrow seems to ease a little. "In part, yes. That is what she became. It is what I made her."

"*You* made her? Why?"

"As punishment," says the goddess. "And as lesson. She was ruthless in her trickery and in her unkindness. She did not know how to care for anyone beyond herself."

"That doesn't sound like Orail," I say, frowning, and now Yslet's smile is like the sun emerging from dense clouds.

"No," she agrees. "It does not. It was her life with you, Áila, that changed her. That redeemed her."

I stare into the fire again. "What you said . . . that she was ruthless and unkind. That sounds like the trickster goddess. Was Orail actually *Arial*?" It doesn't much matter to me, I realize, whether my dog was the fabled trickster bound into creature flesh, but I am curious all the same.

Yslet's laugh is a light exhale, and I realize the sadness I thought I saw earlier is really a kind of relieved exhaustion: the sort of look a person has when they have just come through a long and harrowing ordeal.

The sort of look I am undoubtedly wearing myself.

"She *became* Arial," says Yslet. "Long before I bound her into Púcca form."

"I thought Dhuos had imprisoned Arial in the Halls of Bone—punishment for killing your daughter Ona? None of the legends ever speak of Arial being turned into a Púcca." I'm a little amazed Yslet is answering so many of my questions; after a lifetime of divine silence, it feels suspicious to have such a surplus of replies.

"The legends are not always right," says Yslet gently. "And

Arial didn't kill Ona. Not really. She *was* Ona. She went to Dhuos the Deathkeeper when her first form died, when I wasn't there to protect her, and asked him to remake her after his fashion. Becoming the trickster goddess was her revenge on a mother who had failed her. And when she became cruel and destructive, I remade her after *my* fashion. I bound her into beast form and sent her to serve the very people she had tormented."

I gape at her, connecting the dots. "Ona?" I say. "Orail was . . . *your daughter?*" My hand drifts to my throat, where Hew's painted icon of Ona still hangs. In all the time we were together, Orail never once mentioned it. I wonder if she ever laughed to herself to see the icon around my neck.

Suddenly, I remember my Mind Ordeal in the chapel before Yslet's altar, and how agitated Orail was during it. I remember the disastrous answer she gave me to the question about the healing goddess, Belaine, saying her greatest triumph had been to let Yslet's daughter die after the wolves attacked. She had seemed so furious then, and so triumphant to be feeding me blasphemies. It would have been right around the same time she regained memory of her past, and now I think I understand her anger.

Because she had been angry with her mother for lifetimes—centuries, probably. Angry enough to become Arial, the trickster.

Orail, the trickster.

I shake my head in disbelief.

But I am not yet done with Yslet. I put thoughts of Orail to the side for a moment and fix the goddess with a sharp eye.

"What about Unblessing?" I say. "Why would you condemn children to live lives as Unblessed, shunned by their own friends and family? Why, when they're people like Hew, who have so much to offer?"

And now Yslet does look sad. Grieved, even. She shakes her head, and tears gather in her eyes. Beside her, the unicorn gets to its feet and presses a velvet nose gently against her leg.

"I have never made anyone Unblessed," she says with a fervent shake of her head. "It is you who have done that."

"What?" I say, incredulous. "You're the one who gives out the medallions!"

"*Precisely*," she says. "I give out the medallions, because my children ask for them. They ask to know what lives, what crafts they should pursue. They ask for my guidance. And so I give it to them in the form of medallions. Guidance to point them toward the skills they already have. And to those whose skills are more diverse than one craft or symbol might suggest, whose paths lay open to many possible ends, I give a gold medallion. A blank medallion. And when they come to me, I tell them the same thing I tell everyone else, whose paths are narrower: That I love them. That they are precious to me. But I do not tell them what to do, because their choices are still their own—just like the person given an iron medallion for smithing, or a hoof medallion for shepherding."

"Are there so few whose paths are diverse?"

She smiles sadly. "Many send their children to meet me with an heirloom medallion tucked away in a pocket. For insurance against Unblessing. The sea is full of gold medallions, thrown away by those who might have lived broader lives."

For a moment, I am too stunned to speak. How many Unblessed are wandering around Carrighlas even now, having avoided Hew's sentence through deceit? "But—why didn't you stop it, or do something else when you saw what the people had decided the gold medallion meant?"

"Would you have me stop or fix every bad choice a person makes?"

I start to retort, but break off, scowling.

"I desire to give my children good things," says Yslet, "but I will not force them to do good with them."

My tea has gone cold, and I set it aside, feeling wearier than

I ever have before. There is something else eating away at me, but it's elusive, and I can't quite pin it down. Yslet's answers have made sense, and what's even more amazing, she hasn't turned me into a pile of cinders for asking for them. So when I feel tears spiking the backs of my eyes again, I am bewildered. I have no idea why I'm crying or why I feel so desolate.

Yslet rises from her chair with a soft rustle of wool and comes to crouch beside me. As I blink furiously, her face comes into focus on a level with mine. Her amber eyes, with all their perceptive intelligence, are soft as newly turned earth, and she lifts one slender hand and cups my chin in it.

"Child," she says, "*Áila*. You are precious to me, and I love you. I couldn't tell you before, because you and Orail needed to find each other. But it was no less true then."

The tears fall, hot and fast, but now I am taking great, healing gulps of air. I feel like something in me has unblocked, and I realize that Yslet knew even when I did not what words I most needed to hear.

I nod to her, and she nods back, and she catches my tears in the hollow of her hand. She bends forward and rests her forehead against mine until I feel the truth of what she has said seep through my body and take root inside my heart.

And when at last my tears have stopped and the fire has burned to flickering embers, Yslet sits back from me. She watches my face as a slow, playful smile crooks her mouth.

Outside the cottage, in the cool summer predawn, I hear the unmistakable sound of a dog's bark.

Chapter Seventy-Four

HEW

Though I know there is no place my letter could have gone, I still spend far too long searching for it, until the clock on the wall is ticking out what I already know: I cannot waste any more time. If I don't go now, I will miss my boat.

I feel a frantic fragmentation as I hoist on my rucksack and make my way through the quiet halls of the monastery, out into the dark early morning. With nothing now to deliver to Wellam, I have no reason to disturb his sleep, and I feel the dual disappointments of losing my chance to say goodbye to my friend and being robbed of speaking the hard-won thoughts I wanted to send to Áila. Of course I can write them both once I arrive in Ellisburgh, but it feels wrong to leave this island without a word.

Resisting the urge to walk back up the path to Áila's cottage and bid the dear place farewell, I turn my steps down the track that cuts a tight, snaking trail along the face of the cliffs to the beach at their feet. There, the cliffs make a kind of cove, which is the perfect spot to meet a dinghy without encountering anyone from the village. I walk carefully, for the path is steep, and by the time I reach the pebbly sand at the bottom, night has truly departed, and a fresh, pale gold light suffuses the whole beach. Far out on the water, I see the billowing white sails of the ship that will carry me to the mainland.

I stand and watch it while a strong easterly wind rolls in and buffets the cliffs behind me, creating a sort of echo chamber that turns the wind into a deafening roar. My hair whips about my face, and I shut my eyes, trying not take it as an omen.

I'm trying to be faithful, I tell Lir. Perhaps if I can convince him, I'll also convince myself. *I'm not running away. I'm just try-ing to serve you better.*

I sigh and open my eyes. Out on the water, the ship has sailed quite close, and I can see it lowering a dinghy. I am sud-denly eager—desperate—to be on board and sailing away.

If this isn't what you want me to do, I tell the sea god, *you're just going to have to stop me. Because Áila rejected me, and I don't see that I have any reason to stay here.*

The dinghy is a small rowboat, manned by a single sailor, and it's making good headway. The wind continues to roar about my ears, but I stride toward the water, too anxious to stand still. The sailor in the rowboat waves at me, and I think per-haps this insane wind is just Lir cheering me on with gale-force enthusiasm.

I push my errant hair out of my eyes, hitch my rucksack a little higher, and splash out into the water to meet the boat.

Chapter Seventy-Five

ÁILA

I am out of the cottage before Yslet can say a word, haring through the trees in the lightening morning toward the sound—the impossible sound—and hoping, *praying* it is not my imagination.

And then I laugh aloud, because the goddess I'm praying to is running alongside me with light dancing in her eyes and wind tugging at her hair. But I outpace her, and a moment later I burst out of the trees before the embankment where I left my boat.

There is a dog on the bank.

It's a large dog, and its coat is a swirling medley of sables, ochres, and fawns, with black spots of every shape and size dusted over it like globs and flecks of paint. It is facing the water with batlike ears raised and whippy tail curled in a wide arc over its back. Lithe muscles strain in all its limbs, as if it can't decide whether or not to jump into the sea. My heart did not stop running when I did, and it gallops inside my chest, knocking hard against my sternum, sending blood barreling through my veins.

I would recognize those markings anywhere, no matter where I was or how much time had passed.

My voice breaks as I call out her name. "Orail?"

She spins, stops, stares. And then it's as though she is a bow-string being bent: she tenses into herself and launches forward with terrifying speed, gold eyes bulging and mouth wide in that familiar, manic grin I have seen so often. I brace myself for the impact, but it still knocks me off my feet, and I am crying as she pummels me with her paws, gnaws at my wrists, knocks her stone-hard skull against my jaw—all the while yowling with feverish intensity. Her every movement is painful and offensive, and I have never felt happier or more grateful.

I wrap my arms around her neck, trying to hold her still—though I may as well try and wrestle down the waves of the sea. "Orail," I say, over and over—half sobbing, half laughing. "Orail, be calm just for a minute."

But she doesn't, and after a while I realize something that stills my bursting heart. I look up at Yslet from my seat on the ground. "She—she doesn't understand me, does she?" I say.

A pang of grief shoots through me as the goddess shakes her head, the expression in her eyes mirroring my own devastation.

"It was her only way back to you," she tells me. "To come as an ordinary creature. And she wanted to come as the one you knew, the one you needed. She is a dog, nothing more, and she will be for as long as she lives in this body. But she asked me to tell you that she did not forget what you asked at the Wish Tree, which is why this dog body will last for as long as you yourself live, Áila."

"What I asked . . . ?" I begin, but my whispered words on the night of the Heart Ordeal come flitting back to me: *I wish Orail would be with me always.*

New tears leak out of my eyes, and I finally manage to wrangle Orail into a hug as she stands, panting and grinning beside me. I press my face into her familiar speckled neck and breathe in her doggish scent.

"Thank you," I tell her, regardless of whether she understands. "There has never been a dog as good as you." And then I look up at Yslet. "Thank you too, Yslet. For sharing your daughter with me."

She inclines her head. "There is one more thing, child," she says. "This letter is for you, and I think you will find its contents rather pressing." From the pocket of her skirt, she withdraws a parchment envelope sealed with wax. "I would make for the cliffside cove, if it were me."

I break the seal and read it quickly, feeling colder and clammier with every line. It is a letter written to me from Hew. I look up again, wild with panic, but Yslet is gone. It is just Orail and me now.

Orail the ordinary dog. Orail the extraordinary dog.

"We have to go!" I tell her, scrambling to my feet. "We have to stop him!"

She may no longer have language, but she and her wide grin are immediately at my side. Together, we leap into the boat and cast off.

I start rowing as hard as I can toward the cliffs of Carrighlas.

Orail is more hindrance than help, but I laugh as I fend her off, rowing as hard as I can through the choppy waves—lit like orange and yellow glass in the morning sun. I feel almost manic under the influence of two intense emotions: panic I will lose Hew, and ecstatic joy to have Orail back again.

I row with all my strength, channeling my feelings through my physical movements and out of me through my muscles. I breathe a steady rhythm: in as I push the oars forward above the waves, and out as I pull them back again hard, through the water.

How strange it is to think of all the time I spent with Hew, taking him for granted, choosing someone else over him, when all along he's the person I can't live without. The person whose absence in my life leaves the deepest fissure. Not because he's without fault—I know his faults only too well—but because no one else in the world laughs the way he does. Because no one else can make me angrier or happier, or give such insightful answers to my questions, or act like such a bumbling fool when they're nervous. Because no one else's smile makes me come alive from the inside out.

And most of all, because no one else has a heart like Hew's: bursting with earnestness, determined to do what is right even at his own expense, and always looking for ways to bring more beauty and kindness down into earth.

In the light of the rising sun, I see Carrighlas appearing as if through a lifting fog. I have passed the docks now, and am rowing parallel to the beach, which curves with the line of the cliffs as the island bends out of sight. Salt fills my nostrils and geese cry overhead, while Orail leaps and barks at them in exuberant challenge. Water sloshes into the boat every time she does, and I beg her to calm down. But then I give a shout of laughter. For I have remembered that Orail is *Lir's* daughter, and he surely won't let her drown.

When at last the cove comes into view, my stomach drops. There is a large brig anchored in its mouth, and a rowboat has almost reached the shore—where a solitary figure stands waiting for it: tall and slender, haloed in glowing copper.

"HEW!" I shriek, pulling on the oars with all my strength.

But the wind is against us, both slowing me down and carrying my voice away.

I try again. "HEW! HEW! STOP!"

He doesn't turn. Instead, he starts forward, walking into the sea toward the rowboat.

I cut hard toward the beach. Behind me, Orail gives a mad yodel of a bark: she has caught Hew's scent, borne to us on the breeze.

"Go, Orail!" I gasp.

She leaps out of the boat. My chest is tight with love, with hope—and with fear.

In a few powerful strokes of her legs, she reaches the shore. Then she is off, kicking up a spray of shale and pebbles as she races down the beach. I run the little boat aground and clamber after her, but I am no match for her speed.

And Hew is already climbing into the boat.

"HEW!" I bellow. It feels like my heart is tearing out of my chest with his name. "PLEASE STOP! DON'T GO!"

And then—

The gods grant me a miracle.

The wind changes.

I feel it circle around me like a wheeling flock of starlings before it is suddenly at my back, carrying me toward Hew, carrying my words toward him.

"HEW!"

But it is not my words that he hears—it is the wild, ecstatic sound of Orail's bark.

I see him startle and turn, one leg in the dinghy, the other in the sea. As he catches sight of the blur of canine resolve hurtling toward him down the beach, he falls backward over the lip of the dinghy and disappears into its hull. And then the sailor manning the boat gives a yelp and starts to row hard, away from Orail—who plunges into the water after them.

"No!" I shout, laughing and crying at once. But Hew is pushing his way up again, and I can see him yelling for the sailor to stop. He leaps out of the dinghy and topples gracelessly into the sea—at the same moment Orail reaches him.

I stop, winded, and for a moment all I can see is seething water and flashes of dark fur and pale skin. Then they both emerge, Hew thigh-deep, and Orail up to her neck and grinning like a kelpie. Hew explains something to the man in the dinghy, and he hands out Hew's bag. Then Hew starts wading back through the water toward the shore, Orail beside him, ears lifted and tail thrashing.

He has not spotted me yet. He is too shocked by Orail's arrival to spare a glance anywhere else. I watch him a moment, his auburn curls afire in the sunlight, his smile wide and incredulous. He is crying, I think, and tenderness roots me to the pebbly sand; how could a person such as this love *me*? But then he turns. His eyes lock onto me, and he stops—and my new shyness snaps like a dead twig.

I start forward again, my chest still tight, but this time with something warm and glowing and wild. I break into a jog.

Hew is frozen, a stone megalith on the beach. Orail lopes toward me, though, tongue lolling like she can't imagine a better day in the whole history of the world.

Perhaps there has never been one.

Suddenly Hew laughs, a sound like sun breaking, and takes off after her, arms swinging. My stomach lurches with a joy that feels almost like terror.

And then my arms are around his neck, and his are crushing me to his chest, seawater seeping through his shirt into my dress. For a while we just cling to each other, breathing hard as the wind whips up and the scents of the ocean welcome us both home. Hew buries his face in my neck, and I can feel his hot tears against my skin, hear the thick, broken sound of his voice as he murmurs against my hair.

"She came back," he says. His chest heaves against mine as he both laughs and sobs. Then he steadies himself and pulls back. "How? And how did you know where to find me?"

I slip down through his arms to stand flat on my feet again, then lift my hands to cup his face in my palms. His gray eyes flicker with a carefully dampened fire as he gazes down at me, but I can see them coming alive with hope, radiating a warmth that sparks heat in my veins.

"Yslet," I tell him simply. Laughter bubbles up in my throat. Orail is leaping and cavorting with wild, jubilant yips, snapping at plovers and plunging in and out of the surf. I want to cup this moment in my hands just as I am holding Hew's face—careful, soft, aware of the precious thing that it is—and keep it forever.

But this is the beginning of our story, not the end.

Hew frowns, not understanding my answer, but I merely laugh again. There is plenty of time for explaining, for telling all the tales we have never thought to share before.

There will be days and months and years for that. Maybe even a lifetime.

I draw his face down to mine and kiss him as the sun blazes in the east and the wind swirls in a graceful loop around us, quieting at last. He tastes of honey and saltwater, and his mouth is soft and hesitant on mine. But then he pulls me in tight against him, and the world around us shrinks to insignificance: there is only Hew, strong hands at my back, damp curls beneath my fingertips, warm lips urgent as a promise against mine.

Orail barks again, spraying us with pebbles and seawater as she leaps at us, and we break apart, laughing. I can smell a change in the air—the first hint of autumn. I think of my little cottage, snug and warm with peat fire, and I wonder what it will be like when the world turns bronze and gold. I wonder what we will share there in the seasons to come, Hew and Orail and I.

Hew must study to become a priest, of course, and there is Unblessing to unmake in Carrighlas. And we must both forge new relationships with this dog who will never again speak into our minds or grant our wishes. But all these things we will do together, hand in hand.

"I think I love you, Hew," I tell him with a teasing grin.

His answering smile is brighter than the rising sun. "I love *you*, Áila," he whispers, fingers laced into my hair and stormy eyes clearing as they hold mine. "I don't just think it now. I know it."

I laugh, choke a little on the tears burning my throat.

And then I take his hand in one of mine and tangle the other into the wet fur of Orail's neck. Together we turn to walk back down the beach.

Back toward the village.

Back toward home.

Chapter Seventy-Six

ORAIL

the universe
    tilts
        shifts
            yearns
            is born—

            She
            Is,

And

    I
    am
    born.

she

    she
    she
    she
    she
        is
            here,
        is
        mine,

Is.

"My Ariel...
That is thy charge: then to the elements
Be free, and fare thou well! Please you, draw
near."

—WILLIAM SHAKESPEARE,
THE TEMPEST, ACT V, SCENE I

Acknowledgments

I am grateful to so many people who helped bring this book to life, whether directly or indirectly. At the top of that list, always, is my husband, Dan, who spent his day off every week of the pandemic caring for our son while I wrote, who cooks me dinner every night, and who is always ready to lend his savvy perspective to my plot brambles when I ask. Both Hew and Áila have threads of his character in theirs, and I love them all the more for it.

To my mom: thank you for all your days watching Edmund, and the proliferation of extra help you gave during the revision of this book. To Ted and Jane: thank you for coming to visit so faithfully, for caring for our kids and giving us the kinds of breaks that enable health and sanity. To Adam: thank you for writing the Ilbhan folk song of my dreams. I think it's every bit as good as "Wild Mountain Thyme." To Jordan and Kelsey: thank you for always cheering me on. To Edmund: thank you for napping so consistently while I drafted this book.

To Dad: I miss you always. No story I write will ever be without your influence.

To Joanna Meyer, my long-distance coworker: I couldn't write a book without your commiseration, encouragement, and (entirely biased) support of every idea I ever have. To Rebecca Ross, Anna Bright, Autumn Krause, and Addie Thorley: Thank you for reading early versions of the book and offering your beautiful endorsements. I am so grateful for the YA fantasy community, and I am honored to share shelf space with authors like you.

To my fearless cheerleader of an agent, Hannah VanVels Ausbury: thank you for believing in this weirdo little story, for cheering me on through tough revisions, and for reminding me to take breaks. To my patient and encouraging editor, Katherine Jacobs: thank you for working so hard to bring out the potential in this book and its characters. To Jacque Alberta, copyeditor extraordinaire: thank you for tackling Orail's poetry (especially the sonnets!), and for really *getting* this story. To Sara Merritt, Jessica Westra, Abby Van Wormer, Megan Dobson, and the rest of the Blink team: thank you for believing in me, and working so hard to get this book into the world. To Micah Kandros, who designed this beautiful cover: thank you for granting me a thistle!

To the utter VILLAGE of people in our community: this book would not have come together without your help. Extra thanks to Jaclyn Metcalf for help with babies and relentless encouragement; to the Donohue family for entertaining Edmund on multiple occasions when my deadlines were intense; to Teresa McKinney for driving from Arkansas to watch my girls; and to Bethany Shorey Fennell for rescuing me when my brain was wrung out and helping me find places to cut.

To Ophelia, the dog who inspired this book: you were a legend, a maniac, a hurricane, a miracle. To quote an old greeting card, "I rescued you, but you saved me." I have written us, here, a new ending.

And always, to Jesus, the original storyteller: "Accept the labor of my hands, and dwell within my heart with all Thy Fulness." *Soli Deo Gloria.*

GLOSSARY OF DEITIES
AND SCOTTISH TERMS

All words and names in italics below use the author's definitions.
All other definitions are taken from *The Pocket Guide to Scottish
Words* by Iseabail Macleod (Glasgow: Scaramouche, 1998).

Arial: the trickster goddess
Atobion: god of skies and storms
bannock: a kind of round, flat cake, often made of oatmeal
beithir: Scottish-Gaelic word meaning "serpent,"
    "lightning," or "thunderbolt," used to describe a draconic
    monster often found in mountain caves and corries.
Belaine: goddess of healing; wife to Bréseh
bide: to stay, live
Birgid: goddess of fires and forges; wife to Credne
blether: to talk too much, including about nothing
    important or things that aren't true
bodhrán drum: an early Celtic frame drum
bonny: lovely, pretty, handsome
bothy: a rough hut used by shepherds, fishermen,
    mountaineers, etc.
breeks: trousers
Bréseh: god of compassion, earth, and harvests; husband to
    Belaine
byre: a cowshed
carnaptious: bad-tempered
clan: a family group, especially one that comes from the
    Highlands or Borders
claymore: a basket-hilted broadsword

crabbit: bad-tempered

Credne: the great goldsmith; husband to Birgid

deamhain: demons, servants of Dhuos

dirk: a short dagger, which Highlanders often wear in their belt

dram: a drink of whisky

Dhuos: the Deathkeeper; master of the Halls of Bone

Ecna: goddess of wisdom and the mind

Gaelan: the mother goddess, ruler of fertility and life

gloaming: twilight, usually the evening twilight

kirk: a church

lad(die): a boy, youth, young man

Laird: a landowner, landlord; the clan chieftain

lass(ie): a girl, young woman

Lir: god of the sea; husband to Yslet and father to Ona

loch: a lake (sea loch: an arm of the sea, often used when the body of water is narrow or partially landlocked)

Ona: goddess of light and laughter; deceased child of Yslet and Lir

quaich: a shallow, two-handed drinking bowl

sark: a shirt

scunner: a feeling of nausea or disgust; a thing that or person who causes this

smoored: to suffocate, smother, or extinguish; a process of subduing or spreading out the coals of a fire in order to slow its burning without putting it out

sleekit: smooth, sly, cunning, hypocritical

stramash: a disturbance, uproar

tattie: a potato

tartan: a kind of woolen cloth with a pattern of checks and stripes; also called a plaid

trews: close-fitting, usually tartan trousers

Yslet: goddess of beasts and birds; wife to Lir and mother to Ona

Want More?

Visit hannachoward.com or use the QR code below to download an exclusive recording of "Golden Light and Thistle," written and performed for this book by indie folk artist, The Duke of Norfolk.